EVERYMAN, I will go with thee,

and be thy guide,

In thy most need to go by thy side

JOHN DONNE

Born in 1573. Entered Hart Hall, Oxford.
Admitted to Lincoln's Inn, 1592. Accompanied Essex's expedition to Cadiz, 1596.
Ordained in 1615 and chaplain to James I in
the same year. Dean of St Paul's from 1621
until his death on 31st March 1631.

John Donne
Poems

EDITED WITH
AN INTRODUCTION BY
HUGH I'ANSON FAUSSET

DENT: LONDON, MELBOURNE AND TORONTO
EVERYMAN'S LIBRARY
DUTTON: NEW YORK

© Introduction and editing, J. M. Dent & Sons Ltd, 1958
All rights reserved
Printed in Great Britain by
Biddles Ltd, Guildford, Surrey
and bound at the
Aldine Press · Letchworth · Herts
for
J. M. DENT & SONS LTD
Aldine House · Albemarle Street · London
This edition was first published in
Everyman's Library in 1931
Last reprinted 1978

Published in the U.S.A. by arrangement
with J. M. Dent & Sons Ltd

No. 867 Hardback ISBN 0 460 00867 6
No. 1867 Paperback ISBN 0 460 01867 1

INTRODUCTION

THE remarkable revival of interest, during this century, in the writings and personality of Donne is due to something more than an accidental fashion in taste. It is, in fact, closely connected with the reaction against the Victorian compromise.

The most noticeable characteristic of the Victorian age as a whole was the success with which it evaded facing the stark antagonisms that underlay the polite and smooth appearances of civilized life. This evasion resulted in a blurred association of sentiment and thought, in which a vague high-mindedness was the inevitable issue of a recoil from physical fact, and purity was confused with respectability. But even before the First World War had displayed the reality under the moral professions of the nineteenth century the reaction had already gone far. And we can see now, that despite many perversities, the primary aim, no less than the primary necessity, of the new century has been to break through the stifling embrace of thought and sentiment, to recover, even at the cost of a ruthless violation of conventional sanctities, a sense of vitality and of truth.

In this attempt many have been driven to concentrate upon life on its elementary physical level. Others, in their reasonable suspicion of emotion and of subjective impurities, have cultivated a destructive cynicism, an ingenious wit, or a barren objectivity; while a few, whom I believe to be the vanguard of many, are seeking to define the conditions of a new creative consciousness, in which heart and head, instinct and spirituality, are no longer confused and falsified, but significantly reconciled.

One explanation of the renewed interest in Donne, which

underlies the appeal of a style, at once so passionately stark
and extravagantly ingenious, is that each and all of these
can find in him at some stage of his career, an intensely
concentrated expression of their own efforts and dilemmas.

He, too, as a young man and a rebel against the Pet-
rarchan convention, was in violent reaction against a
mannered age. With a virile, if at times brutal, sincerity
he spurned the dainty elegance of Elizabethan song-
writers, the drowsy enchantments of Spenser, the courtly
appeals of Sidney, the attenuated sweetness of Lodge and
Peele, the pastoral plaintiveness of Greene. A candid and
ruthless realist himself, he challenged alike the idyllic and
the affected, with the words:

> I sing not, siren-like, to tempt, for I
> Am harsh.

And to those of his contemporaries who, in their love poetry,
made of every woman either a goddess or an unreal per-
sonification of chastity he curtly announced out of his
own crude experience:

> Love's not so pure, and abstract, as they use
> To say, which have no Mistress but their Muse.

Donne had, throughout his life, little, if any, sympathy
with Renaissance humanism. He was a medievalist by
nature and training, in his preoccupation with the esoteric
and his attachment to scholasticism. And this, too, ex-
plains his appeal to an age which has begun to question
the whole Renaissance tradition.

But his medievalism would not make this appeal, if it
had not been combined with a quality which we recognize
as distinctively modern and which was also typical of the
Renaissance—I mean his restless and audacious curiosity
for knowledge of all kinds, the "sacred hunger of science,"
as he called it in one of his poems. And this "hydroptique
immoderate desire" was not merely for "humane learning,"
although his knowledge, particularly of medieval literature,
metaphysical, theological, and legal, was both vast and
minute. It was a hunger for vital experience on all the
planes of being from the carnal to the spiritually ecstatic.

In this he did reflect the "universal man" of the Renais-
sance, but with a very significant difference. He was
haunted by a sense of sin. This, again, was a medieval
inheritance, but it was something more. Donne was a
moralist in a sense almost unknown to the Middle Ages,
because he was an extravagant individualist. The ideas
of Augustine and Aquinas may have been the groundwork
of his thought, but he never submitted to their authority.
Even in the days of his later sanctity he twisted them to
his own uses, transforming them at the demands of his own
convulsed, tortured, and casuistical being into strange and
fantastic shapes. He was, in short, a Protestant in the
deepest and most stringent sense of the word, a man who
claimed the rights and responsibilities of discovering truth
and of ordering his life in relation to divine and demoniacal
forces for himself. And his position was complicated by
the fact that he was reared as a Catholic, and so expressed
his own unique and eccentric problems in terms of the
Fathers, the schoolmen, and the medieval jurists.

He was thus both more medieval and more modern
than the Renaissance, sharing with the Middle Ages their
macabre preoccupation with the loathsome aspects of the
physical, and their conviction of the reality of sin, but
forestalling modern psychology in his analytical rationalism.
His peculiar significance, indeed, for us to-day lies in the
fact that he was one of the first men of genius to express,
with frenzied penetration, that state of discord and dis-
integration into which every man falls as he advances
through critical self-consciousness from an instinctive
towards a spiritual harmony. Few, if any, indeed, have left
such an intimate record of all the stages of that self-
martyrdom which lies between a state of nature and a state
of grace.

Behind all the apparent vacillations and contradictions,
then, of his life lies a single, doubtless largely unconscious,
but determining purpose, which was to bring the physical,
intellectual, and spiritual elements in his nature into
harmony. It cannot be said that he ever fully succeeded;
his physical instincts were too strong, his mind too self-
destructive. But it is these very qualities which ensure

the vividness and veracity of his record, as he passes through the valley of carnal avidity and mental cynicism up the tortuous hill of intellectual and moral questioning, and thence has glimpses of an ecstatic delivery, which he can never securely achieve.

As a lover he is in turn the sensualist and the cynic, passion's slave and passion's critic, the mystical Platonist and the devoted husband. In religion he escapes from Catholicism to agnosticism, becomes the paid casuist and the learned theologian; embraces at last, to satisfy his own inner and outer needs, the ministry of the English Church, and in the anguish of his self-enslavement, converts a profession into a spiritual vocation, which, for convulsive intensity of expression, has never been surpassed.

Intensity is the keynote of his career. All his days he is on fire. His experience deepens, his body decays, but the flame of life within him does not languish. Rather it burns brighter and more lurid as emaciation heralds dissolution. For his life is one long battle with Death, with the death of physical grossness and mental conceit, of worldly ambition, and spiritual complacence. And this life-and-death struggle is only comparable, as Walton, his first and tenderest biographer, suggests, with that recorded of some of the Fathers, that of St. Ambrose, for example, or St. Augustine.

II

Donne is best known as a poet for his "Songs and Sonnets," but, in fact, every stage in his development, from the piratical Jack Donne to the penitent John Donne, is registered in his poetry. He was born in London in 1573, the son of a prosperous tradesman, but on his mother's side of a family distinguished both in literature and law, and one which had suffered much for its staunch Catholicism. His father died in 1575, and his early education was entrusted to tutors who were particularly urged to instil into him the principles of the Romish Church, which, however, they could only profess themselves in secret.

Thus his "first breeding and conversation" was "with

men of a suppressed and afflicted religion, accustomed to the despite of death, and hungry of an imagin'd Martyrdome." This very early impression of a world of persecution and intrigue may well have aggravated his innate tendency both to morbidity and independence. At the age of eleven he was sent to Hart Hall, Oxford, where he stayed for three years before being transferred for a similar period to Trinity College, Cambridge. At Oxford he is said to have studied Spanish, and particularly such Spanish mystics as St. Teresa or Luis de Granada, in whom he took a precocious, but wholly characteristic, pleasure.

But if Oxford ministered to his innate mysticism, Cambridge strengthened the faculty for close and ingenious logic which his early Jesuitical training had developed. But it also strengthened his inclination to break with the Faith of his "dear and pious parents." Soon, in fact, after being admitted in 1592 to Lincoln's Inn, his wilful, inquiring nature had cast off the "custom of credulity."

The years immediately subsequent to his admission to Lincoln's Inn were a period of violent and varied experiment, of which his "Satires," many of his "Songs and Sonnets," and the more sensually cynical of his "Elegies" are the fruit in verse, while in the mazes of law and theology he began to take that tense mental exercise which an irritated brain, fermenting with energy, demanded. His "Satires" are certainly the most awkwardly constructed of his poems, but although the earliest of them were little more than conscious experiments in a new kind of versification, calculated affronts to the stylistic graces which he despised as false, they are valuable as the first manifestation of his attitude towards life. In them he lampooned the hypocrisy and arrogance of priests, lawyers, and popinjays, as he was shortly to lampoon the love of women.

And even in the earliest of them his cynicism had its roots in certain deep personal cravings of which it was an inversion, a craving, for example, which was to prove lifelong, for the Court life which he assailed as vain and witless, and for the religious faith which he caricatured in the theological quibblings of combative sectarians. Moreover the satirist gave place, at times, to the preacher, who foretold his own destiny as he acclaimed Truth, standing "on a huge hill, cragged and steep,

> . . . and he that will
> Reach her, about must and about must go
> And what the hill's suddenness resists, win so;
> Yes strive so, that before age, death's twilight,
> Thy soul rest, for none can work in that night."

Not only, then, in the knots and compressions of his prosody, the complicated casuistry of his thought, and the extravagance of his imagery, are Donne's satires, despite their youthful superficiality, characteristic, but in the avid appetite for life which underlay their scorn, and the half-animal, half-moral, disgust of death, which, gathering intensity with every year, was to subject his personality to a continual crisis of battle.

His cravings, however, for sensation which led him to spend nights in the London streets in the company of "fighting and untrussed gallants," involved him increasingly in erotic experiences. The record of these experiences, and the convulsive advance from frank sensuality, spiced with an arrogant cynicism, through self-disgust and self-arraignment, to a mystical apprehension of the potential spirituality of physical love, is to be found in his "Songs and Sonnets" and "Elegies." They belong, for the most part, to the years between 1590 and 1601, but the year 1598, in which he first met the girl whom he was secretly to marry, marked a decisive change in his attitude to women and to love, as it did in his worldly prospects. But this event only confirmed and completed a process of inward growth through licence and disillusionment, which had already gone far.

His earliest lyrics reveal him sowing, in imagination, if not in fact, the wild oats of promiscuous passion, and scoffing at those "poor heretics in love, which think to stablish dangerous constancy." He lets his "body range," loves and hates together with a savage glee and exalts audacity above fear, shame, and honour as the only real principle of purity. The purely predatory phase, however, is short-lived. For as his senses taste satiety, his mind begins to detach itself from the physical impulses which it had previously subserved and exploited. He lashes with a savage self-satisfaction the inconstancy of his victims. He gloats over

Love's deformity as previously over its allurements, expanding all his virtuosity on the delighted imaging of rank physical ugliness. Or he is sufficiently liberated from lust to indulge the fantastical vein in his nature, to extemporize upon the theme of desire in far-fetched allusions and conceits, and even to hint at pathos.

As the virus of consciousness spreads and deepens, and with it the fever of disillusionment, he begins to plead with, and for, the passion and the constancy which he had previously outraged. His prayer would seem to have been answered. He who had been passion's cynic was transformed into passion's slave by, it has been conjectured, the wife of a rich man, a cripple, whom he met at some society function. It is a mistake to read the "Songs and Sonnets" too literally as autobiography. But whatever the experience was which he dramatized so graphically in verse, it was interrupted in 1596 by service abroad, in which he was attached to the Earl of Essex, one of the leaders of a naval expedition against Spain. He was present at the battle of Cadiz, in which the Spanish fleet was defeated, and in the next year he took part in another expedition to intercept the Spanish plate-ships off the Azores. To this voyage we owe the two verse-letters to Christopher Brooke, *The Storm* and *The Calm*, in the latter of which he described one of his motives for volunteering for this expedition as being the desire to escape from "the queasy pain of being belov'd and loving."

Whether, in fact, his latest liaison had run its violent course between the two expeditions to the conclusion of almost demented hate expressed in *The Apparition* is doubtful. But that it brought Donne's career to an end as a piratical lover is certain. His disillusionment of merely physical passion was complete. He had discovered in it the principle of death, and all his efforts were henceforth bent upon discovering a principle of life which would raise love above the tortured ebb and flow of desire. Sensuality, uninformed by spiritual value, was now

> The spider love, which transubstantiates all,
> And can convert Manna to gall.

Yet he was far too physically possessed and far too

potentially real a mystic to react from sensuality into
Platonic abstractions. As he wrote in *The Ecstasy*, which
of all his shorter poems perhaps reveals best his power to
expose the quivering nerves of love and the communion
of souls through bodies:

> So must pure lovers' souls descend
>   T' affections, and to faculties
> Which sense may reach and apprehend,
>   Else a great Prince in prison lies.
> To our bodies turn we then, that so
>   Weak men on love reveal'd may look;
> Love's mysteries in souls do grow,
>   But yet the body is his book.

He found the solution he sought in marriage. In 1598
he had become secretary to Sir Thomas Egerton, the Lord
Keeper, at whose house Ann More, a favourite niece, was
a frequent visitor. On Lady Egerton's death in 1600 she
kept house for her uncle, although only a girl of sixteen.
And in the following year, Donne, casting discretion to
the winds, married her secretly. This so infuriated her
father, Sir George More, that he had Donne arrested and
thrown into prison, and also induced Egerton to dismiss
him from his service. After some months, however, of
which *The Canonization* is essentially the splendid memorial,
the marriage was confirmed, and Ann was allowed to join
her husband.

From the material point of view, Donne was, indeed,
"Undone." His rash action destroyed the promise of a
distinguished secular career, and for fifteen years tied him
to poverty and the humiliations of the mendicant. Yet,
as both the tenderest and the most spiritually ecstatic of
the "Songs and Sonnets" prove, his marriage resolved
for him on the plane of sex the conflict between thought
and instinct which had for so long convulsed him. Hence-
forth the struggle was more and more transferred to the
plane of religion, in which the mystic in him had to oppose
equally his earthly desires and his worldly ambitions.

The Progress of the Soul, which he composed in the year
of his marriage, is at once the most ambitiously planned
and least read of his poems. It was based on the Pytha-
gorean theory of "Metempsychosis," a theory which itself

derived, as Donne may well have known, from the ancient and esoteric doctrine which proclaimed an obligatory pilgrimage for every soul through a cycle of incarnation, that included every elemental form of the phenomenal world. It was never completed, and has generally been dismissed as an extreme example of Donne's worst defects. Yet De Quincey praised, with some reason, the "many diamonds" which compose its very substance, and fanciful and even satirically frivolous as it often is, there is a pregnant force and dark sublimity in parts of it, because the "soul" of the poem, plunged from one natural process into another, with no control over the humiliating experiences to which it is subjected, but obeying a mysterious force which is gradually driving it upward to the plane of human individuality, is essentially the convulsed soul of Donne himself.

The majority of the "Verse Letters" belong to the years between his marriage and his taking of Orders in 1615. During this time his circumstances were, at worst, very straitened, at best, very insecure. He was, to a great extent, dependent on the charity of friends and patrons, and with a family rapidly and regularly increasing, his means were often insufficient. For some years he rented a small house at Mitcham, and divided his time between it and rooms in the Strand, where he collected material from Canon Law for the use of Thomas Morton, later Bishop of Durham, who employed him in the war of pamphlets against the Catholics. In 1607 Morton, on becoming Dean of Gloucester, offered his assistant a comfortable benefice, if he would take Orders. Donne, however, refused, and probably his refusal was equally dictated by a sense of personal unworthiness, by intellectual doubt, and by the hopes he still cherished of promotion in a secular sphere.

Meanwhile his outlook remained gloomy; isolation intensified his morbidity, and owing to the damp conditions of the Mitcham house he and his family were so frequently sick that he headed some of his letters, "From my hospital at Mitcham." The depressed and disordered state of mind which such conditions engendered are evident in many of his "Verse Letters." They are often flat and elaborately

laboured, like the controversial works in prose upon which
he was professionally employed, and from which he turned
with cramped hand to the medium of verse.

During 1608, indeed, he seems to have fallen into so acute
a state of depression as to have even contemplated the idea
of suicide.

In the previous year, however, he had become acquainted
with Magdalen Herbert, the widowed mother of George
Herbert, the poet, And in her he found one, who by her
sanity, piety, and sympathy was, for the rest of his days,
to reinforce his higher self and to strengthen him in hours
of perplexity. Nevertheless, in 1608 he described himself
as "rather a sickness or a disease of the world, than any
part of it," and early in 1609 he experienced the first of
those physical crises which were to prove milestones in his
emancipation from the vanities of the world and the flesh.
During this illness he wrote the first of what have been
called his "Divine Poems"—*The Litany*, and also, probably,
The Cross. His religious, like his erotic, verse, images the
gradual absorption of the casuist in the would-be convert,
and in these two poems each is apparent, lines woven by
ingenious wit alternating with others that express a
passionate contrition and longing for spiritual release.
"Who will deliver me from the burden of this Death?"
is the essence of his appeal and his lament, and in his
relation to God, as earlier in his relation to women, death
meant to him both mental arrogance and physical enslave-
ment. As he wrote in *The Cross*:

> . . . Cross thy senses, else, both they, and thou
> Must perish soon, and to destruction bow.

And again:

> So when thy brain works, ere thou utter it,
> Cross and correct concupiscence of wit.

This tense struggle to subdue a mental and carnal
egotism was to dictate for the rest of his life all his spiritual
activity. As health returned, however, and his fortunes
improved, he relaxed the struggle, and only when sickness
had attacked him again with more severity and his secular
ambitions seemed finally frustrated, did he devote himself
to it with all his heart.

For, late in 1608, the burden of immediate poverty was lifted. Sir George More was persuaded to grant his son-in-law a small regular allowance, while Donne acquired himself a generous patroness in the Countess of Bedford, who gathered about her at Twickenham some of the most gifted and cultivated men of the day. Donne attached himself to her informal court, and "a new world rose from her light." With his talent for spinning allegorical imagery about a theme he found it easy to decorate the nuptials or obsequies of his patroness's relatives with complimentary verses. Moreover, in the excitement of versification the poet often transcended the laureate. Nor was his adulation in this case degrading, as his prostration before rank and influence was often later to be. For the Countess of Bedford he cherished a sincere devotion. She stood to him in the position of a secular Mrs. Herbert. Each personified for him one of the two ambitions which were to dispute his allegiance — the world's charm and the Church's peace. And despite his father-in-law's bounty and his London diversions, he was still at heart unhappy and ill-adjusted. His great gifts were being wasted on trivial activities, his wife's energies were overtaxed by a steadily increasing family, and he was haunted by the thought that he had "transplanted her into a wretched fortune." Consequently, even in the years 1609 and 1610, his preoccupation with religion was quite as insistent as with society, but in 1610 an event occurred which, in delivering him from his "hospital" at Mitcham, arrested his growing inclination to enter the Church.

Sir Robert Drury of Hawstead, in Suffolk, lost his only surviving daughter, Elizabeth, a girl of fourteen, upon whom he had lavished his affections and, according to rumour, centred exorbitant ambitions. The facts and fictions of this "sad history" reached Donne's ears, and he composed a short funeral elegy which he sent to the stricken father. Doubtless his main motive was to attract the notice of one of the wealthiest men of the time, and in this he was completely successful. Sir Robert offered him and his family a set of chambers in his own large house in Drury Lane, and Donne, wishing to make the only return he could to his benefactor, composed successively the *Anatomy of the World*, to celebrate the first anniversary of Elizabeth's death, and *Of the Progress of the Soul*, to celebrate the second. His intention was to continue his tributes yearly, but after these two he wisely desisted.

The circumstances, indeed, of their origin, and the extravagant homage which he offered to a young girl whom he had never known, had already excited some derision, and Ben Jonson's remark that "the Anniversarie was profane and full of blasphemies . . . that if it had been written of the Virgin Marie it had been something," reflected doubtless a very general opinion. Yet although Donne may deserve censure for exploiting to some extent both his muse and a tragic occasion, the poems themselves, despite their artificial excesses, are his sufficient justification. Moreover, the original Elegy and *The First Anniversary*, against which the charge of artificiality can most justly be sustained, were written without any idea of publication, as a private, if interested, offering to a distracted father. And even these contain passages of ecstatic divination.

We do not need the example of other great elegists to inform us that the actual subject of an elegy is of secondary importance. And Donne sufficiently defended himself against Jonson's strictures by saying that it was "the Idea of a Woman and not as she was," that haunted his imagination as he wrote. And in his Idea of Woman he embodied also his Idea of the Divine as pure spirit inviolable by death. Indeed, in *The Second Anniversary* he came nearer, perhaps, expressing that spiritual triumph over the dead-weight of mortality, for which his whole life was a battle, than in any other of his poems. The professional elegist, extravagant eulogist, and quibbling dialectician were, in fact, with each tribute increasingly superseded by a poet possessed of a hunger for "that radiance, which the world sullies, that form which the world fumbles or distorts," and for whom Elizabeth Drury had become nothing less than a symbol of pure spirit, of immortal beauty, harmony, and innocence. As in the sermons of his latter years, this ecstatic intuition of the

Divine was at once crossed and heightened by a fearful sense of the terrors of death and the horrors of corruption. And when the moment of ideal intoxication had passed, the fact of death still remained to convulse him to the end.

In November 1611 Sir Robert Drury wished Donne to accompany him abroad, and the necessity of parting from his wife, who was in poor health and expecting her eighth child, occasioned two of the tenderest of his shorter poems: *A Valediction : forbidding mourning,* and the song, *Sweetest love, I do not go.* He was away almost a year, and on his return, having tasted the sweets of "high life" as a rich and influential man's attendant, he renewed his efforts to obtain some reliable appointment. The pending marriage of the popular Princess Elizabeth with the Elector Palatine offered him an opportunity of engaging the attention of the Court, and when the sudden death of her brother, the young Prince of Wales, delayed the marriage for some months, he embraced the sad theme with the same readiness as the glad. In the *Elegy upon Prince Henry,* however, he produced a poem lamentable only in its laboured obscurity. For his hopes and fears were for the time set on life, and he had recently and sublimely exhausted his powers on the subject of death.

Very different is the *Marriage Song,* dedicated to the radiant princess. Like the Epithalamion which he had written during his residence at Lincoln's Inn, it has a physical candour devoid of all calculated sensuality. But its gleeful naturalism is keyed up to a higher level, at once more recondite, more gracious, and more imaginative than that of the earlier poem. In affirming the generative joy of life, the marriage of its elements, of the earth spirit and the quickening flame of the sun, Donne, for a moment, could forget both the ugly aspect of the physical, and his own morbid introspection.

His homage, however, made no apparent impression upon the Court, and his thoughts turned once more towards the Church, as a possible profession, and a means of harmonizing the warring forces in himself. In October 1612, he addressed himself to Viscount Rochester, the reigning favourite, declaring his resolve to take Holy Orders. That

the hope of worldly preferment still underlay his resolve
cannot be doubted, but sickness was once again to intensify
his longing for sanctity. In March 1613 he announced his
recovery from a short bout of illness in the old dismal
dialect of Mitcham: "I begin to be past hope of dying."
And riding on Good Friday to visit the Herberts at Mont-
gomery Castle he implored punishment and pardon for
the worldly self-debasement of which he had been guilty.
Riding Westward testifies to the sincerity of his contri-
tion, and the lines in which at the same time he associated
his hostess and through her his ideal of womanhood with
the primrose in a love-poem "above all thought of sex"
reveals, as *The Autumnal* was even more rarely to do, the
inspiration, the "warm redeeming hand" of Magdalen
Herbert. On his return to London, however, he relapsed
once again into craven solicitation, composing an Epitha-
lamion to celebrate the scandalous nuptials of Rochester
and the Countess of Essex which was a mere composite of
flagrant flattery, bedizened diction, and carnal conventions,
while in the introductory eclogue to it he paid a politic
tribute to the Court life which he had so often elsewhere
assessed at its true value.

Yet nothing came of these efforts, and from the middle
of 1613 to the end of 1614 continuous sickness and domestic
tragedy reduced him to a state of frenzied anxiety. With
agitated servility he commended himself to every lord and
lady of his acquaintance; yet even the Countess of Bedford,
in memory of whose young brother, Lord Harrington, he
composed some "Obsequies," which were something more
than ceremonial verse, had to refuse him financial help.
At last, however, he wrung from Rochester, now Lord
Somerset, an invitation to meet the king, who, he hoped,
would appoint him to a vacant clerkship of the Council.
But James I had other ideas of preferment, which neces
sitated Donne's entering into sacred Orders. In January
1615 he was ordained and attached as curate to the parish
of Paddington.

If material necessity dictated the step, it answered, too,
an inner need. The conviction, voiced so many years before
that "there is no Virtue, but Religion," had at last almost

triumphed in his heart over the itchings of worldly ambition. In October 1616 he was elected Divinity Reader by the Benchers of Lincoln's Inn, and when in the following August his much tried wife died after giving birth to a twelfth and still-born infant, grief and remorse sealed the contract with religion which he had accepted. Essentially henceforth he stood alone with his God, though it was as a "man that hath seen affliction by the rod of His wrath."

In the "Holy Sonnets," probably composed during 1617 and 1618, he confessed in his approach to God the same remorse for past infidelity as he had shown to his wife at the time of his marriage. Primarily, in all of them he was engaged in asserting that now "wholly on heavenly things" his mind was set and in lamenting past and present sin. Consequently Death, image alike of spiritual emancipation and of physical bondage, is their central theme. For here, as in his sermons, his sense of sin constantly curdled his spiritual exaltation, while his fascinated horror of death embittered his boast of eternal life. In "La Corona," 1609, which follows the Church's festivals in celebrating the life of Christ from the Annunciation to the Ascension, the theologian trespasses as considerably upon the poet as the quibbler did once upon the lover. But in the "Holy Sonnets," the conventional idiom of religion never intrudes upon the drama of his own imperfect conversion, with "Despair behind" and "Death before," of which they are the concentrated expression. His lust for life and his scepticism were not submerged, save in moments of defiant ecstasy, in mystical faith; and it was their persistence which gave so terrible and sublime a reality to his utterance, as of a man who did consciously, in his assault on heaven, "hell's wide mouth o'erstride," and knew that one moment's slackening of effort would change potential victory into actual defeat.

Consequently, Donne now wooed his God with both the fervour and the self-disgust with which he had before addressed his mistresses; even the erotic imagery recurs. His religion was become a personal passion and a personal hazard, to which theology was no more than a prop.   And if, for the most part, he sounded the torments of a frustrated lover to whom death only could bring alleviation, and all a lover's agonized yearning for those ultimate bridals which the flesh, at best, so tantalizingly, at worst, so grossly denies, there were moments, as in his *Hymn to Christ*, composed in 1619, when the tension relaxed, and he confided himself to his Creator with a deep-toned affection, reminiscent of that which he had expressed eight years before in the lines addressed to his wife on parting.

Meanwhile in 1621 the king appointed him Dean of St. Paul's. Two years later, however, he was attacked by a gastric fever more violent than any from which he had yet suffered, and essentially the fire thus kindled was to blaze and smoulder until it had burnt his body away. He had entered on the last stage of his pilgrimage and that which shares with the licentious era of his youth the fascinated amazement of posterity. The reflections which he committed to paper during the height of his fever surpass in vividness and intensity of self-analysis even the *Devotions* which grew out of them, but his *Hymn to God the Father*, written in the spring of 1624, is the perfect epilogue to the tortured analysis of his sick-bed. It contains in its three stanzas the essence of his contrition, and in its conclusion reveals with the unfevered calm of convalescence the doubt and fear which were to haunt his mind to the end.

During the seven remaining years of his life the energies of the poet were, for the most part, exhausted in the pulpit. As he wrote in the lines *To Mr. Tilman after he had taken Orders*:

> What function is so noble, as to be
> Ambassador to God and destiny?

And as a preacher he relieved by expressing, again and again, the life-long conflict in himself between Heaven and Hell, which he could never transform, as Blake was later to do, into a Marriage. To the autumn of 1625, however, belongs the lovely elegy, entitled *The Autumnal*, which he addressed in a period of enforced retirement from London, to Magdalen Herbert, and which comes nearer perhaps the ultimate wisdom of love, in which there is neither expectancy nor regret, than any other of his poems.

But self-renunciation and freedom from attachment were ideals which he could never make constant in his life, of which the last six years were as inwardly convulsed as any that preceded them. And eight days before his end, when fever had almost burnt his flesh away, and he had offered death a last gesture of sardonic defiance by posing for his portrait, clothed only in his shroud, he bade farewell to life in *A Hymn to God, my God, in my Sickness*, with the same chemistry of far-fetched fancy and analogy, of devotion and geographical conceits as he had brought to the celebration of his mistresses in the hey-day of his youth.

In some ways, therefore, the best of Donne's "Divine Poems," like the best of his sermons, are more significant, if less daring, than the early "Songs and Sonnets," for which he is best known. They are the ripe harvest of a life prodigally sown; for it was through the agonies of sex that he mounted to the sublimities of religion. But while he brought the same sensuousness and the same riddling subtlety to his courtship of God, as to his courtship of women, he solicited life in his "Divine Poems" at a deeper and a wider level. Always it is his rich virility which makes him, even in intricate moments of perplexity and self-defeat, passionately expressive; and in his rare moments of imaginative victory, of conflict culminating in unity, only to relapse again into discord, "through the ragged apparel of the afflictions of this life; through the scars and wounds and paleness, and morphews of sin, and corruption, we can look upon the soul itself."

HUGH I'A. FAUSSET.

1958.

ACKNOWLEDGMENTS

Any editor of Donne's poems must be primarily indebted to Professor Grierson, whose masterly critical edition of the poems is substantially final, both for the canon and the text which it has established. To him and the Delegates of the

Clarendon Press, I also owe a particular debt for allowing me to print the Verse Letter, *Henrico Wottini in Hibernia Belligeranti*, from the Burley MS. By the courtesy of Mr. Philip Gosse I have been able to reproduce poems from the Westmorland MS., while to Mr. John Hayward and the Nonesuch Press Ltd. I am indebted for the use of several acceptable new readings from their *Complete Poetry and Selected Prose of John Donne*. My wife has given me much valuable help in modernizing the spelling, while preserving, as far as possible, the distinctive idiosyncrasies of the original text.

H. I'A. F.

SELECT BIBLIOGRAPHY

WORKS. *Poems by J. D. with elegies on the author's death,* 1633; enlarged editions 1635, 1649, 1650 and 1669; *Complete Poems,* ed. A. B. Grosart, 2 vols., 1872; *Poems,* ed. Sir E. K. Chambers, with Introduction by George Saintsbury, 2 vols., 1896; *Poems,* ed. H. J. C. Grierson, 2 vols., 1912 (the standard edition); *Complete Poetry and Selected Prose,* ed. John Hayward, 1929, revised edition 1930; *The Elegies and the Songs and Sonnets,* ed. Helen Gardner, 1967.

BIOGRAPHY AND CRITICISM. Izaak Walton, *The Life of John Donne,* 1658; ed. T. E. Tomlins, 1852; E. Gosse, *The Life and Letters of John Donne,* 1899; H. I'Anson Fausset, *John Donne, A Study in Discord,* 1924; Evelyn M. Simpson, *A Study of the Prose Works of John Donne,* 1924; C. M. Coffin, *John Donne and the New Philosophy,* 1937; Evelyn Hardy, *Donne, a Spirit in Conflict,* 1943; M. F. Moloney, *John Donne, His Flight from Mediaevalism,* 1944; W. S. Scott, *The Fantasticks,* 1945; J. B. Leishman, *The Monarch of Wit: An Analytical and Comparative Study of the Poetry of John Donne,* 1951; K. W. Gransden, *John Donne,* 1954; R. C. Bald, *Donne and the Drurys,* 1959; W. R. Mueller, *John Donne: Preacher,* 1963; Helen Gardner, *Donne,* 1963; E. L. Comte, *Grace to a Willing Sinner: A Life of John Donne,* 1965; N. C. J. Andreasen, *John Donne: Conservative Revolutionary,* 1967; Albert James Smith, ed., *John Donne: Essays in Celebration,* 1972; J. Lovelock, ed., *Donne Songs and Sonnets.* Casebook S., 1973; Albert James Smith, ed., *John Donne,* Crit. Heritage S., 1975.

BIBLIOGRAPHY. Geoffrey Keynes, *A Bibliography of the Works of John Donne,* 1914; revised edition 1932.

CONTENTS

	PAGE
INTRODUCTION by Hugh I'A. Fausset	vii

SONGS AND SONNETS:

The Good-morrow	1
Song	1
Woman's Constancy	2
The Undertaking	3
The Sun Rising	4
The Indifferent	5
Love's Usury	6
The Canonization	6
The Triple Fool	8
Lover's Infiniteness	8
Song	9
The Legacy	11
A Fever	11
Air and Angels	12
Break of Day	13
The Anniversary	14
A Valediction: of my name, in the window	15
Twickenham Garden	17
A Valediction: of the book	18
Community	20
Love's Growth	21
Love's Exchange	21
Confined Love	23
The Dream	23
A Valediction: of weeping	24
Love's Alchemy	25
The Flea	26
The Curse	27
The Message	28
A Nocturnal upon St. Lucy's Day . . .	29
Witchcraft by a Picture	30
The Bait	30
The Apparition	31
The Broken Heart	32
A Valediction: forbidding mourning . . .	33
The Ecstasy	34
Love's Deity	36
Love's Diet	37

CONTENTS

SONGS AND SONNETS—*continued*   PAGE

    The Will 38
    The Funeral 40
    The Blossom 40
    The Primrose 42
    The Relique 43
    The Damp 44
    The Dissolution 44
    A Jet Ring sent 45
    Negative Love 46
    The Prohibition 46
    The Expiration 47
    The Computation 47
    The Paradox 48
    Farewell to Love 48
    A Lecture upon the Shadow 50
    Sonnet: The Token 50
    Self-love 51

EPIGRAMS:

    Hero and Leander 53
    Pyramus and Thisbe 53
    Niobe 53
    A Burnt Ship 53
    Fall of a Wall 53
    A Lame Beggar 54
    Cales and Guiana 54
    Sir John Wingfield 54
    A Self-accuser 54
    A Licentious Person 54
    Antiquary 54
    Disinherited 55
    Phryne 55
    An Obscure Writer 55
    Klockius 55
    Raderus 55
    Mercurius Gallo-Belgicus 55
    Ralphius 56
    The Liar 56

ELEGIES:

    I. Jealousy 57
    II. The Anagram 58
    III. Change 60
    IV. The Perfume 61
    V. His Picture 63
    VI. *Oh, let me not serve* 63
    VII. *Nature's lay Idiot* 65

CONTENTS

ELEGIES—*continued*   PAGE

   VIII. The Comparison 66
    IX. The Autumnal 67
     X. The Dream 69
    XI. The Bracelet 70
   XII. His parting from her 73
  XIII. Julia 76
  XIV. A Tale of a Citizen and his Wife . . . 77
   XV. The Expostulation 79
  XVI. On his Mistress 81
 XVII. Variety 82
XVIII. Love's Progress 85
  XIX. To his Mistress going to Eed . . . 87
   XX. Love's War 89

HEROICAL EPISTLE:

   Sappho to Philænis 90

EPITHALAMIONS, OR MARRIAGE SONGS:

   On the Lady Elizabeth and Count Palatine . . 93
   Eclogue: 1613. December 26 . . . 97
   Epithalamion 100
   Epithalamion made at Lincoln's Inn . . 104

SATIRES:

   Satire   I 108
   Satire   II 111
   Satire III 114
   Satire   IV 117
   Satire   V 123
   Upon Mr. Thomas Coryat's Crudities . . 126
   In Eundem Macaronicon . . . 128

VERSE LETTERS TO SEVERAL PERSONAGES:

   To Mr. Christopher Brooke:
     The Storm 129
     The Calm 131
   To the Countess of Huntingdon . . . 132
   To Sir Henry Wotton 136
   To Sir Henry Goodyere 138
   To Mr. Rowland Woodward 139
   To Sir Henry Wotton 141
   Henrico Wottoni in Hibernia Belligeranti . . 142
   To the Countess of Bedford:
     Madam, Reason is 142
     Madam, you have refin'd 144

VERSE LETTERS TO SEVERAL PERSONAGES—*continued*   PAGE

To Sir Edward Herbert at Juliers 146
To the Countess of Bedford:
    To have written then 147
    This twilight 150
To the Countess of Huntingdon 152
To Mr. T[homas]. W[oodward].:
    All hail, sweet Poet 154
    Haste thee harsh verse 155
    Pregnant again 156
    At once, from hence 156
To Mr. R[owland]. W[oodward].:
    Zealously my Muse 157
    Muse not 157
To Mr. C[hristopher]. B[rooke]. 157
To Mr. E[dward]. G[ilpin?]. 158
To Mr. R[owland]. W[oodward].:
    If, as mine is 158
    Kindly I envy 159
To Mr. S[amuel]. B[rooke?]. 160
To Mr. I. L.:
    Of that short roll 160
    Blest are your north parts 161
To Mr. B[asil]. B[rooke?]. 161
To Sir H[enry]. W[otton]. at his going Ambassador to
    Venice 162
To Mrs. M[agdalen]. H[erbert]. 164
To the Countess of Bedford:
    Honour is so sublime perfection . . . 165
    Though I be dead 167
A Letter to the Lady Carey and Mrs. Essex Rich,
    from Amiens 168
To the Countess of Salisbury 170
To the Lady Bedford 173

AN ANATOMY OF THE WORLD:
To the Praise of the Dead 175
The First Anniversary 176
A Funeral Elegy 189

OF THE PROGRESS OF THE SOUL:
The Harbinger to the Progress 192
The Second Anniversary. 193

CONTENTS

PAGE

EPICEDES AND OBSEQUIES UPON THE DEATHS OF SUNDRY
  PERSONAGES:
  Elegy upon Prince Henry 208
  Obsequies to the Lord Harrington 211
  Elegy on the Lady Markham 218
  Elegy on Mistress Boulstred 219
  Elegy. Death 221
  Elegy on the L[ord]. C[hamberlain]. . . . 223
  An Hymn to the Saints, and to Marquis Hamilton . 224

EPITAPHS:
  On Himself 225
  Omnibus 226

INFINITATI SACRUM:
  The Progress of the Soul 227

DIVINE POEMS:
  To E[arl] . of D[orset]. 245
  To the Lady Magdalen Herbert 245

  HOLY SONNETS:
  La Corona 246
  Annunciation 246
  Nativity 246
  Temple 247
  Crucifying 247
  Resurrection 248
  Ascension 248

  HOLY SONNETS:
    I. Thou hast made me 249
   II. As due by many titles 249
  III. Oh might those sighs and tears . . 249
   IV. Oh my black Soul 250
    V. I am a little world 250
   VI. This is my play's last scene . . 251
  VII. At the round earth's imagin'd corners . 251
 VIII. If faithful souls be alike glorified . . 251
   IX. If poisonous minerals . . . 252
    X. Death be not proud . . . 252
   XI. Spit in my face you Jews . . 253
  XII. Why are we by all creatures waited on ? . 253
 XIII. What if this present were the world's last night? 253
  XIV. Batter my heart 254
   XV. Wilt thou love God . . . 254
  XVI. Father, part of His double interest . . 255

CONTENTS

Holy Sonnets—*continued*   PAGE
  XVII. *Since she whom I lov'd hath paid her last debt* . 255
  XVIII. *Show me dear Christ* 255
  XIX. *Oh, to vex me, contraries meet in one* .   . 256

The Cross 256
Resurrection, imperfect 258
Upon the Annunciation and Passion .   . 259
Good Friday, 1613. Riding Westward .   . 260
The Litany 261
Upon the Translation of the Psalms .   . 270
To Mr. Tilman after he had taken Orders .   . 272
A Hymn to Christ 273
The Lamentations of Jeremy .   .   . 274
Hymn to God my God, in my Sickness .   . 287
A Hymn to God the Father .   .   . 288

LATIN POEMS AND TRANSLATIONS:
To Mr. George Herbert, with one of my Seals .   . 289
Translated out of Gazæus 290

SONGS AND SONNETS

THE GOOD-MORROW

I WONDER by my troth, what thou and I
Did, till we lov'd? were we not wean'd till then?
But suck'd on country pleasures, childishly?
Or snorted we in the seven sleepers' den?
'Twas so; but this, all pleasures fancies be.
If ever any beauty I did see,
Which I desir'd, and got, 'twas but a dream of thee.

And now good-morrow to our waking souls,
Which watch not one another out of fear;
For love all love of other sights controls,
And makes one little room an everywhere.
Let sea-discoverers to new worlds have gone,
Let maps to other, worlds on worlds have shown,
Let us possess one world, each hath one, and is one.

My face in thine eye, thine in mine appears,
And true plain hearts do in the faces rest;
Where can we find two better hemispheres
Without sharp North, without declining West?
What ever dies, was not mixt equally;
If our two loves be one, or thou and I
Love so alike that none do slacken, none can die.

SONG

Go, and catch a falling star,
    Get with child a mandrake root,
Tell me, where all past years are,
    Or who cleft the Devil's foot,

Teach me to hear Mermaids singing,
  Or to keep off envy's stinging,
      And find
      What wind
Serves to advance an honest mind.

If thou be'st born to strange sights,
  Things invisible to see,
Ride ten thousand days and nights,
  Till age snow white hairs on thee,
Thou, when thou return'st, wilt tell me
All strange wonders that befell thee,
      And swear
      No where
Lives a woman true, and fair.

If thou find'st one, let me know,
  Such a Pilgrimage were sweet;
Yet do not, I would not go,
  Though at next door we might meet,
Though she were true, when you met her,
And last, till you write your letter,
      Yet she
      Will be
False, ere I come, to two, or three.

WOMAN'S CONSTANCY

Now thou hast lov'd me one whole day,
To-morrow when thou leav'st, what wilt thou say?
Wilt thou then antedate some new made vow?
    Or say that now
We are not just those persons, which we were?
Or, that oaths made in reverential fear
Of Love, and his wrath, any may forswear?
Or, as true deaths true marriages untie,

So lovers' contracts, images of those,
Bind but till sleep, death's image, them unloose?
      Or, your own end to justify,
For having purpos'd change, and falsehood, you
Can have no way but falsehood to be true?
Vain lunatic, against these 'scapes I could
        Dispute, and conquer, if I would,
        Which I abstain to do,
For by to-morrow, I may think so too.

THE UNDERTAKING

I HAVE done one braver thing
    Than all the *Worthies* did,
And yet a braver thence doth spring,
    Which is, to keep that hid.

It were but madness now to impart
    The skill of specular stone,
When he which can have learn'd the art
    To cut it, can find none.

So, if I now should utter this,
    Others (because no more
Such stuff to work upon, there is,)
    Would love but as before.

But he who loveliness within
    Hath found, all outward loathes,
For he who colour loves, and skin,
    Loves but their oldest clothes.

If, as I have, you also do
    Virtue attired in woman see,
And dare love that, and say so too,
    And forget the He and She;

And if this love, though placèd so,
    From profane men you hide,
Which will no faith on this bestow,
    Or, if they do, deride:

Then you have done a braver thing
    Than all the *Worthies* did;
And a braver thence will spring,
    Which is, to keep that hid.

THE SUN RISING

    Busy old fool, unruly Sun,
      Why dost thou thus,
Through windows, and through curtains call on us?
Must to thy motions lovers' seasons run?
      Saucy, pedantic wretch, go chide
      Late school-boys, and sour prentices,
    Go tell Court-huntsmen, that the King will ride,
    Call country ants to harvest offices;
Love, all alike, no season knows, nor clime,
Nor hours, days, months, which are the rags of time.

      Thy beams so reverend, and strong
      Why shouldst thou think?
I could eclipse and cloud them with a wink,
But that I would not lose her sight so long:
      If her eyes have not blinded thine,
      Look, and to-morrow late, tell me,
    Whether both th' Indias of spice and mine
    Be where thou left'st them, or lie here with me.
Ask for those Kings whom thou saw'st yesterday,
And thou shalt hear, All here in one bed lay.

      She's all States, and all Princes, I,
      Nothing else is.
Princes do but play us; compar'd to this,
All honour's mimic; all wealth alchemy.

Thou sun art half as happy as we,
 In that the world 's contracted thus;
Thine age asks ease, and since thy duties be
To warm the world, that 's done in warming us.
Shine here to us, and thou art everywhere;
This bed thy centre is, these walls, thy sphere.

THE INDIFFERENT

I CAN love both fair and brown,
Her whom abundance melts, and her whom want betrays,
Her who loves loneness best, and her who masks and plays,
Her whom the country form'd, and whom the town,
Her who believes, and her who tries,
Her who still weeps with spongy eyes,
And her who is dry cork, and never cries;
I can love her, and her, and you and you,
I can love any, so she be not true.

Will no other vice content you?
Will it not serve your turn to do as did your mothers?
Or have you all old vices spent, and now would find out
 others?
Or doth a fear, that men are true, torment you?
Oh we are not, be not you so;
Let me, and do you, twenty know.
Rob me, but bind me not, and let me go.
Must I, who came to travail thorough you,
Grow your fixt subject, because you are true?

Venus heard me sigh this song,
And by Love's sweetest part, Variety, she swore,
She heard not this till now; and that it should be so no more.
She went, examin'd, and return'd ere long,
And said, alas, Some two or three
Poor heretics in love there be,
Which think to 'stablish dangerous constancy.
But I have told them, since you will be true,
You shall be true to them, who 're false to you.

LOVE'S USURY

For every hour that thou wilt spare me now,
      I will allow,
Usurious God of Love, twenty to thee,
When with my brown, my grey hairs equal be;
Till then, Love, let my body reign, and let
Me travel, sojourn, snatch, plot, have, forget,
Resume my last year's relict: think that yet
      We 'd never met.

Let me think any rival's letter mine,
      And at next nine
Keep midnight's promise; mistake by the way
The maid, and tell the Lady of that delay;
Only let me love none, no, not the sport;
From country grass, to comfitures of Court,
Or city's *quelque-choses*, let report
      My mind transport.

This bargain 's good; if when I 'm old, I be
      Inflam'd by thee,
If thine own honour, or my shame, or pain,
Thou covet most, at that age thou shalt gain.
Do thy will then, then subject and degree,
And fruit of love, Love, I submit to thee;
Spare me till then, I 'll bear it, though she be
      One that loves me.

THE CANONIZATION

For God's sake hold your tongue, and let me love;
   Or chide my palsy, or my gout,
My five grey hairs, or ruin'd fortune flout;
    With wealth your state, your mind with arts improve,
    Take you a course, get you a place,
    Observe his Honour, or his Grace,

Or the King's real, or his stamped face
  Contemplate; what you will, approve,
  So you will let me love.

Alas, alas, who 's injur'd by my love?
  What merchant's ships have my sighs drown'd?
Who says my tears have overflow'd his ground?
  When did my colds a forward spring remove?
    When did the heats which my veins fill
    Add one more to the plaguy bill?
Soldiers find wars, and lawyers find out still
  Litigious men, which quarrels move,
  Though she and I do love.

Call us what you will, we are made such by love;
  Call her one, me another fly,
We 're tapers too, and at our own cost die,
  And we in us find the Eagle and the Dove.
    The Phœnix riddle hath more wit
    By us; we two being one, are it.
So to one neutral thing both sexes fit,
  We die and rise the same, and prove
  Mysterious by this love.

We can die by it, if not live by love,
  And if unfit for tombs and hearse
Our legend be, it will be fit for verse;
  And if no piece of Chronicle we prove,
    We 'll build in sonnets pretty rooms;
    As well a well-wrought urn becomes
The greatest ashes, as half-acre tombs,
  And by these hymns, all shall approve
  Us canonized for Love:

And thus invoke us; You whom reverend love
  Made one another's hermitage;
You, to whom love was peace, that now is rage;
  Who did the whole world's soul contract, and drove
    Into the glasses of your eyes
    (So made such mirrors, and such spies,

That they did all to you epitomize,)
   Countries, Towns, Courts: beg from above
   A pattern of your love!

THE TRIPLE FOOL

I AM two fools, I know,
For loving, and for saying so
   In whining poetry;
But where 's that wise man, that would not be I,
   If she would not deny?
Then as th' earth's inward narrow crooked lanes
Do purge sea-water's fretful salt away,
   I thought, if I could draw my pains
Through rhyme's vexation, I should them allay.
Grief brought to numbers cannot be so fierce,
For he tames it, that fetters it in verse.

   But when I have done so,
Some man, his art and voice to show,
   Doth set and sing my pain,
And, by delighting many, frees again
   Grief, which verse did restrain.
To Love and Grief tribute of Verse belongs,
But not of such as pleases when 'tis read;
   Both are increasèd by such songs:
For both their triumphs so are publishèd,
And I, which was two fools, do so grow three;
Who are a little wise, the best fools be.

LOVERS' INFINITENESS

IF yet I have not all thy love,
Dear, I shall never have it all,
I cannot breathe one other sigh, to move,
Nor can entreat one other tear to fall,
And all my treasure, which should purchase thee,

Sighs, tears, and oaths, and letters I have spent.
Yet no more can be due to me,
Than at the bargain made was meant.
If then thy gift of love were partial,
That some to me, some should to others fall,
　Dear, I shall never have Thee All.

Or if then thou gavest me all,
All was but all, which thou hadst then;
But if in thy heart, since, there be or shall
New love created be, by other men,
Which have their stocks entire, and can in tears,
In sighs, in oaths, and letters outbid me,
This new love may beget new fears,
For, this love was not vowed by thee.
And yet it was, thy gift being general;
The ground, thy heart, is mine; whatever shall
　Grow there, dear, I should have it all.

Yet I would not have all yet,
He that hath all can have no more,
And since my love doth every day admit
New growth, thou shouldst have new rewards in store;
Thou canst not every day give me thy heart,
If thou canst give it, then thou never gavest it:
Love's riddles are, that though thy heart depart,
It stays at home, and thou with losing savest it:
But we will have a way more liberal,
Than changing hearts, to join them, so we shall
　Be one, and one another's All.

SONG

SWEETEST love, I do not go,
　For weariness of thee,
Nor in hope the world can show
　A fitter Love for me;

But since that I
Must die at last, 'tis best,
To use my self in jest
　　Thus by feign'd deaths to die.

Yesternight the Sun went hence,
　　And yet is here to-day;
He hath no desire nor sense,
　　Nor half so short a way:
　　　Then fear not me,
But believe that I shall make
Speedier journeys, since I take
　　More wings and spurs than he.

O how feeble is man's power,
　　That if good fortune fall,
Cannot add another hour,
　　Nor a lost hour recall!
　　　But come bad chance,
And we join to it our strength,
And we teach it art and length,
　　Itself o'er us to advance.

When thou sigh'st, thou sigh'st not wind,
　　But sigh'st my soul away,
When thou weep'st, unkindly kind,
　　My life's blood doth decay.
　　　It cannot be
That thou lov'st me, as thou say'st,
If in thine my life thou waste,
　　That art the best of me.

Let not thy divining heart
　　Forethink me any ill,
Destiny may take thy part,
　　And may thy fears fulfil;
　　　But think that we
Are but turn'd aside to sleep;
They who one another keep
　　Alive, ne'er parted be.

THE LEGACY

WHEN I died last, and, Dear, I die
  As often as from thee I go,
  Though it be but an hour ago,
And Lovers' hours be full eternity,
I can remember yet, that I
  Something did say, and something did bestow;
Though I be dead, which sent me, I should be
Mine own executor and legacy.

I heard me say, Tell her anon,
  That my self, (that is you, not I,)
  Did kill me, and when I felt me die,
I bid me send my heart, when I was gone;
But I alas could there find none,
  When I had ripp'd me, and search'd where hearts did lie;
It kill'd me again, that I who still was true,
In life, in my last Will should cozen you.

Yet I found something like a heart,
  But colours it, and corners had,
  It was not good, it was not bad,
It was entire to none, and few had part.
As good as could be made by art
  It seem'd; and therefore for our losses sad,
I meant to send this heart instead of mine,
But oh, no man could hold it, for 'twas thine.

A FEVER

OH do not die, for I shall hate
  All women so, when thou art gone,
That thee I shall not celebrate,
  When I remember, thou wast one.

But yet thou canst not die, I know,
  To leave this world behind, is death,
But when thou from this world wilt go,
  The whole world vapours with thy breath.

Or if, when thou, the world's soul, goest,
    It stay, 'tis but thy carcase then,
The fairest woman, but thy ghost,
    But corrupt worms, the worthiest men.

O wrangling schools, that search what fire
    Shall burn this world, had none the wit
Unto this knowledge to aspire,
    That this her fever might be it?

And yet she cannot waste by this,
    Nor long bear this torturing wrong,
For such corruption needful is
    To fuel such a fever long.

These burning fits but meteors be,
    Whose matter in thee is soon spent.
Thy beauty, and all parts, which are thee,
    Are unchangeable firmament.

Yet 'twas of my mind, seizing thee,
    Though it in thee cannot perséver.
For I had rather owner be
    Of thee one hour, than all else ever.

AIR AND ANGELS

TWICE or thrice had I loved thee,
Before I knew thy face or name;
So in a voice, so in a shapeless flame,
Angels affect us oft, and worshipp'd be;
    Still when, to where thou wert, I came,
Some lovely glorious nothing I did see.
    But since my soul, whose child love is,
Takes limbs of flesh, and else could nothing do,
    More subtle than the parent is,
Love must not be, but take a body too,
    And therefore what thou wert, and who,
        I bid Love ask, and now

That it assume thy body, I allow,
And fix itself in thy lip, eye, and brow.

Whilst thus to ballast love, I thought,
And so more steadily to have gone,
With wares which would sink admiration,
I saw, I had love's pinnace overfraught;
   Every thy hair for love to work upon
Is much too much, some fitter must be sought;
   For, nor in nothing, nor in things
Extreme, and scatt'ring bright, can love inhere;
   Then as an Angel, face and wings
Of air, not pure as it, yet pure doth wear,
   So thy love may be my love's sphere;
      Just such disparity
As is 'twixt Air and Angels' purity,
'Twixt women's love, and men's will ever be.

BREAK OF DAY

'Tis true, 'tis day; what though it be?
O wilt thou therefore rise from me?
Why should we rise, because 'tis light?
Did we lie down, because 'twas night?
Love which in spite of darkness brought us hither,
Should in despite of light keep us together.

Light hath no tongue, but is all eye;
If it could speak as well as spy,
This were the worst, that it could say,
That being well, I fain would stay,
And that I lov'd my heart and honour so,
That I would not from him, that had them, go.

Must business thee from hence remove?
Oh, that 's the worst disease of love,
The poor, the foul, the false, love can
Admit, but not the busied man.
He which hath business, and makes love, doth do
Such wrong, as when a married man doth woo.

THE ANNIVERSARY

ALL Kings, and all their favourites,
　　All glory of honours, beauties, wits,
The Sun itself, which makes times, as they pass,
Is elder by a year, now, than it was
When thou and I first one another saw:
All other things to their destruction draw,
　　Only our love hath no decay;
This, no to-morrow hath, nor yesterday,
Running it never runs from us away,
But truly keeps his first, last, everlasting day.

　　Two graves must hide thine and my corse,
　　If one might, death were no divorce.
Alas, as well as other Princes, we,
(Who Prince enough in one another be,)
Must leave at last in death, these eyes, and ears,
Oft fed with true oaths, and with sweet salt tears;
　　But souls where nothing dwells but love
(All other thoughts being inmates) then shall prove
This, or a love increasèd there above,
When bodies to their graves, souls from their graves
　　　remove.

　　And then we shall be throughly blest,
　　But we no more, than all the rest;
Here upon earth, we 're Kings, and none but we
Can be such Kings, nor of such subjects be.
Who is so safe as we? where none can do
Treason to us, except one of us two.
　　True and false fears let us refrain,
Let us love nobly, and live, and add again
Years and years unto years, till we attain
To write threescore: this is the second of our reign.

A VALEDICTION: OF MY NAME, IN THE WINDOW

I

My name engrav'd herein
Doth contribute my firmness to this glass,
    Which, ever since that charm, hath been
    As hard as that which grav'd it was;
Thine eye will give it price enough, to mock
    The diamonds of either rock.

II

'Tis much that glass should be
As all-confessing, and through-shine as I,
    'Tis more, that it shows thee to thee,
    And clear reflects thee to thine eye.
But all such rules, love's magic can undo,
    Here you see me, and I am you.

III

As no one point, nor dash,
Which are but accessories to this name,
    The showers and tempests can outwash,
    So shall all times find me the same;
You this entireness better may fulfil,
    Who have the pattern with you still.

IV

Or if too hard and deep
This learning be, for a scratch'd name to teach,
    It, as a given death's head keep.
    Lovers' mortality to preach,
Or think this ragged bony name to be
    My ruinous anatomy.

V

Then, as all my souls be
Emparadis'd in you, (in whom alone
    I understand, and grow and see,)

The rafters of my body, bone
Being still with you, the Muscle, Sinew, and Vein,
   Which tile this house, will come again.

VI

Till my return, repair
And recompact my scattered body so.
   As all the virtuous powers which are
   Fix'd in the stars, are said to flow
Into such characters, as gravèd be
   When these stars have supremacy:

VII

So since this name was cut
When love and grief their exaltation had,
   No door 'gainst this name's influence shut;
   As much more loving, as more sad,
'Twill make thee; and thou shouldst, till I return,
   Since I die daily, daily mourn.

VIII

When thy inconsiderate hand
Flings ope this casement, with my trembling name,
   To look on one, whose wit or land,
   New battery to thy heart may frame,
Then think this name alive, and that thou thus
   In it offend'st my Genius.

IX

And when thy melted maid,
Corrupted by thy Lover's gold, and page,
   His letter at thy pillow hath laid,
   Disputed it, and tam'd thy rage,
And thou begin'st to thaw towards him, for this,
   May my name step in, and hide his.

x

And if this treason go
To an overt act, and that thou write again:
    In superscribing, this name flow
    Into thy fancy, from the pane.
So, in forgetting thou rememb'rest right,
        And unaware to me shalt write.

xi

But glass and lines must be
No means our firm substantial love to keep;
    Near death inflicts this lethargy.
    And this I murmur in my sleep;
Impute this idle talk, to that I go,
        For dying men talk often so.

TWICKENHAM GARDEN

Blasted with sighs, and surrounded with tears,
    Hither I come to seek the spring,
    And at mine eyes, and at mine ears,
Receive such balms, as else cure everything;
    But O, self-traitor, I do bring
The spider love, which transubstantiates all,
    And can convert Manna to gall,
And that this place may thoroughly be thought
    True Paradise, I have the serpent brought.

'Twere wholesomer for me, that winter did
    Benight the glory of this place,
    And that a grave frost did forbid
These trees to laugh, and mock me to my face;
    But that I may not this disgrace
Endure, nor yet leave loving, Love, let me
    Some senseless piece of this place be;
Make me a mandrake, so I may groan here,
    Or a stone fountain weeping out my year.

Hither with crystal vials, lovers come,
  And take my tears, which are love's wine.
And try your mistress' tears at home,
  For all are false, that taste not just like mine;
    Alas, hearts do not in eyes shine,
  Nor can you more judge woman's thoughts by tears,
    Than by her shadow, what she wears.
O perverse sex, where none is true but she,
  Who 's therefore true, because her truth kills me.

A VALEDICTION: OF THE BOOK

I 'LL tell thee now (dear Love) what thou shalt do
  To anger destiny, as she doth us,
  How I shall stay, though she eloign me thus,
And how posterity shall know it too;
    How thine may out-endure
    Sibyl's glory, and obscure
    Her who from *Pindar* could allure,
  And her, through whose help *Lucan* is not lame,
And her, whose book (they say) *Homer* did find, and name.

Study our manuscripts, those myriads
  Of letters, which have past 'twixt thee and me,
  Thence write our Annals, and in them will be
To all whom love's subliming fire invades,
    Rule and example found;
    There, the faith of any ground
    No schismatic will dare to wound,
  That sees, how Love this grace to us affords,
To make, to keep, to use, to be these his Records.

This Book, as long-liv'd as the elements,
  Or as the world's form, this all-gravèd tome
  In cypher writ, or new made Idiom,
We for Love's clergy only are instruments:
    When this book is made thus,

    Should again the ravenous
    Vandals and Goths inundate us,
  Learning were safe; in this our Universe
Schools might learn Sciences, Spheres Music, Angels Verse.

Here Love's Divines (since all Divinity
    Is love or wonder) may find all they seek,
    Whether abstract spiritual love they like,
Their Souls exhal'd with what they do not see,
      Or, loth so to amuse
      Faith's infirmity, they choose
      Something which they may see and use;
  For, though mind be the heaven, where love doth sit,
Beauty a convenient type may be to figure it.

Here more than in their books may Lawyers find,
    Both by what titles Mistresses are ours,
    And how prerogative these states devours,
Transferr'd from Love himself, to womankind,
      Who though from heart, and eyes,
      They exact great subsidies,
      Forsake him who on them relies,
  And for the cause, honour, or conscience give,
Chimeras, vain as they, or their prerogative.

Here Statesmen, (or of them, they which can read,)
    May of their occupation find the grounds:
    Love and their art alike it deadly wounds,
If to consider what 'tis, one proceed,
      In both they do excel
      Who the present govern well,
      Whose weakness none doth, or dares tell;
  In this thy book, such will their nothing see,
As in the Bible some can find out alchemy.

Thus vent thy thoughts; abroad I 'll study thee,
    As he removes far off, that great heights takes;
    How great love is, presence best trial makes,
But absence tries how long this love will be;

To take a latitude
Sun, or stars, are fitliest view'd
At their brightest, but to conclude
Of longitudes, what other way have we,
But to mark when, and where the dark eclipses be?

COMMUNITY

GOOD we must love, and must hate ill,
For ill is ill, and good good still,
    But there are things indifferent,
Which we may neither hate, nor love,
But one, and then another prove,
    As we shall find our fancy bent.

If then at first wise Nature had
Made women either good or bad,
    Then some we might hate, and some choose,
But since she did them so create,
That we may neither love, nor hate,
    Only this rests, All, all may use.

If they were good it would be seen,
Good is as visible as green,
    And to all eyes itself betrays:
If they were bad, they could not last,
Bad doth itself and others waste;
    So, they deserve nor blame, nor praise.

But they are ours as fruits are ours,
He that but tastes, he that devours,
    And he that leaves all, doth as well:
Chang'd loves are but chang'd sorts of meat,
And when he hath the kernel eat,
    Who doth not fling away the shell?

LOVE'S GROWTH

I scarce believe my love to be so pure
　　As I had thought it was,
　　Because it doth endure
Vicissitude, and season, as the grass;
Methinks I lied all winter; when I swore,
My love was infinite, if spring make it more.
But if this medicine, love, which cures all sorrow
With more, not only be no quintessence,
But mixt of all stuffs, paining soul, or sense,
And of the Sun his working vigour borrow,
Love 's not so pure, and abstract, as they use
To say, which have no Mistress but their Muse,
But as all else, being elemented too,
Love sometimes would contemplate, sometimes do.

And yet no greater, but more eminent,
　　Love by the Spring is grown;
　　As, in the firmament,
Stars by the Sun are not enlarg'd, but shown,
Gentle love deeds, as blossoms on a bough,
From love's awakened root do bud out now.
If, as in water stirr'd more circles be
Produc'd by one, love such additions take,
Those like so many spheres, but one heaven make,
For, they are all concentric unto thee.
And though each spring do add to love new heat,
As princes do in times of action get
New taxes, and remit them not in peace,
No winter shall abate the spring's increase.

LOVE'S EXCHANGE

Love, any devil else but you,
Would for a given Soul give something too.
At Court your fellows every day,
Give th' art of Rhyming, Huntsmanship, or Play,

For them which were their own before;
Only I have nothing which gave more,
But am, alas, by being lowly, lower.

I ask no dispensation now
To falsify a tear, or sigh, or vow,
I do not sue from thee to draw
A *non obstante* on nature's law,
These are prerogatives, they inhere
In thee and thine; none should forswear
Except that he Love's minion were.

Give me thy weakness, make me blind,
Both ways, as thou and thine, in eyes and mind;
Love, let me never know that this
Is love, or, that love childish is.
Let me not know that others know
That she knows my pains, lest that so
A tender shame make me mine own new woe.

If thou give nothing, yet thou 'rt just,
Because I would not thy first motions trust;
Small towns which stand stiff, till great shot
Enforce them, by war's law condition not.
Such in love's warfare is my case,
I may not article for grace,
Having put Love at last to show this face.

This face, by which he could command
And change th' idolatry of any land,
This face, which wheresoe'er it comes,
Can call vow'd men from cloisters, dead from tombs,
And melt both Poles at once, and store
Deserts with cities, and make more
Mines in the earth, than Quarries were before.

For this, Love is enrag'd with me,
Yet kills not. If I must example be
To future Rebels; If th' unborn
Must learn, by my being cut up, and torn:

Kill, and dissect me, Love; for this
Torture against thine own end is,
Rack'd carcases make ill Anatomies.

CONFINED LOVE

SOME man unworthy to be possessor
Of old or new love, himself being false or weak,
　Thought his pain and shame would be lesser,
If on womankind he might his anger wreak,
　　　And thence a law did grow,
　　　One might but one man know;
　　　But are other creatures so?

Are Sun, Moon, or Stars by law forbidden,
To smile where they list, or lend away their light?
　Are birds divorc'd, or are they chidden
If they leave their mate, or lie abroad a-night?
　　　Beasts do no jointures lose
　　　Though they new lovers choose,
　　　But we are made worse than those.

Who e'er rigg'd fair ship to lie in harbours
And not to seek new lands, or not to deal withal?
　Or built fair houses, set trees, and arbours,
Only to lock up, or else to let them fall?
　　　Good is not good, unless
　　　A thousand it possess,
　　　But doth waste with greediness.

THE DREAM

DEAR love, for nothing less than thee
Would I have broke this happy dream,
　　　It was a theme
For reason, much too strong for phantasy,
Therefore thou waked'st me wisely; yet

My Dream thou brok'st not, but continued'st it;
Thou art so truth, that thoughts of thee suffice,
To make dreams truths, and tables histories;
Enter these arms, for since thou thought'st it best,
Not to dream all my dream, let 's act the rest.

As lightning, or a taper's light,
Thine eyes, and not thy noise waked me;
        Yet I thought thee
(For thou lovest truth) an Angel, at first sight,
But when I saw thou sawest my heart,
And knew'st my thoughts, beyond an Angel's art,
When thou knew'st what I dreamt, when thou knew'st
    when
Excess of joy would wake me, and cam'st then,
I must confess, it could not choose but be
Profane, to think thee anything but thee.

Coming and staying show'd thee, thee,
But rising makes me doubt, that now,
        Thou art not thou.
That love is weak, where fear 's as strong as he;
'Tis not all spirit, pure, and brave,
If mixture it of *Fear, Shame, Honour,* have.
Perchance as torches which must ready be,
Men light and put out, so thou deal'st with me,
Thou cam'st to kindle, goest to come; then I
Will dream that hope again, but else would die.

A VALEDICTION: OF WEEPING

    Let me pour forth
My tears before thy face, whilst I stay here,
For thy face coins them, and thy stamp they bear,
And by this Mintage they are something worth,
    For thus they be
    Pregnant of thee;

Fruits of much grief they are, emblems of more;
When a tear falls, that thou falls which it bore,
So thou and I are nothing then, when on a divers shore.

> On a round ball
A workman that hath copies by, can lay
An Europe, Afric, and an Asia,
And quickly make that, which was nothing, *All*,
> So doth each tear,
> Which thee doth wear,
A globe, yea world by that impression grow,
Till thy tears mixt with mine do overflow
This world, by waters sent from thee, my heaven dissolvèd so

> O more than Moon,
Draw not up seas to drown me in thy sphere,
Weep me not dead, in thine arms, but forbear
To teach the sea, what it may do too soon;
> Let not the wind
> Example find,
To do me more harm, than it purposeth;
Since thou and I sigh one another's breath,
Whoe'er sighs most, is cruellest, and hastes the other's death

LOVE'S ALCHEMY

Some that have deeper digg'd love's mine than I,
Say, where his centric happiness doth lie:
> I have lov'd, and got, and told,
But should I love, get, tell, till I were old,
I should not find that hidden mystery;
> Oh, 'tis imposture all:
And as no chemic yet th' Elixir got,
> But glorifies his pregnant pot,
> If by the way to him befall
Some odoriferous thing, or medicinal,
> So, lovers dream a rich and long delight,
> But get a winter-seeming summer's night.

Our ease, our thrift, our honour, and our day,
Shall we, for this vain bubble's shadow pay?
　　　　Ends love in this, that my man,
Can be as happy as I can; if he can
Endure the short scorn of a bridegroom's play?
　　　　That loving wretch that swears,
'Tis not the bodies marry, but the minds,
　　　　Which he in her angelic finds,
　　　　Would swear as justly, that he hears,
In that day's rude hoarse minstrelsy, the spheres.
Hope not for mind in women; at their best
　　Sweetness and wit, they are but *Mummy*, possessed.

THE FLEA

MARK but this flea, and mark in this,
How little that which thou deny'st me is;
It suck'd me first, and now sucks thee,
And in this flea, our two bloods mingled be;
Thou know'st that this cannot be said
A sin, nor shame, nor loss of maidenhead,
　　Yet this enjoys before it woo,
　　And pamper'd swells with one blood made of two,
　　And this, alas, is more than we would do.

Oh stay, three lives in one flea spare,
Where we almost, yea more than married are.
This flea is you and I, and this
Our marriage bed, and marriage temple is;
Though parents grudge, and you, we're met,
And cloistered in these living walls of jet.
　　Though use make you apt to kill me,
　　Let not to that, self murder added be,
　　And sacrilege, three sins in killing three.

Cruel and sudden, hast thou since
Purpled thy nail, in blood of innocence?

Wherein could this flea guilty be,
Except in that drop which it suck'd from thee?
Yet thou triumph'st, and say'st that thou
Find'st not thyself, nor me the weaker now;
   'Tis true, then learn how false, fears be;
   Just so much honour, when thou yield'st to me,
   Will waste, as this flea's death took life from thee

THE CURSE

WHOEVER guesses, thinks, or dreams he knows
Who is my mistress, wither by this curse;
    His only, and only his purse
    May some dull heart to love dispose,
And she yield then to all that are his foes;
   May he be scorn'd by one, whom all else scorn,
   Forswear to others, what to her he hath sworn,
   With fear of missing, shame of getting, torn:

Madness his sorrow, gout his cramp, may he
Make, by but thinking who hath made him such:
    And may he feel no touch
    Of conscience, but of fame, and be
Anguish'd not that 'twas sin, but that 'twas she:
   In early and long scarceness may he rot,
   For land which had been his, if he had not
   Himself incestuously an heir begot:

May he dream Treason, and believe, that he
Meant to perform it, and confess, and die,
    And no record tell why:
    His sons, which none of his may be,
Inherit nothing but his infamy:
   Or may he so long Parasites have fed,
   That he would fain be theirs, whom he hath bred,
   And at the last be circumciz'd for bread:

The venom of all stepdames, gamesters' gall,
What Tyrants, and their subjects interwish,
What Plants, Mines, Beasts, Fowl, Fish,
Can contribute, all ill which all
Prophets, or Poets spake; and all which shall
Be annex'd in schedules unto this by me,
Fall on that man; for if it be a she
Nature before hand hath out-cursèd me.

THE MESSAGE

SEND home my long stray'd eyes to me,
Which O! too long have dwelt on thee;
Yet since there they have learn'd such ill,
Such forc'd fashions,
And false passions,
That they be
Made by thee
Fit for no good sight, keep them still.

Send home my harmless heart again,
Which no unworthy thought could stain;
But if it be taught by thine
To make jestings
Of protestings,
And cross both
Word and oath,
Keep it, for then 'tis none of mine.

Yet send me back my heart and eyes,
That I may know, and see thy lies,
And may laugh and joy, when thou
Art in anguish
And dost languish
For some one
That will none,
Or prove as false as thou art now.

A NOCTURNAL UPON ST. LUCY'S DAY,

BEING THE SHORTEST DAY

'TIS the year's midnight, and it is the day's,
Lucy's, who scarce seven hours herself unmasks;
   The Sun is spent, and now his flasks
   Send forth light squibs, no constant rays;
     The world's whole sap is sunk:
The general balm th' hydroptic earth hath drunk,
Whither, as to the bed's-feet, life is shrunk,
Dead and interr'd; yet all these seem to laugh,
Compar'd with me, who am their Epitaph.

Study me then, you who shall lovers be
At the next world, that is, at the next Spring:
   For I am every dead thing,
   In whom love wrought new alchemy.
     For his art did express
A quintessence even from nothingness,
From dull privations, and lean emptiness:
He ruin'd me, and I am re-begot
Of absence, darkness, death; things which are not.

All others, from all things, draw all that 's good,
Life, soul, form, spirit, whence they being have;
   I, by love's limbec, am the grave
   Of all, that 's nothing.   Oft a flood
     Have we two wept, and so
Drown'd the whole world, us two; oft did we grow
To be two Chaoses, when we did show
Care to aught else; and often absences
Withdrew our souls, and made us carcases.

But I am by her death (which word wrongs her)
Of the first nothing, the Elixir grown;
   Were I a man, that I were one,
   I needs must know; I should prefer,
     If I were any beast,

Some ends, some means; yea plants, yea stones detest,
And love; all, all some properties invest;
If I an ordinary nothing were,
As shadow, a light, and body must be here.

But I am None; nor will my Sun renew.
You lovers, for whose sake, the lesser Sun
  At this time to the Goat is run
  To fetch new lust, and give it you,
    Enjoy your summer all;
Since she enjoys her long night's festival,
Let me prepare towards her, and let me call
This hour her Vigil, and her Eve, since this
Both the year's, and the day's deep midnight is.

WITCHCRAFT BY A PICTURE

I FIX mine eye on thine, and there
  Pity my picture burning in thine eye,
My picture drown'd in a transparent tear,
  When I look lower I espy;
    Hadst thou the wicked skill
By pictures made and marr'd, to kill,
How many ways mightst thou perform thy will?

But now I have drunk thy sweet salt tears,
  And though thou pour more I 'll depart;
My picture vanish'd, vanish fears,
  That I can be endamag'd by that art;
    Though thou retain of me
One picture more, yet that will be,
Being in thine own heart, from all malice free.

THE BAIT

COME live with me, and be my love,
And we will some new pleasures prove
Of golden sands, and crystal brooks,
With silken lines, and silver hooks.

There will the river whispering run
Warm'd by thy eyes, more than the Sun.
And there th' enamour'd fish will stay,
Begging themselves they may betray.

When thou wilt swim in that live bath,
Each fish, which every channel hath,
Will amorously to thee swim,
Gladder to catch thee, than thou him.

If thou, to be so seen, be'st loth,
By Sun, or Moon, thou dark'nest both,
And if myself have leave to see,
I need not their light, having thee.

Let others freeze with angling reeds,
And cut their legs, with shells and weeds,
Or treacherously poor fish beset,
With strangling snare, or windowy net:

Let coarse bold hands, from slimy nest
The bedded fish in banks out-wrest,
Or curious traitors, sleeve-silk flies
Bewitch poor fishes' wand'ring eyes.

For thee, thou need'st no such deceit,
For thou thyself art thine own bait;
That fish, that is not catch'd thereby,
Alas, is wiser far than I.

THE APPARITION

WHEN by thy scorn, O murd'ress, I am dead,
And that thou think'st thee free
From all solicitation from me,
Then shall my ghost come to thy bed,
And thee, feign'd vestal, in worse arms shall see;

Then thy sick taper will begin to wink,
And he, whose thou art then, being tired before,
Will, if thou stir, or pinch to wake him, think
     Thou call'st for more,
And in false sleep will from thee shrink,
And then poor Aspen wretch, neglected thou
Bath'd in a cold quicksilver sweat wilt lie
     A verier ghost than I;
What I will say, I will not tell thee now,
Lest that preserve thee; and since my love is spent,
I 'd rather thou shouldst painfully repent,
Than by my threat'nings rest still innocent.

THE BROKEN HEART

HE is stark mad, who ever says,
  That he hath been in love an hour,
Yet not that love so soon decays,
  But that it can ten in less space devour;
Who will believe me, if I swear
That I have had the plague a year?
  Who would not laugh at me, if I should say,
  I saw a flask of powder burn a day?

Ah, what a trifle is a heart,
  If once into love's hands it come!
All other griefs allow a part
  To other griefs, and ask themselves but some;
They come to us, but us Love draws,
He swallows us, and never chaws:
  By him, as by chain'd shot, whole ranks do die,
  He is the tyrant Pike, our hearts the Fry.

If 'twere not so, what did become
  Of my heart, when I first saw thee?
I brought a heart into the room,
  But from the room, I carried none with me:

If it had gone to thee, I know
Mine would have taught thine heart to show
    More pity unto me: but Love, alas,
    At one first blow did shiver it as glass.

Yet nothing can to nothing fall,
    Nor any place be empty quite,
Therefore I think my breast hath all
    Those pieces still, though they be not unite;
And now as broken glasses show
A hundred lesser faces, so
    My rags of heart canlike, wish, and adore,
    But after one such love, can love no more.

A VALEDICTION: FORBIDDING MOURNING

As virtuous men pass mildly away,
    And whisper to their souls, to go,
Whilst some of their sad friends do say,
    The breath goes now, and some say, no:

So let us melt, and make no noise,
    No tear-floods, nor sigh-tempests move,
'Twere profanation of our joys
    To tell the laity our love.

Moving of th' earth brings harms and fears,
    Men reckon what it did and meant,
But trepidation of the spheres,
    Though greater far, is innocent.

Dull sublunary lovers' love
    (Whose soul is sense) cannot admit
Absence, because it doth remove
    Those things which elemented it.

But we by a love, so much refin'd,
    That ourselves know not what it is,
Inter-assurèd of the mind,
    Care less eyes, lips, and hands to miss.

Our two souls therefore, which are one,
　　Though I must go, endure not yet
A breach, but an expansion,
　　Like gold to aery thinness beat.

If they be two, they are two so
　　As stiff twin compasses are two,
Thy soul the fixed foot, makes no show
　　To move, but doth, if th' other do.

And though it in the centre sit,
　　Yet when the other far doth roam,
It leans, and hearkens after it,
　　And grows erect, as that comes home.

Such wilt thou be to me, who must
　　Like th' other foot, obliquely run;
Thy firmness draws my circle just,
　　And makes me end, where I begun.

THE ECSTASY

WHERE, like a pillow on a bed,
　　A pregnant bank swell'd up, to rest
The violet's reclining head,
　　Sat we two, one another's best.
Our hands were firmly cemented
　　With a fast balm, which thence did spring,
Our eye-beams twisted, and did thread
　　Our eyes, upon one double string;
So t' intergraft our hands, as yet
　　Was all the means to make us one,
And pictures in our eyes to get
　　Was all our propagation.
As 'twixt two equal Armies, Fate
　　Suspends uncertain victory,
Our souls, (which to advance their state,
　　Were gone out,) hung 'twixt her, and me.

And whilst our souls negotiate there,
  We like sepulchral statues lay;
All day, the same our postures were,
  And we said nothing, all the day.
If any, so by love refin'd,
  That he soul's language understood,
And by good love were grown all mind,
  Within convenient distance stood,
He (though he knew not which soul spake,
  Because both meant, both spake the same)
Might thence a new concoction take,
  And part far purer than he came.
This Ecstasy doth unperplex
  (We said) and tell us what we love,
We see by this, it was not sex,
  We see, we saw not what did move:
But as all several souls contain
  Mixture of things, they know not what,
Love these mix'd souls doth mix again,
  And makes both one, each this and that.
A single violet transplant,
  The strength, the colour, and the size,
(All which before was poor, and scant,)
  Redoubles still, and multiplies.
When love, with one another so
  Interinanimates two souls,
That abler soul, which thence doth flow,
  Defects of loneliness controls.
We then, who are this new soul, know,
  Of what we are compos'd, and made,
For, th' Atomies of which we grow,
  Are souls, whom no change can invade.
But O alas, so long, so far
  Our bodies why do we forbear?
They are ours, though they are not we, We are
  The intelligences, they the spheres.
We owe them thanks, because they thus,
  Did us, to us, at first convey,
Yielded their forces, sense, to us,

Nor are dross to us, but allay.
On man heaven's influence works not **so**,
  But that it first imprints the air,
So soul into the soul may flow,
  Though it to body first repair.
As our blood labours to beget
  Spirits, as like souls as it can,
Because such fingers need to knit
  That subtle knot, which makes us man:
So must pure lovers' souls descend
  T' affections, and to faculties,
Which sense may reach and apprehend,
  Else a great Prince in prison lies.
To our bodies turn we then, that so
  Weak men on love reveal'd may look;
Love's mysteries in souls do grow,
  But yet the body is his book,
And if some lover, such as we,
  Have heard this dialogue of one,
Let him still mark us, he shall see
  Small change, when we 're to bodies gone.

LOVE'S DEITY

I LONG to talk with some old lover's ghost,
  Who died before the god of Love was born:
I cannot think that he, who then lov'd most,
  Sunk so low, as to love one which did scorn.
But since this god produc'd a destiny,
And that vice-nature, custom, lets it be;
  I must love her, that loves not me.

Sure, they which made him god, meant not so much,
  Nor he, in his young godhead practis'd it.
But when an even flame two hearts did touch,
  His office was indulgently to fit
Actives to passives.   Correspondency
Only his subject was; it cannot be
  Love, till I love her, that loves me.

But every modern god will now extend
　His vast prerogative, as far as Jove.
To rage, to lust, to write to, to commend,
　All is the purlieu of the God of Love.
Oh were we waken'd by this Tyranny
To ungod this child again, it could not be
　I should love her, who loves not me.

Rebel and Atheist too, why murmur I,
　As though I felt the worst that love could do?
Love might make me leave loving, or might try
　A deeper plague, to make her love me too,
Which, since she loves before, I'm loth to see;
Falsehood is worse than hate; and that must be,
　If she whom I love, should love me.

LOVE'S DIET

To what a cumbersome unwieldiness
And burdenous corpulence my love had grown,
　But that I did, to make it less,
　And keep it in proportion,
Give it a diet, made it feed upon
That which love worst endures, *discretion*.

Above one sigh a day I allow'd him not,
Of which my fortune, and my faults had part;
　And if sometimes by stealth he got
　A she sigh from my mistress' heart,
And thought to feast on that, I let him see
'Twas neither very sound, nor meant to me.

If he wrung from me a tear, I brined it so
With scorn or shame, that him it nourish'd not;
　If he suck'd hers, I let him know
　'Twas not a tear, which he had got,
His drink was counterfeit, as was his meat;
For, eyes which roll towards all, weep not, but sweat.

Whatever he would dictate, I writ that,
But burnt my letters; when she writ to me,
   And that that favour made him fat,
    I said, if any title be
Convey'd by this, Ah, what doth it avail,
To be the fortieth name in an entail?

Thus I reclaim'd my buzzard love, to fly
At what, and when, and how, and where I choose;
   Now negligent of sport I lie,
    And now as other falconers use,
I spring a mistress, swear, write, sigh and weep:
And the game kill'd, or lost, go talk, and sleep.

THE WILL

BEFORE I sigh my last gasp, let me breathe,
Great love, some Legacies; Here I bequeath
Mine eyes to *Argus*, if mine eyes can see,
If they be blind, then Love, I give them thee;
My tongue to Fame; to Ambassadors mine ears;
   To women or the sea, my tears.
  Thou, Love, hast taught me heretofore
By making me serve her who had twenty more,
That I should give to none, but such, as had too much before.

My constancy I to the planets give;
My truth to them, who at the Court do live;
Mine ingenuity and openness,
To Jesuits; to Buffoons my pensiveness;
My silence to any, who abroad hath been;
   My money to a Capuchin.
  Thou Love taught'st me, by appointing me
To love there, where no love receiv'd can be,
Only to give to such as have an incapacity.

My faith I give to Roman Catholics;
All my good works unto the Schismatics

Of Amsterdam: my best civility
And Courtship, to an University;
My modesty I give to soldiers bare;
   My patience let gamesters share.
  Thou Love taught'st me, by making me
 Love her that holds my love disparity,
Only to give to those that count my gifts indignity.

  I give my reputation to those
Which were my friends; mine industry to foes;
To Schoolmen I bequeath my doubtfulness;
My sickness to Physicians, or excess;
To Nature, all that I in Rhyme have writ;
   And to my company my wit.
  Thou Love, by making me adore
 Her, who begot this love in me before,
Taught'st me to make, as though I gave, when I did but
     restore.

To him for whom the passing bell next tolls,
I give my physic books; my written rolls
Of Moral counsels, I to Bedlam give;
My brazen medals, unto them which live
In want of bread; to them which pass among
   All foreigners, mine English tongue.
  Thou, Love, by making me love one
 Who thinks her friendship a fit portion
For younger lovers, dost my gifts thus disproportion.

Therefore I 'll give no more; but I 'll undo
The world by dying; because love dies too.
Then all your beauties will be no more worth
Than gold in Mines, where none doth draw it forth;
And all your graces no more use shall have
   Than a Sun-dial in a grave.
  Thou Love taught'st me, by making me
 Love her, who doth neglect both me and thee,
To invent, and practise this one way, to annihilate all three.

THE FUNERAL

WHOEVER comes to shroud me, do not harm
      Nor question much
That subtle wreath of hair, which crowns my arm;
The mystery, the sign you must not touch,
      For 'tis my outward Soul,
Viceroy to that, which then to heaven being gone,
      Will leave this to control,
And keep these limbs, her Provinces, from dissolution.

For if the sinewy thread my brain lets fall
      Through every part,
Can tie those parts, and make me one of all;
These hairs which upward grew, and strength and art
      Have from a better brain,
Can better do 't; except she meant that I
      By this should know my pain,
As prisoners then are manacled, when they 're condemn'd
      to die.

Whate'er she meant by it, bury it with me,
      For since I am
Love's martyr, it might breed idolatry,
If into others' hands these Reliques came;
      As 'twas humility
To afford to it all that a Soul can do,
      So, 'tis some bravery,
That since you would save none of me, I bury some of you

THE BLOSSOM

LITTLE think'st thou, poor flower,
  Whom I have watch'd six or seven days,
And seen thy birth, and seen what every hour
Gave to thy growth, thee to this height to raise,

THE BLOSSOM

And now dost laugh and triumph on this bough,
    Little think'st thou
That it will freeze anon, and that I shall
To-morrow find thee fal'n, or not at all.

  Little think'st thou, poor heart,
   That labour'st yet to nestle thee,
And think'st by hovering here to get a part
In a forbidden or forbidding tree,
And hop'st her stiffness by long siege to bow:
    Little think'st thou,
That thou to-morrow, ere that Sun doth wake,
Must with this Sun, and me a journey take.

  But thou which lov'st to be
   Subtle to plague thyself, wilt say,
Alas, if you must go, what's that to me?
Here lies my business, and here I will stay:
You go to friends, whose love and means present
    Various content
To your eyes, ears, and tongue, and every part.
If then your body go, what need you a heart?

  Well then, stay here; but know,
   When thou hast stay'd and done thy most;
A naked thinking heart, that makes no show,
Is to a woman, but a kind of Ghost;
How shall she know my heart; or having none,
    Know thee for one?
Practice may make her know some other part,
But take my word, she doth not know a Heart.

  Meet me at London, then,
   Twenty days hence, and thou shalt see
Me fresher, and more fat, by being with men,
Than if I had stayed still with her and thee.
For God's sake, if you can, be you so too:
    I would give you
There, to another friend, whom we shall find
As glad to have my body, as my mind.

THE PRIMROSE, BEING AT MONTGOMERY CASTLE, UPON THE HILL, ON WHICH IT IS SITUATE

Upon this Primrose hill,
 Where, if Heav'n would distil
A shower of rain, each several drop might go
To his own primrose, and grow Manna so;
And where their form, and their infinity
 Make a terrestrial Galaxy,
 As the small stars do in the sky:
I walk to find a true Love; and I see
That 'tis not a mere woman, that is she,
But must or more or less than woman be.

 Yet know I not, which flower
 I wish; a six, or four;
For should my true-Love less than woman be,
She were scarce anything; and then, should she
Be more than woman, she would get above
 All thought of sex, and think to move
 My heart to study her, and not to love;
Both these were monsters; since there must reside
Falsehood in woman, I could more abide,
She were by art, than Nature falsified.

 Live Primrose then, and thrive
 With thy true number five;
And women, whom this flower doth represent,
With this mysterious number be content;
Ten is the farthest number; if half ten
 Belong unto each woman, then
 Each woman may take half us men;
Or if this will not serve their turn, since all
Numbers are odd, or even, and they fall
First into this, five, women may take us all.

THE RELIQUE

WHEN my grave is broke up again
Some second guest to entertain,
(For graves have learn'd that woman-head
To be to more than one a Bed)
    And he that digs it, spies
A bracelet of bright hair about the bone,
    Will he not let us alone,
And think that there a loving couple lies,
Who thought that this device might be some way
To make their souls, at the last busy day,
Meet at this grave, and make a little stay?

If this fall in a time, or land,
Where mis-devotion doth command,
Then, he that digs us up, will bring
Us, to the Bishop, and the King,
    To make us Reliques; then
Thou shalt be a Mary Magdalen, and I
    A something else thereby;
All women shall adore us, and some men;
And since at such time, miracles are sought,
I would have that age by this paper taught
What miracles we harmless lovers wrought.

First, we lov'd well and faithfully,
Yet knew not what we lov'd, nor why,
Difference of sex no more we knew,
Than our Guardian Angels do;
    Coming and going, we
Perchance might kiss, but not between those meals;
    Our hands ne'er touched the seals,
Which nature, injur'd by late law, sets free:
These miracles we did; but now alas,
All measure, and all language, I should pass,
Should I tell what a miracle she was.

THE DAMP

WHEN I am dead, and Doctors know not why,
        And my friends' curiosity
Will have me cut up to survey each part,
When they shall find your Picture in my heart,
        You think a sudden damp of love
        Will through all their senses move,
And work on them as me, and so prefer
Your murder, to the name of Massacre.

Poor victories!   But if you dare be brave,
        And pleasure in your conquest have,
First kill th' enormous Giant, your *Disdain*,
And let th' enchantress *Honour*, next be slain,
        And like a Goth and Vandal rise,
        Deface Records, and Histories
Of your own arts and triumphs over men,
And without such advantage kill me then.

For I could muster up as well as you
        My Giants, and my Witches too,
Which are vast *Constancy*, and *Secretness*,
But these I neither look for, nor profess;
        Kill me as Woman, let me die
        As a mere man; do you but try
Your passive valour, and you shall find then,
Naked you have odds enough of any man.

THE DISSOLUTION

SHE's dead; and all which die
    To their first Elements resolve;
And we were mutual Elements to us,
    And made of one another.
My body then doth hers involve,
And those things whereof I consist, hereby

In me abundant grow, and burdenous,
    And nourish not, but smother.
  My fire of Passion, sighs of air,
Water of tears, and earthy sad despair,
    Which my materials be,
But near worn out by love's security,
She, to my loss, doth by her death repair,
    And I might live long wretched so
But that my fire doth with my fuel grow.
    Now as those Active Kings
    Whose foreign conquest treasure brings,
Receive more, and spend more, and soonest break:
This (which I am amaz'd that I can speak)
      This death, hath with my store
        My use increas'd.
And so my soul more earnestly releas'd,
Will outstrip hers; as bullets flown before
A latter bullet may o'ertake, the powder being more.

A JET RING SENT

Thou art not so black as my heart,
  Nor half so brittle as her heart, thou art;
What would'st thou say? shall both our properties by thee
    be spoke,
  Nothing more endless, nothing sooner broke?

    Marriage rings are not of this stuff;
  Oh, why should aught less precious, or less tough
Figure our loves? Except in thy name thou have bid it say,
  I'm cheap, and naught but fashion, fling me away.

    Yet stay with me since thou art come,
  Circle this finger's top, which didst her thumb.
Be justly proud, and gladly safe, that thou dost dwell with
    me,
  She that, Oh, broke her faith, would soon break thee.

NEGATIVE LOVE

I NEVER stoop'd so low, as they
Which on an eye, cheek, lip, can prey,
   Seldom to them, which soar no higher
   Than virtue or the mind to admire,
For sense, and understanding may
   Know, what gives fuel to their fire:
My love, though silly, is more brave,
For may I miss, whene'er I crave,
If I know yet what I would have.

If that be simply perfectest
Which can by no way be exprest
   But *Negatives*, my love is so.
   To All, which all love, I say no.
If any who decipher best,
   What we know not, ourselves, can know,
Let him teach me that nothing; this
As yet my ease, and comfort is,
Though I speed not, I cannot miss.

THE PROHIBITION

TAKE heed of loving me,
At least remember, I forbade it thee;
Not that I shall repair my unthrifty waste
Of Breath and Blood, upon thy sighs, and tears,
By being to thee then what to me thou wast;
But so great Joy our life at once outwears,
Then, lest thy love, by my death, frustrate be,
If thou love me, take heed of loving me.

Take heed of hating me,
Or too much triumph in the Victory.
Not that I shall be mine own officer,
And hate with hate again retaliate;
But thou wilt lose the style of conqueror,

If I, thy conquest, perish by thy hate.
Then, lest my being nothing lessen thee,
If thou hate me, take heed of hating me.

       Yet, love and hate me too,
So, these extremes shall neither's office do;
Love me, that I may die the gentler way;
Hate me, because thy love is too great for me;
Or let these two, themselves, not me decay;
So shall I, live, thy Stage, not triumph be;
Lest thou thy love and hate and me undo,
To let me live, O love and hate me too.

THE EXPIRATION

So, so, break off this last lamenting kiss,
   Which sucks two souls, and vapours both away;
Turn thou ghost that way, and let me turn this,
   And let ourselves benight our happiest day;
We ask'd none leave to love; nor will we owe
   Any, so cheap a death, as saying, Go;

Go; and if that word have not quite killed thee,
   Ease me with death, by bidding me go too.
Oh, if it have, let my word work on me,
   And a just office on a murderer do.
Except it be too late, to kill me so,
   Being double dead, going, and bidding, Go.

THE COMPUTATION

For the first twenty years, since yesterday,
   I scarce believed, thou could'st be gone away,
For forty more, I fed on favours past,
   And forty on hopes, that thou would'st, they might last.
Tears drown'd one hundred, and sighs blew out two,
   A thousand, I did neither think, nor do,

Or not divide, all being one thought of you;
Or in a thousand more, forgot that too.
Yet call not this long life; but think that I
Am, by being dead, Immortal; can ghosts die?

THE PARADOX

No Lover saith, I love, nor any other
    Can judge a perfect Lover;
He thinks that else none can, nor will agree
    That any loves but he:
I cannot say I lov'd, for who can say
    He was kill'd yesterday?
Love with excess of heat, more young than old,
    Death kills with too much cold;
We die but once, and who lov'd last did die,
    He that saith twice, doth lie:
For though he seem to move, and stir a while,
    It doth the sense beguile.
Such life is like the light which bideth yet
    When the light's life is set,
Or like the heat, which fire in solid matter
    Leaves behind, two hours after.
Once I lov'd and died; and am now become
    Mine Epitaph and Tomb.
Here dead men speak their last, and so do I;
    Love-slain, lo, here I lie.

FAREWELL TO LOVE

WHILST yet to prove,
I thought there was some Deity in love
    So did I reverence, and gave
Worship; as Atheists at their dying hour
Call, what they cannot name, an unknown power,
    As ignorantly did I crave:

Thus when
Things not yet known are coveted by men,
  Our desires give them fashion, and so
As they wax lesser, fall, as they size, grow.

  But, from late fair
His highness sitting in a golden Chair,
  Is not less cared for after three days
By children, than the thing which lovers so
Blindly admire, and with such worship woo;
  Being had, enjoying it decays:
        And thence,
What before pleas'd them all, takes but one sense,
  And that so lamely, as it leaves behind
A kind of sorrowing dullness to the mind.

  Ah cannot we,
As well as Cocks and Lions jocund be,
  After such pleasures?   Unless wise
Nature decreed (since each such Act, they say,
Diminisheth the length of life a day)
  This, as she would man should despise
        The sport;
Because that other curse of being short,
  And only for a minute made to be,
Eagers desire to raise posterity.

  Since so, my mind
Shall not desire what no man else can find,
  I'll no more dote and run
To pursue things which had endamaged me.
And when I come where moving beauties be,
  As men do when the summer's Sun
        Grows great,
Though I admire their greatness, shun their heat;
  Each place can afford shadows.   If all fail,
'Tis but applying worm-seed to the Tail.

A LECTURE UPON THE SHADOW

STAND still, and I will read to thee
A Lecture, love, in Love's philosophy.
    These three hours that we have spent,
    Walking here, two shadows went
Along with us, which we ourselves produc'd;
But, now the Sun is just above our head,
    We do those shadows tread;
    And to brave clearness all things are reduc'd.
  So whilst our infant loves did grow,
  Disguises did, and shadows, flow,
  From us, and our cares; but, now 'tis not so.

That love hath not attain'd the high'st degree,
Which is still diligent lest others see.

Except our loves at this noon stay,
We shall new shadows make the other way.
    As the first were made to blind
    Others; these which come behind
Will work upon ourselves, and blind our eyes.
If our loves faint, and westwardly decline;
    To me thou, falsely, thine,
    And I to thee mine actions shall disguise.
  The morning shadows wear away,
  But these grow longer all the day,
  But oh, love's day is short, if love decay.

Love is a growing, or full constant light;
And his first minute, after noon, is night.

SONNET: THE TOKEN

SEND me some token, that my hope may live,
  Or that my easeless thoughts may sleep and rest;
Send me some honey to make sweet my hive,
  That in my passion I may hope the best.

I beg no riband wrought with thine own hands,
   To knit our loves in the fantastic strain
Of new-touched youth; nor Ring to show the stands
   Of our affection, that as that 's round and plain,
So should our loves meet in simplicity.
   No, nor the Corals which thy wrist enfold,
Lac'd up together in congruity,
   To show our thoughts should rest in the same hold;
No, nor thy picture, though most gracious,
   And most desir'd, because best like the best;
Nor witty Lines, which are most copious,
   Within the Writings which thou hast addrest.

Send me nor this, nor that, t' increase my store,
But swear thou think'st I love thee, and no more.

SELF-LOVE

He that cannot choose but love,
And strives against it still,
Never shall my fancy move;
For he loves 'gainst his will;
Nor he which is all his own,
And can at pleasure choose,
When I am caught he can be gone,
And when he list refuse.
Nor he that loves none but fair,
For such by all are sought;
Nor he that can for foul ones care,
For his Judgment then is naught:
Nor he that hath wit, for he
Will make me his jest or slave;
Nor a fool, for when others . . . ,
He can neither . . .
Nor he that still his Mistress pays,
For she is thrall'd therefore,

SELF-LOVE

Nor he that pays not, for he says
Within, she 's worth no more.
Is there then no kind of men
Whom I may freely prove?
I will vent that humour then
In mine own self-love.

EPIGRAMS

HERO AND LEANDER

Both robb'd of air, we both lie in one ground,
Both whom one fire had burnt, one water drown'd.

PYRAMUS AND THISBE

Two, by themselves, each other, love and fear
Slain, cruel friends, by parting have join'd here.

NIOBE

By children's births, and death, I am become
So dry, that I am now mine own sad tomb.

A BURNT SHIP

Out of a fired ship, which, by no way
But drowning, could be rescued from the flame,
Some men leap'd forth, and ever as they came
Near the foes' ships, did by their shot decay;
So all were lost, which in the ship were found,
  They in the sea being burnt, they in the burnt ship
    drown'd.

FALL OF A WALL

Under an undermin'd, and shot-bruis'd wall
A too-bold Captain perish'd by the fall,
Whose brave misfortune, happiest men envied,
That had a town for tomb, his bones to hide.

A LAME BEGGAR

I AM unable, yonder beggar cries,
To stand, or move; if he say true, he *lies*.

CALES AND GUIANA

IF you from spoil of th' old world's farthest end
To the new world your kindled valours bend,
What brave examples then do prove it true
That one thing's end doth still begin a new.

SIR JOHN WINGFIELD

BEYOND th' old Pillars many have travailed
Towards the Sun's cradle, and his throne, and bed.
A fitter Pillar our Earl did bestow
In that late Island; for he well did know
Farther than Wingfield no man dares to go.

A SELF-ACCUSER

YOUR mistress, that you follow whores, still taxeth you:
'Tis strange that she should thus confess it, though it be true.

A LICENTIOUS PERSON

THY sins and hairs may no man equal call,
For, as thy sins increase, thy hairs do fall.

ANTIQUARY

IF in his study he hath so much care
To hang all old strange things, let his wife beware.

DISINHERITED

Thy father all from thee, by his last Will,
Gave to the poor; thou hast good title still.

PHRYNE

Thy flattering picture, *Phryne*, is like thee,
Only in this, that you both painted be.

AN OBSCURE WRITER

Philo, with twelve years' study, hath been griev'd
To be understood; when will he be believ'd?

KLOCKIUS

Klockius so deeply hath sworn, ne'er more to come
In bawdy house, that he dares not go home.

RADERUS

Why this man gelded *Martial* I muse,
Except himself alone his tricks would use,
As *Katherine*, for the Court's sake, put down Stews.

MERCURIUS GALLO-BELGICUS

Like *Esop's* fellow-slaves, O *Mercury*,
Which could do all things, thy faith is; and I
Like *Esop's* self, which nothing; I confess
I should have had more faith, if thou hadst less;
Thy credit lost thy credit: 'Tis sin to do,
In this case, as thou wouldst be done unto,
To believe all.   Change thy name: thou art like
Mercury in stealing, but liest like a *Greek*.

RALPHIUS

COMPASSION in the world again is bred:
   Ralphius is sick, the broker keeps his bed.

THE LIAR

THOU in the fields walk'st out thy supping hours
   And yet thou swear'st thou has supp'd like a king:
Like Nebuchadnezzar perchance with grass and flowers,
   A salad worse than Spanish dieting.

ELEGIES AND HEROICAL EPISTLE

ELEGY I

JEALOUSY

FOND woman, which wouldst have thy husband die,
And yet complain'st of his great jealousy;
If swoln with poison, he lay in his last bed,
His body with a sere-bark covered,
Drawing his breath, as thick and short, as can
The nimblest crocheting Musician,
Ready with loathsome vomiting to spew
His Soul out of one hell, into a new,
Made deaf with his poor kindred's howling cries,
Begging with few feign'd tears, great legacies,
Thou wouldst not weep, but jolly, and frolic be,
As a slave, which to-morrow should be free;
Yet weep'st thou, when thou seest him hungerly
Swallow his own death, heart's-bane jealousy.
O give him many thanks, he is courteous,
That in suspecting kindly warneth us.
We must not, as we us'd, flout openly,
In scoffing riddles, his deformity;
Nor at his board together being sat,
With words, nor touch, scarce looks adulterate.
Nor when he swoln and pamper'd with great fare
Sits down, and snorts, cag'd in his basket chair,
Must we usurp his own bed any more,
Nor kiss and play in his house, as before.
Now I see many dangers; for that is
His realm, his castle, and his diocese.
But if, as envious men, which would revile
Their Prince, or coin his gold, themselves exile

57

Into another country, and do it there,
We play in another house, what should we fear?
There we will scorn his household policies,
His silly plots, and pensionary spies,
As the inhabitants of Thames' right side
Do London's Mayor; or Germans, the Pope's pride.

ELEGY II

THE ANAGRAM

MARRY, and love thy *Flavia*, for, she
Hath all things, whereby others beauteous be,
For, though her eyes be small, her mouth is great,
Though they be Ivory, yet her teeth be jet,
Though they be dim, yet she is light enough,
And though her harsh hair fall, her skin is rough;
What though her cheeks be yellow, her hair 's red,
Give her thine, and she hath a maidenhead.
These things are beauty's elements, where these
Meet in one, that one must, as perfect, please.
If red and white and each good quality
Be in thy wench, ne'er ask where it doth lie.
In buying things perfum'd, we ask, if there
Be musk and amber in it, but not where.
Though all her parts be not in th' usual place,
She hath yet an Anagram of a good face.
If we might put the letters but one way,
In the lean dearth of words, what could we say?
When by the Gamut some Musicians make
A perfect song, others will undertake,
By the same Gamut chang'd, to equal it.
Things simply good, can never be unfit.
She 's fair as any, if all be like her,
And if none be, then she is singular.
All love is wonder; if we justly do
Account her wonderful, why not lovely too?

Love built on beauty, soon as beauty, dies;
Choose this face, chang'd by no deformities.
Women are all like Angels; the fair be
Like those which fell to worse; but such as she
Like to good Angels, nothing can impair:
'Tis less grief to be foul, than to have been fair.
For one night's revels, silk and gold we choose,
But, in long journeys, cloth, and leather use.
Beauty is barren oft; best husbands say,
There is best land, where there is foulest way.
Of what a sovereign Plaster will she be,
If thy past sins have taught thee jealousy!
Here needs no spies, nor eunuchs; her commit
Safe to thy foes; yea, to a Marmoset.
When Belgia's cities, the round countries drown,
That dirty foulness guards, and arms the town:
So doth her face guard her; and so, for thee,
Which, forc'd by business, absent oft must be,
She, whose face, like clouds, turns the day to night,
Who, mightier than the sea, makes Moors seem white,
Who, though seven years, she in the Stews had laid,
A Nunnery durst receive, and think a maid,
And though in childbed's labour she did lie,
Midwives would swear, 'twere but a tympany,
Whom, if she accuse herself, I credit less
Than witches, which impossibles confess,
Whom Dildoes, Bedstaves, and her Velvet Glass
Would be as loth to touch as Joseph was:
One like none, and lik'd of none, fittest were,
For, things in fashion every man will wear.

ELEGY III

CHANGE

ALTHOUGH thy hand and faith, and good works too,
Have seal'd thy love which nothing should undo,
Yea though thou fall back, that apostasy
Confirm thy love; yet much, much I fear thee.
Women are like the Arts, forc'd unto none,
Open to all searchers, unpriz'd, if unknown.
If I have caught a bird, and let him fly,
Another fowler using these means, as I,
May catch the same bird; and, as these things be.
Women are made for men, not him, nor me.
Foxes and goats, all beasts change when they please,
Shall women, more hot, wily, wild than these,
Be bound to one man, and did Nature then
Idly make them apter to endure than men?
They're our clogs, not their own; if a man be
Chain'd to a galley, yet the galley's free;
Who hath a plow-land, casts all his seed corn there,
And yet allows his ground more corn should bear;
Though Danuby into the sea must flow,
The sea receives the Rhine, Volga, and Po.
By nature, which gave it, this liberty
Thou lov'st, but Oh! canst thou love it and me?
Likeness glues love: and if that thou so do,
To make us like and love, must I change too?
More than thy hate, I hate it, rather let me
Allow her change, than change as oft as she,
And so not teach, but force my opinion
To love not any one, nor every one.
To live in one land, is captivity,
To run all countries, a wild roguery;
Waters stink soon, if in one place they bide,
And in the vast sea are more putrefied:
But when they kiss one bank, and leaving this
Never look back, but the next bank do kiss,
Then are they purest; Change is the nursery
Of music, joy, life and eternity.

ELEGY IV

THE PERFUME

ONCE, and but once found in thy company,
All thy suppos'd escapes are laid on me;
And as a thief at bar, is question'd there
By all the men, that have been robb'd that year,
So am I, (by this traitorous means surpris'd)
By thy Hydroptic father catechiz'd.
Though he had wont to search with glazed eyes,
As though he came to kill a Cockatrice,
Though he hath oft sworn, that he would remove
Thy beauty's beauty, and food of our love,
Hope of his goods, if I with thee were seen,
Yet close and secret, as our souls, we have been.
Though thy immortal mother which doth lie
Still buried in her bed, yet will not die,
Takes this advantage to sleep out day-light,
And watch thy entries, and returns all night,
And, when she takes thy hand, and would seem kind,
Doth search what rings, and armlets she can find,
And kissing notes the colour of thy face,
And fearing lest thou 'rt swoln, doth thee embrace;
To try if thou long, doth name strange meats,
And notes thy paleness, blushing, sighs, and sweats;
And politiquely will to thee confess
The sins of her own youth's rank lustiness;
Yet love these Sorceries did remove, and move
Thee to gull thine own mother for my love.
Thy little brethren, which like Faery Sprites
Oft skipped into our chamber, those sweet nights,
And kissed, and ingled on thy father's knee,
Were brib'd next day, to tell what they did see:
The grim eight-foot-high iron-bound serving-man,
That oft names God in oaths, and only then,
He that to bar the first gate, doth as wide
As the great Rhodian Colossus stride,

Which, if in hell no other pains there were,
Makes me fear hell, because he must be there:
Though by thy father he were hir'd to this,
Could never witness any touch or kiss.
But Oh, too common ill, I brought with me
That, which betray'd me to my enemy:
A loud perfume, which at my entrance cried
Even at thy father's nose, so were we spied.
When, like a tyrant King, that in his bed
Smelt gunpowder, the pale wretch shivered.
Had it been some bad smell, he would have thought
That his own feet, or breath, that smell had wrought.
But as we in our Isle imprisoned,
Where cattle only, and diverse dogs are bred,
The precious Unicorns, strange monsters call,
So thought he good, strange, that had none at all.
I taught my silks, their whistling to forbear,
Even my opprest shoes, dumb and speechless were,
Only, thou bitter-sweet, whom I had laid
Next me, me traitorously hast betray'd,
And unsuspected hast invisibly
At once fled unto him, and stay'd with me.
Base excrement of earth, which dost confound
Sense, from distinguishing the sick from sound;
By thee the silly Amorous sucks his death
By drawing in a leprous harlot's breath;
By thee, the greatest stain to man's estate
Falls on us, to be call'd effeminate;
Though you be much lov'd in the Prince's hall,
There, things that seem, exceed substantial.
Gods, when ye fum'd on altars, were pleas'd well,
Because you were burnt, not that they lik'd your smell;
You're loathsome all, being taken simply alone,
Shall we love ill things join'd, and hate each one?
If you were good, your good doth soon decay;
And you are rare, that takes the good away.
All my perfumes, I give most willingly
To embalm thy father's corpse; What? will he die?

ELEGY V

HIS PICTURE

Here take my Picture; though I bid farewell,
Thine, in my heart, where my soul dwells, shall dwell.
'Tis like me now, but I dead, 'twill be more
When we are shadows both, than 'twas before.
When weather-beaten I come back; my hand,
Perhaps with rude oars torn, or Sun-beams tann'd,
My face and breast of haircloth, and my head
With care's rash sudden storms being o'erspread,
My body a sack of bones, broken within,
And powder's blue stains scatter'd on my skin;
If rival fools tax thee to have lov'd a man,
So foul, and coarse, as Oh, I may seem then,
This shall say what I was: and thou shalt say,
Do his hurts reach me? doth my worth decay?
Or do they reach his judging mind, that he
Should now love less, what he did love to see?
That which in him was fair and delicate,
Was but the milk, which in love's childish state
Did nurse it: who now is grown strong enough
To feed on that, which to disus'd tastes seems tough.

ELEGY VI

Oh, let me not serve so, as those men serve
Whom honour's smokes at once fatten and starve;
Poorly enrich'd with great men's words or looks;
Nor so write my name in thy loving books
As those Idolatrous flatterers, which still
Their Princes' styles with many Realms fulfil
Whence they no tribute have, and where no sway.
Such services I offer as shall pay
Themselves, I hate dead names: Oh then let me
Favourite in Ordinary, or no favourite be.

When my Soul was in her own body sheath'd,
Nor yet by oaths betroth'd, nor kisses breath'd
Into my Purgatory, faithless thee,
Thy heart seem'd wax, and steel thy constancy:
So, careless flowers strow'd on the water's face,
The curled whirlpools suck, smack, and embrace,
Yet drown them; so, the taper's beamy eye
Amorously twinkling, beckons the giddy fly,
Yet burns his wings; and such the devil is,
Scarce visiting them, who are entirely his.
When I behold a stream, which, from the spring,
Doth with doubtful melodious murmuring,
Or in a speechless slumber, calmly ride
Her wedded channel's bosom, and then chide
And bend her brows, and swell if any bough
Do but stoop down, or kiss her upmost brow:
Yet, if her often gnawing kisses win
The traitorous bank to gape, and let her in,
She rusheth violently, and doth divorce
Her from her native, and her long-kept course,
And roars, and braves it, and in gallant scorn,
In flattering eddies promising return,
She flouts the channel, who thenceforth is dry;
Then say I; that is she, and this am I.
Yet let not thy deep bitterness beget
Careless despair in me, for that will whet
My mind to scorn; and Oh, love dull'd with pain
Was ne'er so wise, nor well arm'd as disdain.
Then with new eyes I shall survey thee, and spy
Death in thy cheeks, and darkness in thine eye.
Though hope bred faith and love: thus taught, I shall
As nations do from Rome, from thy love fall.
My hate shall outgrow thine, and utterly
I will renounce thy dalliance: and when I
Am the Recusant, in that resolute state,
What hurts it me to be excommunicate?

ELEGY VII

NATURE's lay Idiot, I taught thee to love,
And in that sophistry, Oh, thou dost prove
Too subtle: Fool, thou didst not understand
The mystic language of the eye nor hand:
Nor couldst thou judge the difference of the air
Of sighs, and say, this lies, this sounds despair:
Nor by th' eye's water call a malady
Desperately hot, or changing feverously.
I had not taught thee then, the Alphabet
Of flowers, how they devisefully being set
And bound up, might with speechless secrecy
Deliver errands mutely, and mutually.
Remember since all thy words us'd to be
To every suitor; *Ay, if my friends agree*;
Since, household charms, thy husband's name to teach,
Were all the love-tricks, that thy wit could reach;
And since, an hour's discourse could scarce have made
One answer in thee, and that ill array'd
In broken proverbs, and torn sentences.
Thou art not by so many duties his,
That from the world's Common having sever'd thee,
Inlaid thee, neither to be seen, nor see,
As mine: who have with amorous delicacies
Refin'd thee into a blissful Paradise.
Thy graces and good words my creatures be;
I planted knowledge and life's tree in thee,
Which Oh, shall strangers taste? Must I alas
Frame and enamel Plate, and drink in Glass?
Chafe wax for others' seals? break a colt's force
And leave him then, being made a ready horse?

ELEGY VIII

THE COMPARISON

As the sweet sweat of Roses in a Still,
As that which from chaf'd musk cat's pores doth trill,
As the Almighty Balm of th' early East,
Such are the sweat drops of my Mistress' breast,
And on her [brow] her skin such lustre sets,
They seem no sweat drops, but pearl coronets.
Rank sweaty froth thy Mistress' brow defiles,
Like spermatic issue of ripe menstruous boils,
Or like the scum, which, by need's lawless law
Enforc'd, Sanserra's starvèd men did draw
From parboil'd shoes, and boots, and all the rest
Which were with any sovereign fatness blest,
And like vile lying stones in saffron'd tin,
Or warts, or weals, they hang upon her skin.
Round as the world's her head, on every side,
Like to the fatal Ball which fell on Ide,
Or that whereof God had such jealousy,
As for the ravishing thereof we die.
Thy head is like a rough-hewn statue of jet,
Where marks for eyes, nose, mouth, are yet scarce set;
Like the first Chaos, or flat seeming face
Of Cynthia, when th' earth's shadows her embrace.
Like Proserpine's white beauty-keeping chest,
Or Jove's best fortune's urn, is her fair breast.
Thine 's like worm-eaten trunks, cloth'd in seal's skin,
Or grave, that 's dust without, and stink within.
And like that slender stalk, at whose end stands
The woodbine quivering, are her arms and hands.
Like rough-bark'd elmboughs, or the russet skin
Of men late scourg'd for madness, or for sin,
Like Sun-parch'd quarters on the city gate,
Such is thy tann'd skin's lamentable state.
And like a bunch of ragged carrots stand
The short swoln fingers of thy gouty hand.

Then like the Chemic's masculine equal fire,
Which in the Limbec's warm womb doth inspire
Into th' earth's worthless dirt a soul of gold,
Such cherishing heat her best lov'd part doth hold.
Thine 's like the dread mouth of a fired gun,
Or like hot liquid metals newly run
Into clay moulds, or like to that Ætna
Where round about the grass is burnt away.
Are not your kisses then as filthy, and more,
As a worm sucking an envenom'd sore?
Doth not thy fearful hand in feeling quake,
As one which gath'ring flowers, still fears a snake?
Is not your last act harsh, and violent,
As when a Plough a stony ground doth rent?
So kiss good Turtles, so devoutly nice
Are Priests in handling reverent sacrifice,
And such in searching wounds the Surgeon is
As we, when we embrace, or touch, or kiss.
Leave her, and I will leave comparing thus,
She and comparisons are odious.

ELEGY IX

THE AUTUMNAL

No Spring, nor Summer Beauty hath such grace,
   As I have seen in one Autumnal face.
Young Beauties force our love, and that 's a Rape,
   This doth but counsel, yet you cannot scape.
If 'twere a shame to love, here 'twere no shame,
   Affection here takes Reverence's name.
Were her first years the Golden Age; that 's true,
   But now she 's gold oft tried, and ever new.
That was her torrid and inflaming time,
   This is her tolerable tropic clime.
Fair eyes, who asks more heat than comes from hence,
   He in a fever wishes pestilence.

D 867

Call not these wrinkles, graves; If graves they were,
  They were Love's graves; for else he is no where.
Yet lies not Love dead here, but here doth sit
  Vow'd to this trench, like an Anachorite.
And here, till hers, which must be his death, come,
  He doth not dig a Grave, but build a Tomb.
Here dwells he, though he sojourn ev'rywhere,
  In Progress, yet his standing house is here.
Here, where still Evening is; not noon, nor night;
  Where no voluptuousness, yet all delight.
In all her words, unto all hearers fit,
  You may at Revels, you at Council, sit.
This is love's timber, youth his underwood;
  There he, as wine in June, enrages blood,
Which then comes seasonabliest, when our taste
  And appetite to other things is past.
Xerxes' strange Lydian love, the Platane tree,
  Was lov'd for age, none being so large as she,
Or else because, being young, nature did bless
  Her youth with age's glory, Barrenness.
If we love things long sought, Age is a thing
  Which we are fifty years in compassing;
If transitory things, which soon decay,
  Age must be loveliest at the latest day.
But name not Winter-faces, whose skin's slack;
  Lank, as an unthrift's purse; but a soul's sack;
Whose Eyes seek light within, for all here's shade;
  Whose mouths are holes, rather worn out, than made;
Whose every tooth to a several place is gone,
  To vex their souls at Resurrection;
Name not these living Death's-heads unto me,
  For these, not Ancient, but Antique be.
I hate extremes; yet I had rather stay
  With Tombs, than Cradles, to wear out a day.
Since such love's natural lation is, may still
  My love descend, and journey down the hill,
Not panting after growing beauties, so,
  I shall ebb out with them, who homeward go.

ELEGY X

THE DREAM

IMAGE of her whom I love, more than she,
  Whose fair impression in my faithful heart,
Makes me her medal, and makes her love me,
  As Kings do coins, to which their stamps impart
The value: go, and take my heart from hence,
  Which now is grown too great and good for me:
Honours oppress weak spirits, and our sense
  Strong objects dull; the more, the less we see.
When you are gone, and Reason gone with you,
  Then Fantasy is Queen and Soul, and all;
She can present joys meaner than you do;
  Convenient, and more proportional.
So, if I dream I have you, I have you,
  For, all our joys are but fantastical.
And so I scape the pain, for pain is true;
  And sleep which locks up sense, doth lock out all.
After a such fruition I shall wake,
  And, but the waking, nothing shall repent;
And shall to love more thankful Sonnets make,
  Than if more honour, tears, and pains were spent.
But dearest heart, and dearer image, stay;
  Alas, true joys at best are dream enough;
Though you stay here you pass too fast away:
  For even at first life's Taper is a snuff.
Fill'd with her love, may I be rather grown
Mad with much heart, than idiot with none.

ELEGY XI

THE BRACELET

*Upon the loss of his Mistress' Chain, for which he
made satisfaction*

Not that in colour it was like thy hair,
For Armlets of that thou mayst let me wear:
Nor that thy hand it oft embrac'd and kiss'd,
For so it had that good, which oft I miss'd:
Nor for that silly old morality,
That as these links were knit, our love should be:
Mourn I that I thy sevenfold chain have lost;
Nor for the luck sake; but the bitter cost.
Oh, shall twelve righteous Angels, which as yet
No leaven of vile solder did admit;
Nor yet by any way have stray'd or gone
From the first state of their Creation;
Angels, which heaven commanded to provide
All things to me, and be my faithful guide;
To gain new friends, t' appease great enemies;
To comfort my soul, when I lie or rise;
Shall these twelve innocents, by thy severe
Sentence (dread judge) my sins' great burden bear?
Shall they be damn'd, and in the furnace thrown,
And punish'd for offences not their own?
They save not me, they do not ease my pains,
When in that hell they 're burnt and tied in chains.
Were they but Crowns of France, I carèd not,
For, most of these, their natural Country's rot
I think possesseth, they come here to us,
So pale, so lame, so lean, so ruinous;
And howsoe'er French Kings most Christian be,
Their Crowns are circumcis'd most Jewishly.
Or were they Spanish Stamps, still travelling,
That are become as Catholic as their King,
Those unlick'd bear-whelps, unfil'd pistolets
That (more than Cannon shot) avails or lets;

Which negligently left unrounded, look
Like many-angled figures, in the book
Of some great Conjurer that would enforce
Nature, as these do justice, from her course;
Which, as the soul quickens head, feet and heart,
As streams, like veins, run through th' earth's every part,
Visit all Countries, and have slily made
Gorgeous *France*, ruin'd, ragged and decay'd;
Scotland, which knew no State, proud in one day:
And mangled seventeen-headed *Belgia*.
Or were it such gold as that wherewithal
Almighty Chemics from each mineral
Having by subtle fire a soul out-pull'd,
Are dirtily and desperately gull'd:
I would not spit to quench the fire they 're in,
For, they are guilty of much heinous Sin.
But, shall my harmless angels perish? Shall
I lose my guard, my ease, my food, my all?
Much hope which they should nourish will be dead,
Much of my able youth, and lustihead
Will vanish; if thou love let them alone,
For thou wilt love me less when they are gone;
And be content that some loud squeaking Crier
Well-pleas'd with one lean thread-bare groat, for hire,
May like a devil roar through every street;
And gall the finder's conscience, if they meet.
Or let me creep to some dread Conjurer,
That with fantastic schemes fills full much paper;
Which hath divided heaven in tenements,
And with whores, thieves, and murderers stuff'd his rents,
So full, that though he pass them all in sin,
He leaves himself no room to enter in.
But if, when all his art and time is spent,
He say 'twill ne'er be found; yet be content;
Receive from him that doom ungrudgingly,
Because he is the mouth of destiny.
 Thou say'st (alas) the gold doth still remain,
Though it be chang'd, and put into a chain;
So in the first fal'n angels, resteth still

Wisdom and knowledge; but, 'tis turn'd to ill:
As these should do good works; and should provide
Necessities; but now must nurse thy pride.
And they are still bad angels; mine are none;
For, form gives being, and their form is gone:
Pity these Angels; yet their dignities
Pass Virtues, Powers, and Principalities.

　　But, thou art resolute; thy will be done!
Yet with such anguish, as her only son
The Mother in the hungry grave doth lay,
Unto the fire these Martyrs I betray.
Good souls, (for you give life to everything)
Good Angels, (for good messages you bring)
Destin'd you might have been to such an one,
As would have lov'd and worshipp'd you alone:
One that would suffer hunger, nakedness,
Yea, death, ere he would make your number less.
But, I am guilty of your sad decay;
May your few fellows longer with me stay.

　　But Oh thou wretched finder whom I hate
So, that I almost pity thy estate:
Gold being the heaviest metal amongst all,
May my most heavy curse upon thee fall:
Here fetter'd, manacled, and hang'd in chains,
First mayst thou be; then chain'd to hellish pains:
Or be with foreign gold brib'd to betray
Thy Country, and fail both of that and thy pay,
May the next thing thou stoop'st to reach, contain
Poison, whose nimble fume rot thy moist brain;
Or libels, or some interdicted thing,
Which negligently kept, thy ruin bring.
Lust-bred diseases rot thee; and dwell with thee
Itchy desire, and no ability.
May all the evils that gold ever wrought;
All mischiefs that all devils ever thought;
Want after plenty; poor and gouty age;
The plagues of travellers; love; marriage
Afflict thee, and at thy life's last moment,
May thy swoln sins themselves to thee present.

But, I forgive; repent thee honest man:
Gold is Restorative, restore it then:
But if from it thou be'st loth to depart,
Because 'tis cordial, would 'twere at thy heart.

ELEGY XII

HIS PARTING FROM HER

SINCE she must go, and I must mourn, come Night,
Environ me with darkness, whilst I write:
Shadow that hell unto me, which alone
I am to suffer when my Love is gone.
Alas the darkest Magic cannot do it,
Thou and great Hell to boot are shadows to it.
Should Cynthia quit thee, Venus, and each star,
It would not form one thought dark as mine are.
I could lend thee obscureness now, and say,
Out of my self, There should be no more Day,
Such is already my felt want of sight,
Did not the fires within me force a light.
O Love, that fire and darkness should be mix'd,
Or to thy Triumphs so strange torments fix'd!
Is 't because thou thyself art blind, that we
Thy Martyrs must no more each other see?
Or tak'st thou pride to break us on the wheel,
And view old Chaos in the Pains we feel?
Or have we left undone some mutual Rite,
Through holy fear, that merits thy despite?
No, no. The fault was mine, impute it to me,
Or rather to conspiring destiny,
Which (since I lov'd for form before) decreed,
That I should suffer when I lov'd indeed:
And therefore now, sooner than I can say,
I saw the golden fruit, 'tis rapt away.
Or as I had watch'd one drop in a vast stream,
And I left wealthy only in a dream.

Yet Love, thou 'rt blinder than thyself in this,
To vex my Dove-like friend for my amiss:
And, where my own sad truth may expiate
Thy wrath, to make her fortune run my fate:
So blinded Justice doth, when Favourites fall,
Strike them, their house, their friends, their followers all.
Was 't not enough that thou didst dart thy fires
Into our bloods, inflaming our desires,
And madest us sigh and glow, and pant, and burn,
And then thyself into our flame didst turn?
Was 't not enough, that thou didst hazard us
To paths in love so dark, so dangerous:
And those so ambush'd round with household spies,
And over all, thy husband's towering eyes
That flam'd with oily sweat of jealousy:
Yet went we not still on with constancy?
Have we not kept our guards, like spy on spy?
Had correspondence whilst the foe stood by?
Stol'n (more to sweeten them) our many blisses
Of meetings, conference, embracements, kisses?
Shadow'd with negligence our most respects?
Varied our language through all dialects,
Of becks, winks, looks, and often under-boards
Spoke dialogues with our feet far from our words?
Have we prov'd all these secrets of our Art,
Yea, thy pale inwards, and thy panting heart?
And, after all this passed Purgatory,
Must sad divorce make us the vulgar story?
First let our eyes be riveted quite through
Our turning brains, and both our lips grow to:
Let our arms clasp like Ivy, and our fear
Freeze us together, that we may stick here,
Till Fortune, that would rive us, with the deed,
Strain her eyes open, and it make them bleed.
For Love it cannot be, whom hitherto
I have accus'd, should such a mischief do.
O Fortune, thou'rt not worth my least exclaim
And plague enough thou hast in thy own shame.
Do thy great worst, my friend and I have arms,

Though not against thy strokes, against thy harms
Rend us in sunder, thou canst not divide
Our bodies so, but that our souls are tied,
And we can love by letters still and gifts,
And thoughts and dreams; Love never wanteth shifts.
I will not look upon the quickening Sun,
But straight her beauty to my sense shall run;
The air shall note her soft, the fire most pure;
Water suggest her clear, and the earth sure.
Time shall not lose our passages; the Spring
How fresh our love was in the beginning;
The Summer how it ripened in the ear;
And Autumn, what our golden harvests were.
The Winter I'll not think on to spite thee,
But count it a lost season, so shall she.
And dearest Friend, since we must part, drown night
With hope of Day, burthens well borne are light.
Though cold and darkness longer hang somewhere,
Yet Phœbus equally lights all the Sphere.
And what he cannot in like Portions pay,
The world enjoys in Mass, and so we may.
Be then ever yourself, and let no woe
Win on your health, your youth, your beauty: so
Declare youself base fortune's Enemy,
No less by your contempt than constancy;
That I may grow enamoured on your mind,
When my own thoughts I there reflected find.
For this to th' comfort of my Dear I vow,
My Deeds shall still be what my words are now;
The Poles shall move to teach me ere I start;
And when I change my Love, I 'll change my heart;
Nay, if I wax but cold in my desire,
Think, heaven hath motion lost, and the world, fire:
Much more I could, but many words have made
That, oft, suspected which men would persuade;
Take therefore all in this: I love so true,
As I will never look for less in you.

ELEGY XIII

JULIA

HARK news, O envy, thou shalt hear descried
My *Julia*; who as yet was ne'er envied.
To vomit gall in slander, swell her veins
With calumny, that hell itself disdains,
Is her continual practice; does her best,
To tear opinion even out of the breast
Of dearest friends, and (which is worse than vile)
Sticks jealousy in wedlock; her own child
Scapes not the showers of envy.   To repeat
The monstrous fashions, how, were alive to eat
Dear reputation.   Would to God she were
But half so loth to act vice, as to hear
My mild reproof.   Liv'd *Mantuan* now again,
That female Mastix, to limn with his pen
This she Chimera, that hath eyes of fire,
Burning with anger, anger feeds desire,
Tongued like the night-crow, whose ill-boding cries
Give out for nothing but new injuries,
Her breath like to the juice in *Tenarus*
That blasts the springs, though ne'er so prosperous,
Her hands, I know not how, us'd more to spill
The food of others, than herself to fill.
But oh her mind, that *Orcus*, which includes
Legions of mischiefs, countless multitudes
Of formless curses, projects unmade up,
Abuses yet unfashion'd, thoughts corrupt,
Misshapen Cavils, palpable untroths,
Inevitable errors, self-accusing oaths:
These, like those Atoms swarming in the Sun,
Throng in her bosom for creation.
I blush to give her half her due; yet say,
No poison's half so bad as *Julia*.

ELEGY XIV

A TALE OF A CITIZEN AND HIS WIFE

I SING no harm good sooth to any wight,
To Lord or fool, Cuckold, beggar or knight,
To peace-teaching Lawyer, Proctor, or brave
Reformèd or reducèd Captain, Knave,
Officer, Juggler, or Justice of peace,
Juror or Judge; I touch no fat sow's grease,
I am no Libeller, nor will be any,
But (like a true man) say there are too many.
I fear not *ore tenus*; for my tale,
Nor Count nor Counsellor will red or pale.
   A citizen and his wife the other day
Both riding on one horse, upon the way
I overtook, the wench a pretty peat,
And (by her eye) well fitting for the feat.
I saw the lecherous Citizen turn back
His head, and on his wife's lip steal a smack,
Whence apprehending that the man was kind,
Riding before, to kiss his wife behind,
To get acquaintance with him I began
To sort discourse fit for so fine a man:
I ask'd the number of the Plaguy Bill,
Ask'd if the Custom Farmers held out still,
Of the Virginian plot, and whether Ward
The traffic of the I[n]land seas had marr'd,
Whether the Britain *Burse* did fill apace,
And likely were to give th' Exchange disgrace;
Of new-built Aldgate, and the Moor-field crosses,
Of store of bankrupts, and poor Merchants' losses
I urgèd him to speak; But he (as mute
As an old Courtier worn to his last suit)
Replies with only yeas and nays; at last
(To fit his element) my theme I cast
On Tradesmen's gains; that set his tongue a-going:
Alas, good sir (quoth he) *There is no doing*

In Court nor City now; she smil'd and I,
And (in my conscience) both gave him the lie
In one met thought: but he went on apace,
And at the present time with such a face
He rail'd, as fray'd me; for he gave no praise,
To any but my Lord of *Essex*' days;
Call'd those the age of action; true (quoth he)
There 's now as great an itch of bravery,
And heat of taking up, but cold lay down,
For, put to push of pay, away they run;
Our only City trades of hope now are
Bawd, Tavern-keeper, Whore and Scrivener;
The much of privileged kingsmen, and the store
Of fresh protections make the rest all poor;
In the first state of their Creation,
Though many stoutly stand, yet proves not one
A righteous paymaster.   Thus ran he on
In a continued rage: so void of reason
Seem'd his harsh talk, I sweat for fear of treason.
And (troth) how could I less? when in the prayer
For the protection of the wise Lord Mayor,
And his wise brethren's worships, when one prayeth,
He swore that none could say Amen with faith.
To get him off from what I glowed to hear,
(In happy time) an Angel did appear,
The bright Sign of a lov'd and well-tried Inn,
Where many Citizens with their wives have been
Well used and often; here I pray'd him stay,
To take some due refreshment by the way.
Look how he look'd that hid the gold (his hope)
And at 's return found nothing but a Rope,
So he on me, refus'd and made away,
Though willing she pleaded a weary day:
I found my miss, struck hands, and pray'd him tell
(To hold acquaintance still) where he did dwell;
He barely nam'd the street, promis'd the Wine.
But his kind wife gave me the very Sign.

ELEGY XV

THE EXPOSTULATION

To make the doubt clear, that no woman 's true,
    Was it my fate to prove it strong in you?
Thought I, but one had breathèd purest air,
    And must she needs be false because she 's fair?
Is it your beauty's mark, or of your youth,
    Or your perfection, not to study truth?
Or think you heaven is deaf, or hath no eyes?
    Or those it hath, smile at your perjuries?
Are vows so cheap with women, or the matter
    Whereof they are made, that they are writ in water,
And blown away with wind?   Or doth their breath
    (Both hot and cold at once) make life and death?
Who could have thought so many accents sweet
    Form'd into words, so many sighs should meet
As from our hearts, so many oaths, and tears
    Sprinkled among (all sweeter by our fears
And the divine impression of stolen kisses,
    That seal'd the rest) should now prove empty blisses?
Did you draw bonds to forfeit? sign to break?
    Or must we read you quite from what you speak,
And find the truth out the wrong way? or must
    He first desire you false, would wish you just?
O I profane, though most of women be
    This kind of beast, my thought shall except thee;
My dearest love, though froward jealousy,
    With circumstance might urge thy inconstancy,
Sooner I 'll think the Sun will cease to cheer
    The teeming earth, and *that* forget to bear,
Sooner that rivers will run back, or Thames
    With ribs of ice in June would bind his streams,
Or Nature, by whose strength the world endures,
    Would change her course, before you alter yours.
But O that treacherous breast to whom weak you
    Did trust our Counsels, and we both may rue,

Having his falsehood found too late, 'twas he
   That made me cast you guilty, and you me,
Whilst he, black wretch, betray'd each simple word
   We spake, unto the cunning of a third.
Curst may he be, that so our love hath slain,
   And wander on the earth, wretched as *Cain*,
Wretched as he, and not deserve least pity;
   In plaguing him, let misery be witty;
Let all eyes shun him, and he shun each eye,
   Till he be noisome as his infamy;
May he without remorse deny God thrice,
   And not be trusted more on his soul's price;
And after all self-torment, when he dies,
   May Wolves tear out his heart, Vultures his eyes,
Swine eat his bowels, and his falser tongue
   That utter'd all, be to some Raven flung,
And let his carrion corse be a longer feast
   To the King's dogs, than any other beast.
Now have I curst, let us our love revive;
   In me the flame was never more alive;
I could begin again to court and praise,
   And in that pleasure lengthen the short days
Of my life's lease; like Painters that do take
   Delight, not in made work, but whiles they make;
I could renew those times, when first I saw
   Love in your eyes, that gave my tongue the law
To like what you lik'd; and at masks and plays
   Commend the self-same Actors, the same ways;
Ask how you did, and often with intent
   Of being officious, be impertinent;
All which were such soft pastimes, as in these
   Love was as subtly catch'd, as a disease;
But being got it is a treasure sweet,
   Which to defend is harder than to get:
And ought not be profan'd on either part,
   For though 'tis got by *chance*, 'tis kept by *art*.

ELEGY XVI

ON HIS MISTRESS

By our first strange and fatal interview,
By all desires which thereof did ensue,
By our long starving hopes, by that remorse
Which my words' masculine persuasive force
Begot in thee, and by the memory
Of hurts, which spies and rivals threatened me,
I calmly beg: but by thy father's wrath,
By all pains, which want and divorcement hath,
I conjure thee, and all the oaths which I
And thou have sworn to seal joint constancy,
Here I unswear, and overswear them thus,
Thou shalt not love by ways so dangerous.
Temper, O fair Love, love's impetuous rage,
Be my true Mistress still, not my feign'd Page;
I'll go, and, by thy kind leave, leave behind
Thee, only worthy to nurse in my mind
Thirst to come back; O if thou die before,
My soul from other lands to thee shall soar.
Thy (else Almighty) beauty cannot move
Rage from the Seas, nor thy love teach them love,
Nor tame wild Boreas' harshness; thou hast read
How roughly he in pieces shivered
Fair Orithea, whom he swore he lov'd.
Fall ill or good, 'tis madness to have prov'd
Dangers unurg'd; feed on this flattery,
That absent Lovers one in th' other be.
Dissemble nothing, not a boy, nor change
Thy body's habit, nor mind's; be not strange
To thyself only; all will spy in thy face
A blushing womanly discovering grace;
Richly cloth'd Apes, are call'd Apes, and as soon
Eclips'd as bright we call the Moon the Moon.
Men of France, changeable chameleons,
Spitals of diseases, shops of fashions,

Love's fuellers, and the rightest company
Of Players, which upon the world's stage be,
Will quickly know thee, and no less, alas!
Th' indifferent Italian, as we pass
His warm land, well content to think thee Page,
Will hunt thee with such lust, and hideous rage,
As Lot's fair guests were vex'd.   But none of these
Nor spongy hydroptic Dutch shall thee displease,
If thou stay here.   O stay here, for, for thee
England is only a worthy gallery,
To walk in expectation, till from thence
Our greatest King call thee to his presence.
When I am gone, dream me some happiness,
Nor let thy looks our long-hid love confess,
Nor praise, nor dispraise me, nor bless nor curse
Openly love's force, nor in bed fright thy Nurse
With midnight's startings, crying out, oh, oh
Nurse, O my love is slain, I saw him go
O'er the white Alps alone; I saw him, I,
Assail'd, fight, taken, stabb'd, bleed, fall, and die.
Augur me better chance, except dread Jove
Think it enough for me to have had thy love.

ELEGY XVII

VARIETY

THE heavens rejoice in motion, why should I
Abjure my so much lov'd variety,
And not with many youth and love divide?
Pleasure is none, if not diversified:
The sun that sitting in the chair of light
Sheds flame into what else soever doth seem bright,
Is not contented at one Sign to Inn,
But ends his year and with a new begins.
All things do willingly in change delight,
The fruitful mother of our appetite:

Rivers the clearer and more pleasing are,
Where their fair spreading streams run wide and far;
And a dead lake that no strange bark doth greet,
Corrupts itself and what doth live in it.
Let no man tell me such a one is fair,
And worthy all alone my love to share.
Nature in her hath done the liberal part
Of a kind Mistress, and employ'd her art
To make her lovable, and I aver
Him not humane that would turn back from her:
I love her well, and would, if need were, die
To do her service. But follows it that I
Must serve her only, when I may have choice
Of other beauties, and in change rejoice?
The law is hard, and shall not have my voice.
The last I saw in all extremes is fair,
And holds me in the Sun-beams of her hair;
Her nymph-like features such agreements have
That I could venture with her to the grave:
Another's brown, I like her not the worse,
Her tongue is soft and takes me with discourse:
Others, for that they well descended are,
Do in my love obtain as large a share;
And though they be not fair, 'tis much with me
To win their love only for their degree.
And though I fail of my required ends,
The attempt is glorious and itself commends.
How happy were our Sires in ancient time,
Who held plurality of loves no crime!
With them it was accounted charity
To stir up race of all indifferently;
Kindreds were not exempted from the bands:
Which with the Persian still in usage stands.
Women were then no sooner asked than won,
And what they did was honest and well done.
But since this title honour hath been used
Our weak credulity hath been abused;
The golden laws of nature are repeal'd,
Which our first Fathers in such reverence held;

Our liberty 's revers'd, our Charter 's gone,
And we 're made servants to opinion,
A monster in no certain shape attir'd,
And whose original is much desir'd,
Formless at first, but growing on it fashions,
And doth prescribe manners and laws to nations.
Here love receiv'd immedicable harms,
And was despoiled of his daring arms.
A greater want than is his daring eyes,
He lost those awful wings with which he flies;
His sinewy bow, and those immortal darts
Wherewith he 's wont to bruise resisting hearts.
Only some few strong in themselves and free
Retain the seeds of ancient liberty,
Following that part of Love although depressed,
And make a throne for him within their breast,
In spite of modern censures him avowing
Their Sovereign, all service him allowing.
Amongst which troop although I am the least,
Yet equal in perfection with the best,
I glory in subjection of his hand,
Nor ever did decline his least command:
For in whatever form the message came
My heart did open and receive the same.
But time will in his course a point descry
When I this loved service must deny,
For our allegiance temporary is,
With firmer age returns our liberties.
What time in years and judgment we repos'd,
Shall not so easily be to change dispos'd,
Nor to the art of several eyes obeying;
But beauty with true worth securely weighing,
Which being found assembled in some one,
We 'll love her ever, and love her alone.

ELEGY XVIII

LOVE'S PROGRESS

WHOEVER loves, if he do not propose
The right true end of love, he 's one that goes
To sea for nothing but to make him sick:
Love is a bear-whelp born, if we o'er-lick
Our love, and force it new strange shapes to take,
We err, and of a lump a monster make.
Were not a Calf a monster that were grown
Faced like a man, though better than his own?
Perfection is in unity: prefer
One woman first, and then one thing in her.
I, when I value gold, may think upon
The ductileness, the application,
The wholesomeness, the ingenuity,
From rust, from soil, from fire ever free:
But if I love it, 'tis because 'tis made
By our new nature (Use) the soul of trade.
   All these in women we might think upon
(If women had them) and yet love but one.
Can men more injure women than to say
They love them for that, by which they 're not they?
Makes virtue woman? must I cool my blood
Till I both be, and find one wise and good?
May barren Angels love so.   But if we
Make love to woman; virtue is not she:
As beauty 's not nor wealth: he that strays thus
From her to hers, is more adulterous
Than if he took her maid.   Search every sphere
And firmament, our *Cupid* is not there:
He 's an infernal god and underground
With *Pluto* dwells, where gold and fire abound:
Men to such Gods, their sacrificing coals
Did not in Altars lay, but pits and holes.
Although we see Celestial bodies move
Above the earth, the earth we till and love:

So we her airs contemplate, words and heart,
And virtues; but we love the centric part.
   Nor is the soul more worthy, or more fit
For love, than this, as infinite as it.
But in attaining this desired place
How much they err, that set out at the face?
The hair a Forest is of Ambushes,
Of springs, snares, fetters and manacles:
The brow becalms us when 'tis smooth and plain,
And when 'tis wrinkled, shipwrecks us again.
Smooth, 'tis a Paradise, where we would have
Immortal stay, and wrinkled 'tis our grave.
The Nose (like to the first Meridian) runs
Not 'twixt an East and West, but 'twixt two suns;
It leaves a Cheek, a rosy Hemisphere
On either side, and then directs us where
Upon the Islands fortunate we fall,
(Not faint *Canaries*, but ambrosial)
Her swelling lips; to which when we are come,
We anchor there, and think ourselves at home,
For they seem all: there sirens' songs, and there
Wise Delphic Oracles do fill the ear;
There in a Creek where chosen pearls do swell,
The Remora, her cleaving tongue doth dwell.
These, and the glorious Promontory, her Chin
O'erpast; and the strait *Hellespont* between
The *Sestos* and *Abydos* of her breasts,
(Not of two Lovers, but two Loves the nests)
Succeeds a boundless sea, but yet thine eye
Some Island moles may scattered there descry;
And sailing towards her *India*, in that way
Shall at her fair Atlantic Navel stay;
Though thence the Current be thy Pilot made,
Yet ere thou be where thou wouldst be embay'd,
Thou shalt upon another Forest set,
Where many shipwreck, and no further get.
When thou art there, consider what this chase
Misspent by thy beginning at the face.
   Rather set out below; practise my Art,

Some Symmetry the foot hath with that part
Which thou dost seek, and is thy Map for that
Lovely enough to stop, but not stay at:
Least subject to disguise and change it is;
Men say the Devil never can change his.
It is the Emblem that hath figured
Firmness; 'tis the first part that comes to bed.
Civility we see refin'd: the kiss
Which at the face began, transplanted is,
Since to the hand, since to the Imperial knee,
Now at the Papal foot delights to be:
If Kings think that the nearer way, and do
Rise from the foot, Lovers may do so too;
For as free Spheres move faster far than can
Birds, whom the air resists, so may that man
Which goes this empty and Æthereal way,
Than if at beauty's elements he stay.
Rich Nature hath in women wisely made
Two purses, and their mouths aversely laid:
They then, which to the lower tribute owe,
That way which that Exchequer looks, must go:
He which doth not, his error is as great,
As who by Clyster gave the Stomach meat.

ELEGY XIX

TO HIS MISTRESS GOING TO BED

COME, Madam, come, all rest my powers defy,
Until I labour, I in labour lie.
The foe oft-times having the foe in sight,
Is tired with standing though he never fight.
Off with that girdle, like heaven's Zone glistering,
But a far fairer world encompassing.
Unpin that spangled breastplate which you wear,
That th' eyes of busy fools may be stopt there.
Unlace yourself, for that harmonious chime

Tells me from you, that now it is bed time.
Off with that happy busk, which I envy,
That still can be, and still can stand so nigh.
Your gown going off, such beauteous state reveals,
As when from flowry meads th' hill's shadow steals.
Off with that wiry Coronet and show
The hairy Diadem which on you doth grow:
Now off with those shoes, and then safely tread
In this love's hallow'd temple, this soft bed.
In such white robes, heaven's Angels used to be
Receiv'd by men; thou Angel bring'st with thee
A heaven like Mahomet's Paradise; and though
Ill spirits walk in white, we easily know,
By this these Angels from an evil sprite,
Those set our hairs, but these our flesh upright.
    Licence my roving hands, and let them go,
Before, behind, between, above, below.
O my America! my new-found-land,
My kingdom, safeliest when with one man mann'd,
My Mine of precious stones, My Empery,
How blest am I in this discovering thee!
To enter in these bonds, is to be free;
Then where my hand is set, my seal shall be.
    Full nakedness!   All joys are due to thee,
As souls unbodied, bodies uncloth'd must be,
To taste whole joys.   Gems wh.ch you women use
Are like Atlanta's balls, cast in men's views,
That when a fool's eye lighteth on a Gem,
His earthly soul may covet theirs, not them.
Like pictures, or like books' gay coverings made
For lay-men, are all women thus array'd;
Themselves are mystic books, which only we
(Whom their imputed grace will dignify)
Must see reveal'd.   Then since that I may know,
As liberally, as to a Midwife, show
Thyself: cast all, yea, this white linen hence,
There is no penance due to innocence.
    To teach thee, I am naked first; why then
What needst thou have more covering than a man.

ELEGY XX

LOVE'S WAR

TILL I have peace with thee, war other men,
And when I have peace, can I leave thee then?
All other Wars are scrupulous; only thou
O fair free City, may'st thyself allow
To any one.   In Flanders, who can tell
Whether the Master press; or men rebel?
Only we know, that which all idiots say,
They bear most blows which come to part the fray.
France in her lunatic giddiness did hate
Ever our men, yea and our God of late;
Yet she relies upon our Angels well,
Which ne'er return; no more than they which fell.
Sick Ireland is with a strange war possessed
Like to an Ague; now raging, now at rest;
Which time will cure: yet it must do her good
If she were purg'd, and her head-vein let blood.
And Midas' joys our Spanish journeys give,
We touch all gold, but find no food to live.
And I should be in the hot parching clime,
To dust and ashes turn'd before my time.
To mew me in a Ship, is to enthral
Me in a prison, that were like to fall;
Or in a cloister; save that there men dwell
In a calm heaven, here in a swaggering hell.
Long voyages are long consumptions,
And ships are carts for executions.
Yea they are Deaths; is 't not all one to fly
Into an other World, as 'tis to die?
Here let me war; in these arms let me lie;
Here let me parley, batter, bleed, and die.
Thine arms imprison me, and mine arms thee,
Thy heart thy ransom is, take mine for me.
Other men war that they their rest may gain;
But we will rest that we may fight again.

Those wars the ignorant, these th' experienc'd love.
There we are always under, here above.
There Engines far off breed a just true fear,
Near thrusts, pikes, stabs, yea bullets hurt not here.
There lies are wrongs; here safe uprightly lie;
There men kill men, we 'll make one by and by.
Thou nothing; I not half so much shall do
In these Wars, as they may which from us two
Shall spring.   Thousands we see which travel not
To wars, but stay swords, arms, and shot
To make at home; and shall not I do then
More glorious service, staying to make men?

HEROICAL EPISTLE

SAPPHO TO PHILÆNIS

WHERE is that holy fire, which Verse is said
    To have? is that enchanting force decay'd?
Verse that draws Nature's works, from Nature's law,
    Thee, her best work, to her work cannot draw.
Have my tears quench'd my old Poetic fire;
    Why quench'd they not as well, that of desire?
Thoughts, my mind's creatures, often are with thee,
    But I, their maker, want their liberty.
Only thine image, in my heart, doth sit,
    But that is wax, and fires environ it.
My fires have driven, thine have drawn it hence;
    And I am robb'd of Picture, Heart, and Sense.
Dwells with me still mine irksome Memory,
    Which, both to keep, and lose, grieves equally.
That tells me how fair thou art: Thou art so fair,
    As gods, when gods to thee I do compare,
Are graced thereby; and to make blind men see,
    What things gods are, I say they 're like to thee.
For, if we justly call each silly man

A little world, What shall we call thee then?
Thou art not soft, and clear, and straight, and fair,
    As Down, as Stars, Cedars, and Lilies are,
But thy right hand, and cheek, and eye, only
    Are like thy other hand, and cheek, and eye.
Such was my Phao awhile, but shall be never,
    As thou wast, art, and, oh, may'st thou be ever.
Here lovers swear in their idolatry,
    That I am such; but Grief discolours me.
And yet I grieve the less, lest Grief remove
    My beauty, and make me unworthy of thy love.
Plays some soft boy with thee, oh there wants yet
    A mutual feeling which should sweeten it.
His chin, a thorny hairy unevenness
    Doth threaten, and some daily change possess.
Thy body is a natural Paradise,
    In whose self, unmanur'd, all pleasure lies,
Nor needs perfection; why shouldst thou then
    Admit the tillage of a harsh rough man?
Men leave behind them that which their sin shows,
    And are as thieves traced, which rob when it snows.
But of our dalliance no more signs there are,
    Than fishes leave in streams, or Birds in air.
And between us all sweetness may be had;
    All, all that Nature yields, or Art can add.
My two lips, eyes, thighs, differ from thy two,
    But so, as thine from one another do;
And, oh, no more; the likeness being such,
    Why should they not alike in all parts touch?
Hand to strange hand, lip to lip none denies;
    Why should they breast to breast, or thighs to thighs?
Likeness begets such strange self-flattery,
    That touching myself, all seems done to thee.
Myself I embrace, and mine own hands I kiss,
    And amorously thank myself for this.
Me, in my glass, I call thee; but alas,
    When I would kiss, tears dim mine eyes, and glass.
O cure this loving madness, and restore
    Me to me; thee, my half, my all, my more.

So may thy cheeks' red outwear scarlet dye,
    And their white, whiteness of the Galaxy,
So may thy mighty, amazing beauty move
    Envy in all women, and in all men, love,
And so be change, and sickness, far from thee,
    As thou by coming near, keep'st them from me.

EPITHALAMIONS OR MARRIAGE SONGS

AN EPITHALAMION, OR MARRIAGE SONG

ON THE LADY ELIZABETH AND COUNT PALATINE BEING
MARRIED ON ST. VALENTINE'S DAY

I

HAIL Bishop Valentine, whose day this is,
  All the Air is thy Diocese,
  And all the chirping Choristers
And other birds are thy Parishioners,
  Thou marriest every year
The lyric Lark, and the grave whispering Dove,
The Sparrow that neglects his life for love,
The household Bird, with the red stomacher;
  Thou mak'st the blackbird speed as soon,
As doth the Goldfinch, or the Halcyon;
The husband cock looks out, and straight is sped,
And meets his wife, which brings her feather-bed.
This day more cheerfully than ever shine,
This day, which might inflame thyself, Old Valentine.

II

Till now, Thou warm'd'st with multiplying loves
  Two larks, two sparrows, or two Doves,
  All that is nothing unto this,
For thou this day couplest two Phœnixes;
  Thou mak'st a Taper see
What the sun never saw, and what the Ark
(Which was of fowls, and beasts, the cage, and park,)
Did not contain, one bed contains, through Thee,
  Two Phœnixes, whose joined breasts
Are unto one another mutual nests,

93

Where motion kindles such fires, as shall give
Young Phœnixes, and yet the old shall live;
Whose love and courage never shall decline,
But make the whole year through, thy day, O Valentine.

III

Up then fair Phœnix Bride, frustrate the Sun,
  Thyself from thine affection
  Takest warmth enough, and from thine eye
All lesser birds will take their jollity.
  Up, up, fair Bride, and call,
Thy stars, from out their several boxes, take
Thy Rubies, Pearls, and Diamonds forth, and make
Thyself a constellation, of them All,
  And by their blazing, signify,
That a Great Princess falls, but doth not die;
Be thou a new star, that to us portends
Ends of much wonder; and be Thou those ends.
Since thou dost this day in new glory shine,
May all men date Records, from this thy Valentine.

IV

Come forth, come forth, and as one glorious flame
  Meeting Another, grows the same,
  So meet thy Frederick, and so
To an unseparable union grow.
  Since separation
Falls not on such things as are infinite,
Nor things which are but one, can disunite,
You 're twice inseparable, great, and one;
  Go, then to where the Bishop stays,
To make you one, his way, which divers ways
Must be effected; and when all is past,
And that you 're one, by hearts and hands made fast,
You two have one way left, yourselves to entwine,
Besides this Bishop's knot, or Bishop Valentine.

V

But oh, what ails the Sun, that here he stays,
  Longer to-day, than other days?
  Stays he new light from these to get?
And finding here such store, is loth to set?
   And why do you two walk,
So slowly paced in this procession?
Is all your care but to be look'd upon,
And be to others spectacle, and talk?
   The feast, with gluttonous delays,
Is eaten, and too long their meat they praise,
The masquers come too late, and I think, will stay,
Like fairies, till the Cock crow them away.
Alas, did not Antiquity assign
A night, as well as day, to thee, O Valentine?

VI

They did, and night is come; and yet we see
  Formalities retarding thee.
  What mean these Ladies, which (as though
They were to take a clock in pieces,) go
   So nicely about the Bride;
A Bride, before a good-night could be said,
Should vanish from her clothes, into her bed,
As Souls from bodies steal, and are not spied.
   But now she is laid; what though she be?
Yet there are more delays, for, where is he?
He comes, and passes through Sphere after Sphere,
First her sheets, then her Arms, then any where.
Let not this day, then, but this night be thine,
Thy day was but the eve to this, O Valentine.

VII

Here lies a she Sun, and a he Moon here,
  She gives the best light to his Sphere,
  Or each is both, and all, and so

They unto one another nothing owe,
  And yet they do, but are
So just and rich in that coin, which they pay,
That neither would, nor needs forbear nor stay;
Neither desires to be spared, nor to spare,
  They quickly pay their debt, and then
Take no acquittances, but pay again;
They pay, they give, they lend, and so let fall
No such occasion to be liberal.
More truth, more courage in these two do shine,
Than all thy turtles have, and sparrows, Valentine.

VIII

And by this act of these two Phœnixes
  Nature again restored is,
  For since these two are two no more,
There's but one Phœnix still, as was before.
  Rest now at last, and we
As Satyrs watch the Sun's uprise, will stay
Waiting, when your eyes opened, let out day,
Only desired, because your face we see;
  Others near you shall whispering speak,
And wagers lay, at which side day will break,
And win by observing, then, whose hand it is
That opens first a curtain, hers or his;
This will be tried to-morrow after nine,
Till which hour, we thy day enlarge, O Valentine.

ECLOGUE

1613. *December* 26

Allophanes *finding* Idios *in the country in Christmas time,
reprehends his absence from court, at the marriage of the
Earl of Somerset*; Idios *gives an account of his purpose
therein, and of his absence thence.*

Allophanes.

UNSEASONABLE man, statue of ice,
   What could to country's solitude entice
Thee, in this year's cold and decrepit time?
   Nature's instinct draws to the warmer clime
Even small birds, who by that courage dare,
   In numerous fleets, sail through their Sea, the air.
What delicacy can in fields appear,
   Whilst Flora herself doth a frieze jerkin wear?
Whilst winds do all the trees and hedges strip
   Of leaves, to furnish rods enough to whip
Thy madness from thee; and all springs by frost
   Have taken cold, and their sweet murmur lost;
If thou thy faults or fortunes wouldst lament
   With just solemnity, do it in Lent;
At Court the spring already advanced is,
   The Sun stays longer up; and yet not his
The glory is, far other, other fires.
   First, zeal to Prince and State; then love's desires
Burn in one breast, and like heaven's two great lights,
   The first doth govern days, the other nights.
And then that early light, which did appear
   Before the Sun and Moon created were,
The Prince's favour is diffused o'er all,
   From which all Fortunes, Names, and Natures fall;
Then from those wombs of stars, the Bride's bright eyes,
   At every glance, a constellation flies,
And sows the Court with stars, and doth prevent
   In light and power, the all-eyed firmament;
First her eyes kindle other Ladies' eyes,
   Then from their beams their jewels' lustres rise,

And from their jewels torches do take fire,
　　And all is warmth, and light, and good desire;
Most other Courts, alas, are like to hell,
　　Where in dark plots, fire without light doth dwell;
Or but like Stoves, for lust and envy get
　　Continual, but artificial heat;
Here zeal and love grown one, all clouds digest,
　　And make our Court an everlasting East.
And can'st thou be from thence?

Idios.　　　　　　　　　No, I am there.
　As heaven, to men dispos'd, is everywhere,
So are those Courts, whose Princes animate,
　　Not only all their house, but all their State.
Let no man think, because he is full, he hath all.
　　Kings (as their pattern, God) are liberal
Not only in fullness, but capacity,
　　Enlarging narrow men, to feel and see,
And comprehend the blessings they bestow.
　　So, reclus'd hermits oftentimes do know
More of heaven's glory, than a worldling can.
　　As man is of the world, the heart of man,
Is an epitome of God's great book
　　Of creatures, and man need no farther look;
So is the Country of Courts, where sweet peace doth,
　　As their one common soul, give life to both,
I am not then from Court.

Allophanes.　　　　　　Dreamer, thou art.
　Think'st thou fantastic that thou hast a part
In the East-Indian fleet, because thou hast
　　A little spice, or Amber in thy taste?
Because thou art not frozen, art thou warm?
　　Seest thou all good because thou seest no harm?
The earth doth in her inward bowels hold
　　Stuff well dispos'd, and which would fain be gold,
But never shall, except it chance to lie,
　　So upward, that heaven gild it with his eye;
As, for divine things, faith comes from above,
　　So, for best civil use, all tinctures move

From higher powers; from God religion springs,
   Wisdom, and honour from the use of Kings.
Then unbeguile thyself, and know with me,
   That angels, though on earth employ'd they be,
Are still in heav'n, so is he still at home
   That doth, abroad, to honest actions come.
Chide thyself then, O fool, which yesterday
   Might'st have read more than all thy books bewray;
Hast thou a history, which doth present
   A Court, where all affections do assent
Unto the King's, and that, that King's are just?
   And where it is no levity to trust?
Where there is no ambition, but to obey,
   Where men need whisper nothing, and yet may;
Where the King's favours are so placed, that all
   Find that the King therein is liberal
To them, in him, because his favours bend
   To virtue, to the which they all pretend?
Thou hast no such; yet here was this, and more,
   An earnest lover, wise then, and before.
Our little Cupid hath sued Livery,
   And is no more in his minority,
He is admitted now into that breast
   Where the King's Counsels and his secrets rest.
What hast thou lost, O ignorant man?

Idios.   I knew
   All this, and only therefore I withdrew.
To know and feel all this, and not to have
   Words to express it, makes a man a grave
Of his own thoughts; I would not therefore stay
   At a great feast, having no grace to say.
And yet I 'scaped not here; for being come
   Full of the common joy, I utter'd some;
Read then this nuptial song, which was not made
   Either the Court or men's hearts to invade,
But since I am dead, and buried, I could frame
   No epitaph, which might advance my fame
So much as this poor song, which testifies
   I did unto that day some sacrifice.

E 867

EPITHALAMION

I. THE TIME OF THE MARRIAGE

THOU art reprieved, old year, thou shalt not die,
Though thou upon thy death-bed lie,
 And should'st within five days expire,
Yet thou art rescued by a mightier fire,
 Than thy old Soul, the Sun,
When he doth in his largest circle run.
The passage of the West or East would thaw,
And open wide their easy liquid jaw
To all our ships, could a Promethean art
Either unto the Northern Pole impart
The fire of these inflaming eyes, or of this loving heart.

II. EQUALITY OF PERSONS

BUT undiscerning Muse, which heart, which eyes,
 In this new couple, dost thou prize,
 When his eye as inflaming is
As hers, and her heart loves as well as his?
 Be tried by beauty, and then
The bridegroom is a maid, and not a man.
If by that manly courage they be tried,
Which scorns unjust opinion; then the bride
Becomes a man.   Should chance or envy's art
Divide these two, whom nature scarce did part?
Since both have both th' inflaming eyes, and both the
  loving heart.

III. RAISING OF THE BRIDEGROOM

THOUGH it be some divorce to think of you
 Singly, so much one are you two,
 Yet let me here contemplate thee,
First, cheerful Bridegroom, and first let me see,
 How thou prevent'st the Sun,

And his red foaming horses dost outrun,
How, having laid down in thy Sovereign's breast
All businesses, from thence to reinvest
Them, when these triumphs cease, thou forward art
To show to her, who doth the like impart,
The fire of thy inflaming eyes, and of thy loving heart.

IV. RAISING OF THE BRIDE

But now, to Thee, fair Bride, it is some wrong,
 To think thou wert in Bed so long,
  Since soon thou liest down first, 'tis fit
Thou in first rising should'st allow for it.
 Powder thy Radiant hair,
Which if without such ashes thou would'st wear,
Thou, which to all which come to look upon,
Art meant for Phœbus, would'st be Phaëton.
For our ease, give thine eyes th' unusual part
Of joy, a Tear; so quench'd, thou may'st impart,
To us that come, thy inflaming eyes, to him, thy loving
   heart.

V. HER APPARELLING

Thus thou descend'st to our infirmity,
 Who can the Sun in water see.
  So dost thou, when in silk and gold,
Thou cloud'st thyself; since we which do behold,
 Are dust, and worms, 'tis just
Our objects be the fruits of worms and dust;
Let every Jewel be a glorious star,
Yet stars are not so pure, as their spheres are.
And though thou stoop, to appear to us in part,
Still in that Picture thou entirely art,
Which thy inflaming eyes have made within his loving
   heart.

VI. GOING TO THE CHAPEL

Now from your Easts you issue forth, and we,
　　As men which through a Cypress see
　　The rising sun, do think it two,
So, as you go to Church, do think of you,
　　But that veil being gone,
By the Church rites you are from thenceforth one.
The Church Triumphant made this match before,
And now the Militant doth strive no more;
Then, reverend Priest, who God's Recorder art,
Do, from his Dictates, to these two impart
All blessings, which are seen, or thought, by Angel's eye
　　　　or heart.

VII. THE BENEDICTION

Blest pair of Swans, Oh may you interbring
　　Daily new joys, and never sing;
　　Live, till all grounds of wishes fail,
Till honour, yea till wisdom grow so stale,
　　That, new great heights to try,
It must serve your ambition, to die;
Raise heirs, and may here, to the world's end, live
Heirs from this King, to take thanks, you, to give,
Nature and grace do all, and nothing Art.
May never age, or error overthwart
With any West, these radiant eyes, with any North, this
　　　　heart.

VIII. FEASTS AND REVELS

But you are over-blest. Plenty this day
　　Injures; it causeth time to stay;
　　The tables groan, as though this feast
Would, as the flood, destroy all fowl and beast.

And were the doctrine new
That the earth mov'd, this day would make it true;
For every part to dance and revel goes.
They tread the air, and fall not where they rose.
Though six hours since, the Sun to bed did part,
The masks and banquets will not yet impart
A sunset to these weary eyes, a centre to this heart.

IX. THE BRIDE'S GOING TO BED

WHAT mean'st thou, Bride, this company to keep?
    To sit up, till thou fain would'st sleep?
    Thou may'st not, when thou art laid, do so.
Thyself must to him a new banquet grow,
    And you must entertain
And do all this day's dances o'er again.
Know that if Sun and Moon together do
Rise in one point, they do not set so too;
Therefore thou may'st, fair Bride, to bed depart,
Thou art not gone, being gone; where'er thou art,
Thou leav'st in him thy watchful eyes, in him thy loving
        heart.

X. THE BRIDEGROOM'S COMING

As he that sees a star fall, runs apace,
    And finds a jelly in the place,
    So doth the Bridegroom haste as much,
Being told this star is fal'n, and finds her such.
    And as friends may look strange,
By a new fashion, or apparel's change,
Their souls, though long acquainted they had been,
These clothes, their bodies, never yet had seen;
Therefore at first she modestly might start,
But must forthwith surrender every part,
As freely, as each to each before, gave either eye or heart.

XI. THE GOOD-NIGHT

Now, as in Tullia's tomb, one lamp burnt clear,
    Unchang'd for fifteen hundred year,
    May these love-lamps we here enshrine,
In warmth, light, lasting, equal the divine.
    Fire ever doth aspire,
And makes all like itself, turns all to fire,
But ends in ashes, which these cannot do,
For none of these is fuel, but fire too.
This is joy's bonfire, then, where love's strong Arts
Make of so noble individual parts
One fire of four inflaming eyes, and of two loving hearts.

Idios.

As I have brought this song, that I may do
    A perfect sacrifice, I 'll burn it too.

Allophanes.

No, Sir.   This paper I have justly got,
    For, in burnt incense, the perfume is not
His only that presents it, but of all;
    Whatever celebrates this Festival
Is common, since the joy thereof is so.
    Nor may yourself be Priest: but let me go
Back to the Court, and I will lay it upon
    Such Altars, as prize your devotion.

EPITHALAMION MADE AT LINCOLN'S INN

THE Sun-beams in the East are spread,
Leave, leave, fair Bride, your solitary bed,
    No more shall you return to it alone,
It nurseth sadness, and your body's print,
Like to a grave, the yielding down doth dint;
    You and your other you meet there anon;
      Put forth, put forth that warm balm-breathing thigh,

Which when next time you in these sheets will smother,
There it must meet another,
    Which never was, but must be, oft, more nigh;
Come glad from thence, go gladder than you came,
To-day put on perfection, and a woman's name.

Daughters of London, you which be
Our Golden Mines, and furnish'd Treasury,
   You which are Angels, yet still bring with you
Thousands of Angels on your marriage days,
Help with your presence and devise to praise
   These rites, which also unto you grow due;
    Conceitedly dress her, and be assign'd,
By you, fit place for every flower and jewel,
Make her for love fit fuel
    As gay as Flora, and as rich as Ind;
So may she fair, rich, glad, and in nothing lame,
To-day put on perfection, and a woman's name.

And you frolic Patricians,
Sons of these Senators, wealth's deep oceans,
   Ye painted courtiers, barrels of others' wits,
Ye country men, who but your beasts love none,
Ye of those fellowships whereof he 's one,
   Of study and play made strange Hermaphrodites,
    Here shine; this Bridegroom to the Temple bring.
Lo, in yon path which store of strew'd flowers graceth,
The sober virgin paceth;
    Except my sight fails, 'tis no other thing;
Weep not nor blush, here is no grief nor shame,
To-day put on perfection, and a woman's name.

Thy two-leav'd gates, fair Temple, unfold,
And these two in thy sacred bosom hold,
   Till, mystically join'd, but one they be;
Then may thy lean and hunger-starved womb
Long time expect their bodies and their tomb,
   Long after their own parents fatten thee.
    All elder claims, and all cold barrenness,

All yielding to new loves be far for ever,
Which might these two dissever,
    All ways all th' other may each one possess;
For, the best Bride, best worthy of praise and fame,
To-day puts on perfection, and a woman's name.

Oh winter days bring much delight,
Not for themselves, but for they soon bring night;
  Other sweets wait thee than these diverse meats,
Other disports than dancing jollities,
Other love tricks than glancing with the eyes,
    But that the Sun still in our half Sphere sweats;
      He flies in winter, but he now stands still.
Yet shadows turn; Noon point he hath attain'd,
His steeds nill be restrain'd,
    But gallop lively down the Western hill;
Thou shalt, when he hath run the world's half frame,
To-night put on perfection, and a woman's name.

The amorous evening star is rose,
Why then should not our amorous star inclose
  Herself in her wish'd bed?   Release your strings
Musicians, and dancers take some truce
With these your pleasing labours, for great use
    As much weariness as perfection brings;
      You, and not only you, but all toiled beasts
Rest duly; at night all their toils are dispensed;
But in their beds commenced
    Are other labours, and more dainty feasts;
She goes a maid, who, lest she turn the same,
To-night puts on perfection, and a woman's name.

Thy virgin's girdle now untie,
And in thy nuptial bed (love's altar) lie
  A pleasing sacrifice; now dispossess
Thee of these chains and robes which were put on
T' adorn the day, not thee; for thou, alone,
    Like virtue and truth, art best in nakedness;
      This bed is only to virginity

A grave, but, to a better state, a cradle;
Till now thou wast but able
    To be what now thou art; then that by thee
No more be said, *I may be*, but, *I am*,
To-night put on perfection, and a woman's name.

Even like a faithful man content,
That this life for a better should be spent,
   So, she a mother's rich style doth prefer,
And at the Bridegroom's wish'd approach doth lie,
Like an appointed lamb, when tenderly
    The priest comes on his knees t' embowel her;
     Now sleep or watch with more joy; and O light
Of heaven, to morrow rise thou hot, and early;
This Sun will love so dearly
    Her rest, that long, long we shall want her sight;
Wonders are wrought, for she which had no maim,
To-night puts on perfection, and a woman's name.

SATIRES

SATIRE I

AWAY thou fondling motley humourist,
Leave me, and in this standing wooden chest,
Consorted with these few books, let me lie
In prison, and here be coffin'd, when I die;
Here are God's conduits, grave Divines; and here
Nature's Secretary, the Philosopher;
And jolly Statesmen, which teach how to tie
The sinews of a city's mystic body;
Here gathering Chroniclers, and by them stand
Giddy fantastic Poets of each land.
Shall I leave all this constant company,
And follow headlong, wild uncertain thee?
First swear by thy best love in earnest
(If thou which lov'st all, canst love any best)
Thou wilt not leave me in the middle street,
Though some more spruce companion thou dost meet,
Not though a Captain do come in thy way
Bright parcel-gilt, with forty dead men's pay,
Not though a brisk perfum'd pert Courtier
Deign with a nod, thy courtesy to answer.
Nor come a velvet Justice with a long
Great train of blue coats, twelve, or fourteen strong,
Wilt thou grin or fawn on him, or prepare
A speech to court his beauteous son and heir!
For better or worse take me, or leave me:
To take, and leave me is adultery.
Oh monstrous, superstitious puritan,
Of refin'd manners, yet ceremonial man,
That when thou meet'st one, with inquiring eyes
Dost search, and like a needy broker prize

The silk, and gold he wears, and to that rate
So high or low, dost raise thy formal hat:
That wilt consort none, until thou have known
What lands he hath in hope, or of his own,
As though all thy companions should make thee
Jointures, and marry thy dear company.
Why should'st thou (that dost not only approve,
But in rank itchy lust, desire, and love
The nakedness and bareness to enjoy,
Of thy plump muddy whore, or prostitute boy)
Hate virtue, though she be naked, and bare?
At birth, and death, our bodies naked are;
And till our Souls be unapparelled
Of bodies, they from bliss are banished.
Man's first blest state was naked, when by sin
He lost that, yet he was cloth'd but in beast's skin,
And in this coarse attire, which I now wear,
With God, and with the Muses I confer.
But since thou like a contrite penitent,
Charitably warn'd of thy sins, dost repent
These vanities, and giddinesses, lo
I shut my chamber door, and come, let's go.
But sooner may a cheap whore, who hath been
Worn by as many several men in sin,
As are black feathers, or musk-colour hose,
Name her child's right true father, 'mongst all those:
Sooner may one guess, who shall bear away
The Infanta of London, Heir to an India;
And sooner may a gulling weather spy
By drawing forth heaven's Scheme tell certainly
What fashioned hats, or ruffs, or suits next year
Our subtle-witted antic youths will wear;
Than thou, when thou depart'st from me, canst show
Whither, why, when, or with whom thou wouldst go.
But how shall I be pardon'd my offence
That thus have sinn'd against my conscience?
Now we are in the street; he first of all
Improvidently proud, creeps to the wall,
And so imprisoned, and hemm'd in by me

Sells for a little state his liberty;
Yet though he cannot skip forth now to greet
Every fine silken painted fool we meet,
He them to him with amorous smiles allures,
And grins, smacks, shrugs, and such an itch endures,
As 'prentices, or school-boys which do know
Of some gay sport abroad, yet dare not go.
And as fiddlers stop lowest, at highest sound,
So to the most brave, stoops he nigh'st the ground.
But to a grave man, he doth move no more
Than the wise politic horse would heretofore,
Or thou O Elephant or Ape wilt do,
When any names the King of Spain to you.
Now leaps he upright, jogs me, and cries, Do you see
Yonder well-favoured youth? Which? Oh, 'tis he
That dances so divinely; Oh, said I,
Stand still, must you dance here for company?
He droopt, we went, till one (which did excel
Th' Indians, in drinking his Tobacco well)
Met us; they talk'd; I whispered, Let us go,
'T may be you smell him not, truly I do;
He hears not me, but, on the other side
A many-coloured Peacock having spied,
Leaves him and me; I for my lost sheep stay;
He follows, overtakes, goes on the way,
Saying, Him whom I last left, all repute
For his device, in handsoming a suit,
To judge of lace, pink, panes, print, cut, and pleat
Of all the Court, to have the best conceit.
Our dull Comedians want him, let him go;
But Oh, God strengthen thee, why stoop'st thou so?
Why? he hath travelled. Long? No; but to me
(Which understand none,) he doth seem to be
Perfect French, and Italian; I replied,
So is the Pox; he answered not, but spied
More men of sort, of parts, and qualities;
At last his Love he in a window spies,
And like light dew exhal'd, he flings from me
Violently ravish'd to his lechery.

Many were there, he could command no more;
He quarrell'd, fought, bled; and turn'd out of door
  Directly came to me hanging the head,
  And constantly a while must keep his bed.

SATIRE II

Sir; though (I thank God for it) I do hate
Perfectly all this town, yet there 's one state
In all ill things so excellently best,
That hate toward them, breeds pity towards the rest.
Though Poetry indeed be such a sin
As I think that brings dearth and Spaniards in,
Though like the Pestilence and old-fashion'd love,
Riddlingly it catch men; and doth remove
Never, till it be starved out; yet their state
Is poor, disarm'd, like Papists, not worth hate.
One (like a wretch, which at Bar judg'd as dead,
Yet prompts him which stands next, and cannot read,
And saves his life) gives idiot actors means
(Starving himself) to live by his labour'd scenes;
As in some Organ, puppets dance above
And bellows pant below, which them do move.
One would move Love by rhythms; but witchcraft's charms
Bring not now their old fears, nor their old harms:
Rams and slings now are silly battery,
Pistolets are the best artillery.
And they who write to Lords, rewards to get,
Are they not like singers at doors for meat?
And they who write, because all write, have still
That excuse for writing, and for writing ill;
But he is worst, who (beggarly) doth chaw
Others' wits' fruits, and in his ravenous maw
Rankly digested, doth those things out spew,
As his own things; and they are his own, 'tis true,
For if one eat my meat, though it be known
The meat was mine, th' excrement is his own:
But these do me no harm, nor they which use

To out-do Dildoes, and out-usure Jews;
To out-drink the sea, to out-swear the Litany;
Who with sins all kinds as familiar be
As Confessors; and for whose sinful sake,
Schoolmen new tenements in hell must make:
Whose strange sins, Canonists could hardly tell
In which Commandment's large receipt they dwell.
But these punish themselves; the insolence
Of Coscus only breeds my just offence,
Whom time (which rots all, and makes botches pox,
And plodding on, must make a calf an ox)
Hath made a Lawyer, which was (alas) of late
But a scarce Poet; jollier of this state,
Than are new benefic'd ministers, he throws
Like nets, or lime-twigs, wheresoever he goes,
His title of Barrister, on every wench,
And woos in language of the Pleas, and Bench:
A motion, Lady; Speak Coscus; I have been
In love, ever since *tricesimo* of the Queen,
Continual claims I have made, injunctions got
To stay my rival's suit, that he should not
Proceed; Spare me; In Hilary term I went,
You said, If I return'd next 'size in Lent,
I should be in remitter of your grace;
In th' interim my letters should take place
Of affidavits: words, words, which would tear
The tender labyrinth of a soft maid's ear,
More, more, than ten Sclavonians scolding, more
Than when winds in our ruin'd Abbeys roar.
When sick with poetry, and possess'd with Muse
Thou wast, and mad, I hop'd; but men which choose
Law-practice for mere gain, bold soul, repute
Worse then embrothell'd strumpets prostitute.
Now like an owl-like watchman, he must walk
His hand still at a bill, now he must talk
Idly, like prisoners, which whole months will swear
That only suretyship hath brought them there,
And to every suitor lie in everything,
Like a King's favourite, yea like a King;

Like a wedge in a block, wring to the bar,
Bearing like Asses; and more shameless far
Than carted whores, lie, to the grave Judge; for
Bastardy abounds not in King's titles, nor
Simony and Sodomy in Churchmen's lives,
As these things do in him; by these he thrives.
Shortly (as the sea) he will compass all our land;
From Scots, to Wight; from Mount, to Dover strand.
And spying heirs melting with luxury,
Satan will not joy at their sins, as he.
For as a thrifty wench scrapes kitchen stuff,
And barrelling the droppings, and the snuff,
Of wasting candles, which in thirty year
(Relique-like kept) perchance buys wedding gear;
Piecemeal he gets lands, and spends as much time
Wringing each Acre, as men pulling prime.
In parchments then, large as his fields, he draws
Assurances, big, as gloss'd civil laws,
So huge, that men (in our time's forwardness)
Are Fathers of the Church for writing less.
These he writes not; nor for these written pays,
Therefore spares no length; as in those first days
When Luther was professed, he did desire
Short *Pater nosters*, saying as a Friar
Each day his beads, but having left those laws,
Adds to Christ's prayer, the Power and glory clause.
But when he sells or changes land, he impairs
His writings, and (unwatch'd) leaves out, *ses heires*,
As slily as any Commenter goes by
Hard words, or sense; or in Divinity
As controverters, in vouch'd Texts, leave out
Shrewd words, which might against them clear the doubt.
Where are those spread woods which cloth'd heretofore
Those bought lands? not built, nor burnt within door.
Where 's th' old landlord's troops, and alms? In great halls
Carthusian fasts, and fulsome Bacchanals
Equally I hate; means bless; in rich men's homes
I bid kill some beasts, but no Hecatombs,
None starve, none surfeit so; but Oh we allow,

Good works as good, but out of fashion now,
Like old rich wardrobes; but my words none draws
Within the vast reach of the huge statute laws.

SATIRE III

KIND pity chokes my spleen; brave scorn forbids
Those tears to issue which swell my eye-lids;
I must not laugh, nor weep sins, and be wise,
Can railing then cure these worn maladies?
Is not our Mistress fair Religion,
As worthy of all our Soul's devotion,
As virtue was to the first blinded age?
Are not heaven's joys as valiant to assuage
Lusts, as earth's honour was to them? Alas,
As we do them in means, shall they surpass
Us in the end, and shall thy father's spirit
Meet blind Philosophers in heaven, whose merit
Of strict life may be imputed faith, and hear
Thee, whom he taught so easy ways and near
To follow, damn'd? O if thou dar'st, fear this;
This fear great courage, and high valour is.
Dar'st thou aid mutinous Dutch, and dar'st thou lay
Thee in ships' wooden sepulchres, a prey
To leaders' rage, to storms, to shot, to dearth?
Dar'st thou dive seas, and dungeons of the earth?
Hast thou courageous fire to thaw the ice
Of frozen North discoveries? and thrice
Colder than Salamanders, like divine
Children in th' oven, fires of Spain, and the line,
Whose countries limbecks to our bodies be,
Canst thou for gain bear? and must every he
Which cries not, Goddess, to thy Mistress, draw,
Or eat thy poisonous words? courage of straw!
O desperate coward, wilt thou seem bold, and
To thy foes and his (who made thee to stand
Sentinel in his world's garrison) thus yield,
And for the forbidden wars, leave th' appointed field?

Know thy foes: the foul Devil (whom thou
Strivest to please,) for hate, not love, would allow
Thee fain, his whole Realm to be quit; and as
The world's all parts wither away and pass,
So the world's self, thy other lov'd foe, is
In her decrepit wane, and thou loving this,
Dost love a withered and worn strumpet; last,
Flesh (itself's death) and joys which flesh can taste,
Thou lovest; and thy fair goodly soul, which doth
Give this flesh power to taste joy, thou dost loathe.
Seek true religion.   O where? Mirreus
Thinking her unhous'd here, and fled from us,
Seeks her at Rome; there, because he doth know
That she was there a thousand years ago;
He loves her rags so, as we here obey
The statecloth where the Prince sate yesterday.
Crantz to such brave Loves will not be enthrall'd,
But loves her only, who at Geneva is call'd
Religion, plain, simple, sullen, young,
Contemptuous, yet unhandsome; as among
Lecherous humours, there is one that judges
No wenches wholesome, but coarse country drudges.
Graius stays still at home here, and because
Some Preachers, vile ambitious bawds, and laws
Still new like fashions, bid him think that she
Which dwells with us, is only perfect, he
Embraceth her, whom his Godfathers will
Tender to him, being tender, as Wards still
Take such wives as their Guardians offer, or
Pay values.   Careless Phrygius doth abhor
All, because all cannot be good, as one
Knowing some women whores, dares marry none.
Gracchus loves all as one, and thinks that so
As women do in divers countries go
In divers habits, yet are still one kind,
So doth, so is Religion; and this blind-
ness too much light breeds; but unmoved thou
Of force must one, and forc'd but one allow;
And the right; ask thy father which is she,

Let him ask his; though truth and falsehood be
Near twins, yet truth a little elder is;
Be busy to seek her, believe me this,
He 's not of none, nor worst, that seeks the best.
To adore, or scorn an image, or protest,
May all be bad; doubt wisely; in strange way
To stand inquiring right, is not to stray;
To sleep, or run wrong is.   On a huge hill,
Cragged, and steep, Truth stands, and he that will
Reach her, about must, and about must go;
And what the hill's suddenness resists, win so;
Yet strive so, that before age, death's twilight,
Thy Soul rest, for none can work in that night.
To will, implies delay, therefore now do:
Hard deeds, the body's pains; hard knowledge too
The mind's endeavours reach, and mysteries
Are like the Sun, dazzling, yet plain to all eyes.
Keep the truth which thou hast found; men do not stand
In so ill case here, that God hath with His hand
Sign'd Kings blank-charters to kill whom they hate,
Nor are they Vicars, but hangmen to Fate.
Fool and wretch, wilt thou let thy Soul be tied
To man's laws, by which she shall not be tried
At the last day?   Oh, will it then boot thee
To say a Philip, or a Gregory,
A Harry, or a Martin taught thee this?
Is not this excuse for mere contraries,
Equally strong? cannot both sides say so?
That thou mayest rightly obey power, her bounds know;
Those past, her nature, and name is chang'd; to be
Then humble to her is idolatry.
As streams are, Power is; those blest flowers that dwell
At the rough stream's calm head, thrive and do well,
But having left their roots, and themselves given
To the stream's tyrannous rage, alas are driven
Through mills, and rocks, and woods, and at last, almost
Consum'd in going, in the sea are lost:
So perish Souls, which more choose men's unjust
Power from God claimed, than God Himself to trust.

SATIRE IV

WELL; I may now receive, and die. My sin
Indeed is great, but I have been in
A Purgatory, such as fear'd hell is
A recreation to, and scarce map of this.
My mind, neither with pride's itch, nor yet hath been
Poisoned with love to see, or to be seen.
I had no suit there, nor new suit to show,
Yet went to Court; but as Glaze which did go
To a Mass in jest, catch'd, was fain to disburse
The hundred marks, which is the Statute's curse,
Before he 'scaped, so it pleas'd my destiny
(Guilty of my sin of going), to think me
As prone to all ill, and of good as forget-
ful, as proud, as lustful, and as much in debt,
As vain, as witless, and as false as they
Which dwell at Court, for once going that way.
Therefore I suffered this; towards me did run
A thing more strange than on Nile's slime the Sun
E'er bred; or all which into Noah's Ark came;
A thing, which would have pos'd Adam to name;
Stranger than seven Antiquaries' studies,
Than Afric's Monsters; Guiana's rarities.
Stranger than strangers; one, who for a Dane,
In the Danes' Massacre had sure been slain,
If he had liv'd then; and without help dies,
When next the 'prentices 'gainst Strangers rise.
One, whom the watch at noon lets scarce go by,
One, to whom, the examining Justice sure would cry,
Sir, by your priesthood tell me what you are.
His clothes were strange, though coarse; and black, though
        bare;
Sleeveless his jerkin was, and it had been
Velvet, but 'twas now (so much ground was seen)
Become tufftaffaty; and our children shall
See it plain Rash awhile, then naught at all.
This thing hath travell'd, and saith, speaks all tongues

And only knoweth what to all States belongs.
Made of th' Accents, and best phrase of all these,
He speaks one language; if strange meats displease,
Art can deceive, or hunger force my taste,
But Pedant's motley tongue, soldier's bombast,
Mountebank's drugtongue, nor the terms of law
Are strong enough preparatives, to draw
Me to bear this: yet I must be content
With his tongue, in his tongue, call'd compliment:
In which he can win widows, and pay scores,
Make men speak treason, cozen subtlest whores,
Out-flatter favourites, or out-lie either
Jovius, or Surius, or both together.
He names me, and comes to me; I whisper, God!
How have I sinn'd, that Thy wrath's furious rod,
This fellow, chooseth me?   He saith, Sir,
I love your judgment; Whom do you prefer,
For the best linguist?   And I sillily
Said, that I thought Calepine's Dictionary;
Nay but of men, most sweet Sir; Beza then,
Some other Jesuits, and two reverend men
Of our two Academies, I named.   There
He stopp'd me, and said; Nay, your Apostles were
Good pretty linguists, and so Panurge was;
Yet a poor gentleman, all these may pass
By travail.   Then, as if he would have sold
His tongue, he praised it, and such wonders told
That I was fain to say, If you had liv'd, Sir,
Time enough to have been Interpreter
To Babel's bricklayers, sure the Tower had stood.
He adds, If of court life you knew the good,
You would leave loneness.   I said, Not alone
My loneness is, but Spartan's fashion,
To teach by painting drunkards, doth not last
Now; Aretine's pictures have made few chaste;
No more can Princes' courts, though there be few
Better pictures of vice, teach me virtue;
He, like to a high-stretched lute-string squeaked, O Sir,
'Tis sweet to talk of Kings.   At Westminster,

Said I, the man that keeps the Abbey tombs,
And for his price doth with whoever comes,
Of all our Harrys, and our Edwards talk,
From King to King and all their kin can walk:
Your ears shall hear naught, but Kings; your eyes meet
Kings only; The way to it, is King Street.
He smack'd, and cried, He 's base, mechanic, coarse,
So are all your Englishmen in their discourse.
Are not your Frenchmen neat? Mine? as you see,
I have but one Frenchman, look, he follows me.
Certes they are neatly cloth'd; I of this mind am,
Your only wearing is your Grogaram.
Not so Sir, I have more. Under this pitch
He would not fly; I chaff'd him; but as Itch
Scratch'd into smart, and as blunt iron ground
Into an edge, hurts worse: so, I (fool) found,
Crossing hurt me; to fit my sullenness,
He to another key his style doth address,
And asks, what news? I tell him of new plays.
He takes my hand, and as a Still, which stays
A semi-breve 'twixt each drop, he niggardly,
As loth to enrich me, so tells many a lie.
More than ten Holinsheds, or Halls, or Stows,
Of trivial household trash he knows; he knows
When the Queen frown'd, or smil'd, and he knows what
A subtle Statesman may gather of that;
He knows who loves, whom; and who by poison
Hastes to an Office's reversion;
He knows who hath sold his land, and now doth beg
A licence, old iron, boots, shoes, and egg-
shells to transport; shortly boys shall not play
At span-counter, or blow-point, but they pay
Toll to some Courtier; and wiser than all us,
He knows what lady is not painted; thus
He with home-meats tries me; I belch, spew, spit,
Look pale, and sickly, like a Patient; yet
He thrusts on more; and as if he 'd undertook
To say Gallo-Belgicus without book
Speaks of all States, and deeds, that have been since

The Spaniards came, to the loss of Amiens.
Like a big wife, at sight of loathed meat,
Ready to travail, so I sigh, and sweat
To hear this Macaron talk: in vain; for yet,
Either my humour, or his own to fit,
He like a privileged spy, whom nothing can
Discredit, libels now 'gainst each great man.
He names a price for every office paid;
He saith, our wars thrive ill, because delayed;
That offices are entail'd, and that there are
Perpetuities of them, lasting as far
As the last day; and that great officers,
Do with the Pirates share, and Dunkirkers.
Who wastes in meat, in clothes, in horse, he notes;
Who loves whores, who boys, and who goats.
I more amazed than Circe's prisoners, when
They felt themselves turn beasts, felt myself then
Becoming Traitor, and methought I saw
One of our Giant Statutes ope his jaw
To suck me in; for hearing him, I found
That as burnt venom Lechers do grow sound
By giving others their sores, I might grow
Guilty, and he free: therefore I did show
All signs of loathing; but since I am in,
I must pay mine, and my forefathers' sin
To the last farthing.   Therefore to my power
Toughly and stubbornly I bear this cross; but the hour
Of mercy now was come; he tries to bring
Me to pay a fine to 'scape his torturing,
And says, Sir, can you spare me; I said, willingly;
Nay, Sir, can you spare me a crown? Thankfully I
Gave it, as Ransom; but as fiddlers, still,
Though they be paid to be gone, yet needs will
Thrust one more jig upon you: so did he
With his long complimental thanks vex me.
But he is gone, thanks to his needy want,
And the prerogative of my Crown: scant
His thanks were ended, when I, (which did see
All the court fill'd with more strange things than he)

Ran from thence with such or more haste, than one
Who fears more actions, doth make from prison.
At home in wholesome solitariness
My precious soul began the wretchedness
Of suitors at court to mourn, and a trance
Like his, who dreamt he saw hell, did advance
Itself on me. Such men as he saw there,
I saw at court, and worse, and more. Low fear
Becomes the guilty, not the accuser; then,
Shall I, none's slave, of high-born, or rais'd men
Fear frowns? And, my Mistress Truth, betray thee
To th' huffing braggart, puffed Nobility?
No, no, thou which since yesterday hast been
Almost about the whole world, hast thou seen,
O Sun, in all thy journey, vanity,
Such as swells the bladder of our court? I
Think he which made your waxen garden, and
Transported it from Italy to stand
With us, at London, flouts our Presence, for
Just such gay painted things, which no sap, nor
Taste have in them, ours are; and natural
Some of the stocks are, their fruits, bastard all.
'Tis ten a-clock and past; all whom the Mews,
Baloon, Tennis, Diet, or the stews,
Had all the morning held, now the second
Time made ready, that day, in flocks, are found
In the Presence, and I, (God pardon me.)
As fresh, and sweet their Apparels be, as be
The fields they sold to buy them; for a King
Those hose are, cry the flatterers; and bring
Them next week to the Theatre to sell;
Wants reach all states; meseems they do as well
At stage, as court; All are players; whoe'er looks
(For themselves dare not go) o'er Cheapside books,
Shall find their wardrobe's Inventory. Now,
The Ladies come. As Pirates, which do know
That there came weak ships fraught with Cutchannel,
The men board them; and praise, as they think, well,
Their beauties; they the men's wits; both are bought.

Why good wits ne'er wear scarlet gowns, I thought
This cause; these men, men's wits for speeches buy,
And women buy all reds which scarlets dye.
He call'd her beauty lime-twigs, her hair net;
She fears her drugs ill laid, her hair loose set.
Would not Heraclitus laugh to see Macrine,
From hat to shoe, himself at door refine,
As if the Presence were a Moschite, and lift
His skirts and hose, and call his clothes to shrift,
Making them confess not only mortal
Great stains and holes in them, but venial
Feathers and dust, wherewith they fornicate:
And then by Dürer's rules survey the state
Of his each limb, and with strings the odds try
Of his neck to his leg, and waist to thigh.
So in immaculate clothes, and symmetry
Perfect as circles, with such nicety
As a young Preacher at his first time goes
To preach, he enters, and a Lady which owes
Him not so much as good will, he arrests,
And unto her protests, protests, protests,
So much as at Rome would serve to have thrown
Ten Cardinals into the Inquisition;
And whisper'd by Jesu, so often, that a
Pursuivant would have ravish'd him away
For saying of our Lady's psalter; but 'tis fit
That they each other plague, they merit it.
But here comes Glorius that will plague them both,
Who, in the other extreme, only doth
Call a rough carelessness, good fashion;
Whose cloak his spurs tear; whom he spits on
He cares not, his ill words do no harm
To him; he rusheth in, as if Arm, arm,
He meant to cry; And though his face be as ill
As theirs which in old hangings whip Christ, still
He strives to look worse, he keeps all in awe;
Jests like a licensed fool, commands like law.
Tired, now I leave this place, and but pleas'd so
As men which from gaols to execution go,

Go through the great chamber (why is it hung
With the seven deadly sins?).   Being among
Those Ascaparts, men big enough to throw
Charing Cross for a bar, men that do know
No token of worth, but Queen's man, and fine
Living, barrels of beef, flagons of wine;
I shook like a spied spy.   Preachers which are
Seas of Wit and Arts, you can, then dare,
Drown the sins of this place, for, for me
Which am but a scarce brook, it enough shall be
To wash the stains away; although I yet
With Macchabee's modesty, the known merit
Of my work lessen: yet some wise man shall,
I hope, esteem my writs Canonical.

SATIRE V

Thou shalt not laugh in this leaf, Muse, nor they
Whom any pity warms.   He which did lay
Rules to make Courtiers, (he being understood
May make good Courtiers, but who Courtiers good?)
Frees from the sting of jests all who in extreme
Are wretched or wicked: of these two a theme
Charity and liberty give me.   What is he
Who Officer's rage, and suitor's misery
Can write, and jest?   If all things be in all,
As I think, since all, which were, are, and shall
Be, be made of the same elements:
Each thing, each thing implies or represents.
Then man is a world; in which, Officers
Are the vast ravishing seas; and suitors,
Springs; now full, now shallow, now dry; which, to
That which drowns them, run: these self reasons do
Prove the world a man, in which, Officers
Are the devouring stomachs, and suitors
The excrements, which they void.   All men are dust;
How much worse are suitors, who to men's lust

Are made preys? O worse than dust, or worm's meat,
For they do eat you now, whose selves worms shall eat.
They are the mills which grind you, yet you are
The wind which drives them; and a wasteful war
Is fought against you, and you fight it; they
Adulterate law, and you prepare their way
Like wittols; th' issue your own ruin is.
Greatest and fairest Empress, know you this?
Alas, no more than Thames' calm head doth know
Whose meads her arms drown, or whose corn o'erflow:
You Sir, whose righteousness she loves, whom I
By having leave to serve, am most richly
For service paid, authoriz'd, now begin
To know and weed out this enormous sin.
O Age of rusty iron! Some better wit
Call it some worse name, if aught equal it;
The iron Age *that* was, when justice was sold; now
Injustice is sold dearer far.   Allow
All demands, fees, and duties, gamesters, anon
The money which you sweat, and swear for, is gone
Into other hands: so controverted lands
'Scape, like Angelica, the strivers' hands.
If Law be the Judge's heart, and he
Have no heart to resist letter, or fee,
Where wilt thou appeal? power of the Courts below
Flow from the first main head, and these can throw
Thee, if they suck thee in, to misery,
To fetters, halters; but if the injury
Steel thee to dare complain, alas, thou go'st
Against the stream, when upwards: when thou art most
Heavy and most faint; and in these labours they,
'Gainst whom thou should'st complain, will in the way
Become great seas, o'er which, when thou shalt be
Forc'd to make golden bridges, thou shalt see
That all thy gold was drown'd in them before;
All things follow their like, only who have may have more.
Judges are Gods; he who made and said them so,
Meant not that men should be forc'd to them to go,
By means of Angels; when supplications

We send to God, to Dominations,
Powers, Cherubins, and all heaven's Courts, if we
Should pay fees as here, daily bread would be
Scarce to Kings; so 'tis.   Would it not anger
A Stoic, a coward, yea a Martyr,
To see a Pursuivant come in, and call
All his clothes, Copes; Books, Primers; and all
His Plate, Chalices; and mistake them away,
And ask a fee for coming?   Oh, ne'er may
Fair law's white reverend name be strumpeted,
To warrant thefts: she is established
Recorder to Destiny, on earth, and she
Speaks Fate's words, and but tells us who must be
Rich, who poor, who in chairs, who in gaols:
She is all fair, but yet hath foul long nails,
With which she scratcheth suitors; in bodies
Of men, so in law, nails are th' extremities,
So Officers stretch to more than Law can do,
As our nails reach what no else part comes to.
Why barest thou to yon Officer?   Fool, hath he
Got those goods, for which erst men bar'd to thee?
Fool, twice, thrice, thou hast bought wrong, and now
      hungerly
Beg'st right; but that dole comes not till these die.
Thou had'st much, and laws Urim and Thummim try
Thou wouldst for more; and for all hast paper
Enough to clothe all the great Carrick's Pepper.
Sell that, and by that thou much more shalt leese,
Than Haman, when he sold his Antiquities.
O wretch, that thy fortunes should moralize
Esop's fables, and make tales, prophecies.
Thou art the swimming dog whom shadows cozened,
And div'st, near drowning, for what 's vanished.

UPON MR. THOMAS CORYAT'S CRUDITIES

Oh to what height will love of greatness drive
Thy leavened spirit, *Sesqui-superlative?*
Venice' vast lake thou hadst seen, and wouldst seek then
Some vaster thing, and found'st a Courtesan.
That inland Sea having discovered well,
A Cellar gulf, where one might sail to hell
From Heidelberg, thou long'dst to see: and thou
This Book, greater than all, producest now.
Infinite work, which doth so far extend,
That none can study it to any end.
'Tis no one thing, it is not fruit nor root;
Nor poorly limited with head or foot.
If man be therefore man, because he can
Reason, and laugh, thy book doth half make man.
One half being made, thy modesty was such,
That thou on th' other half wouldst never touch.
When wilt thou be at full, great Lunatic?
Not till thou exceed the world? Canst thou be like
A prosperous nose-born wen, which sometimes grows
To be far greater than the Mother-nose?
Go then; and as to thee, when thou didst go,
Munster did Towns, and *Gesner* Authors show,
Mount now to *Gallo-belgicus;* appear
As deep a Statesman, as a Gazetteer.
Homely and familiarly, when thou com'st back,
Talk of *Will. Conqueror,* and *Prester Jack.*
Go bashful man, lest here thou blush to look
Upon the progress of thy glorious book,
To which both Indies sacrifices send;
The West sent gold, which thou didst freely spend,
(Meaning to see 't no more) upon the press.
The East sends hither her deliciousness;
And thy leaves must embrace what comes from thence,
The Myrrh, the Pepper, and the Frankincense.
This magnifies thy leaves; but if they stoop

To neighbour wares, when Merchants do unhoop
Voluminous barrels; if thy leaves do then
Convey these wares in parcels unto men;
If for vast Tons of Currants, and of Figs,
Of Medicinal and Aromatic twigs,
Thy leaves a better method do provide,
Divide to pounds, and ounces sub-divide;
If they stoop lower yet, and vent our wares,
Home-manufactures, to thick popular Fairs,
If *omni-prægnant* there, upon warm stalls,
They hatch all wares for which the buyer calls;
Then thus thy leaves we justly may commend,
That they all kind of matter comprehend.
Thus thou, by means which th'Ancients never took,
A Pandect makest, and Universal Book.
The bravest Heroes, for public good,
Scattered in divers Lands their limbs and blood.
Worst malefactors, to whom men are prize,
Do public good, cut in Anatomies;
So will thy book in pieces; for a Lord
Which casts at Portescues, and all the board,
Provide whole books; each leaf enough will be
For friends to pass time, and keep company.
Can all carouse up thee? no, thou must fit
Measures; and fill out for the half-pint wit:
Some shall wrap pills, and save a friend's life so,
Some shall stop muskets, and so kill a foe.
Thou shalt not ease the Critics of next age
So much, at once their hunger to assuage:
Nor shall wit-pirates hope to find thee lie
All in one bottom, in one Library.
Some Leaves may paste strings there in other books,
And so one may, which on another looks,
Pilfer, alas, a little wit from you;
But hardly [1] much; and yet I think this true;
As *Sibyl's* was, your book is mystical,
For every piece is as much worth as all.
Therefore mine impotency I confess,

[1] I mean from one page which shall paste strings in a book.

The healths which my brain bears must be far less:
Thy Giant wit o'erthrows me, I am gone;
And rather than read all, I would read none.

IN EUNDEM MACARONICON

Quot, dos haec, **Linguists** perfetti, *Disticha* fairont,
Tot cuerdos **States=men,** *hic* livre fara *tuus.*
Es *sat* a my l'honneur estre hic inteso; Car **J leave**
L'honra, de personne n'estre creduto, *tibi.*

Explicit Joannes Donne.

VERSE LETTERS TO SEVERAL PERSONAGES

TO Mr. CHRISTOPHER BROOKE

THE STORM

THOU which art I, ('tis nothing to be so)
Thou which art still thyself, by these shalt know
Part of our passage; and, a hand, or eye
By *Hilliard* drawn, is worth an history,
By a worse painter made; and (without pride)
When by thy judgment they are dignified,
My lines are such: 'tis the pre-eminence
Of friendship only to impute excellence.
England to whom we owe, what we be, and have,
Sad that her sons did seek a foreign grave
(For, Fate's, or Fortune's drifts none can soothsay,
Honour and misery have one face and way,)
From out her pregnant entrails sigh'd a wind
Which at th' air's middle marble room did find
Such strong resistance, that itself it threw
Downward again; and so when it did view
How in the port, our fleet dear time did leese,
Withering like prisoners, which lie but for fees,
Mildly it kissed our sails, and, fresh and sweet,
As to a stomach starv'd, whose insides meet,
Meat comes, it came; and swole our sails, when we
So joy'd, as *Sara* her swelling joy'd to see.
But 'twas but so kind, as our countrymen,
Which bring friends one day's way, and leave them then.
Then like two mighty Kings, which dwelling far
Asunder, meet against a third to war,
The South and West winds join'd, and, as they blew,
Waves like a rolling trench before them threw.

Sooner than you read this line, did the gale,
Like shot, not fear'd till felt, our sails assail;
And what at first was call'd a gust, the same
Hath now a storm's, anon a tempest's name.
Jonas, I pity thee, and curse those men,
Who when the storm rag'd most, did wake thee then;
Sleep is pain's easiest salve, and doth fulfil
All offices of death, except to kill.
But when I waked, I saw, that I saw not;
Ay, and the Sun, which should teach me had forgot
East, West, Day, Night, and I could only say,
If the world had lasted, now it had been day.
Thousands our noises were, yet we 'mongst all
Could none by his right name, but thunder call:
Lightning was all our light, and it rain'd more
Than if the Sun had drunk the sea before.
Some coffin'd in their cabins lie, equally
Griev'd that they are not dead, and yet must die;
And as sin-burden'd souls from graves will creep,
At the last day, some forth their cabins peep:
And tremblingly ask what news, and do hear so,
Like jealous husbands, what they would not know.
Some sitting on the hatches, would seem there,
With hideous gazing to fear away fear.
Then note they the ship's sicknesses, the Mast
Shak'd with this ague, and the Hold and Waist
With a salt dropsy clogged, and all our tacklings
Snapping, like too-high-stretched treble strings.
And from our totter'd sails, rags drop down so,
As from one hang'd in chains, a year ago.
Even our Ordnance plac'd for our defence,
Strive to break loose, and 'scape away from thence.
Pumping hath tired our men, and what 's the gain?
Seas into seas thrown, we suck in again;
Hearing hath deaf'd our sailors; and if they
Knew how to hear, there 's none knows what to say.
Compar'd to these storms, death is but a qualm,
Hell somewhat lightsome, and the Bermuda calm.
Darkness, light's elder brother, his birth-right

Claims o'er this world, and to heaven hath chas'd light.
All things are one, and that one none can be,
Since all forms, uniform deformity
Doth cover, so that we, except God say
Another *Fiat*, shall have no more day.
So violent, yet long these furies be,
That though thine absence starve me, I wish not thee.

THE CALM

Our storm is past, and that storm's tyrannous rage,
A stupid calm, but nothing it, doth 'suage.
The fable is inverted, and far more
A block afflicts, now, than a stork before.
Storms chafe, and soon wear out themselves, or us;
In calms, Heaven laughs to see us languish thus.
As steady as I can wish, that my thoughts were,
Smooth as thy mistress' glass, or what shines there,
The sea is now.   And, as the Isles which we
Seek, when we can move, our ships rooted be.
As water did in storms, now pitch runs out:
As lead, when a fired Church becomes one spout.
And all our beauty, and our trim, decays,
Like courts removing, or like ended plays.
The fighting place now seamen's rags supply;
And all the tackling is a frippery.
No use of lanthorns; and in one place lay
Feathers and dust, to-day and yesterday.
Earth's hollownesses, which the world's lungs are,
Have no more wind than the upper vault of air.
We can nor lost friends, nor sought foes recover,
But meteor-like, save that we move not, hover.
Only the Calenture together draws
Dear friends, which meet dead in great fishes' jaws:
And on the hatches as on Altars lies
Each one, his own Priest, and own Sacrifice.
Who live, that miracle do multiply

Where walkers in hot Ovens, do not die.
If in despite of these, we swim, that hath
No more refreshing, than our brimstone Bath,
But from the sea, into the ship we turn,
Like parboiled wretches, on the coals to burn.
Like *Bajazet* encag'd, the shepherds' scoff,
Or like slack-sinew'd Samson, his hair off,
Languish our ships.   Now, as a Myriad
Of Ants, durst th' Emperor's lov'd snake invade,
The crawling Gallies, Sea-gaols, finny chips,
Might brave our Pinnaces, now bed-rid ships.
Whether a rotten state, and hope of gain,
Or to disuse me from the queasy pain
Of being belov'd, and loving, or the thirst
Of honour, or fair death, out pushed me first,
I lose my end: for here as well as I
A desperate may live, and a coward die.
Stag, dog, and all which from, or towards flies,
Is paid with life, or prey, or doing dies.
Fate grudges us all, and doth subtly lay
A scourge, 'gainst which we all forget to pray,
He that at sea prays for more wind, as well
Under the poles may beg cold, heat in hell.
What are we then? How little more alas
Is man now, than before he was? he was
Nothing; for us, we are for nothing fit;
Chance, or ourselves still disproportion it.
We have no power, no will, no sense; I lie,
I should not then thus feel this misery.

TO THE COUNTESS OF HUNTINGDON

THAT unripe side of earth, that heavy clime
That gives us man up now, like *Adam's* time
Before he ate; man's shape, that would yet be
(Knew they not it, and fear'd beasts' company)
So naked at this day, as though man there
From Paradise so great a distance were,

As yet the news could not arrived be
Of *Adam's* tasting the forbidden tree;
Depriv'd of that free state which they were in,
And wanting the reward, yet bear the sin.
　　But, as from extreme heights who downward looks,
Sees men at children's shapes, rivers at brooks,
And loseth younger forms; so, to your eye,
These (Madam) that without your distance lie,
Must either mist, or nothing seem to be,
Who are at home but wit's mere *Atomi*.
But, I who can behold them move, and stay,
Have found myself to you, just their midway;
And now must pity them; for, as they do
Seem sick to me, just so must I to you.
Yet neither will I vex your eyes to see
A sighing Ode, nor cross-arm'd Elegy.
I come not to call pity from your heart,
Like some white-liver'd dotard that would part
Else from his slippery soul with a faint groan,
And faithfully, (without you smil'd) were gone.
I cannot feel the tempest of a frown,
I may be rais'd by love, but not thrown down.
Though I can pity those sigh twice a day,
I hate that thing whispers itself away.
Yet since all love is fever, who to trees
Doth talk, doth yet in love's cold ague freeze.
'Tis love, but, with such fatal weakness made,
That it destroys itself with its own shade.
Who first look'd sad, griev'd, pin'd, and show'd his pains.
Was he that first taught women to disdain.
　　As all things were one nothing, dull and weak,
Until this raw disordered heap did break,
And several desires led parts away,
Water declin'd with earth, the air did stay,
Fire rose, and each from other but untied,
Themselves unprison'd were and purified;
So was love, first in vast confusion hid,
An unripe willingness which nothing did,
A thirst, an Appetite which had no ease,

That found a want, but knew not what would please.
What pretty innocence in those days mov'd!
Man ignorantly walk'd by her he lov'd;
Both sigh'd and interchang'd a speaking eye,
Both trembled and were sick, both knew not why.
That natural fearfulness that struck man dumb,
Might well (those times consider'd) man become.
As all discoverers whose first assay
Finds but the place, after, the nearest way:
So passion is to woman's love, about,
Nay, farther off, than when we first set out.
It is not love that sueth, or doth contend;
Love either conquers, or but meets a friend.
Man's better part consists of purer fire,
And finds itself allow'd, ere it desire.
Love is wise here, keeps home, gives reason sway,
And journeys not till it find summer-way.
A weather-beaten Lover but once known,
Is sport for every girl to practise on.
Who strives through woman's scorns, women to know,
Is lost, and seeks his shadow to outgo;
It must be sickness, after one disdain,
Though he be call'd aloud, to look again.
Let others sigh, and grieve; one cunning sleight
Shall freeze my Love to crystal in a night.
I can love first, and (if I win) love still;
And cannot be remov'd, unless she will.
It is her fault if I unsure remain,
She only can untie, and bind again.
The honesties of love with ease I do,
But am no porter for a tedious woo.

    But (Madam) I now think on you; and here
Where we are at our heights, you but appear,
We are but clouds you rise from, our noon-ray
But a foul shadow, not your break of day.
You are at first hand all that's fair and right,
And others' good reflects but back your light.
You are a perfectness, so curious hit,
That youngest flatteries do scandal it.

For, what is more doth what you are restrain,
And though beyond, is down the hill again.
We 've no next way to you, we cross to it:
You are the straight line, thing prais'd, attribute;
Each good in you 's a light; so many a shade
You make, and in them are your motions made.
These are your pictures to the life.   From far
We see you move, and here your Zanies are:
So that no fountain good there is, doth grow
In you, but our dim actions faintly show.

Then find I, if man's noblest part be love,
Your purest lustre must that shadow move.
The soul, with body, is a heaven combin'd
With earth, and for man's ease, but nearer join'd,
Where thoughts the stars of soul we understand.
We guess not their large natures, but command.
And love in you, that bounty is of light,
That gives to all, and yet hath infinite.
Whose heat doth force us thither to intend,
But soul we find too earthly to ascend,
'Till slow access hath made it wholly pure,
Able immortal clearness to endure.
Who dare aspire this journey with a stain,
Hath weight will force him headlong back again.
No more can impure man retain and move
In that pure region of a worthy love,
Than earthly substance can unforc'd aspire,
And leave his nature to converse with fire:
Such may have eye, and hand; may sigh, may speak;
But like swoln bubbles, when they are high'st they break.

Though far removèd Northern fleets scarce find
The Sun's comfort; others think him too kind.
There is an equal distance from her eye,
Men perish too far off, and burn too nigh.
But as air takes the Sun-beams equal bright
From the first Rays, to his last opposite:
So able men, blest with a virtuous Love,
Remote or near, or howsoe'er they move;
Their virtue breaks all clouds that might annoy,

There is no Emptiness, but all is Joy.
He much profanes whom violent heats do move
To style his wand'ring rage of passion, *Love*.
Love that imparts in everything delight,
Is feign'd, which only tempts man's appetite.
Why love among the virtues is not known
Is, that love is them all contract in one.

TO SIR HENRY WOTTON

SIR, more than kisses, letters mingle Souls;
For, thus friends absent speak.   This ease controls
The tediousness of my life: but for these
I could ideate nothing, which could please,
But I should wither in one day, and pass
To a bottle of Hay, that am a lock of Grass.
Life is a voyage, and in our life's ways
Countries, Courts, Towns are Rocks, or Remoras;
They break or stop all ships, yet our state 's such,
That though than pitch they stain worse, we must touch.
If in the furnace of the even line,
Or under th' adverse icy poles thou pine,
Thou know'st two temperate Regions girded in,
Dwell there: But Oh, what refuge canst thou win
Parch'd in the Court, and in the country frozen?
Shall cities, built of both extremes, be chosen?
Can dung and garlic be a perfume? or can
A Scorpion and Torpedo cure a man?
Cities are worst of all three; of all three
(O knotty riddle) each is worst equally.
Cities are sepulchres; they who dwell there
Are carcases, as if none such there were.
And Courts are Theatres, where some men play
Princes, some slaves, all to one end, and of one clay.
The Country is a desert, where no good,
Gain'd (as habits, not born,) is understood.
There men become beasts, and prone to more evils;
In cities blocks, and in a lewd court, devils.

As in the first Chaos confusedly
Each element's qualities were in the other three;
So pride, lust, covetize, being several
To these three places, yet all are in all,
And mingled thus, their issue incestuous.
Falsehood is denizen'd.   Virtue is barbarous.
Let no man say there, Virtue's flinty wall
Shall lock vice in me, I 'll do none, but know all.
Men are sponges, which to pour out, receive;
Who know false play, rather than lose, deceive.
For in best understandings, sin began,
Angels sinn'd first, then Devils, and then man.
Only perchance beasts sin not; wretched we
Are beasts in all, but white integrity.
I think if men, which in these places live
Durst look for themselves, and themselves retrieve,
They would like strangers greet themselves, seeing then
Utopian youth, grown old Italian.
    Be thou thine own home, and in thyself dwell;
Inn anywhere, continuance maketh hell.
And seeing the snail, which everywhere doth roam,
Carrying his own house still, still is at home,
Follow (for he is easy paced) this snail,
Be thine own Palace, or the world 's thy gaol.
And in the world's sea, do not like cork sleep
Upon the water's face; nor in the deep
Sink like a lead without a line: but as
Fishes glide, leaving no print where they pass,
Nor making sound; so closely thy course go,
Let men dispute, whether thou breathe, or no.
Only in this one thing, be no Galenist: to make
Courts' hot ambitions wholesome, do not take
A dram of Country's dullness; do not add
Correctives, but as chemics, purge the bad.
But, Sir, I advise not you, I rather do
Say o'er those lessons, which I learn'd of you:
Whom, free from German schisms, and lightness
Of France, and fair Italy's faithlessness,
Having from these suck'd all they had of worth,

And brought home that faith, which you carried forth,
I throughly love.   But if myself, I have won
To know my rules, I have, and you have

DONNE.

TO SIR HENRY GOODYERE

WHO makes the Past, a pattern for next year,
   Turns no new leaf, but still the same things reads,
Seen things, he sees again, Heard things doth hear,
   And makes his life but like a pair of beads.

A Palace, when 'tis that, which it should be,
   Leaves growing, and stands such, or else decays:
But he, which dwells there, is not so; for he
   Strives to urge upward, and his fortune raise;

So had your body her morning, hath her noon,
   And shall not better; her next change is night:
But her fair larger guest, to whom Sun and Moon
   Are sparks, and short-lived, claims another right.

The noble Soul by age grows lustier,
   Her appetite and her digestion mend,
We must not starve, nor hope to pamper her
   With women's milk, and pap unto the end.

Provide you manlier diet; you have seen
   All libraries, which are Schools, Camps, and Courts;
But ask your Garners if you have not been
   In harvests, too indulgent to your sports.

Would you redeem it? then yourself transplant
   A while from hence.   Perchance outlandish ground
Bears no more wit, than ours, but yet more scant
   Are those diversions there, which here abound.

To be a stranger hath that benefit,
  We can beginnings, but not habits choke.
Go; whither? Hence; you get, if you forget;
  New faults, till they prescribe in us, are smoke.

Our soul, whose country's heaven, and God her father,
  Into this world, corruption's sink, is sent,
Yet, so much in her travail she doth gather,
  That she returns home, wiser than she went;

It pays you well, if it teach you to spare,
  And make you asham'd to make your hawk's praise
    yours,
Which when herself she lessens in the air,
  You then first say, that high enough she towers.

However, keep the lively taste you hold
  Of God, love Him as now, but fear Him more,
And in your afternoons think what you told
  And promis'd Him, at morning prayer before.

Let falsehood like a discord anger you,
  Else be not froward.   But why do I touch
Things, of which none is in your practice new,
  And Tables, or fruit-trenchers teach as much;

But thus I make you keep your promise Sir,
  Riding I had you, though you still stay'd there,
And in these thoughts, although you never stir,
  You came with me to Mitcham, and are here.

TO MR. ROWLAND WOODWARD

LIKE one who in her third widowhood doth profess
Herself a Nun, tied to retiredness,
So affects my muse now, a chaste fallowness;

Since she to few, yet to too many hath shown
How love-song weeds, and Satiric thorn are grown
Where seeds of better Arts, were early sown.

Though to use and love Poetry, to me,
Betrothed to no one Art, be no adultery;
Omissions of good, ill, as ill deeds be.

For though to us it seem, and be light and thin,
Yet in those faithful scales, where God throws in
Men's works, vanity weighs as much as sin.

If our Souls have stain'd their first white, yet we
May clothe them with faith, and dear honesty,
Which God imputes, as native purity.

There is no Virtue, but Religion:
Wise, valiant, sober, just, are names, which none
Want, which want not Vice-covering discretion.

Seek we then ourselves in ourselves; for as
Men force the Sun with much more force to pass,
By gathering his beams with a crystal glass;

So we, if we into ourselves will turn,
Blowing our sparks of virtue, may outburn
The straw, which doth about our hearts sojourn.

You know, Physicians, when they would infuse
Into any oil, the Souls of Simples, use
Places, where they may lie still warm, to choose.

So works retiredness in us; to roam
Giddily, and be everywhere, but at home,
Such freedom doth a banishment become.

We are but farmers of ourselves, yet may,
If we can stock ourselves, and thrive, uplay
Much, much dear treasure for the great rent day.

Manure thyself then, to thyself be approv'd,
And with vain outward things be no more mov'd,
But to know, that I love thee and would be lov'd.

TO SIR HENRY WOTTON

HERE's no more news, than virtue, I may as well
Tell you *Calais*, or *Saint Michael's* tale for news, as tell
That vice doth here habitually dwell.

Yet, as to get stomachs, we walk up and down,
And toil to sweeten rest, so, may God frown,
If, but to loathe both, I haunt Court, or Town.

For here no one is from th' extremity
Of vice, by any other reason free,
But that the next to him still is worse than he.

In this world's warfare, they whom rugged Fate,
(God's Commissary,) doth so throughly hate,
As in the Court's Squadron to marshal their state:

If they stand arm'd with silly honesty,
With wishing prayers, and neat integrity,
Like Indian 'gainst Spanish hosts they be.

Suspicious boldness to this place belongs,
And to have as many ears as all have tongues;
Tender to know, tough to acknowledge wrongs.

Believe me, Sir, in my youth's giddiest days,
When to be like the Court, was a play's praise,
Plays were not so like Courts, as Courts are like plays.

Then let us at these mimic antics jest,
Whose deepest projects, and egregious gests
Are but dull Morals of a game at Chests.

But now 'tis incongruity to smile,
Therefore I end; and bid farewell a while,
At Court; though *From Court*, were the better style.

HENRICO WOTTONI IN HIBERNIA
BELLIGERANTI

WENT you to conquer? and have so much lost
Yourself, that what in you was best and most,
Respective friendship, should so quickly die?
In public gain my share 's not such that I
Would lose your love for Ireland: better cheap
I pardon death (who though he do not reap
Yet gleans he many of our friends away)
Than that your waking mind should be a prey
To lethargies.　Let shot, and bogs, and skeins
With bodies deal, as fate bids and restrains;
Ere sicknesses attack, young death is best,
Who pays before his death doth 'scape arrest.
Let not your soul (at first with graces fill'd,
And since, and thorough crooked limbecs, still'd
In many schools and courts, which quicken it,)
Itself unto the Irish negligence submit.
I ask not laboured letters which should wear
Long papers out: nor letters which should fear
Dishonest carriage: or a seer's art:
Nor such as from the brain come, but the heart.

TO THE COUNTESS OF BEDFORD

MADAM,

REASON is our Soul's left hand, Faith her right,
By these we reach divinity, that 's you;
Their loves, who have the blessings of your light,
Grew from their reason, mine from fair faith grew.

But as, although a squint lefthandedness
Be ungracious, yet we cannot want that hand,
So would I, not to increase, but to express
My faith, as I believe, so understand.

Therefore I study you first in your Saints,
Those friends, whom your election glorifies,
Then in your deeds, accesses, and restraints,
And what you read, and what yourself devise.

But soon, the reasons why you 're lov'd by all,
Grow infinite, and so pass reason's reach,
Then back again to implicit faith I fall,
And rest on what the Catholic voice doth teach;

That you are good: and not one Heretic
Denies it: if he did, yet you are so,
For, rocks, which high-topp'd and deep-rooted stick,
Waves wash, not undermine, nor overthrow.

In everything there naturally grows
A *Balsamum* to keep it fresh, and new,
If 'twere not injur'd by extrinsic blows;
Your birth and beauty are this Balm in you.

But you of learning and religion,
And virtue, and such ingredients, have made
A mithridate, whose operation
Keeps off, or cures what can be done or said.

Yet, this is not your physic, but your food,
A diet fit for you; for you are here
The first good Angel, since the world's frame stood,
That ever did in woman's shape appear.

Since you are then God's masterpiece, and so
His Factor for our loves; do as you do,
Make your return home gracious; and bestow
This life on that; so make one life of two.
    For so God help me, I would not miss you there
    For all the good which you can do me here.

TO THE COUNTESS OF BEDFORD

Madam,

You have refin'd me, and to worthiest things
(Virtue, Art, Beauty, Fortune,) now I see
Rareness, or use, not nature value brings;
And such, as they are circumstanc'd, they be.
  Two ills can ne'er perplex us, sin to excuse;
  But of two good things, we may leave and choose.

Therefore at Court, which is not virtue's clime,
(Where a transcendent height, (as, lowness me)
Makes her not be, or not show) all my rhyme
Your virtues challenge, which there rarest be;
  For, as dark texts need notes: there some must be
  To usher virtue, and say, *This is she*.

So in the country's beauty; to this place
You are the season (Madam) you the day,
'Tis but a grave of spices, till your face
Exhale them, and a thick close bud display.
  Widow'd and reclus'd else, her sweets she enshrines;
  As China, when the Sun at Brazil dines.

Out from your chariot, morning breaks at night,
And falsifies both computations so;
Since a new world doth rise here from your light,
We your new creatures, by new reckonings go.
  This shows that you from nature lothly stray,
  That suffer not an artificial day.

In this you 've made the Court the Antipodes,
And will'd your Delegate, the vulgar Sun.
To do profane autumnal offices,
Whilst here to you, we sacrificers run;
  And whether Priests, or Organs, you we obey,
  We sound your influence, and your Dictates say.

Yet to that Deity which dwells in you,
Your virtuous Soul, I now not sacrifice;
These are *Petitions*, and not *Hymns*; they sue
But that I may survey the edifice.
    In all Religions as much care hath been
    Of Temples' frames, and beauty, as Rites within.

As all which go to Rome, do not thereby
Esteem religions, and hold fast the best,
But serve discourse, and curiosity,
With that which doth religion but invest,
    And shun th' entangling labyrinths of Schools,
    And make it wit, to think the wiser fools:

So in this pilgrimage I would behold
You as you 're Virtue's temple, not as she,
What walls of tender crystal her enfold,
What eyes, hands, bosom, her pure Altars be;
    And after this survey, oppose to all
    Babblers of Chapels, you th' Escurial.

Yet not as consecrate, but merely as fair,
On these I cast a lay and country eye.
Of past and future stories, which are rare,
I find you all record, and prophecy.
    Purge but the book of Fate, that it admit
    No sad nor guilty legends, you are it.

If good and lovely were not one, of both
You were the transcript, and original,
The Elements, the Parent, and the Growth,
And every piece of you, is both their All:
    So entire are all your deeds, and you, that you
    Must do the same thing still; you cannot two.

But these (as nice thin School divinity
Serves heresy to further or repress)
Taste of Poetic rage, or flattery,
And need not, where all hearts one truth profess;

Oft from new proofs, and new phrase, new doubts
  grow,
As strange attire aliens the men we know.

Leaving then busy praise, and all appeal
To higher Courts, sense's decree is true,
The Mine, the Magazine, the Commonweal,
The story of beauty, in Twickenham is, and you.
    Who hath seen one, would both; as, who had been
    In Paradise, would seek the Cherubin.

TO SIR EDWARD HERBERT AT JULIERS

MAN is a lump, where all beasts kneaded be,
  Wisdom makes him an Ark where all agree;
The fool, in whom these beasts do live at jar,
  Is sport to others, and a theatre;
Nor 'scapes he so, but is himself their prey,
  All which was man in him, is eat away,
And now his beasts on one another feed,
  Yet couple in anger, and new monsters breed.
How happy is he, which hath due place assign'd
  To his beasts, and disafforested his mind!
Empal'd himself to keep them out, not in;
  Can sow, and dares trust corn, where they have been;
Can use his horse, goat, wolf, and every beast,
  And is not Ass himself to all the rest.
Else, man not only is the herd of swine,
  But he 's those devils too, which did incline
Them to a headlong rage, and made them worse:
  For man can add weight to heaven's heaviest curse.
As Souls (they say) by our first touch, take in
  The poisonous tincture of Original sin,
So, to the punishments which God doth fling,
  Our apprehension contributes the sting.
To us, as to His chickens, He doth cast
  Hemlock, and we as men, His hemlock taste;

We do infuse to what He meant for meat,
    Corrosiveness, or intense cold or heat.
For, God no such specific poison hath
    As kills we know not how; His fiercest wrath
Hath no antipathy, but may be good
    At least for physic, if not for our food.
Thus man, that might be His pleasure, is His rod,
    And is His devil, that might be his God.
Since then our business is, to rectify
    Nature, to what she was, we are led awry
By them, who man to us in little show;
    Greater than due, no form we can bestow
On him; for Man into himself can draw
    All; all his faith can swallow, or reason chaw.
All that is fill'd, and all that which doth fill,
    All the round world, to man is but a pill;
In all it works not, but it is in all
    Poisonous, or purgative, or cordial,
For, knowledge kindles Calentures in some,
    And is to others icy *Opium*.
As brave as true, is that profession then
    Which you do use to make; that you know man.
This makes it credible; you have dwelt upon
    All worthy books, and now are such an one.
Actions are authors, and of those in you
    Your friends find every day a mart of new.

TO THE COUNTESS OF BEDFORD

To have written then, when you writ, seem'd to me
    Worst of spiritual vices, Simony,
And not to have written then, seems little less
    Than worst of civil vices, thanklessness.
In this, my debt I seem'd loth to confess,
    In that, I seem'd to shun beholdingness.
But 'tis not so; nothings, as I am, may
    Pay all they have, and yet have all to pay.

Such borrow in their payments, and owe more
    By having leave to write so, than before.
Yet since rich mines in barren grounds are shown,
    May not I yield (not gold) but coal or stone?
Temples were not demolish'd, though profane:
    Here *Peter Jove's*, there *Paul* hath *Dian's* Fane.
So whether my hymns you admit or choose,
    In me you have hallowed a Pagan Muse,
And denizen'd a stranger, who, mistaught
    By blamers of the times they marr'd, hath sought
Virtues in corners, which now bravely do
    Shine in the world's best part, or all it; you.
I have been told, that virtue in Courtiers' hearts
    Suffers an Ostracism, and departs.
Profit, ease, fitness, plenty, bid it go,
    But whither, only knowing you, I know;
Your (or you) virtue two vast uses serves,
    It ransoms one sex, and one Court preserves.
There 's nothing but your worth, which being true,
    Is known to any other, not to you:
And you can never know it; to admit
    No knowledge of your worth, is some of it.
But since to you, your praises discords be,
    Stoop, others' ills to meditate with me.
Oh! to confess we know not what we should,
    Is half excuse; we know not what we would:
Lightness depresseth us, emptiness fills,
    We sweat and faint, yet still go down the hills.
As new Philosophy arrests the Sun,
    And bids the passive earth about it run,
So we have dull'd our mind, it hath no ends;
    Only the body 's busy, and pretends;
As dead low earth eclipses and controls
    The quick high Moon: so doth the body, Souls.
In none but us, are such mix'd engines found,
    As hands of double office: for, the ground
We till with them; and them to heav'n we raise;
    Who prayerless labours, or, without this, prays,
Doth but one half, that 's none; He which said, *Plough*

And look not back, to look up doth allow.
Good seed degenerates, and oft obeys
   The soil's disease, and into cockle strays;
Let the mind's thoughts be but transplanted so,
   Into the body, and bastardly they grow.
What hate could hurt our bodies like our love?
   We (but no foreign tyrants could) remove
These not engrav'd, but inborn dignities,
   Caskets of souls; Temples, and Palaces:
For, bodies shall from death redeemed be,
   Souls but preserv'd, not naturally free.
As men to our prisons, new souls to us are sent,
   Which learn vice there, and come in innocent.
First seeds of every creature are in us,
   Whate'er the world hath bad, or precious,
Man's body can produce, hence hath it been
   That stones, worms, frogs, and snakes in man are seen:
But who e'er saw, though nature can work so,
   That pearl, or gold, or corn in man did grow?
We 've added to the world Virginia, and sent
   Two new stars lately to the firmament;
Why grudge we us (not heaven) the dignity
   T' increase with ours, those fair souls' company?
But I must end this letter, though it do
   Stand on two truths, neither is true to you.
Virtue hath some perverseness; For she will
   Neither believe her good, nor others' ill.
Even in you, Virtue's best paradise,
   Virtue hath some, but wise degrees of vice.
Too many virtues, or too much of one
   Begets in you unjust suspicion;
And ignorance of vice makes virtue less,
   Quenching compassion of our wretchedness.
But these are riddles; some aspersion
   Of vice becomes well some complexion.
Statesmen purge vice with vice, and may corrode
   The bad with bad, a spider with a toad:
For so, ill thralls not them, but they tame ill
   And make her do much good against her will,

But in your Commonwealth, or world in you,
   Vice hath no office, or good work to do.
Take then no vicious purge, but be content
   With cordial virtue, your known nourishment.

TO THE COUNTESS OF BEDFORD

ON NEW YEAR'S DAY

THIS twilight of two years, not past nor next,
   Some emblem is of me, or I of this,
Who Meteor-like, of stuff and form perplext,
   Whose *what*, and *where*, in disputation is,
   If I should call me *anything*, should miss.

I sum the years, and me, and find me not
   Debtor to th' old, nor Creditor to th' new,
That cannot say, My thanks, I have forgot,
   Nor trust I this with hopes, and yet scarce true
   This bravery is, since these times show'd me you.

In recompense I would show future times
   What you were, and teach them to urge towards such.
Verse embalms virtue; and Tombs, or Thrones of rhymes,
   Preserve frail transitory fame, as much
   As spice doth bodies from corrupt air's touch.

Mine are short-lived; the tincture of your name
   Creates in them, but dissipates as fast,
New spirits: for, strong agents with the same
   Force that doth warm and cherish, us do waste;
   Kept hot with strong extracts, no bodies last:

So, my verse built of your just praise, might want
   Reason and likelihood, the firmest Base,
And made of miracle, now faith is scant,
   Will vanish soon, and so possess no place,
   And you, and it, too much grace might disgrace.

When all (as truth commands assent) confess
  All truth of you, yet they will doubt how I,
One corn of one low anthill's dust, and less,
  Should name, know, or express a thing so high,
And, not an inch, measure infinity.

I cannot tell them, nor myself, nor you,
  But leave, lest truth be endanger'd by my praise,
And turn to God, who knows I think this true,
  And useth oft, when such a heart mis-says,
  To make it good, for, such a praiser prays.

He will best teach you, how you should lay out
  His stock of *beauty, learning, favour, blood*;
He will perplex security with doubt,
  And clear those doubts; hide from you and show you good,
  And so increase your appetite and food;

He will teach you, that good and bad have not
  One latitude in cloisters, and in Court;
Indifferent there the greatest space hath got;
  Some pity 's not good there, some vain disport,
  On this side sin, with that place may comport.

Yet He, as He bounds seas, will fix your hours,
  Which pleasure, and delight may not ingress,
And though what none else lost, be truliest yours,
  He will make you, what you did not, possess,
  By using others', not vice, but weakness.

He will make you speak truths, and credibly,
  And make you doubt, that others do not so:
He will provide you keys, and locks, to spy,
  And 'scape spies, to good ends, and He wi'l show
  What you may not acknowledge, what not know.

For your own conscience, He gives innocence,
  But for your fame, a discreet wariness,
And though to 'scape, than to revenge offence
  Be better, He shows both, and to repress
  Joy, when your state swells, *sadness* when 'tis less.

From need of tears He will defend your soul,
   Or make a rebaptizing of one tear;
He cannot, (that 's, He will not) dis-enrol
   Your name; and when with active joy we hear
   This private Gospel, then 'tis our New Year.

TO THE COUNTESS OF HUNTINGDON

MADAM,

MAN to God's image, *Eve* to man's was made,
   Nor find we that God breath'd a soul in her;
Canons will not Church functions you invade,
   Nor laws to civil office you prefer.

Who vagrant transitory Comets sees,
   Wonders, because they 're rare; but a new star
Whose motion with the firmament agrees,
   Is miracle; for, there no new things are.

In woman so perchance mild innocence
   A seldom comet is, but active good
A miracle, which reason 'scapes, and sense;
   For, Art and Nature this in them withstood.

As such a star, the *Magi* led to view
   The manger-cradled infant, God below:
By virtue's beams by fame deriv'd from you,
   May apt souls, and the worst may, virtue know.

If the world's age, and death be argued well
   By the Sun's fall, which now towards earth doth bend,
Then we might fear that virtue, since she fell
   So low as woman, should be near her end.

But she 's not stoop'd, but rais'd; exil'd by men
   She fled to heaven, that 's heavenly things, that 's you;
She was in all men, thinly scatter'd then,
   But now amass'd, contracted in a few.

She gilded us: but you are gold, and she;
 Us she inform'd, but transubstantiates you;
Soft dispositions which ductile be,
 Elixir-like, she makes not clean, but new.

Though you a wife's and mother's name retain,
 'Tis not as woman, for all are not so,
But virtue having made you virtue, is fain
 To adhere in these names, her and you to show,

Else, being alike pure, we should neither see;
 As, water being into air rarefied,
Neither appear, till in one cloud they be,
 So, for our sakes you do low names abide;

Taught by great constellations, which being fram'd,
 Of the most stars, take low names, *Crab*, and *Bull*,
When single planets by the *Gods* are nam'd,
 You covet not great names, of great things full.

So you, as woman, one doth comprehend,
 And in the vale of kindred others see;
To some ye are reveal'd, as in a friend,
 And as a virtuous Prince far off, to me.

To whom, because from you all virtues flow,
 And 'tis not none, to dare contemplate you,
I, which do so, as your true subject owe
 Some tribute for that, so these lines are due.

If you can think these flatteries, they are,
 For then your judgment is below my praise,
If they were so, oft, flatteries work as far,
 As Counsels, and as far th' endeavour raise.

So my ill reaching you might there grow good,
 But I remain a poison'd fountain still;
But not your beauty, virtue, knowledge, blood
 Are more above all flattery, than my will.

And if I flatter any, 'tis not you
　　But my own judgment, who did long ago
Pronounce, that all these praises should be true,
　　And Virtue should your beauty, and birth outgrow.

Now that my prophecies are all fulfill'd,
　　Rather than God should not be honour'd too,
And all these gifts confess'd, which He instill'd,
　　Yourself were bound to say that which I do.

So I, but your Recorder am in this,
　　Or mouth, or Speaker of the universe,
A ministerial Notary, for 'tis
　　Not I, but you and fame, that make this verse;

I was your Prophet in your younger days,
And now your Chaplain, God in you to praise.

TO MR. T[HOMAS]. W[OODWARD].

All hail, sweet Poet, more full of more strong fire,
　　Than hath or shall enkindle any spirit,
　　I lov'd what nature gave thee, but this merit
Of wit and Art I love not but admire;
Who have before or shall write after thee,
Their works, though toughly laboured, will be
　　Like infancy or age to man's firm stay,
　　Or early and late twilights to mid-day.

Men say, and truly, that they better be
　　Which be envied than pitied: therefore I,
　　Because I wish thee best, do thee envy:
O wouldst thou, by like reason, pity me!
But care not for me: I, that ever was
In Nature's, and in Fortune's gifts, alas,
　　(Before thy grace got in the Muses' School)
　　A monster and a beggar, am now a fool.

Oh how I grieve, that late-born modesty
    Hath got such root in easy waxen hearts,
    That men may not themselves, their own good parts
Extol, without suspect of surquedry,
For, but thyself, no subject can be found
Worthy thy quill, nor any quill resound
    Thy worth but thine: how good it were to see
    A Poem in thy praise, and writ by thee.

Now if this song be too harsh for rhyme, yet, as
    The Painters' bad god made a good devil,
    'Twill be good prose, although the verse be evil,
If thou forget the rhyme as thou dost pass.
Then write, that I may follow, and so be
Thy debtor, thy echo, thy foil, thy zany.
    I shall be thought, if mine like thine I shape,
    All the world's Lion, though I be thy Ape.

TO MR. T[HOMAS]. W[OODWARD].

HASTE thee harsh verse, as fast as thy lame measure
    Will give thee leave, to him, my pain and pleasure.
I have given thee, and yet thou art too weak,
    Feet, and a reasoning soul and tongue to speak.
Plead for me, and so by thine and my labour
    I am thy Creator, thou my Saviour.
Tell him, all questions, which men have defended
    Both of the place and pains of hell, are ended;
And 'tis decreed our hell is but privation
    Of him, at least in this earth's habitation:
And 'tis where I am, where in every street
    Infections follow, overtake, and meet:
Live I or die, by you my love is sent,
    And you 're my pawns, or else my Testament.

TO MR. T[HOMAS]. W[OODWARD].

PREGNANT again with th' old twins Hope and Fear,
Oft have I asked for thee, both how and where
Thou wert, and what my hopes of letters were;

As in the streets sly beggars narrowly
Watch motions of the giver's hand and eye,
And evermore conceive some hope thereby.

And now thy Alms is given, thy letter 's read,
The body risen again, the which was dead,
And thy poor starveling bountifully fed.

After this banquet my Soul doth say grace,
And praise thee for 't, and zealously embrace
Thy love; though I think thy love in this case
    To be as gluttons, which say 'midst their meat,
    They love that best of which they most do eat.

TO MR. T[HOMAS]. W[OODWARD].

AT once, from hence, my lines and I depart,
I to my soft still walks, they to my Heart;
I to the Nurse, they to the child of Art;

Yet as a firm house, though the Carpenter
Perish, doth stand: as an Ambassador
Lies safe, howe'er his king be in danger:

So, though I languish, prest with Melancholy,
My verse, the strict Map of my misery,
Shall live to see that, for whose want I die.

Therefore I envy them, and do repent,
That from unhappy me, things happy are sent;
Yet as a Picture, or bare Sacrament,
    Accept these lines, and if in them there be
    Merit of love, bestow that love on me.

TO MR. R[OWLAND]. W[OODWARD].

ZEALOUSLY my Muse doth salute all thee,
Inquiring of that mystic trinity
Whereof thou and all to whom heavens do infuse
Like fire, are made; thy body, mind, and Muse.
Dost thou recover sickness, or prevent?
Or is thy Mind travail'd with discontent?
Or art thou parted from the world and me,
In a good scorn of the world's vanity?
Or is thy devout Muse retired to sing
Upon her tender Elegiac string?
Our Minds part not, join then thy Muse with mine,
For mine is barren thus divorced from thine.

TO MR. R[OWLAND]. W[OODWARD].

MUSE not that by thy Mind thy body is led:
For by thy Mind, my Mind 's distempered.
So thy Care lives long, for I bearing part
It eats not only thine, but my swoln heart.
And when it gives us intermission
We take new hearts for it to feed upon.
But as a Lay Man's Genius doth control
Body and mind; the Muse being the Soul's Soul
Of Poets, that methinks should ease our anguish,
Although our bodies wither and minds languish.
Write then, that my griefs which thine got may be
Cur'd by thy charming sovereign melody.

TO MR. C[HRISTOPHER]. B[ROOKE].

THY friend, whom thy deserts to thee enchain,
  Urg'd by this unexcusable occasion,
  Thee and the Saint of his affection
Leaving behind, doth of both wants complain;
And let the love I bear to both sustain
  No blot nor maim by this division;

Strong is this love which ties our hearts in one,
And strong that love pursu'd with amorous pain;
But though besides thyself I leave behind
   Heaven's liberal, and earth's thrice-fairer Sun,
   Going to where stern winter aye doth won,
Yet, love's hot fires, which martyr my sad mind,
   Do send forth scalding sighs, which have the Art
   To melt all Ice, but that which walls her heart.

TO MR. E[DWARD]. G[ILPIN?].

EVEN as lame things thirst their perfection, so
The slimy rhymes bred in our vale below,
Bearing with them much of my love and heart,
Fly unto that Parnassus, where thou art.
There thou o'erseest London: here I have been,
By staying in London, too much overseen.
Now pleasure's dearth our City doth possess,
Our Theatres are fill'd with emptiness;
As lank and thin is every street and way
As a woman deliver'd yesterday.
Nothing whereat to laugh my spleen espies
But bearbaitings or Law exercise.
Therefore I 'll leave it, and in the Country strive
Pleasure, now fled from London, to retrieve.
Do thou so too: and fill not like a Bee
Thy thighs with honey, but as plenteously
As Russian Merchants, thyself's whole vessel load,
And then at Winter retail it here abroad.
Bless us with Suffolk's Sweets; and as it is
Thy garden, make thy hive and warehouse this.

TO MR. R[OWLAND]. W[OODWARD].

IF, as mine is, thy life a slumber be,
  Seem, when thou read'st these lines, to dream of me,
Never did Morpheus nor his brother wear
  Shapes so like those Shapes, whom they would appear,

As this my letter is like me, for it
  Hath my name, words, hand, feet, heart, mind and wit;
It is my deed of gift of me to thee,
  It is my Will, myself the Legacy.
So thy retirings I love, yea envy,
  Bred in thee by a wise melancholy,
That I rejoice, that unto where thou art,
  Though I stay here, I can thus send my heart,
As kindly as any enamoured Patient
  His Picture to his absent Love hath sent.

All news I think sooner reach thee than me;
  Havens are Heavens, and Ships wing'd Angels be,
The which both Gospel, and stern threat'nings bring;
  Guiana's harvest is nipp'd in the spring,
I fear; and with us (methinks) Fate deals so
  As with the Jews' guide God did; He did show
Him the rich land, but barr'd his entry in:
  Oh, slowness is our punishment and sin.
Perchance, these Spanish business being done,
  Which as the Earth between the Moon and Sun
Eclipse the light which Guiana would give,
  Our discontinued hopes we shall retrieve:
But if (as all th' All must) hopes smoke away,
  Is not Almighty Virtue an India?
If men be worlds, there is in every one
  Something to answer in some proportion
All the world's riches: and in good men, this,
  Virtue, our form's form and our soul's soul, is.

TO MR. R[OWLAND]. W[OODWARD].

KINDLY I envy thy song's perfection
  Built of all th' elements as our bodies are:
  That Little of earth that is in it, is a fair
Delicious garden where all sweets are sown.
In it is cherishing fire which dries in me

Grief which did drown me: and half quench'd by it
Are satiric fires which urg'd me to have writ
In scorn of all: for now I admire thee.
And as Air doth fulfil the hollowness
Of rotten walls; so it mine emptiness,
Where toss'd and mov'd it did beget this sound
Which as a lame Echo of thine doth rebound.
Oh, I was dead; but since thy song new Life did give,
I recreated, even by thy creature, live.

TO MR. S[AMUEL]. B[ROOKE].

O THOU which to search out the secret parts
    Of the India, or rather Paradise
    Of knowledge, hast with courage and advice
Lately launch'd into the vast Sea of Arts,
Disdain not in thy constant travailing
    To do as other Voyagers, and make
    Some turns into less Creeks, and wisely take
Fresh water at the Heliconian spring;
I sing not, Siren-like, to tempt; for I
    Am harsh; nor as those Schismatics with you,
    Which draw all wits of good hope to their crew;
But seeing in you bright sparks of Poetry,
    I, though I brought no fuel, had desire
With these Articulate blasts to blow the fire.

TO MR. I. L.

OF that short Roll of friends writ in my heart
    Which with thy name begins, since their depart,
Whether in the English Provinces they be,
    Or drink of Po, Sequan, or Danuby,
There 's none that sometimes greets us not, and yet
    Your Trent is Lethe; that past, us you forget.
You do not duties of Societies,
    If from the embrace of a lov'd wife you rise,

View your fat Beasts, stretch'd Barns, and labour'd fields,
　Eat, play, ride, take all joys which all day yields,
And then again to your embracements go:
　Some hours on us your friends, and some bestow
Upon your Muse, else both we shall repent,
　I that my love, she that her gifts on you are spent.

TO MR. I. L.

Blest are your North parts, for all this long time
　My Sun is with you, cold and dark is our Clime;
Heaven's Sun, which stay'd so long from us this year,
　Stay'd in your North (I think) for she was there,
And hither by kind nature drawn from thence,
　Here rages, chafes, and threatens pestilence;
Yet I, as long as she from hence doth stay,
　Think this no South, no Summer, nor no day.
With thee my kind and unkind heart is run,
　There sacrifice it to that beauteous Sun:
And since thou art in Paradise and need'st crave
　No joy's addition, help thy friend to save.
So may thy pastures with their flowery feasts,
　As suddenly as Lard, fat thy lean beasts;
So may thy woods oft poll'd, yet ever wear
　A green, and when thee list, a golden hair;
So may all thy sheep bring forth Twins; and so
　In chase and race may thy horse all outgo;
So may thy love and courage ne'er be cold;
　Thy Son ne'er Ward; thy lov'd wife ne'er seem old;
But may'st thou wish great things, and them attain,
　As thou tell'st her, and none but her, my pain.

TO MR. B[ASIL]. B[ROOKE].

Is not thy sacred hunger of science
　Yet satisfied? Is not thy brain's rich hive
　Fulfill'd with honey which thou dost derive
From the Arts' spirits and their Quintessence?

Then wean thyself at last, and thee withdraw
  From Cambridge thy old nurse, and, as the rest,
  Here toughly chew, and sturdily digest
Th' immense vast volumes of our common law;
And begin soon, lest my grief grieve thee too,
  Which is, that that which I should have begun
  In my youth's morning, now late must be done;
And I as Giddy Travellers must do,
  Which stray or sleep all day, and having lost
  Light and strength, dark and tired must then ride post.

If thou unto thy Muse be married,
  Embrace her ever, ever multiply,
  Be far from me that strange Adultery
To tempt thee and procure her widowhood.
My Muse, (for I had one,) because I'm cold,
  Divorc'd herself: the cause being in me,
  That I can take no new in Bigamy,
Not my will only but power doth withhold.
Hence comes it, that these Rhymes which never had
  Mother, want matter, and they only have
  A little form, the which their Father gave;
They are profane, imperfect, oh, too bad
  To be counted Children of Poetry
  Except confirm'd and Bishoped by thee.

TO SIR H[ENRY]. W[OTTON]. AT HIS GOING AMBASSADOR TO VENICE

AFTER those reverend papers, whose soul is
  Our good and great King's lov'd hand and fear'd name,
By which to you he derives much of his,
  And (how he may) makes you almost the same,

A Taper of his Torch, a copy writ
  From his Original, and a fair beam
Of the same warm, and dazzling Sun, though it
  Must in another Sphere his virtue stream:

After those learned papers which your hand
  Hath stor'd with notes of use and pleasure too,
From which rich treasury you may command
  Fit matter whether you will write or do:

After those loving papers, where friends send
  With glad grief, to your Sea-ward steps, farewell,
Which thicken on you now, as prayers ascend
  To heaven in troops at a good man's passing bell:

Admit this honest paper, and allow
  It such an audience as yourself would ask;
What you must say at Venice this means now,
  And hath for nature, what you have for task:

To swear much love, not to be chang'd before
  Honour alone will to your fortune fit;
Nor shall I then honour your fortune, more
  Than I have done your honour wanting it.

But 'tis an easier load (though both oppress)
  To want, than govern greatness, for we are
In that, our own and only business,
  In this, we must for others' vices care;

'Tis therefore well your spirits now are plac'd
  In their last Furnace, in activity;
Which fits them (Schools and Courts and Wars o'erpast)
  To touch and test in any best degree.

For me, (if there be such a thing as I)
  Fortune (if there be such a thing as she)
Spies that I bear so well her tyranny,
  That she thinks nothing else so fit for me;

But though she part us, to hear my oft prayers
  For your increase, God is as near me here;
And to send you what I shall beg, His stairs
  In length and ease are alike everywhere.

TO MRS. M[AGDALEN]. H[ERBERT].

MAD paper, stay, and grudge not here to burn
   With all those sons whom my brain did create,
At least lie hid with me, till thou return
   To rags again, which is thy native state.

What though thou have enough unworthiness
   To come unto great place as others do,
That 's much; emboldens, pulls, thrusts I confess,
   But 'tis not all; thou should'st be wicked too.

And, that thou canst not learn, or not of me;
   Yet thou wilt go?   Go, since thou goest to her
Who lacks but faults to be a Prince, for she,
   Truth, whom they dare not pardon, dares prefer.

But when thou com'st to that perplexing eye
   Which equally claims *love* and *reverence*,
Thou wilt not long dispute it, thou wilt die;
   And, having little now, have then no sense.

Yet when her warm redeeming hand, which is
   A miracle; and made such to work more,
Doth touch thee, sapless leaf, thou grow'st by this
   Her creature; glorified more than before.

Then as a mother which delights to hear
   Her early child mis-speak half-uttered words,
Or, because majesty doth never fear
   Ill or bold speech, she Audience affords.

And then, cold speechless wretch, thou diest again,
   And wisely; what discourse is left for thee?
For, speech of ill, and her, thou must abstain,
   And is there any good which is not she?

Yet may'st thou praise her servants, though not her,
　And wit, and virtue, and honour her attend,
And since they 're but her clothes, thou shalt not err,
　If thou her shape and beauty and grace commend.

Who knows thy destiny? when thou hast done,
　Perchance her Cabinet may harbour thee,
Whither all noble ambitious wits do run,
　A nest almost as full of Good as she.

When thou art there, if any, whom we know,
　Were sav'd before, and did that heaven partake,
When she revolves his papers, mark what show
　Of favour, she alone, to them doth make.

Mark, if to get them, she o'erskip the rest,
　Mark, if she read them twice, or kiss the name;
Mark, if she do the same that they protest,
　Mark, if she mark whether her woman came.

Mark, if slight things be objected, and o'erblown,
　Mark, if her oaths against him be not still
Reserv'd, and that she grieves she 's not her own,
　And chides the doctrine that denies Freewill.

I bid thee not do this to be my spy;
　Nor to make myself her familiar;
But so much I do love her choice, that I
　Would fain love him that shall be lov'd of her.

TO THE COUNTESS OF BEDFORD

Honour is so sublime perfection,
　And so refined; that when God was alone
　And creatureless at first, Himself had none;

But as of the elements, these which we tread,
　Produce all things with which we 're joy'd or fed,
　And, those are barren both above our head:

So from low persons doth all honour flow;
Kings, whom they would have honoured, to us show,
And but *direct* our honour, not *bestow*.

For when from herbs the pure part must be won
From gross, by Stilling, this is better done
By despis'd dung, than by the fire or Sun.

Care not then, Madam, how low your praisers lie;
In labourers' ballads oft more piety
God finds, than in *Te Deums'* melody.

And, ordnance rais'd on Towers, so many mile
Send not their voice, nor last so long a while
As fires from th' earth's low vaults in *Sicil* Isle.

Should I say I liv'd darker than were true,
Your radiation can all clouds subdue;
But one, 'tis best light to contemplate you.

You, for whose body God made better clay,
Or took Soul's stuff such as shall late decay,
Or such as needs small change at the last day.

This, as an Amber drop enwraps a Bee,
Covering discovers your quick Soul; that we
May in your through-shine front your heart's thoughts
    see.

You teach (though we learn not) a thing unknown
To our late times, the use of specular stone,
Through which all things within without were shown.

Of such were Temples; so and of such you are;
Being and *seeming* is your equal care,
And virtue's whole sum is but *know* and *dare*.

But as our Souls of growth and Souls of sense
Have birthright of our reason's Soul, yet hence
They fly not from that, nor seek presidence:

Nature's first lesson, so, discretion,
Must not grudge zeal a place, nor yet keep none.
Not banish itself, nor religion.

Discretion is a wiseman's Soul, and so
Religion is a Christian's, and you know
How these are one; her *yea*, is not her *no*.

Nor may we hope to solder still and knit
These two, and dare to break them; nor must wit
Be colleague to religion, but be it.

In those poor types of God (round circles) so
Religion's types, the pieceless centres flow,
And are in all the lines which all ways go.

If either ever wrought in you alone
Or principally, then religion
Wrought your ends, and your ways discretion.

Go thither still, go the same way you went,
Who so would change, do covet or repent;
Neither can reach you, great and innocent.

TO THE COUNTESS OF BEDFORD

BEGUN IN FRANCE BUT NEVER PERFECTED

THOUGH I be dead, and buried, yet I have
   (Living in you,) Court enough in my grave,
As oft as there I think myself to be,
   So many resurrections waken me.
That thankfulness your favours have begot
   In me, embalms me, that I do not rot.
This season as 'tis Easter, as 'tis spring,
   Must both to growth and to confession bring
My thoughts dispos'd unto your influence; so,
   These verses bud, so these confessions grow.

First I confess I have to others lent
   Your stock, and over prodigally spent
Your treasure, for since I had never known
   Virtue or beauty, but as they are grown
In you, I should not think or say they shine,
   (So as I have) in any other Mine.
Next I confess this my confession,
   For, 'tis some fault thus much to touch upon
Your praise to you, where half rights seem too much,
   And make your mind's sincere complexion blush.
Next I confess my impenitence, for I
   Can scarce repent my first fault, since thereby
Remote low Spirits, which shall ne'er read you,
   May in less lessons find enough to do,
By studying copies, not Originals,
           Desunt cætera.

A LETTER TO THE LADY CAREY AND MRS. ESSEX RICH, FROM AMIENS

MADAM,

HERE where by all All Saints invoked are,
'Twere too much schism to be singular,
And 'gainst a practice general to war.

Yet turning to Saints, should my humility
To other Saint than you directed be,
That were to make my schism, heresy.

Nor would I be a Convertite so cold,
As not to tell it; If this be too bold,
Pardons are in this market cheaply sold.

Where, because Faith is in too low degree,
I thought it some Apostleship in me
To speak things which by faith alone I see.

That is, of you, who are a firmament
Of virtues, where no one is grown, or spent,
They 're your materials, not your ornament.

Others whom we call virtuous, are not so
In their whole substance, but, their virtues grow
But in their humours, and at seasons show.

For when through tasteless flat humi'ity
In dough-baked men some harmlessness we see,
'Tis but his phlegm that 's Virtuous, and not he:

So is the Blood sometimes; who ever ran
To danger unimportun'd, he was then
No better than a sanguine Virtuous man.

So cloistral men, who, in pretence of fear
All contributions to this life forbear,
Have Virtue in Melancholy, and only there.

Spiritual choleric Critics, which in all
Religions find faults, and forgive no fall,
Have, through this zeal, Virtue but in their Gall.

We 're thus but parcel guilt; to Gold we 're grown
When Virtue is our Soul's complexion;
Who knows his Virtue's name or place, hath none.

Virtue 's but aguish, when 'tis several,
By occasion wak'd and circumstantial.
True Virtue is Soul, always in all deeds All.

This Virtue thinking to give dignity
To your soul, found there no infirmity,
For, your soul was as good Virtue, as she;

She therefore wrought upon that part of you
Which is scarce less than soul, as she could do.
And so hath made your beauty, Virtue too.

Hence comes it, that your Beauty wounds not hearts,
As Others, with profane and sensual Darts,
But as an influence, virtuous thoughts imparts.

But if such friends by the honour of your sight
Grow capable of this so great a light,
As to partake your virtues, and their might,

What must I think that influence must do,
Where it finds sympathy and matter too,
Virtue, and beauty of the same stuff, as you?

Which is, your noble worthy sister, she
Of whom, if what in this my Ecstasy
And revelation of you both I see,

I should write here, as in short Galleries
The Master at the end large glasses ties,
So to present the room twice to our eyes,

So I should give this letter length, and say
That which I said of you; there is no way
From either, but by the other, not to stray.

May therefore this be enough to testify
My true devotion, free from flattery;
He that believes himself, doth never lie.

TO THE COUNTESS OF SALISBURY

AUGUST, 1614

FAIR, great, and good, since seeing you, we see
What Heaven can do, and what any Earth can be:
Since now your beauty shines, now when the Sun
Grown stale, is to so low a value run,
That his dishevell'd beams and scattered fires
Serve but for Ladies' Periwigs and Tires
In lovers' Sonnets: you come to repair
God's book of creatures, teaching what is fair.
Since now, when all is withered, shrunk, and dried,
All Virtues ebb'd out to a dead low tide,

All the world's frame being crumbled into sand,
Where every man thinks by himself to stand,
Integrity, friendship, and confidence,
(Cements of greatness) being vapour'd hence,
And narrow man being fill'd with little shares,
Court, City, Church, are all shops of small-wares,
All having blown to sparks their noble fire,
And drawn their sound gold-ingot into wire;
All trying by a love of littleness
To make abridgments, and to draw to less
Even that nothing, which at first we were;
Since in these times, your greatness doth appear,
And that we learn by it, that man to get
Towards him that 's infinite, must first be great.
Since in an age so ill, as none is fit
So much as to accuse, much less mend it,
(For who can judge, or witness of those times
Where all alike are guilty of the crimes?)
Where he that would be good, is thought by all
A monster, or at best fantastical:
Since now you durst be good, and that I do
Discern, by daring to contemplate you,
That there may be degrees of fair, great, good,
Through your light, largeness, virtue understood:
If in this sacrifice of mine, be shown
Any small spark of these, call it your own.
And if things like these, have been said by me
Of others; call not that Idolatry.
For had God made man first, and man had seen
The third day's fruits, and flowers, and various green,
He might have said the best that he could say
Of those fair creatures, which were made that day;
And when next day, he had admir'd the birth
Of Sun, Moon, Stars, fairer than late-prais'd earth,
He might have said the best that he could say,
And not be chid for praising yesterday:
So though some things are not together true
As, that another 's worthiest, and, that you:
Yet, to say so, doth not condemn a man,

If when he spoke them, they were both true then.
How fair a proof of this, in our soul grows?
We first have souls of growth, and sense, and those,
When our last soul, our soul immortal came,
Were swallowed into it, and have no name.
Nor doth he injure those souls, which doth cast,
The power and praise of both them, on the last;
No more do I wrong any; I adore
The same things now, which I ador'd before,
The subject chang'd, and measure; the same thing
In a low constable, and in the King
I reverence; His power to work on me:
So did I humbly reverence each degree
Of fair, great, good; but more, now I am come
From having found their *walks*, to find their *home*.
And as I owe my first souls thanks, that they
For my last soul did fit and mould my clay,
So am I debtor unto them, whose worth,
Enabled me to profit, and take forth
This new great lesson, thus to study you;
Which none, not reading others, first, could do.
Nor lack I light to read this book, though I
In a dark Cave, yea in a Grave do lie;
For as your fellow-Angels, so you do
Illustrate them who come to study you.
The first whom we in Histories do find
To have profess'd all Arts, was one born blind:
He lack'd those eyes beasts have as well as we,
Not those, by which Angels are seen and see;
So, though I 'm born without those eyes to live,
Which fortune, who hath none herself, doth give,
Which are, fit means to see bright courts and you,
Yet may I see you thus, as now I do;
I shall by that, all goodness have discern'd,
And though I burn my library, be learn'd.

TO THE LADY BEDFORD

You that are she and you, that 's double she,
  In her dead face, half of yourself shall see;
She was the other part, for so they do
  Which build them friendships, become one of two;
So two, that but themselves no third can fit,
  Which were to be so, when they were not yet;
Twins, though their birth *Cusco*, and *Musco* take,
  As divers stars one Constellation make,
Pair'd like two eyes, have equal motion, so
  Both but one means to see, one way to go.
Had you died first, a carcase she had been;
  And we your rich Tomb in her face had seen;
She like the Soul is gone, and you here stay,
  Not a live friend; but th' other half of clay;
And since you act that part, as men say, Here
  Lies such a Prince, when but one part is there,
And do all honour and devotion due
  Unto the whole, so we all reverence you;
For such a friendship who would not adore
  In you, who are all what both were before,
Not all, as if some perished by this,
  But so, as all in you contracted is.
As of this all, though many parts decay,
  The pure which elemented them shall stay;
And though diffus'd, and spread in infinite,
  Shall recollect, and in one All unite:
So madam, as her Soul to heaven is fled,
  Her flesh rests in the earth, as in the bed;
Her virtues do, as to their proper sphere,
  Return to dwell with you, of whom they were;
As perfect motions are all circular,
  So they to you, their sea, whence less streams are.
She was all spices, you all metals; so
  In you two we did both rich Indies know;
And as no fire, nor rust can spend or waste
  One dram of gold, but what was first shall last,

Though it be forc'd in water, earth, salt, air,
    Expans'd in infinite, none will impair;
So, to yourself you may additions take,
    But nothing can you less, or changed make.
Seek not in seeking new, to seem to doubt,
    That you can match her, or not be without
But let some faithful book in her room be,
    Yet but of *Judith* no such book as she.

AN ANATOMY OF THE WORLD

WHEREIN,

BY OCCASION OF THE UNTIMELY DEATH OF

MISTRESS ELIZABETH DRURY, THE FRAILTY AND THE

DECAY OF THIS WHOLE WORLD IS REPRESENTED

THE FIRST ANNIVERSARY

TO THE PRAISE OF THE DEAD, AND THE ANATOMY

WELL *died the World, that we might live to see*
This world of wit, in his Anatomy:
No evil wants his good; so wilder heirs
Bedew their Fathers' Tombs, with forcèd tears,
Whose state requites their loss: whiles thus we gain,
Well may we walk in blacks, but not complain.
Yet how can I consent the world is dead
While this Muse lives? which in his spirit's stead
Seems to inform a World; and bids it be,
In spite of loss or frail mortality?
And thou the subject of this well-born thought,
Thrice noble maid, couldst not have found nor sought
A fitter time to yield to thy sad Fate,
Than whiles this spirit lives, that can relate
Thy worth so well to our last Nephews' eyne,
That they shall wonder both at his and thine:
Admired match! where strive in mutual grace
The cunning pencil, and the comely face:
A task which thy fair goodness made too much
For the bold pride of vulgar pens to touch;
Enough is us to praise them that praise thee,
And say, that but enough those praises be,

Which hadst thou liv'd, had hid their fearful head
From th' angry checkings of thy modest red:
Death bars reward and shame: when envy 's gone,
And gain, 'tis safe to give the dead their own.
As then the wise Egyptians wont to lay
More on their Tombs than houses: these of clay,
But those of brass, or marble were: so we
Give more unto thy Ghost, than unto thee.
Yet what we give to thee, thou gav'st to us,
And may'st but thank thyself, for being thus:
Yet what thou gav'st, and wert, O happy maid,
Thy grace profess'd all due, where 'tis repaid.
So these high songs that to thee suited bin
Serve to but sound thy Maker's praise, in thine,
Which thy dear soul as sweetly sings to him
Amid the Quire of Saints, and Seraphim,
As any Angel's tongue can sing of thee;
The subjects differ, though the skill agree:
For as by infant-years men judge of age,
Thy early love, thy virtues, did presage
What an high part thou bear'st in those best songs,
Whereto no burden, nor no end belongs.
Sing on thou virgin Soul, whose lossful gain
Thy lovesick parents have bewail'd in vain;
Never may thy Name be in our songs forgot,
Till we shall sing thy ditty and thy note.

AN ANATOMY OF THE WORLD

THE FIRST ANNIVERSARY

WHEN that rich Soul which to her heaven is gone,   *The entry*
Whom all do celebrate, who know they have one,   *into the*
(For who is sure he hath a Soul, unless   *work.*
It see, and judge, and follow worthiness,
And by Deeds praise it? he who doth not this,
May lodge an In-mate soul, but 'tis not his.)

When that Queen ended here her progress time,
And, as to her standing house, to heaven did climb,
Where loth to make the Saints attend her long,
She 's now a part both of the Quire, and Song,
This World, in that great earthquake languished;
For in a common bath of tears it bled,
Which drew the strongest vital spirits out:
But succour'd then with a perplexed doubt,
Whether the world did lose, or gain in this,
(Because since now no other way there is,
But goodness, to see her, whom all would see,
All must endeavour to be good as she,)
This great consumption to a fever turn'd,
And so the world had fits; it joy'd, it mourn'd;
And, as men think, that Agues physic are,
And th' Ague being spent, give over care,
So thou sick World, mistak'st thyself to be
Well, when alas, thou 'rt in a Lethargy.
Her death did wound and tame thee then, and then
Thou might'st have better spar'd the Sun, or Man.
That wound was deep, but 'tis more misery,
That thou hast lost thy sense and memory.
'Twas heavy then to hear thy voice of moan,
But this is worse, that thou art speechless grown.
Thou hast forgot thy name, thou hadst; thou wast
Nothing but she, and her thou hast o'erpast.
For as a child kept from the Font, until
A prince, expected long, come to fulfil
The ceremonies, thou unnam'd had'st laid,
Had not her coming, thee her Palace made:
Her name defin'd thee, gave thee form, and frame,
And thou forget'st to celebrate thy name.
Some months she hath been dead (but being dead,
Measures of times are all determined)
But long she hath been away, long, long, yet none
Offers to tell us who it is that 's gone.
But as in states doubtful of future heirs,
When sickness without remedy impairs
The present Prince, they 're loth it should be said,

The Prince doth languish, or the Prince is dead:
So mankind feeling now a general thaw,
A strong example gone, equal to law,
The cement which did faithfully compact,
And glue all virtues, now resolv'd, and slack'd,
Thought it some blasphemy to say she was dead,
Or that our weakness was discovered
In that confession; therefore spoke no more
Than tongues, the Soul being gone, the loss deplore.
But though it be too late to succour thee,
Sick World, yea, dead, yea putrefied, since she
Thy intrinsic balm, and thy preservative,
Can never be renew'd, thou never live,
I (since no man can make thee live) will try,
What we may gain by thy Anatomy.
Her death hath taught us dearly, that thou art
Corrupt and mortal in thy purest part.
Let no man say, the world itself being dead,
'Tis labour lost to have discovered
The world's infirmities, since there is none
Alive to study this dissection;
For there's a kind of World remaining still, *What life*
Though she which did inanimate and fill *the world*
The world, be gone, yet in this last long night, *hath still.*
Her Ghost doth walk; that is, a glimmering light,
A faint weak love of virtue, and of good,
Reflects from her, on them which understood
Her worth; and though she have shut in all day,
The twilight of her memory doth stay;
Which, from the carcase of the old world, free,
Creates a new world, and new creatures be
Produc'd: the matter and the stuff of this,
Her virtue, and the form our practice is:
And though to be thus elemented, arm
These creatures, from home-born intrinsic harm,
(For all assumed unto this dignity,
So many weedless Paradises be,
Which of themselves produce no venomous sin,
Except some foreign Serpent bring it in)

Yet, because outward storms the strongest break,
And strength itself by confidence grows weak,
This new world may be safer, being told
The dangers and diseases of the old:
For with due temper men do then forgo,
Or covet things, when they their true worth know.
There is no health; Physicians say that we,
At best, enjoy but a neutrality.
And can there be worse sickness, than to know
That we are never well, nor can be so?
We are born ruinous: poor mothers cry,
That children come not right, nor orderly;
Except they headlong come and fall upon
An ominous precipitation.
How witty 's ruin! how importunate
Upon mankind! it labour'd to frustrate
Even God's purpose; and made woman, sent
For man's relief, cause of his languishment.
They were to good ends, and they are so still,
But accessory, and principal in ill;
For that first marriage was our funeral:
One woman at one blow, then kill'd us all,
And singly, one by one, they kill us now.
We do delightfully ourselves allow
To that consumption; and profusely blind,
We kill ourselves to propagate our kind.
And yet we do not that; we are not men:
There is not now that mankind, which was then,
When as the Sun and man did seem to strive,
(Joint tenants of the world) who should survive;
When Stag, and Raven, and the long-liv'd tree,
Compar'd with man, died in minority;
When, if a slow-pac'd star had stolen away
From the observer's marking, he might stay
Two or three hundred years to see it again,
And then make up his observation plain;
When, as the age was long, the size was great;
Man's growth confess'd, and recompensed the meat;
So spacious and large, that every Soul

The sick-
nesses of
the world.
Impossi-
bility of
health.

Shortness
of life.

Did a fair Kingdom, and large Realm control:
And when the very stature, thus erect,
Did that soul a good way towards heaven direct.
Where is this mankind now? who lives to age,
Fit to be made *Methusalem* his page?
Alas, we scarce live long enough to try
Whether a true-made clock run right, or lie.
Old Grandsires talk of yesterday with sorrow,
And for our children we reserve to-morrow.
So short is life, that every peasant strives,
In a torn house, or field, to have three lives.
And as in lasting, so in length is man
Contracted to an inch, who was a span;
For had a man at first in forests stray'd,
Or shipwreck'd in the Sea, one would have laid
A wager, that an Elephant, or Whale,
That met him, would not hastily assail
A thing so equal to him: now alas,
The Fairies, and the Pigmies well may pass
As credible; mankind decays so soon,
We 're scarce our Fathers' shadows cast at noon:
Only death adds to our length: nor are we grown
In stature to be men, till we are none.
But this were light, did our less volume hold
All the old Text; or had we chang'd to gold
Their silver; or dispos'd into less glass
Spirits of virtue, which then scatter'd was.
But 'tis not so: we 're not retir'd, but damp'd;
And as our bodies, so our minds are cramp'd:
'Tis shrinking, not close weaving that hath thus,
In mind, and body both bedwarfed us.
We seem ambitious, God's whole work to undo;
Of nothing He made us, and we strive too,
To bring ourselves to nothing back; and we
Do what we can, to do 't so soon as He.
With new diseases on ourselves we war,
And with new Physic, a worse Engine far.
Thus man, this world's Vice-Emperor, in whom
All faculties, all graces are at home;

*Smallness
of stature.*

And if in other creatures they appear,
They 're but man's Ministers, and Legates there,
To work on their rebellions, and reduce
Them to Civility, and to man's use:
This man, whom God did woo, and loth to attend
Till man came up, did down to man descend,
This man, so great, that all that is, is his,
Oh what a trifle, and poor thing he is!
If man were anything, he 's nothing now:
Help, or at least some time to waste, allow
To his other wants, yet when he did depart
With her whom we lament, he lost his heart.
She, of whom th' Ancients seem'd to prophesy,
When they call'd virtues by the name of *she*;
She in whom virtue was so much refin'd,
That for Allay unto so pure a mind
She took the weaker Sex; she that could drive
The poisonous tincture, and the stain of *Eve*,
Out of her thoughts, and deeds; and purify
All, by a true religious Alchemy;
She, she is dead; she 's dead: when thou knowest this,
Thou knowest how poor a trifling thing man is.
And learn'st thus much by our Anatomy,
The heart being perish'd, no part can be free.
And that except thou feed (not banquet) on
The supernatural food, Religion,
Thy better Growth grows withered, and scant;
Be more than man, or thou 'rt less than an Ant.
Then, as mankind, so is the world's whole frame
Quite out of joint, almost created lame:
For, before God had made up all the rest,
Corruption entered, and deprav'd the best.
It seized the Angels, and then first of all
The world did in her cradle take a fall,
And turn'd her brains, and took a general maim,
Wronging each joint of th' universal frame.
The noblest part, man, felt it first; and then   *Decay of*
Both beasts and plants, curst in the curse of man.   *nature in*
So did the world from the first hour decay,   *other parts.*

That evening was beginning of the day,
And now the Springs and Summers which we see,
Like sons of women after fifty be.
And new Philosophy calls all in doubt,
The Element of fire is quite put out;
The Sun is lost, and th' earth, and no man's wit
Can well direct him where to look for it.
And freely men confess that this world 's spent,
When in the Planets, and the Firmament
They seek so many new; then see that this
Is crumbled out again to his Atomies.
'Tis all in pieces, all coherence gone;
All just supply, and all Relation:
Prince, Subject, Father, Son, are things forgot,
For every man alone thinks he hath got
To be a Phœnix, and that then can be
None of that kind, of which he is, but he.
This is the world's condition now, and now
She that should all parts to reunion bow,
She that had all magnetic force alone,
To draw, and fasten sundered parts in one;
She whom wise nature had invented then
When she observ'd that every sort of men
Did in their voyage in this world's Sea stray,
And needed a new compass for their way;
She that was best, and first original
Of all fair copies, and the general
Steward to Fate; she whose rich eyes, and breast
Gilt the West Indies, and perfum'd the East;
Whose having breath'd in this world, did bestow
Spice on those Isles, and bade them still smell so,
And that rich Indy which doth gold inter,
Is but as single money, coined from her:
She to whom this world must itself refer,
As Suburbs, or the Microcosm of her,
She, she is dead; she 's dead: when thou know'st this,
Thou know'st how lame a cripple this world is.
And learn'st thus much by our Anatomy,
That this world's general sickness doth not lie

In any humour, or one certain part;
But as thou sawest it rotten at the heart,
Thou seest a hectic fever hath got hold
Of the whole substance, not to be controlled,
And that thou hast but one way, not to admit
The world's infection, to be none of it.
For the world's subtlest immaterial parts
Feel this consuming wound, and age's darts.
For the world's beauty is decay'd or gone,   *Disformity*
Beauty, that's colour, and proportion.   *of parts.*
We think the heavens enjoy their Spherical,
Their round proportion embracing all.
But yet their various and perplexed course,
Observ'd in divers ages, doth enforce
Men to find out so many eccentric parts,
Such divers down-right lines, such overthwarts,
As disproportion that pure form: it tears
The Firmament in eight and forty shares,
And in these Constellations then arise
New stars, and old do vanish from our eyes:
As though heav'n suffered earthquakes, peace or
      war,
When new Towers rise, and old demolish'd are.
They have impal'd within a Zodiac
The free-born Sun, and keep twelve Signs awake
To watch his steps; the Goat and Crab control,
And fright him back, who else to either Pole
(Did not these Tropics fetter him) might run:
For his course is not round; nor can the Sun
Perfect a Circle, or maintain his way
One inch direct; but where he rose to-day
He comes no more, but with a cozening line,
Steals by that point, and so is Serpentine:
And seeming weary with his reeling thus,
He means to sleep, being now fall'n nearer us.
So, of the Stars, which boast that they do run
In Circle still, none ends where he begun.
All their proportion's lame, it sinks, it swells.
For of Meridians, and Parallels,

Man hath weav'd out a net, and this net thrown
Upon the Heavens, and now they are his own.
Loth to go up the hill, or labour thus
To go to heaven, we make heaven come to us.
We spur, we rein the stars, and in their race
They 're diversely content t' obey our pace.
But keeps the earth her round proportion still?
Doth not a Teneriffe, or higher Hill
Rise so high like a Rock, that one might think
The floating Moon would shipwreck there, and sink?
Seas are so deep, that Whales being struck to-day,
Perchance to-morrow, scarce at middle way
Of their wish'd journey's end, the bottom, die.
And men, to sound depths, so much line untie,
As one might justly think that there would rise
At end thereof, one of th' Antipodies:
If under all, a Vault infernal be,
(Which sure is spacious, except that we
Invent another torment, that there must
Millions into a strait hot room be thrust)
Then solidness, and roundness have no place.
Are these but warts, and pock-holes in the face
Of th' earth?   Think so: but yet confess, in this
The world's proportion disfigured is;
That those two legs whereon it doth rely, *Disorder*
Reward and punishment are bent awry. *in the*
And, Oh, it can no more be questioned, *world.*
That beauty's best, proportion, is dead,
Since even grief itself, which now alone
Is left us, is without proportion.
She by whose lines proportion should be
Examin'd, measure of all Symmetry,
Whom had that Ancient seen, who thought souls
      made
Of Harmony, he would at next have said
That Harmony was she, and thence infer,
That souls were but Resultances from her,
And did from her into our bodies go,
As to our eyes, the forms from objects flow:

She, who if those great Doctors truly said
That the Ark to man's proportions was made,
Had been a type for that, as that might be
A type of her in this, that contrary
Both Elements, and Passions liv'd at peace
In her, who caus'd all Civil war to cease.
She, after whom, what form soe'er we see,
Is discord, and rude incongruity;
She, she is dead, she 's dead; when thou know'st this.
Thou know'st how ugly a monster this world is:
And learn'st thus much by our Anatomy,
That here is nothing to enamour thee:
And that, not only faults in inward parts,
Corruptions in our brains, or in our hearts,
Poisoning the fountains, whence our actions spring
Endanger us: but that if everything
Be not done fitly and in proportion,
To satisfy wise, and good lookers-on,
(Since most men be such as most think they be)
They 're loathsome too, by this Deformity.
For good, and well, must in our actions meet;
Wicked is not much worse than indiscreet.
But beauty's other second Element,
Colour, and lustre now, is as near spent.
And had the world his just proportion,
Were it a ring still, yet the stone is gone.
As a compassionate Turquoise which doth tell
By looking pale, the wearer is not well,
As gold falls sick being stung with Mercury,
All the world's parts of such complexion be.
When nature was most busy, the first week,
Swaddling the new-born earth, God seem'd to like
That she should sport herself sometimes, and play,
To mingle, and vary colours every day:
And then, as though she could not make enow,
Himself His various Rainbow did allow.
Sight is the noblest sense of any one,
Yet sight hath only colour to feed on,
And colour is decay'd: summer's robe grows

Dusky, and like an oft-dyed garment shows.
Our blushing red, which used in cheeks to spread,
Is inward sunk, and only our souls are red.
Perchance the world might have recovered,
If she whom we lament had not been dead:
But she, in whom all white, and red, and blue
(Beauty's ingredients) voluntary grew,
As in an unvext Paradise; from whom
Did all things verdure, and their lustre come,
Whose composition was miraculous,
Being all colour, all Diaphanous,
(For Air, and Fire but thick gross bodies were,
And liveliest stones but drowsy, and pale to her,)
She, she, is dead; she's dead: when thou know'st this,
Thou know'st how wan a Ghost this our world is:
And learn'st thus much by our Anatomy,
That it should more affright, than pleasure thee.
And that, since all fair colour then did sink,
'Tis now but wicked vanity, to think
To colour vicious deeds with good pretence,
Or with bought colours to illude men's sense.
Nor in aught more this world's decay appears
Than that her influence the heav'n forbears,
Or that the Elements do not feel this,
The father, or the mother barren is.
The clouds conceive not rain, or do not pour,
In the due birth-time, down the balmy shower;
Th' Air doth not motherly sit on the earth,
To hatch her seasons, and give all things birth;
Spring-times were common cradles, but are tombs;
And false-conceptions fill the general wombs;
Th' Air shows such Meteors, as none can see,
Not only what they mean, but what they be;
Earth such new worms, as would have troubled much
Th' Ægyptian *Mages* to have made more such.
What Artist now dares boast that he can bring
Heaven hither, or constellate anything,
So as the influence of those stars may be
Imprison'd in an Herb, or Charm, or Tree,

Weakness in the want of corre- spond- ence of heaven and earth

And do by touch, all which those stars could do?
The art is lost, and correspondence too.
For heaven gives little, and the earth takes less,
And man least knows their trade and purposes.
If this commerce 'twixt heaven and earth were not
Embarr'd, and all this traffic quite forgot,
She, for whose loss we have lamented thus,
Would work more fully, and pow'rfully on us:
Since herbs, and roots, by dying lose not all,
But they, yea Ashes too, are medicinal,
Death could not quench her virtue so, but that
It would be (if not follow'd) wonder'd at:
And all the world would be one dying Swan,
To sing her funeral praise, and vanish then.
But as some Serpents' poison hurteth not,
Except it be from the live Serpent shot,
So doth her virtue need her here, to fit
That unto us; she working more than it.
But she, in whom to such maturity
Virtue was grown, past growth, that it must die;
She, from whose influence all Impressions came,
But, by Receivers' impotencies, lame,
Who, though she could not transubstantiate
All states to gold, yet gilded every state,
So that some Princes have some temperance;
Some Counsellors some purpose to advance
The common profit; and some people have
Some stay, no more than Kings should give, to crave;
Some women have some taciturnity,
Some nunneries some grains of chastity.
She that did thus much, and much more could do,
But that our age was Iron, and rusty too,
She, she is dead; she 's dead; when thou know'st this,
Thou know'st how dry a Cinder this world is.
And learn'st thus much by our Anatomy,
That 'tis in vain to dew, or mollify
It with thy tears, or sweat, or blood: nothing
Is worth our travail, grief, or perishing,
But those rich joys, which did possess her heart,

Of which she 's now partaker, and a part.
But as in cutting up a man that 's dead,   *Con-*
The body will not last out, to have read   *clusion.*
On every part, and therefore men direct
Their speech to parts, that are of most effect;
So the world's carcase would not last, if I
Were punctual in this Anatomy;
Nor smells it well to hearers, if one tell
Them their disease, who fain would think they 're
    well.
Here therefore be the end: and, blessed maid,
Of whom is meant whatever hath been said,
Or shall be spoken well by any tongue,
Whose name refines coarse lines, and makes prose
    song,
Accept this tribute, and his first year's rent,
Who till his dark short taper's end be spent,
As oft as thy feast sees this widowed earth,
Will yearly celebrate thy second birth,
That is, thy death; for though the soul of man
Be got when man is made, 'tis born but then
When man doth die; our body 's as the womb,
And, as a Mid-wife, death directs it home.
And you her creatures, whom she works upon,
And have your last, and best concoction
From her example, and her virtue, if you
In reverence to her, do think it due,
That no one should her praises thus rehearse,
As matter fit for Chronicle, not verse;
Vouchsafe to call to mind that God did make
A last, and lasting'st piece, a song.   He spake
To *Moses* to deliver unto all,
That song, because He knew they would let fall
The Law, the Prophets, and the History,
But keep the song still in their memory:
Such an opinion (in due measure) made
Me this great Office boldly to invade:
Nor could incomprehensibleness deter
Me, from thus trying to emprison her,

Which when I saw that a strict grave could do,
I saw not why verse might not do so too.
Verse hath a middle nature: heaven keeps Souls,
The Grave keeps bodies, Verse the Fame enrols.

A FUNERAL ELEGY

'TIS lost, to trust a Tomb with such a guest,
Or to confine her in a marble chest.
Alas, what 's Marble, Jet, or Porphyry,
Priz'd with the Chrysolite of either eye,
Or with those Pearls, and Rubies, which she was?
Join the two Indies in one Tomb, 'tis glass;
And so is all to her materials,
Though every inch were ten Escurials,
Yet she 's demolish'd: can we keep her then
In works of hands, or of the wits of men?
Can these memorials, rags of paper, give
Life to that name, by which name they must live?
Sickly, alas, short-liv'd, aborted be
Those carcase verses, whose soul is not she.
And can she, who no longer would be she,
Being such a Tabernacle, stoop to be
In paper wrapt; or, when she would not lie
In such a house, dwell in an Elegy?
But 'tis no matter; we may well allow
Verse to live so long as the world will now,
For her death wounded it.   The world contains
Princes for arms, and Counsellors for brains,
Lawyers for tongues, Divines for hearts, and more,
The Rich for stomachs, and for backs, the Poor;
The Officers for hands, Merchants for feet,
By which, remote and distant Countries meet.
But those fine spirits which do tune, and set
This organ, are those pieces which beget
Wonder and love; and these were she; and she
Being spent, the world must needs decrepit be;

For since death will proceed to triumph still,
He can find nothing, after her, to kill,
Except the world itself, so great as she.
Thus brave and confident may Nature be,
Death cannot give her such another blow,
Because she cannot such another show.
But must we say she's dead? may't not be said
That as a sunder'd clock is piecemeal laid,
Not to be lost, but by the maker's hand
Repolish'd, without error then to stand,
Or as the Afric Niger stream enwombs
Itself into the earth, and after comes
(Having first made a natural bridge, to pass
For many leagues) far greater than it was,
May't not be said, that her grave shall restore
Her, greater, purer, firmer, than before?
Heaven may say this, and joy in 't, but can we
Who live, and lack her, here this vantage see?
What is 't to us, alas, if there have been
An Angel made a Throne, or Cherubin?
We lose by 't: and as aged men are glad
Being tasteless grown, to joy in joys they had,
So now the sick starv'd world must feed upon
This joy, that we had her, who now is gone.
Rejoice then Nature, and this World, that you,
Fearing the last fires hast'ning to subdue
Your force and vigour, ere it were near gone,
Wisely bestow'd and laid it all on one.
One, whose clear body was so pure and thin,
Because it need disguise no thought within.
'Twas but a through-light scarf, her mind to enrol;
Or exhalation breath'd out from her Soul.
One, whom all men who durst no more, admir'd:
And whom, whoe'er had worth enough, desir'd;
As when a Temple 's built, Saints emulate
To which of them, it shall be consecrate.
But, as when heaven looks on us with new eyes,
Those new stars every Artist exercise,
What place they should assign to them they doubt,

Argue, and agree not, till those stars go out:
So the world studied whose this piece should be,
Till she can be nobody's else, nor she:
But like a Lamp of Balsamum, desir'd
Rather to adorn, than last, she soon expir'd,
Cloth'd in her virgin white integrity,
For marriage, though it do not stain, doth dye.
To 'scape th' infirmities which wait upon
Woman, she went away, before she was one;
And the world's busy noise to overcome,
Took so much death, as serv'd for *opium*;
For though she could not, nor could choose to die,
She hath yielded to too long an ecstasy:
He which not knowing her said History,
Should come to read the book of destiny,
How fair, and chaste, humble, and high she had been,
Much promis'd, much perform'd, at not fifteen,
And measuring future things, by things before,
Should turn the leaf to read, and read no more,
Would think that either destiny mistook,
Or that some leaves were torn out of the book.
But 'tis not so; Fate did but usher her
To years of reason's use, and then infer
Her destiny to herself, which liberty
She took but for thus much, thus much to die.
Her modesty not suffering her to be
Fellow-Commissioner with Destiny,
She did no more but die; if after her
Any shall live, which dare true good prefer,
Every such person is her delegate,
T' accomplish that which should have been her Fate.
They shall make up that Book and shall have thanks
Of Fate, and her, for filling up their blanks.
For future virtuous deeds are Legacies,
Which from the gift of her example rise;
And 'tis in heav'n part of spiritual mirth,
To see how well the good play her, on earth.

THE PROGRESS OF THE SOUL

WHEREIN,

BY OCCASION OF THE RELIGIOUS DEATH OF

MISTRESS ELIZABETH DRURY, THE INCOMMODITIES OF THE SOUL IN THIS LIFE, AND HER EXALTATION IN THE NEXT, ARE CONTEMPLATED

THE SECOND ANNIVERSARY

THE HARBINGER TO THE PROGRESS

Two Souls move here, and mine (a third) must move
Paces of admiration and of love;
Thy Soul (dear virgin) whose this tribute is,
Mov'd from this mortal Sphere to lively bliss;
And yet moves still, and still aspires to see
The world's last day, thy glory's full degree:
Like as those stars which thou o'erlookest far,
Are in their place, and yet still moved are:
No soul (whiles with the luggage of this clay
It clogged is) can follow thee half way;
Or see thy flight, which doth our thoughts outgo
So fast, that now the lightning moves but slow:
But now thou art as high in heaven flown
As heaven's from us; what soul besides thine own
Can tell thy joys, or say he can relate
Thy glorious Journals in that blessed state?
I envy thee (rich soul) I envy thee,
Although I cannot yet thy glory see:
And thou (great spirit) which hers follow'd hast
So fast, as none can follow thine so fast;
So far, as none can follow thine so far,
(And if this flesh did not the passage bar

Hadst caught her) let me wonder at thy flight
Which long agone hadst lost the vulgar sight,
And now mak'st proud the better eyes, that they
Can see thee lessened in thine aery way;
So while thou mak'st her soul by progress known
Thou mak'st a noble progress of thine own,
From this world's carcase having mounted high
To that pure life of immortality.
Since thine aspiring thoughts themselves so raise
That more may not beseem a creature's praise,
Yet still thou vow'st her more; and every year
Mak'st a new progress, while thou wand'rest here;
Still upward mount; and let thy Maker's praise
Honour thy Laura, and adorn thy lays.
And since thy Muse her head in heaven shrouds,
Oh let her never stoop below the clouds:
And if those glorious sainted souls may know
Or what we do, or what we sing below,
Those acts, those songs, shall still content them best
Which praise those awful Powers that make them blest.

OF THE PROGRESS OF THE SOUL

THE SECOND ANNIVERSARY

NOTHING could make me sooner to confess
That this world had an everlastingness,
Than to consider, that a year is run,
Since both this lower world's, and the Sun's Sun,
The Lustre, and the vigour of this All,
Did set; 'twere blasphemy to say, did fall,
But as a ship which hath struck sail, doth run
By force of that force which before, it won:
Or as sometimes in a beheaded man,
Though at those two Red seas, which freely ran,
One from the Trunk, another from the Head,
His soul be sail'd, to her eternal bed,

*The
entrance.*

His eyes will twinkle, and his tongue will roll,
As though he beckoned, and called back his soul,
He grasps his hands, and he pulls up his feet,
And seems to reach, and to step forth to meet
His soul; when all these motions which we saw,
Are but as Ice, which crackles at a thaw:
Or as a Lute, which in moist weather, rings
Her knell alone, by cracking of her strings:
So struggles this dead world, now she is gone;
For there is motion in corruption.
As some days are at the Creation nam'd,
Before the Sun, the which fram'd days, was fram'd,
So after this Sun 's set, some show appears,
And orderly vicissitude of years.
Yet a new Deluge, and of *Lethe* flood,
Hath drown'd us all, all have forgot all good,
Forgetting her, the main reserve of all.
Yet in this deluge, gross and general,
Thou seest me strive for life; my life shall be,
To be hereafter prais'd, for praising thee;
Immortal Maid, who though thou would'st refuse
The name of Mother, be unto my Muse
A Father, since her chaste Ambition is,.
Yearly to bring forth such a child as this.
These Hymns may work on future wits, and so
May great-grand-children of thy praises grow.
And so, though not revive, embalm and spice
The world, which else would putrefy with vice.
For thus, Man may extend thy progeny,
Until man do but vanish, and not die.
These Hymns thy issue, may increase so long,
As till God's great *Venite* change the song.
Thirst for that time, O my insatiate soul,
And serve thy thirst, with God's safe-sealing Bowl   *A just*
Be thirsty still, and drink still till thou go   *disesti*
To th' only Health, to be hydroptic so.   *mation*
Forget this rotten world; and unto thee   *of the*
Let thine own times as an old story be.   *world.*
Be not concern'd: study not why, nor when;

Do not so much as not believe a man.
For though to err, be worst, to try truths forth,
Is far more business than this world is worth.
The world is but a carcase; thou art fed
By it, but as a worm, that carcase bred;
And why should'st thou, poor worm, consider more,
When this world will grow better than before,
Than those thy fellow worms do think upon
That carcase's last resurrection.
Forget this world, and scarce think of it so,
As of old clothes, cast off a year ago.
To be thus stupid is Alacrity;
Men thus lethargic have best Memory.
Look upward; that 's towards her, whose happy state
We now lament not, but congratulate.
She, to whom all this world was but a stage,
Where all sat heark'ning how her youthful age
Should be employ'd, because in all she did,
Some Figure of the Golden times was hid.
Who could not lack, whate'er this world could give,
Because she was the form, that made it live;
Nor could complain, that this world was unfit
To be stay'd in, then when she was in it;
She that first tried indifferent desires
By virtue, and virtue by religious fires,
She to whose person Paradise adher'd,
As Courts to Princes, she whose eyes enspher'd
Star-light enough, to have made the South control,
(Had she been there) the Star-full Northern Pole,
She, she is gone; she is gone; when thou knowest this,
What fragmentary rubbish this world is
Thou knowest, and that it is not worth a thought;
He honours it too much that thinks it naught.
Think then, my soul, that death is but a Groom,   *Contem-*
Which brings a Taper to the outward room,   *plation of*
Whence thou spiest first a little glimmering light, *our state*
And after brings it nearer to thy sight: *in our*
For such approaches doth heaven make in death.   *death-*
Think thyself labouring now with broken breath,   *bed.*

And think those broken and soft Notes to be
Division, and thy happiest Harmony.
Think thee laid on thy death-bed, loose and slack;
And think that, but unbinding of a pack,
To take one precious thing, thy soul from thence.
Think thyself parch'd with fever's violence,
Anger thine ague more, by calling it
Thy Physic; chide the slackness of the fit.
Think that thou hear'st thy knell, and think no more,
But that, as Bells called thee to Church before,
So this, to the Triumphant Church, calls thee.
Think Satan's Sergeants round about thee be,
And think that but for Legacies they thrust;
Give one thy Pride, to another give thy Lust:
Give them those sins which they gave thee before,
And trust th' immaculate blood to wash thy score.
Think thy friends weeping round, and think that they
Weep but because they go not yet thy way.
Think that they close thine eyes, and think in this,
That they confess much in the world, amiss,
Who dare not trust a dead man's eye with that,
Which they from God, and Angels cover not.
Think that they shroud thee up, and think from thence
They re-invest thee in white innocence.
Think that thy body rots, and (if so low,
Thy soul exalted so, thy thoughts can go),
Think thee a Prince, who of themselves create
Worms which insensibly devour their State.
Think that they bury thee, and think that rite
Lays thee to sleep but a Saint Lucy's night.
Think these things cheerfully: and if thou be
Drowsy or slack, remember then that she,
She whose Complexion was so even made,
That which of her Ingredients should invade
The other three, no Fear, no Art could guess:
So far were all remov'd from more or less.
But as in Mithridate, or just perfumes,
Where all good things being met, no one presumes
To govern, or to triumph on the rest,

Only because all were, no part was best.
And as, though all do know, that quantities
Are made of lines, and lines from Points arise,
None can these lines or quantities unjoint,
And say this is a line, or this a point,
So though the Elements and Humours were
In her, one could not say, this governs there.
Whose even constitution might have won
Any disease to venture on the Sun,
Rather than her: and make a spirit fear,
That he to disuniting subject were.
To whose proportions if we would compare
Cubes, they 're unstable; Circles, Angular;
She who was such a chain as Fate employs
To bring mankind all Fortunes it enjoys;
So fast, so even wrought, as one would think,
No Accident could threaten any link;
She, she embrac'd a sickness, gave it meat,
The purest blood, and breath, that e'er it eat;
And hath taught us, that though a good man hath
Title to heaven, and plead it by his Faith,
And though he may pretend a conquest, since
Heaven was content to suffer violence,
Yea though he plead a long possession too,
(For they 're in heaven on earth who heaven's works do)
Though he had right and power and place, before,
Yet Death must usher, and unlock the door.
Think further on thy self, my Soul, and think   *Incom-*
How thou at first was made but in a sink;   *modities*
Think that it argued some infirmity,   *of the*
That those two souls, which then thou found'st in me, *Soul in*
Thou fed'st upon, and drew'st into thee, both   *the Body.*
My second soul of sense, and first of growth.
Think but how poor thou wast, how obnoxious;
Whom a small lump of flesh could poison thus.
This curded milk, this poor unlittered whelp
My body, could, beyond escape or help,
Infect thee with Original sin, and thou
Couldst neither then refuse, nor leave it now.

Think that no stubborn sullen Anchorite,
Which fixt to a pillar, or a grave, doth sit
Bedded, and bath'd in all his ordures, dwells
So foully as our Souls in their first-built Cells.
Think in how poor a prison thou didst lie
After, enabled but to suck and cry.
Think, when 'twas grown to most, 'twas a poor Inn,
A Province pack'd up in two yards of skin,
And that usurp'd or threatened with the rage
Of sicknesses, or their true mother, Age.
But think that Death hath now enfranchis'd thee,
Thou hast thy expansion now, and liberty;
Think that a rusty Piece, discharg'd, is flown   *Her lib-*
In pieces, and the bullet is his own,   *erty by*
And freely flies: this to thy Soul allow,   *death.*
Think thy shell broke, think thy Soul hatch'd but now.
And think this slow-pac'd soul, which late did cleave
To a body, and went but by the body's leave,
Twenty, perchance, or thirty mile a day,
Dispatches in a minute all the way
'Twixt heaven, and earth; she stays not in the air,
To look what Meteors there themselves prepare;
She carries no desire to know, nor sense,
Whether th' air's middle region be intense;
For th' Element of fire, she doth not know,
Whether she passed by such a place or no;
She baits not at the Moon, nor cares to try
Whether in that new world, men live, and die.
Venus retards her not, to enquire, how she
Can, (being one star) *Hesper*, and *Vesper* be;
He that charm'd *Argus*' eyes, sweet *Mercury*,
Works not on her, who now is grown all eye;
Who, if she meet the body of the Sun,
Goes through, not staying till his course be run;
Who finds in *Mars* his Camp no corps of Guard;
Nor is by *Jove*, nor by his father barr'd;
But ere she can consider how she went,
At once is at, and through the Firmament.
And as these stars were but so many beads

Strung on one string, speed undistinguish'd leads
Her through those Spheres, as through the beads, a string,
Whose quick succession makes it still one thing:
As doth the pith, which, lest our bodies slack,
Strings fast the little bones of neck, and back;
So by the Soul doth death string Heaven and Earth;
For when our Soul enjoys this her third birth,
(Creation gave her one, a second, grace),
Heaven is as near, and present to her face,
As colours are, and objects, in a room
Where darkness was before, when Tapers come.
This must, my Soul, thy long-short Progress be;
To advance these thoughts, remember then, that she,
She, whose fair body no such prison was,
But that a Soul might well be pleas'd to pass
An age in her; she whose rich beauty lent
Mintage to other beauties, for they went
But for so much as they were like to her;
She, in whose body (if we dare prefer
This low world, to so high a mark as she),
The Western treasure, Eastern spicery,
Europe, and Afric, and the unknown rest
Were easily found, or what in them was best;
And when we have made this large discovery
Of all, in her some one part then will be
Twenty such parts, whose plenty and riches is
Enough to make twenty such worlds as this;
She, whom had they known who did first betroth
The Tutelar Angels, and assign'd one, both
To Nations, Cities, and to Companies,
To Functions, Offices, and Dignities,
And to each several man, to him, and him,
They would have given her one for every limb;
She, of whose soul, if we may say, 'twas Gold,
Her body was th' Electrum, and did hold
Many degrees of that; we understood
Her by her sight; her pure, and eloquent blood
Spoke in her cheeks, and so distinctly wrought,
That one might almost say, her body thought;

She, she, thus richly and largely hous'd, is gone:
And chides us slow-pac'd snails who crawl upon
Our prison's prison, earth, nor think us well,
Longer, than whilst we bear our brittle shell.
But 'twere but little to have chang'd our room, *Her ig-*
If, as we were in this our living Tomb *norance*
Oppress'd with ignorance, we still were so. *in this*
Poor soul, in this thy flesh what dost thou know? *life and*
Thou know'st thyself so little, as thou know'st not, *know-*
How thou didst die, nor how thou wast begot. *ledge in*
Thou neither know'st, how thou at first cam'st in, *the next.*
Nor how thou took'st the poison of man's sin.
Nor dost thou, (though thou know'st, that thou art so)
By what way thou art made immortal, know.
Thou art too narrow, wretch, to comprehend
Even thyself: yea though thou wouldst but bend
To know thy body. Have not all souls thought
For many ages, that our body is wrought
Of Air, and Fire, and other Elements?
And now they think of new ingredients,
And one Soul thinks one, and another way
Another thinks, and 'tis an even lay.
Know'st thou but how the stone doth enter in
The bladder's cave, and never break the skin?
Know'st thou how blood, which to the heart doth flow,
Doth from one ventricle to th' other go?
And for the putrid stuff, which thou dost spit,
Know'st thou how thy lungs have attracted it?
There are no passages, so that there is
(For aught thou know'st) piercing of substances.
And of those many opinions which men raise
Of Nails and Hairs, dost thou know which to praise?
What hope have we to know our selves, when we
Know not the least things, which for our use be?
We see in Authors, too stiff to recant,
A hundred controversies of an Ant;
And yet one watches, starves, freezes, and sweats,
To know but Catechisms and Alphabets
Of unconcerning things, matters of fact;

How others on our stage their parts did Act;
What *Cæsar* did, yea, and what *Cicero* said.
Why grass is green, or why our blood is red,
Are mysteries which none have reach'd unto.
In this low form, poor soul, what wilt thou do?
When wilt thou shake off this Pedantry,
Of being taught by sense, and Fantasy?
Thou look'st through spectacles; small things seem great
Below; but up unto the watch-tower get,
And see all things despoiled of fallacies:
Thou shalt not peep through lattices of eyes,
Nor hear through Labyrinths of ears, nor learn
By circuit, or collections to discern.
In heaven thou straight know'st all, concerning it,
And what concerns it not, shalt straight forget.
There thou (but in no other school) may'st be
Perchance, as learned, and as full, as she,
She who all libraries had throughly read
At home in her own thoughts, and practisèd
So much good as would make as many more:
She whose example they must all implore,
Who would or do, or think well, and confess
That all the virtuous Actions they express,
Are but a new, and worse edition
Of her some one thought, or one action:
She who in th' art of knowing Heaven, was grown
Here upon earth, to such perfection,
That she hath, ever since to Heaven she came,
(In a far fairer print), but read the same:
She, she not satisfied with all this weight,
(For so much knowledge, as would over-freight
Another, did but ballast her) is gone
As well t' enjoy, as get perfection.
And calls us after her, in that she took,
(Taking herself) our best, and worthiest book.
Return not, my Soul, from this ecstasy,
And meditation of what thou shalt be,
To earthly thoughts, till it to thee appear,
With whom thy conversation must be there.

Of our company in this life, and in the next.

With whom wilt thou converse? what station
Canst thou choose out, free from infection,
That will not give thee theirs, nor drink in thine?
Shalt thou not find a spongy slack Divine
Drink and suck in th' instructions of Great men,
And for the word of God, vent them again?
Are there not some Courts (and then, no things be
So like as Courts) which, in this let us see,
That wits and tongues of Libellers are weak,
Because they do more ill, than these can speak?
The poison 's gone through all, poisons affect
Chiefly the chiefest parts, but some effect
In nails, and hairs, yea excrements, will show;
So lies the poison of sin in the most low.
Up, up, my drowsy Soul, where thy new ear
Shall in the Angels' songs no discord hear;
Where thou shalt see the blessed Mother-maid
Joy in not being that, which men have said.
Where she is exalted more for being good,
Than for her interest of Mother-hood.
Up to those Patriarchs, which did longer sit
Expecting Christ, than they have enjoy'd Him yet.
Up to those Prophets, which now gladly see
Their Prophecies grown to be History.
Up to th' Apostles, who did bravely run
All the Sun's course, with more light than the Sun.
Up to those Martyrs, who did calmly bleed
Oil to th' Apostles' Lamps, dew to their seed.
Up to those Virgins, who thought, that almost
They made joint-tenants with the Holy Ghost,
If they to any should his Temple give.
Up, up, for in that squadron there doth live
She, who hath carried thither new degrees
(As to their number) to their dignities.
She, who being to herself a State, enjoy'd
All royalties which any State employ'd;
For she made wars, and triumph'd; reason still
Did not o'erthrow, but rectify her will:
And she made peace, for no peace is like this,

That beauty, and chastity together kiss:
She did high justice, for she crucified
Every first motion of rebellious pride:
And she gave pardons, and was liberal,
For, only herself except, she pardon'd all:
She coin'd, in this, that her impressions gave
To all our actions all the worth they have:
She gave protections; the thoughts of her breast
Satan's rude Officers could ne'er arrest.
As these prerogatives being met in one,
Made her a sovereign State; religion
Made her a Church; and these two made her all.
She who was all this All, and could not fall
To worse, by company, (for she was still
More Antidote, than all the world was ill,)
She, she doth leave it, and by Death, survive
All this, in Heaven; whither who doth not strive
The more, because she 's there, he doth not know
That accidental joys in Heaven do grow.
But pause, my soul; and study, ere thou fall
On accidental joys, th' essential.
Still before Accessories do abide
A trial, must the principal be tried.
And what essential joy canst thou expect
Here upon earth? what permanent effect
Of transitory causes? Dost thou love
Beauty? (And beauty worthiest is to move)
Poor cozened cozener, *that* she, and *that* thou,
Which did begin to love, are neither now;
You are both fluid, chang'd since yesterday;
Next day repairs, (but ill) last day's decay.
Nor are, (although the river keep the name)
Yesterday's waters, and to-day's the same.
So flows her face, and thine eyes, neither now
That Saint, nor Pilgrim, which your loving vow
Concern'd, remains; but whilst you think you be
Constant, you 're hourly in inconstancy.
Honour may have pretence unto our love,
Because that God did live so long above

Of essen-
tial joy in
this life
and in
the next.

Without this Honour, and then lov'd it so,
That He at last made Creatures to bestow
Honour on Him; not that He needed it,
But that, to His hands, man might grow more fit.
But since all Honours from inferiors flow,
(For they do give it; Princes do but show
Whom they would have so honour'd) and that this
On such opinions, and capacities
Is built, as rise and fall, to more and less:
Alas, 'tis but a casual happiness.
Hath ever any man to himself assign'd
This or that happiness to arrest his mind,
But that another man which takes a worse,
Thinks him a fool for having ta'en that course?
They who did labour Babel's tower to erect,
Might have considered, that for that effect,
All this whole solid Earth could not allow
Nor furnish forth materials enow;
And that this Centre, to raise such a place,
Was far too little, to have been the Base;
No more affords this world, foundation
To erect true joy, were all the means in one.
But as the Heathen made them several gods,
Of all God's Benefits, and all his Rods,
(For as the Wine, and Corn, and Onions are
Gods unto them, so Agues be, and War)
And as by changing that whole precious Gold
To such small Copper coins, they lost the old,
And lost their only God, who ever must
Be sought alone, and not in such a thrust:
So much mankind true happiness mistakes;
No Joy enjoys that man, that many makes.
Then, Soul, to thy first pitch work up again;
Know that all lines which circles do contain,
For once that they the Centre touch, do touch
Twice the circumference; and be thou such;
Double on heaven thy thoughts on earth employ'd;
All will not serve; only who have enjoy'd
The sight of God, in fulness, can think it;

For it is both the object, and the wit.
This is essential joy, where neither He
Can suffer diminution, nor we;
'Tis such a full, and such a filling good;
Had th' Angels once look'd on Him, they had stood.
To fill the place of one of them, or more,
She whom we celebrate, is gone before.
She, who had Here so much essential joy,
As no chance could distract, much less destroy;
Who with God's presence was acquainted so,
(Hearing, and speaking to Him) as to know
His face in any natural Stone, or Tree,
Better than when in Images they be:
Who kept by diligent devotion,
God's Image, in such reparation,
Within her heart, that what decay was grown,
Was her first Parents' fault, and not her own:
Who being solicited to any act,
Still heard God pleading His safe precontract;
Who by a faithful confidence, was here
Betroth'd to God, and now is married there;
Whose twilights were more clear, than our mid-day;
Who dreamt devoutlier, than most use to pray;
Who being here fill'd with grace, yet strove to be,
Both where more grace, and more capacity
At once is given: she to Heaven is gone,
Who made this world in some proportion
A heaven, and here, became unto us all,
Joy, (as our joys admit) essential.
But could this low world joys essential touch,   *Of acci-*
Heaven's accidental joys would pass them much.   *dental*
How poor and lame, must then our casual be?   *joys in*
If thy Prince will his subjects to call thee   *both*
My Lord, and this do swell thee, thou art then,   *places.*
By being greater, grown to be less Man.
When no Physician of redress can speak,
A joyful casual violence may break
A dangerous Aposteme in thy breast;
And whilst thou joyest in this, the dangerous rest,

The bag may rise up, and so strangle thee.
Whate'er was casual, may ever be.
What should the nature change? Or make the same
Certain, which was but casual, when it came?
All casual joy doth loud and plainly say,
Only by coming, that it can away.
Only in Heaven joy's strength is never spent;
And accidental things are permanent.
Joy of a soul's arrival ne'er decays;
For that soul ever joys and ever stays.
Joy that their last great Consummation
Approaches in the resurrection;
When earthly bodies more celestial
Shall be, than Angels were, for they could fall;
This kind of joy doth every day admit
Degrees of growth, but none of losing it.
In this fresh joy, 'tis no small part, that she,
She, in whose goodness, he that names degree,
Doth injure her; ('tis loss to be call'd best,
There where the stuff is not such as the rest)
She, who left such a body, as even she
Only in Heaven could learn, how it can be
Made better; for she rather was two souls,
Or like to full on both sides written Rolls,
Where eyes might read upon the outward skin,
As strong Records for God, as minds within;
She, who by making full perfection grow,
Pieces a Circle, and still keeps it so,
Long'd for, and longing for it, to heaven is gone,
Where she receives, and gives addition.
Here in a place, where mis-devotion frames   *Con-*
A thousand Prayers to Saints, whose very names   *clusion.*
The ancient Church knew not, Heaven knows not yet:
And where, what laws of Poetry admit,
Laws of Religion have at least the same,
Immortal Maid, I might invoke thy name.
Could any Saint provoke that appetite,
Thou here should'st make me a French convertite.
But thou would'st not; nor would'st thou be content,

To take this, for my second year's true Rent,
Did this Coin bear any other stamp, than His,
That gave thee power to do, me, to say this.
Since His will is, that to posterity,
Thou should'st for life, and death, a pattern be,
And that the world should notice have of this,
The purpose, and th' authority is His;
Thou art the Proclamation; and I am
The Trumpet, at whose voice the people came.

EPICEDES AND OBSEQUIES

UPON THE DEATHS OF SUNDRY PERSONAGES

ELEGY ON THE UNTIMELY DEATH

OF THE

INCOMPARABLE PRINCE HENRY

LOOK to me, Faith; and look to my Faith, God:
For, both my centres feel this period.
Of weight, one centre; one of greatness is:
And Reason is that centre; Faith is this.
For into our Reason flow, and there do end,
All that this natural world doth comprehend;
Quotidian things, and equi-distant hence,
Shut-in for man in one circumference:
But, for th' enormous greatnesses, which are
So disproportion'd and so angular
As in God's essence, place, and providence,
Where, how, when, what, souls do, departed hence:
These things (eccentric else) on Faith do strike;
Yet neither all, nor upon all alike:
For, Reason, put to her best extension,
Almost meets Faith, and makes both centres one:
And nothing ever came so near to this,
As contemplation of that Prince, we miss.
For, all that Faith might credit mankind could,
Reason still seconded that this Prince would.
If then, least movings of the centre make
(More than if whole hell belched) the world to shake,
What must this do, centres distracted so,
That we see not what to believe or know?
Was it not well believ'd, till now, that he,
Whose reputation was an ecstasy
On neighbour States; which knew not why to wake

208

Till he discovered what ways he would take:
For whom what Princes angled (when they tried)
Met a Torpedo, and were stupefied:
And others' studies, how he would be bent;
Was his great father's greatest instrument,
And activest spirit to convey and tie
This soul of peace through Christianity?
Was it not well believ'd, that he would make
This general peace th'eternal overtake?
And that his times might have stretched out so far
As to touch those of which they emblems are?
For, to confirm this just belief, that now
The last days came, we saw Heaven did allow
That but from his aspect and exercise,
In peaceful times, Rumours of wars did rise.
But now this faith is heresy: we must
Still stay, and vex our great-grand-mother, Dust.
Oh, is God prodigal?   Hath He spent His store
Of plagues on us? and only now, when more
Would ease us much, doth He grudge misery,
And will not let 's enjoy our curse, to die?
As, for the Earth thrown lowest down of all,
'Twere an ambition to desire to fall:
So God, in our desire to die, doth know
Our plot for ease, in being wretched so.
Therefore we live: though such a life we have
As but so many mandrakes on his grave.

    What had his growth and generation done?
When what we are, his putrefaction
Sustains in us; Earth, which griefs animate?
Nor hath our world now other soul than That.
And could grief get so high as Heav'n, that Quire
Forgetting this, their new joy, would desire
(With grief to see him) he had stay'd below,
To rectify our errors they foreknow.

    Is th' other centre, Reason, faster, then?
Where should we look for that, now we 're not men?
For, if our Reason be our connexion
Of causes, now to us there can be none.

For, as, if all the substances were spent,
'Twere madness to enquire of accident:
So is 't to look for Reason, he being gone,
The only subject Reason wrought upon.
    If Fate have such a chain, whose divers links,
Industrious man discerneth, as he thinks,
When miracle doth join, and so steal-in
A new link, man knows not where to begin:
At a much deader fault must Reason be,
Death having broke-off such a link as he.
But, now, for us with busy proof to come
That we 've no Reason, would prove we had some:
So would just lamentations.   Therefore we
May safelier say, that we are dead, than he
So, if our griefs we do not well declare,
We 've double excuse; he is not dead, we are.
Yet would not I die yet; for though I be
Too narrow, to think him, as he is he
(Our Soul's best baiting and mid-period
In her long journey of considering God)
Yet (no dishonour) I can reach him thus;
As he embraced the fires of love with us.
Oh may I (since I live) but see or hear
That she-Intelligence which mov'd this sphere,
I pardon Fate, my life.   Whoe'er thou be
Which hast the noble conscience, thou art she.
I conjure thee by all the charms he spoke,
By th' oaths which only you two never broke,
By all the souls ye sigh'd; that if you see
These lines, you wish I knew your history:
So, much as you two mutual heavens were here,
I were an Angel singing what you were.

TO THE COUNTESS OF BEDFORD

MADAM,
    *I have learn'd by those laws wherein I am a little conversant,
that he which bestows any cost upon the dead, obliges him which
is dead, but not the heir; I do not therefore send this paper to*

*your Ladyship, that you should thank me for it, or think that
I thank you in it; your favours and benefits to me are so much
above my merits, that they are even above my gratitude, if that
were to be judged by words which must express it : but, Madam,
since your noble brother's fortune being yours, the evidences also
concerning it are yours, so his virtue being yours, the evidences
concerning it, belong also to you, of which by your acceptance
this may be one piece, in which quality I humbly present it,
and as a testimony how entirely your family possesseth*

Your Ladyship's most humble
and thankful servant
JOHN DONNE.

OBSEQUIES TO THE LORD HARRINGTON

BROTHER TO THE LADY LUCY, COUNTESS OF BEDFORD

FAIR soul, which wast, not only, as all souls be,
Then when thou wast infusèd, harmony,
But didst continue so; and now dost bear
A part in God's great organ, this whole Sphere:
If looking up to God; or down to us,
Thou find that any way is pervious,
Twixt heav'n and earth, and that man's actions do
Come to your knowledge, and affections too,
See, and with joy, me to that good degree
Of goodness grown, that I can study thee,
And, by these meditations refin'd,
Can unapparel and enlarge my mind,
And so can make by this soft ecstasy,
This place a map of heav'n, myself of thee.
Thou seest me here at midnight, now all rest;
Time's dead-low water; when all minds divest
To-morrow's business, when the labourers have
Such rest in bed, that their last Church-yard grave,
Subject to change, will scarce be a type of this,
Now when the client, whose last hearing is
To-morrow, sleeps, when the condemned man,

(Who when he opens his eyes, must shut them then
Again by death), although sad watch he keep,
Doth practice dying by a little sleep,
Thou at this midnight seest me, and as soon
As that Sun rises to me, midnight's noon,
All the world grows transparent, and I see
Through all, both Church and State, in seeing thee;
And I discern by favour of this light,
Myself, the hardest object of the sight.
God is the glass; as thou when thou dost see
Him who sees all, seest all concerning thee,
So, yet unglorified, I comprehend
All, in these mirrors of thy ways, and end.
Though God be our true glass, through which we see
All, since the being of all things is He,
Yet are the trunks which do to us derive
Things, in proportion fit, by perspective,
Deeds of good men; for by their living here,
Virtues, indeed remote, seem to be near.
But where can I affirm, or where arrest
My thoughts on his deeds? which shall I call best?
For fluid virtue cannot be look'd on,
Nor can endure a contemplation.
As bodies change, and as I do not wear
Those Spirits, humours, blood I did last year,
And, as if on a stream I fix mine eye,
That drop, which I looked on, is presently
Pusht with more waters from my sight, and gone,
So in this sea of virtues, can no one
Be insisted on; virtues, as rivers, pass,
Yet still remains that virtuous man there was;
And as if man feed on man's flesh, and so
Part of his body to another owe,
Yet at the last two perfect bodies rise,
Because God knows where every Atom lies;
So, if one knowledge were made of all those,
Who knew his minutes well, he might dispose
His virtues into names, and ranks; but I
Should injure Nature, Virtue, and Destiny,

Should I divide and discontinue so,
Virtue, which did in one entireness grow.
For as, he that would say, spirits are fram'd
Of all the purest parts that can be nam'd,
Honours not spirits half so much, as he
Which says, they have no parts, but simple be;
So is 't of virtue; for a point and one
Are much entirer than a million.
And had Fate meant to have his virtues told,
It would have let him live to have been old;
So, then that virtue in season, and then this,
We might have seen, and said, that now he is
Witty, now wise, now temperate, now just;
In good short lives, virtues are fain to thrust,
And to be sure betimes to get a place,
When they would exercise, lack time, and space.
So was it in this person, forc'd to be
For lack of time, his own epitome:
So to exhibit in few years as much,
As all the long-breath'd Chronicles can touch.
As when an Angel down from heav'n doth fly,
Our quick thought cannot keep him company,
We cannot think, now he is at the Sun,
Now through the Moon, now he through th' air doth run,
Yet when he 's come, we know he did repair
To all 'twixt Heav'n and Earth, Sun, Moon, and Air;
And as this Angel in an instant knows,
And yet we know, this sudden knowledge grows
By quick amassing several forms of things,
Which he successively to order brings;
When they, whose slow-pac'd lame thoughts cannot go
So fast as he, think that he doth not so;
Just as a perfect reader doth not dwell,
On every syllable, nor stay to spell,
Yet without doubt, he doth distinctly see
And lay together every A, and B;
So, in short-lived good men, is not understood
Each several virtue, but the compound good;
For, they all virtue's paths in that pace tread,

As Angels go, and know, and as men read.
O why should then these men, these lumps of Balm
Sent hither, this world's tempests to becalm,
Before by deeds they are diffus'd and spread,
And so make us alive, themselves be dead?
O Soul, O circle, why so quickly be
Thy ends, thy birth and death, clos'd up in thee?
Since one foot of thy compass still was plac'd
In heav'n, the other might securely have pac'd
In the most large extent, through every path,
Which the whole world, or man the abridgment hath.
Thou know'st, that though the tropic circles have
(Yea and those small ones which the Poles engrave),
All the same roundness, evenness, and all
The endlessness of the equinoctial;
Yet, when we come to measure distances,
How here, how there, the Sun affected is,
When he doth faintly work, and when prevail,
Only great circles, then can be our scale:
So, though thy circle to thyself express
All, tending to thy endless happiness,
And we, by our good use of it may try,
Both how to live well young, and how to die,
Yet, since we must be old, and age endures
His Torrid Zone at Court, and calentures
Of hot ambitions, irreligion's ice,
Zeal's agues, and hydroptic avarice,
Infirmities which need the scale of truth,
As well as lust, and ignorance of youth;
Why didst thou not for these give medicines too,
And by thy doing tell us what to do?
Though as small pocket-clocks, whose every wheel
Doth each mismotion and distemper feel,
Whose hand gets shaking palsies, and whose string
(His sinews) slackens, and whose Soul, the spring,
Expires, or languishes, whose pulse, the fly,
Either beats not, or beats unevenly,
Whose voice, the Bell, doth rattle, or grow dumb,
Or idle, as men, which to their last hours come,

If these clocks be not wound, or be wound still,
Or be not set, or set at every will;
So, youth is easiest to destruction,
If then we follow all, or follow none.
Yet, as in great clocks, which in steeples chime,
Plac'd to inform whole towns, to employ their time,
An error doth more harm, being general,
When, small clocks' faults, only on the wearer fall;
So work the faults of age, on which the eye
Of children, servants, or the State rely.
Why wouldst not thou then, which hadst such a soul,
A clock so true, as might the Sun control,
And daily hadst from Him, who gave it thee,
Instructions, such as it could never be
Disordered, stay here, as a general
And great Sun-dial, to have set us All?
O why wouldst thou be any instrument
To this unnatural course, or why consent
To this, not miracle, but Prodigy
That when the ebbs, longer than flowings be,
Virtue, whose flood did with thy youth begin,
Should so much faster ebb out, than flow in?
Though her flood was blown in, by thy first breath,
All is at once sunk in the whirl-pool death.
Which word I would not name, but that I see
Death, else a desert, grown a Court by thee.
Now I grow sure, that if a man would have
Good company, his entry is a grave.
Methinks all Cities now, but Anthills be,
Where, when the several labourers I see,
For children, house, provision, taking pain,
They 're all but Ants, carrying eggs, straw, and grain;
And Church-yards are our cities, unto which
The most repair, that are in goodness rich.
There is the best concourse, and confluence,
There are the holy suburbs, and from thence
Begins God's City, New Jerusalem,
Which doth extend her utmost gates to them.
At that gate then Triumphant soul, dost thou

Begin thy Triumph; but since laws allow
That at the Triumph day, the people may,
All that they will, 'gainst the Triumpher say,
Let me here use that freedom, and express
My grief, though not to make thy Triumph less.
By law, to Triumphs none admitted be,
Till they as Magistrates get victory;
Though then to thy force, all youth's foes did yield,
Yet till fit time had brought thee to that field,
To which thy rank in this state destin'd thee,
That there thy counsels might get victory,
And so in that capacity remove
All jealousies 'twixt Prince and subject's love,
Thou couldst no title, to this triumph have,
Thou didst intrude on death, usurp'dst a grave.
Then (though victoriously) thou hadst fought as yet
But with thine own affections, with the heat
Of youth's desires, and colds of ignorance,
But till thou shouldst successfully advance
Thine arms 'gainst foreign enemies, which are
Both Envy, and acclamations popular,
(For, both these engines equally defeat,
Though by a divers Mine, those which are great,)
Till then thy War was but a civil War,
For which to triumph, none admitted are.
No more are they, who though with good success,
In a defensive war, their power express;
Before men triumph, the dominion
Must be enlarg'd and not preserv'd alone;
Why shouldst thou then, whose battles were to win
Thyself, from those straits nature put thee in,
And to deliver up to God that state,
Of which He gave thee the vicariate,
(Which is thy soul and body) as entire
As he, who takes endeavours, doth require,
But didst not stay, to enlarge His kingdom too,
By making others, what thou didst, to do;
Why shouldst thou Triumph now, when Heav'n no more
Hath got, by getting thee, than it had before?

For, Heav'n and thou, even when thou livedst here,
Of one another in possession were.
But this from Triumph most disables thee,
That, that place which is conquered, must be
Left safe from present war, and likely doubt
Of imminent commotions to break out:
And hath he left us so? or can it be
His territory was no more than He?
No, we were all his charge, the Diocese
Of ev'ry exemplar man, the whole world is,
And he was joined in commission
With Tutelar Angels, sent to every one.
But though his freedom to upbraid, and chide
Him who Triumph'd, were lawful, it was tied
With this, that it might never reference have
Unto the Senate, who this triumph gave;
Men might at Pompey jest, but they might not
At that authority, by which he got
Leave to Triumph, before, by age, he might;
So, though, triumphant soul, I dare to write,
Mov'd with a reverential anger, thus,
That thou so early wouldst abandon us;
Yet I am far from daring to dispute
With that great sovereignty, whose absolute
Prerogative hath thus dispens'd with thee,
'Gainst nature's laws, which just impugners be
Of early triumphs; and I (though with pain)
Lessen our loss, to magnify thy gain
Of triumph, when I say, It was more fit,
That all men should lack thee, than thou lack it.
Though then in our time, be not suffered
That testimony of love, unto the dead,
To die with them, and in their graves be hid,
As Saxon wives, and French *soldarii* did;
And though in no degree I can express
Grief in great Alexander's great excess,
Who at his friend's death, made whole towns divest
Their walls and bulwarks which became them best:
Do not, fair soul, this sacrifice refuse,

That in thy grave I do inter my Muse,
Who, by my grief, great as thy worth, being cast
Behind hand, yet hath spoke, and spoke her last.

ELEGY ON THE LADY MARKHAM

MAN is the World, and death th' Ocean,
  To which God gives the lower parts of man.
This Sea environs all, and though as yet
  God hath set marks, and bounds, 'twixt us and it,
Yet doth it roar, and gnaw, and still pretend,
  And breaks our banks, whene'er it takes a friend.
Then our land waters (tears of passion) vent;
  Our waters, then, above our firmament,
(Tears which our Soul doth for her sins let fall)
  Take all a brackish taste, and funeral,
And even these tears, which should wash sin, are sin.
We, after God's *No*, drown our world again.
Nothing but man of all envenom'd things
  Doth work upon itself, with inborn stings.
Tears are false Spectacles, we cannot see
  Through passion's mist, what we are, or what she.
In her this sea of death hath made no breach,
  But as the tide doth wash the slimy beach,
And leaves embroider'd works upon the sand,
  So is her flesh refin'd by death's cold hand.
As men of China, after an age's stay,
  Do take up Porcelain, where they buried Clay;
So at this grave, her limbeck, which refines
  The Diamonds, Rubies, Sapphires, Pearls, and Mines,
Of which this flesh was, her soul shall inspire
  Flesh of such stuff, as God, when His last fire
Annuls this world, to recompense it, shall,
  Make and name then, th' Elixir of this All.
They say, the sea, when it gains, loseth too;
  If carnal Death (the younger brother) do
Usurp the body, our soul, which subject is
  To th' elder death, by sin, is freed by this;

They perish both, when they attempt the just;
  For, graves our trophies are, and both deaths' dust.
So, unobnoxious now, she hath buried both;
  For, none to death sins, that to sin is loth,
Nor do they die, which are not loth to die;
  So hath she this, and that virginity.
Grace was in her extremely diligent,
  That kept her from sin, yet made her repent.
Of what small spots pure white complains!   Alas,
  How little poison cracks a crystal glass!
She sinn'd, but just enough to let us see
  That God's word must be true, All, sinners be.
So much did zeal her conscience rarefy,
  That, extreme truth lack'd little of a lie,
Making omissions, acts; laying the touch
  Of sin, on things that sometimes may be such.
As *Moses*' Cherubins, whose natures do
  Surpass all speed, by him are winged too:
So would her soul, already in heaven, seem then,
  To climb by tears, the common stairs of men.
How fit she was for God, I am content
  To speak, that Death his vain haste may repent.
How fit for us, how even and how sweet,
  How good in all her titles, and how meet,
To have reform'd this forward heresy,
  That women can no parts of friendship be;
How Moral, how Divine shall not be told,
  Lest they that hear her virtues, think her old:
And lest we take Death's part, and make him glad
  Of such a prey, and to his triumph add.

ELEGY ON MISTRESS BOULSTRED

DEATH I recant, and say, unsaid by me
  Whate'er hath slipp'd, that might diminish thee.
Spiritual treason, atheism 'tis, to say,
  That any can thy Summons disobey.
Th' earth's face is but thy Table; there are set
  Plants, cattle, men, dishes for Death to eat.

In a rude hunger now he millions draws
   Into his bloody, or plaguey, or starv'd jaws.
Now he will seem to spare, and doth more waste,
   Eating the best first, well preserv'd to last.
Now wantonly he spoils, and eats us not,
   But breaks off friends, and lets us piecemeal rot.
Nor will this earth serve him; he sinks the deep
   Where harmless fish monastic silence keep,
Who (were Death dead) by Roes of living sand,
   Might sponge that element, and make it land.
He rounds the air, and breaks the hymnic notes
   In birds (Heaven's choristers), organic throats,
Which (if they did not die) might seem to be
   A tenth rank in the heavenly hierarchy.
O strong and long-liv'd death, how cam'st thou in?
   And how without Creation didst begin?
Thou hast, and shalt see dead, before thou diest,
   All the four Monarchies, and Antichrist.
How could I think thee nothing, that see now
   In all this All, nothing else is, but thou.
Our births and lives, vices, and virtues, be
   Wasteful consumptions, and degrees of thee.
For, we to live, our bellows wear, and breath,
   Nor are we mortal, dying, dead, but death.
And though thou be'st, O mighty bird of prey,
   So much reclaim'd by God, that thou must lay
All that thou kill'st at His feet, yet doth He
   Reserve but few, and leaves the most to thee.
And of those few, now thou hast overthrown
   One whom thy blow makes, not ours, nor thine own.
She was more storeys high: hopeless to come
   To her Soul, thou hast offer'd at her lower room.
Her Soul and body was a King and Court:
   But thou hast both of Captain miss'd and fort.
As houses fall not, though the King remove,
   Bodies of Saints rest for their souls above.
Death gets 'twixt souls and bodies such a place
   As sin insinuates 'twixt just men and grace,
Both work a separation, no divorce.

Her Soul is gone to usher up her corse,
Which shall be almost another soul, for there
  Bodies are purer, than best Souls are here.
Because in her, her virtues did outgo
  Her years, wouldst thou, O emulous death, do so?
And kiil her young to thy loss? must the cost
  Of beauty, and wit, apt to do harm, be lost?
What though thou found'st her proof 'gainst sins of youth?
  Oh, every age a diverse sin pursueth.
Thou shouldst have stay'd, and taken better hold,
  Shortly, ambitious; covetous, when old,
She might have prov'd: and such devotion
  Might once have stray'd to superstition.
If all her virtues must have grown, yet might
  Abundant virtue have bred a proud delight.
Had she persever'd just, there would have been
  Some that would sin, mis-thinking she did sin.
Such as would call her friendship, love, and feign
  To sociableness, a name profane;
Or sin, by tempting, or, not daring that,
  By wishing, though they never told her what.
Thus might'st thou have slain more souls, hadst thou not crost
  Thyself, and to triumph, thine army lost.
Yet though these ways be lost, thou hast left one,
  Which is, immoderate grief that she is gone.
But we may 'scape that sin, yet weep as much,
  Our tears are due, because we are not such.
Some tears, that knot of friends, her death must cost,
  Because the chain is broke, though no link lost.

ELEGY

DEATH

LANGUAGE, thou art too narrow, and too weak
  To ease us now; great sorrow cannot speak;
If we could sigh out accents, and weep words,
  Grief wears, and lessens, that tears breath affords.
Sad hearts, the less they seem the more they are,

(So guiltiest men stand mutest at the bar)
Not that they know not, feel not their estate,
    But extreme sense hath made them desperate.
Sorrow, to whom we owe all that we be;
    Tyrant, in the fifth and greatest Monarchy,
Was 't, that she did possess all hearts before,
    Thou hast killed her, to make thy Empire more?
Knew'st thou some would, that knew her not, lament,
    As in a deluge perish th' innocent?
Was 't not enough to have that palace won,
    But thou must raze it too, that was undone?
Hadst thou stay'd there, and look'd out at her eyes,
    All had ador'd thee that now from thee flies,
For they let out more light, than they took in,
    They told not when, but did the day begin.
She was too Sapphirine, and clear for thee;
    Clay, flint, and jet now thy fit dwellings be;
Alas, she was too pure, but not too weak;
    Whoe'er saw crystal ordnance but would break?
And if we be thy conquest, by her fall
    Thou 'st lost thy end, for in her perish all;
Or if we live, we live but to rebel,
    They know her better now, that knew her well.
If we should vapour out, and pine, and die;
    Since, she first went, that were not misery.
She chang'd our world with hers; now she is gone,
    Mirth and prosperity is oppression;
For of all moral virtues she was all,
    The Ethics speak of virtues cardinal.
Her soul was Paradise; the Cherubin
    Set to keep it was grace, that kept out sin.
She had no more than let in death, for we
    All reap consumption from one fruitful tree.
God took her hence, lest some of us should love
    Her, like that plant, Him and His laws above,
And when we tears, He mercy shed in this,
    To raise our minds to heaven where now she is;
Who if her virtues would have let her stay
    We had had a Saint, have now a holiday.

Her heart was that strange bush, where sacred fire,
  Religion, did not consume, but inspire
Such piety, so chaste use of God's day,
  That what we turn to *feast*, she turn'd to *pray*,
And did prefigure here, in devout taste,
  The rest of her high Sabaoth, which shall last.
Angels did hand her up, who next God dwell,
  (For she was of that order whence most fell)
Her body left with us, lest some had said,
  She could not die, except they saw her dead;
For from less virtue, and less beauteousness,
  The Gentiles fram'd them Gods and Goddesses.
The ravenous earth that now woos her to be
  Earth too, will be a *Lemnia*; and the tree
That wraps that crystal in a wooden Tomb,
  Shall be took up spruce, fill'd with diamond;
And we her sad glad friends all bear a part
  Of grief, for all would waste a Stoic's heart.

ELEGY ON THE L[ORD]. C[HAMBERLAIN].

SORROW, who to this house scarce knew the way:
Is, Oh, heir of it, our All is his prey.
This strange chance claims strange wonder, and to us
Nothing can be so strange, as to weep thus.
'Tis well his life's loud speaking works deserve,
And give praise too, our cold tongues could not serve:
'Tis well, he kept tears from our eyes before,
That to fit this deep ill, we might have store.
Oh, if a sweet briar climb up by a tree,
If to a paradise that transplanted be,
Or fell'd, and burnt for holy sacrifice,
Yet, that must wither, which by it did rise,
As we for him dead: though no family
E'er rigg'd a soul for heaven's discovery
With whom more Venturers more boldly dare
Venture their states, with him in joy to share.
We lose what all friends lov'd, him; he gains now
But life by death, which worst foes would allow,

If he could have foes, in whose practice grew
All virtues, whose names subtle Schoolmen knew
What ease, can hope that we shall see him, beget,
When we must die first, and cannot die yet?
His children are his pictures, Oh they be
Pictures of him dead, senseless, cold as he.
Here needs no marble Tomb, since he is gone,
He, and about him, his, are turn'd to stone.

AN HYMN TO THE SAINTS, AND TO
MARQUIS HAMILTON

To Sir Robert Carr

SIR,
  *I presume you rather try what you can do in me, than what
I can do in verse; you know my uttermost when it was best,
and even then I did best when I had least truth for my subjects.
In this present case there is so much truth as it defeats all
Poetry. Call therefore this paper by what name you will, and,
if it be not worthy of him, nor of you, nor of me, smother it,
and be that the sacrifice. If you had commanded me to have
waited on his body to Scotland and preached there, I would
have embraced the obligation with more alacrity; but, I thank
you that you would command me that which I was loth to do,
for, even that hath given a tincture of merit to the obedience of*
                    Your poor friend and servant in Christ Jesus
                                                        J. D.

WHETHER that soul which now comes up to you
Fill any former rank or make a new,
Whether it take a name nam'd there before,
Or be a name itself, and order more
Than was in heaven till now; (for may not he
Be so, if every several Angel be
A kind alone?) What ever order grow
Greater by him in heaven, we do not so.
One of your orders grows by his access;
But, by his loss grow all our orders less;
The name of Father, Master, Friend, the name
Of Subject and of Prince, in one are lame;

Fair mirth is dampt, and coversation black,
The household widow'd, and the garter slack;
The Chapel wants an ear, Council a tongue;
Story, a theme; and Music lacks a song;
Blest order that hath him! the loss of him
Gangrened all Orders here; all lost a limb.
Never made body such haste to confess
What a soul was; all former comeliness
Fled, in a minute, when the soul was gone,
And, having lost that beauty, would have none;
So fell our Monasteries, in one instant grown
Not to less houses, but, to heaps of stone;
So sent this body that fair form it wore,
Unto the sphere of forms, and doth (before
His soul shall fill up his sepulchral stone),
Anticipate a Resurrection;
For, as in his fame, now, his soul is here,
So, in the form thereof his body 's there;
And if, fair soul, not with first Innocents
Thy station be, but with the Penitents,
(And, who shall dare to ask then when I am
Dyed scarlet in the blood of that pure Lamb,
Whether that colour, which is scarlet then,
Were black or white before in eyes of men?)
When thou rememb'rest what sins thou didst find
Amongst those many friends now left behind,
And seest such sinners as they are, with thee
Got thither by repentance, let it be
Thy wish to wish all there, to wish them clean;
Wish him a David, her a Magdalen.

EPITAPHS

EPITAPH ON HIMSELF

MADAM,   *To the Countess of Bedford*
 That I might make your Cabinet my tomb,
  And for my fame which I love next my soul,

Next to my soul provide the happiest room,
    Admit to that place this last funeral Scroll.
        Others by Wills give Legacies, but I
        Dying, of you do beg a Legacy.

My fortune and my will this custom break,
When we are senseless grown to make stones speak,
Though no stone tell thee what I was, yet thou
In my grave's inside see what thou art now:
Yet thou 'rt not yet so good; till us death lay
To ripe and mellow there, we 're stubborn clay,
Parents make us earth, and souls dignify
Us to be glass, here to grow gold we lie;
Whilst in our souls sin bred and pampered is,
Our souls become worm-eaten carcases.

OMNIBUS

My Fortune and my choice this custom break,
When we are speechless grown, to make stones speak,
Though no stone tell thee what I was, yet thou
In my grave's inside seest what thou art now:
Yet thou 'rt not yet so good, till death us lay
To ripe and mellow here, we are stubborn Clay.
Parents make us earth, and souls dignify
Us to be glass; here to grow gold we lie.
Whilst in our souls sin bred and pamper'd is,
Our souls become worm-eaten carcases;
So we ourselves miraculously destroy.
Here bodies with less miracle enjoy
Such privileges, enabled here to scale
Heaven, when the Trumpet's air shall them exhale.
Hear this, and mend thyself, and thou mend'st me,
By making me being dead, do good to thee,
    And think me well compos'd, that I could now
    A last-sick hour to syllables allow.

THE PROGRESS OF THE SOUL

INFINITATI SACRUM

16. *Augusti* 1601.

METEMPSYCHOSIS

POËMA SATYRICON

EPISTLE

OTHERS at the Porches and entries of their Buildings set
their Arms; I, my picture; if any colours can deliver a mind
so plain, and flat, and through-light as mine. Naturally at
a new Author, I doubt, and stick, and do not say quickly,
good. I censure much and tax; and this liberty costs me
more than others, by how much my own things are worse
than others. Yet I would not be so rebellious against
myself, as not to do it, since I love it; nor so unjust to
others, to do it *sine talione*. As long as I give them as
good hold upon me, they must pardon me my bitings. I
forbid no reprehender, but him that like the Trent Council
forbids not books, but Authors, damning whatever such a
name hath or shall write. None writes so ill, that he gives
not some thing exemplary, to follow, or fly. Now when I
begin this book, I have no purpose to come into any man's
debt; how my stock will hold out I know not; perchance
waste, perchance increase in use; if I do borrow any thing
of Antiquity, besides that I make account that I pay it to
posterity, with as much and as good: you shall still find me
to acknowledge it, and to thank not him only that hath
digg'd out treasure for me, but that hath lighted me a candle
to the place. All which I will bid you remember, (for I will
have no such Readers as I can teach) is, that the Pytha-
gorean doctrine doth not only carry one soul from man to
man, nor man to beast, but indifferently to plants also: and

227

therefore you must not grudge to find the same soul in an Emperor, in a Post-horse, and in a Mushroom, since no unreadiness in the soul, but an indisposition in the organs works this. And therefore though this soul could not move when it was a Melon, yet it may remember, and now tell me, at what lascivious banquet it was serv'd. And though it could not speak, when it was a spider, yet it can remember, and now tell me, who used it for poison to attain dignity. However the bodies have dull'd her other faculties, her memory hath ever been her own, which makes me so seriously deliver you by her relation all her passages from her first making when she was that apple which Eve eat, to this time when she is he, whose life you shall find in the end of this book.

THE PROGRESS OF THE SOUL

FIRST SONG

I

I sing the progress of a deathless soul,
Whom Fate, which God made, but doth not control,
Plac'd in most shapes; all times before the law
Yok'd us, and when, and since, in this I sing.
And the great world to his aged evening;
From infant morn, through manly noon I draw.
What the gold Chaldee, or silver Persian saw,
Greek brass, or Roman iron, is in this one;
A work to outwear *Seth's* pillars, brick and stone,
    And (Holy Writ excepted) made to yield to none.

II

Thee, eye of heaven, this great Soul envies not,
By thy male force, is all we have, begot.
In the first East, thou now begin'st to shine,
Suck'st early balm, and island spices there,
And wilt anon in thy loose-reined career
At Tagus, Po, Seine, Thames, and Danow dine,

And see at night thy Western land of Myne,
Yet hast thou not more nations seen than she,
That before thee, one day began to be,
   And thy frail light being quench'd, shall long, long out-
      live thee.

III

Nor, holy *Janus*, in whose sovereign boat
The Church, and all the Monarchies did float;
That swimming College, and free Hospital
Of all mankind, that cage and vivary
Of fowls, and beasts, in whose womb, Destiny
Us, and our latest nephews did instal
(From thence are all deriv'd, that fill this All),
Didst thou in that great stewardship embark
So diverse shapes into that floating park,
   As have been moved, and inform'd by this heavenly spark.

IV

Great Destiny the Commissary of God,
That hast mark'd out a path and period
For every thing; who, where we off-spring took,
Our ways and ends seest at one instant; thou
Knot of all causes, thou whose changeless brow
Ne'er smiles nor frowns, O vouch thou safe to look
And show my story, in thy eternal book:
That (if my prayer be fit) I may understand
So much myself, as to know with what hand,
   How scant, or liberal this my life's race is spann'd.

V

To my six lustres almost now outwore,
Except thy book owe me so many more,
Except my legend be free from the lets
Of steep ambition, sleepy poverty,
Spirit-quenching sickness, dull captivity,
Distracting business, and from beauty's nets,
And all that calls from this, and to others whets,

O let me not launch out, but let me save
Th' expense of brain and spirit; that my grave
  His right and due, a whole unwasted man may have.

VI

But if my days be long, and good enough,
In vain this sea shall enlarge, or enrough
Itself; for I will through the wave, and foam,
And shall, in sad lone ways a lively sprite,
Make my dark heavy Poem light, and light.
For though through many straits, and lands I roam,
I launch at paradise, and I sail towards home;
The course I there began, shall here be stay'd,
Sails hoisted there, struck here, and anchors laid
  In Thames, which were at Tigris, and Euphrates weigh'd.

VII

For the great soul which here amongst us now
Doth dwell, and moves that hand, and tongue, and brow,
Which, as the Moon the sea, moves us; to hear
Whose story, with long patience you will long;
(For 'tis the crown, and last strain of my song)
This soul to whom *Luther*, and *Mahomet* were
Prisons of flesh; this soul which oft did tear,
And mend the wracks of th' Empire, and late Rome,
And liv'd when every great change did come,
  Had first in paradise, a low, but fatal room.

VIII

Yet no low room, nor than the greatest, less,
If (as devout and sharp men fitly guess)
That Cross, our joy, and grief, where nails did tie
That All, which always was all, everywhere;
Which could not sin, and yet all sins did bear;
Which could not die, yet could not choose but die;
Stood in the self-same room in Calvary,
Where first grew the forbidden learned tree,
For on that tree hung in security
  This Soul, made by the Maker's will from pulling free.

IX

Prince of the orchard, fair as dawning morn,
Fenc'd with the law, and ripe as soon as born
That apple grew, which this Soul did enlive,
Till the then climbing serpent, that now creeps
For that offence, for which all mankind weeps,
Took it, and to her whom the first man did wive
(Whom and her race, only forbiddings drive)
He gave it, she to her husband, both did eat;
So perished the eaters, and the meat:
   And we (for treason taints the blood) thence die and
      sweat.

X

Man all at once was there by woman slain,
And one by one we 're here slain o'er again
By them. The mother poison'd the well-head,
The daughters here corrupt us, rivulets;
No smallness 'scapes, no greatness breaks their nets;
She thrust us out, and by them we are led
Astray, from turning to whence we are fled.
Were prisoners Judges, 'twould seem rigorous,
She sinn'd, we bear; part of our pain is, thus
   To love them, whose fault to this painful love yok'd us.

XI

So fast in us doth this corruption grow,
That now we dare ask why we should be so.
Would God (disputes the curious Rebel) make
A law, and would not have it kept? Or can
His creatures' will, cross His? Of every man
For one, will God (and be just) vengeance take?
Who sinn'd? 'twas not forbidden to the snake
Nor her, who was not then made; nor is 't writ
   That Adam cropt, or knew the apple; yet
   The worm and she, and he, and we endure for it.

XII

But snatch me, heavenly Spirit, from this vain
Reckoning their vanities, less is their gain

Than hazard still, to meditate on ill,
Though with good mind; their reasons, like those toys
Of glassy bubbles, which the gamesome boys
Stretch to so nice a thinness through a quill
That they themselves break, do themselves spill:
Arguing is heretics' game, and Exercise
As wrestlers, perfects them; not liberties
   Of speech, but silence; hands, not tongues, end heresies.

XIII

Just in that instant when the serpent's gripe,
Broke the slight veins, and tender conduit-pipe,
Through which this soul from the tree's root did draw
Life, and growth to this apple. fled away
This loose soul, old, one and another day.
As lightning, which one scarce dares say, he saw,
'Tis so soon gone, (and better proof the law
Of sense, than faith requires) swiftly she flew
To a dark and foggy Plot; her, her fates threw
   There through th' earth's pores, and in a Plant hous'd her
     anew.

XIV

The plant thus abled, to itself did force
A place, where no place was; by nature's course
As air from water, water fleets away
From thicker bodies, by this root thronged so
His spongy confines gave him place to grow;
Just as in our streets, when the people stay
To see the Prince, and have so fill'd the way
That weasels scarce could pass, when she comes near
They throng and cleave up, and a passage clear,
   As if, for that time, their round bodies flatten'd were.

XV

His right arm he thrust out towards the East,
Weatward his left; th' ends did themselves digest
Into ten lesser strings, these fingers were:
And as a slumberer stretching on his bed,

This way he this, and that way scattered
His other leg, which feet with toes upbear.
Grew on his middle parts, the first day, hair,
To show, that in love's business he should still
A dealer be, and be us'd well, or ill:
   His apples kindle, his leaves, force of conception kill.

XVI

A mouth, but dumb, he hath; blind eyes, deaf ears,
And to his shoulders dangle subtle hairs;
A young *Colossus* there he stands upright,
And as that ground by him were conquered
A leafy garland wears he on his head
Enchas'd with little fruits, so red and bright
That for them you would call your Love's lips white;
So, of a lone unhaunted place possest,
Did this soul's second Inn, built by the guest,
   This living buried man, this quiet mandrake, rest.

XVII

No lustful woman came this plant to grieve,
But 'twas because there was none yet but Eve;
And she (with other purpose) kill'd it quite;
Her sin had now brought in infirmities,
And so her cradled child, the moist red eyes
Had never shut, nor slept since it saw light;
Poppy she knew, she knew the mandrake's might,
And tore up both, and so cool'd her child's blood;
Unvirtuous weeds might long unvex'd have stood;
   But he's short-liv'd, that with his death can do most
     good.

XVIII

To an unfetter'd soul's quick nimble haste
Are falling stars, and heart's thoughts, but slow-pac'd:
Thinner than burnt air flies this soul, and she
Whom four new coming, and four parting Suns
Had found, and left the Mandrake's tenant, runs

Thoughtless of change, when her firm destiny
Confin'd, and enjail'd her, that seem'd so free,
Into a small blue shell, the which a poor
Warm bird o'erspread, and sat still evermore,
    Till her enclos'd child kick'd, and pick'd itself a door.

XIX

Outcrept a sparrow, this soul's moving Inn,
On whose raw arms stiff feathers now begin,
As children's teeth through gums, to break with pain,
His flesh is jelly yet, and his bones threads,
All a new downy mantle overspreads,
A mouth he opes, which would as much contain
As his late house, and the first hour speaks plain,
And chirps aloud for meat.   Meat fit for men
His father steals for him, and so feeds then
    One, that within a month, will beat him from his hen.

XX

In this world's youth wise nature did make haste,
Things ripened sooner, and did longer last;
Already this hot cock, in bush and tree,
In field and tent, o'erflutters his next hen;
He asks her not, who did so last, nor when,
Nor if his sister, or his niece she be;
Nor doth she pule for his inconstancy
If in her sight he change, nor doth refuse
The next that calls; both liberty do use,
    Where store is of both kinds, both kinds may freely choose.

XXI

Men, till they took laws which made freedom less,
Their daughters, and their sisters did ingress;
Till now unlawful, therefore ill, 'twas not.
So jolly, that it can move, this soul is,
The body so free of his kindnesses,
That self-preserving it hath now forgot,
And slack'neth so the soul's, and body's knot

Which temperance straitens; freely on his she friends
He blood, and spirit, pith, and marrow spends,
   Ill steward of himself, himself in three years ends.

XXII

Else might he long have liv'd; man did not know
Of gummy blood, which doth in holly grow,
How to make bird-lime, nor how to deceive
With feigned calls, hid nets, or enwrapping snare,
The free inhabitants of the pliant air.
Man to beget, and woman to conceive
Asked not of roots, nor of cock-sparrows, leave:
Yet chooseth he, though none of these he fears,
Pleasantly three, than straitened twenty years
   To live; and to increase his race, himself outwears.

XXIII

This coal with overblowing quench'd and dead,
The Soul from her too active organs fled
To a brook.   A female fish's sandy Roe
With the male's jelly, newly leavened was,
For they had intertouch'd as they did pass,
And one of those small bodies, fitted so,
This soul inform'd, and abled it to row
Itself with finny oars, which she did fit:
Her scales seem'd yet of parchment, and as yet
   Perchance a fish, but by no name you could call it.

XXIV

When goodly, like a ship in her full trim,
A swan, so white that you may unto him
Compare all whiteness, but himself to none,
Glided along, and as he glided watch'd,
And with his arched neck this poor fish catch'd.
It mov'd with state, as if to look upon
Low things it scorn'd, and yet before that one
Could think he sought it, he had swallowed clear
This, and much such, and unblam'd devour'd there
   All, but who too swift, too great, or well armed were.

XXV

Now swam a prison in a prison put,
And now this Soul in double walls was shut,
Till melted with the Swan's digestive fire,
She left her house the fish, and vapour'd forth;
Fate not affording bodies of more worth
For her as yet, bids her again retire
To another fish, to any new desire
Made a new prey; for, he that can to none
Resistance make, nor complaint, sure is gone.
    Weakness invites, but silence feasts oppression.

XXVI

Pace with her native stream, this fish doth keep,
And journeys with her, towards the glassy deep,
But oft retarded, once with a hidden net
Though with great windows, for when Need first taught
These tricks to catch food, then they were not wrought
As now, with curious greediness to let
None 'scape, but few, and fit for use, to get,
As, in this trap a ravenous pike was ta'en,
Who, though himself distress'd, would fain have slain
    This wretch; so hardly are ill habits left again.

XXVII

Here by her smallness she two deaths o'erpast,
Once innocence 'scaped, and left the oppressor fast.
The net through-swum, she keeps the liquid path,
And whether she leap up sometimes to breathe
And suck in air, or find it underneath,
Or working parts like mills or limbecks hath
To make the water thin and airlike, faith
Cares not; but safe the Place she 's come unto
Where fresh, with salt waves meet, and what to do
    She knows not, but between both makes a board or two.

XXVIII

So far from hiding her guests, water is,
That she shows them in bigger quantities

Than they are.   Thus doubtful of her way,
For game and not for hunger a sea Pie
Spied through this traitorous spectacle, from high
The silly fish where it disputing lay,
And to end her doubts and her, bears her away:
Exalted she is, but to the exalter's good,
As are by great ones, men which lowly stood.
   It 's rais'd, to be the Raiser's instrument and food.

XXIX

Is any kind subject to rape like fish?
Ill unto man, they neither do, nor wish:
Fishers they kill not, nor with noise awake,
They do not hunt, nor strive to make a prey
Of beasts, nor their young sons to bear away;
Fowls they pursue not, nor do undertake
To spoil the nests industrious birds do make;
Yet them all these unkind kinds feed upon,
To kill them is an occupation,
   And laws make Fasts, and Lents for their destruction.

XXX

A sudden stiff land-wind in that self hour
To sea-ward forc'd this bird, that did devour
The fish; he cares not, for with ease he flies,
Fat gluttony's best orator: at last
So long he hath flown, and hath flown so fast
That many leagues at sea, now tired he lies,
And with his prey, that till then languished, dies:
The souls no longer foes, two ways did err,
The fish I follow, and keep no calendar
   Of the other; he lives yet in some great officer.

XXXI

Into an embryon fish, our Soul is thrown,
And in due time thrown out again, and grown
To such vastness as, if unmanacled
From Greece, Morea were, and that by some
Earthquake unrooted, loose Morea swum,

Or seas from Afric's body had severed
And torn the hopeful promontory's head,
This fish would seem these, and, when all hopes fail,
A great ship overset, or without sail
   Hulling, might (when this was a whelp) be like this whale.

XXXII

At every stroke his brazen fins do take,
More circles in the broken sea they make
Than cannons' voices, when the air they tear:
His ribs are pillars, and his high arch'd roof
Of bark that blunts best steel, is thunder-proof:
Swim in him swallow'd Dolphins, without fear,
And feel no sides, as if his vast womb were
Some inland sea, and ever as he went
He spouted rivers up, as if he meant
   To join our seas, with seas above the firmament.

XXXIII

He hunts not fish, but as an officer,
Stays in his court, at his own net, and there
All suitors of all sorts themselves enthral;
So on his back lies this whale wantoning,
And in his gulf-like throat, sucks every thing
That passeth near.   Fish chaseth fish, and all,
Flyer and follower, in this whirlpool fall;
O might not states of more equality
Consist? and is it of necessity
   That thousand guiltless smalls, to make one great, must
     die?

XXXIV

Now drinks he up seas, and he eats up flocks,
He jostles Islands, and he shakes firm rocks.
Now in a roomful house this Soul doth float,
And like a Prince she sends her faculties
To all her limbs, distant as Provinces.
The Sun hath twenty times both crab and goat

Parched, since first launched forth this living boat;
'Tis greatest now, and to destruction
Nearest; there's no pause at perfection;
   Greatness a period hath, but hath no station.

XXXV

Two little fishes whom he never harm'd,
Nor fed on their kind, two not throughly arm'd
With hope that they could kill him, nor could do
Good to themselves by his death (they did not eat
His flesh, nor suck those oils, which thence outstreat)
Conspir'd against him, and it might undo
The plot of all, that the plotters were two,
But that they fishes were, and could not speak.
How shall a Tyrant wise strong projects break,
   If wretches can on them the common anger wreak?

XXXVI

The flail-finn'd Thresher, and steel-beak'd Sword-fish
Only attempt to do, what all do wish.
The Thresher backs him, and to beat begins;
The sluggard Whale yields to oppression,
And to hide himself from shame and danger, down
Begins to sink; the Swordfish upward spins,
And gores him with his beak; his staff-like fins,
So well the one, his sword the other plies,
That now a scoff, and prey, this tyrant dies,
   And (his own dole) feeds with himself all companies.

XXXVII

Who will revenge his death? or who will call
Those to account, that thought, and wrought his fall?
The heirs of slain kings, we see are often so
Transported with the joy of what they get,
That they, revenge and obsequies forget,
Nor will against such men the people go,
Because he's now dead, to whom they should show
Love in that act; some kings by vice being grown

So needy of subjects' love, that of their own
   They think they lose, if love be to the dead Prince shown.

XXXVIII

This Soul, now free from prison, and passion,
Hath yet a little indignation
That so small hammers should so soon down beat
So great a castle.   And having for her house
Got the strait cloister of a wretched mouse
(As basest men that have not what to eat,
Nor enjoy aught, do far more hate the great
Than they, who good repos'd estates possess)
This Soul, late taught that great things might by less
   Be slain, to gallant mischief doth herself address.

XXXIX

Nature's great masterpiece, an Elephant,
The only harmless great thing; the giant
Of beasts; who thought, no more had gone, to make one wise
But to be just, and thankful, loth to offend,
(Yet nature hath given him no knees to bend)
Himself he up-props, on himself relies,
And foe to none, suspects no enemies,
Still sleeping stood; vexed not his fantasy
Black dreams; like an unbent bow, carelessly
   His sinewy Proboscis did remissly lie:

XL

In which as in a gallery this mouse
Walk'd, and survey'd the rooms of this vast house,
And to the brain, the soul's bedchamber, went,
And gnaw'd the life cords there; like a whole town
Clean undermin'd, the slain beast tumbled down;
With him the murderer dies, whom envy sent
To kill, not 'scape, (for, only he that meant
To die, did ever kill a man of better room),
And thus he made his foe, his prey, and tomb:
   Who cares not to turn back, may any whither come.

XLI

Next, hous'd this Soul a Wolf's yet unborn whelp,
Till the best midwife, Nature, gave it help,
To issue.   It could kill, as soon as go.
Abel, as white, and mild as his sheep were,
(Who, in that trade, of Church, and kingdoms, there
Was the first type) was still infested so,
With this wolf, that it bred his loss and woe;
And yet his bitch, his sentinel attends
The flock so near, so well warns and defends,
    That the wolf, (hopeless else) to corrupt her, intends.

XLII

He took a course, which since, successfully,
Great men have often taken, to espy
The counsels, or to break the plots of foes.
To Abel's tent he stealeth in the dark,
On whose skirts the bitch slept; ere she could bark,
Attach'd her with strait grips, yet he call'd those,
Embracements of love; to love's work he goes
Where deeds move more than words; nor doth she show,
Nor much resist, nor needs he straiten so
    His prey, for, were she loose, she would nor bark, nor go.

XLIII

He hath engag'd her; his, she wholly bides;
Who not her own, none other's secrets hides.
If to the flock he come, and Abel there,
She feigns hoarse barkings, but she biteth not,
Her faith is quite, but not her love forgot.
At last a trap, of which some every where
Abel had plac'd, ends all his loss, and fear,
By the Wolf's death; and now just time it was
That a quick soul should give life to that mass
    Of blood in Abel's bitch, and thither this did pass.

XLIV

Some have their wives, their sisters some begot,
But in the lives of Emperors you shall not

Read of a lust the which may equal this;
This wolf begot himself, and finished
What he began alive, when he was dead;
Son to himself, and father too, he is
A riddling lust, for which Schoolmen would miss
A proper name. The whelp of both these lay
In Abel's tent, and with soft Moaba,
  His sister, being young, it us'd to sport and play.

XLV

He soon for her too harsh, and churlish grew,
And Abel (the dam dead) would use this new
For the field. Being of two kinds thus made,
He, as his dam, from sheep drove wolves away,
And as his Sire, he made them his own prey.
Five years he liv'd, and cozened with his trade,
Then hopeless that his faults were hid, betrayed
Himself by flight, and by all followed,
From dogs, a wolf; from wolves, a dog he fled;
  And, like a spy to both sides false, he perished.

XLVI

It quicken'd next a toyful Ape, and so
Gamesome it was, that it might freely go
From tent to tent, and with the children play.
His organs now so like theirs he doth find,
That why he cannot laugh, and speak his mind,
He wonders. Much with all, most he doth stay
With Adam's fifth daughter *Siphatecia*,
Doth gaze on her, and, where she passeth, pass,
Gathers her fruits, and tumbles on the grass,
  And wisest of that kind, the first true lover was.

XLVII

He was the first that more desir'd to have
One than another; first that e'er did crave
Love by mute signs, and had no power to speak;
First that could make love faces, or could do

The vaulter's somersaults, or us'd to woo
With hoiting gambols, his own bones to break
To make his mistress merry; or to wreak
Her anger on himself.   Sins against kind
They easily do, that can let feed their mind
  With outward beauty; beauty they in boys and beasts do
  find.

XLVIII

By this misled, too low things men have prov'd,
And too high; beasts and angels have been lov'd.
This Ape, though else through-vain, in this was wise,
He reach'd at things too high, but open way
There was, and he knew not she would say nay;
His toys prevail not, likelier means he tries,
He gazeth on her face with tear-shot eyes,
And up lifts subtly with his russet paw
Her kidskin apron without fear or awe
  Of Nature; Nature hath no gaol, though she hath law.

XLIX

First she was silly and knew not what he meant.
That virtue, by his touches, chafed and spent,
Succeeds an itchy warmth, that melts her quite;
She knew not first, now cares not what he doth,
And willing half and more, more than half loth,
She neither pulls nor pushes, but outright
Now cries, and now repents; when *Tethlemite*
Her brother, enter'd, and a great stone threw
After the Ape, who, thus prevented, flew.
This house thus batter'd down, the Soul possessed a new.

L

And whether by this change she lose or win,
She comes out next, where the Ape would have gone in.
Adam and *Eve* had mingled bloods, and now
Like chemic's equal fires, her temperate womb
Had stew'd and form'd it: and part did become

A spongy liver, that did richly allow,
Like a free conduit, on a high hill's brow,
Life-keeping moisture unto every part;
Part hardened itself to a thicker heart,
    Whose busy furnaces life's spirits do impart.

LI

Another part became the well of sense,
The tender well-arm'd feeling brain, from whence,
Those sinewy strings which do our bodies tie,
Are ravelled out; and fast there by one end,
Did this Soul limbs, these limbs a soul attend;
And now they join'd; keeping some quality
Of every past shape, she knew treachery,
Rapine, deceit, and lust, and ills enow
To be a woman. *Themech* she is now,
    Sister and wife to *Cain*, *Cain* that first did plow.

LII

Whoe'er thou be'st that read'st this sullen Writ,
Which just so much courts thee, as thou dost it,
Let me arrest thy thoughts; wonder with me,
Why plowing, building, ruling and the rest,
Or most of those arts, whence our lives are blest,
By cursed *Cain's* race invented be,
And blest *Seth* vexed us with Astronomy.
There's nothing simply good, nor ill alone,
Of every quality comparison,
    The only measure is, and judge, opinion.

DIVINE POEMS

TO E[ARL]. OF D[ORSET]. WITH SIX
HOLY SONNETS

SEE Sir, how as the Sun's hot Masculine flame
    Begets strange creatures on Nile's dirty slime,
    In me, your fatherly yet lusty Rhyme
(For, these songs are their fruits) have wrought the same;
But though the engend'ring force from whence they came
    Be strong enough, and nature do admit
    Seven to be born at once, I send as yet
But six; they say, the seventh hath still some maim.
    I choose your judgment, which the same degree
    Doth with her sister, your invention, hold,
As fire these drossy Rhymes to purify,
    Or as Elixir, to change them to gold;
You are that Alchemist which always had
Wit, whose one spark could make good things of bad.

TO THE LADY MAGDALEN HERBERT:
OF ST. MARY MAGDALEN

HER of your name, whose fair inheritance
    Bethina was, and jointure Magdalo:
An active faith so highly did advance,
    That she once knew, more than the Church did know,
The Resurrection; so much good there is
    Deliver'd of her, that some Fathers be
Loth to believe one Woman could do this;
    But, think these Magdalens were two or three.
Increase their number, Lady, and their fame:
    To their Devotion, add your Innocence;
Take so much of th' example, as of the name;
    The latter half; and in some recompense
That they did harbour Christ himself, a Guest,
    Harbour these Hymns, to his dear name address'd.

LA CORONA

HOLY SONNETS

LA CORONA

1

Deign at my hands this crown of prayer and praise,
Weav'd in my low devout melancholy,
Thou which of good, hast, yea art treasury,
All changing unchang'd Ancient of days;
But do not, with a vile crown of frail bays,
Reward my muse's white sincerity,
But what Thy thorny crown gain'd, that give me,
A crown of Glory, which doth flower always;
The ends crown our works, but Thou crown'st our ends,
For, at our end begins our endless rest;
The first last end, now zealously possess'd,
With a strong sober thirst, my soul attends.
'Tis time that heart and voice be lifted high,
Salvation to all that will is nigh.

2

ANNUNCIATION

Salvation to all that will is nigh ;
That All, which always is All everywhere,
Which cannot sin, and yet all sins must bear,
Which cannot die, yet cannot choose but die,
Lo, faithful Virgin, yields Himself to lie
In prison, in thy womb; and though He there
Can take no sin, nor thou give, yet He 'll wear
Taken from thence, flesh, which death's force may try.
Ere by the spheres time was created, thou
Wast in His mind, who is thy Son, and Brother;
Whom thou conceiv'st, conceiv'd; yea thou art now
Thy Maker's maker, and thy Father's mother;
Thou hast light in dark; and shutt'st in little room,
Immensity cloister'd in thy dear womb.

3

NATIVITY

Immensity cloister'd in thy dear womb,
Now leaves His well-beloved imprisonment,

There he hath made Himself to His intent
Weak enough, now into our world to come;
But Oh, for thee, for Him, hath th' Inn no room?
Yet lay Him in this stall, and from the Orient,
Stars, and wisemen will travel to prevent
Th' effect of Herod's jealous general doom.
See'st thou, my Soul, with thy faith's eyes, how He
Which fills all place, yet none holds Him, doth lie?
Was not His pity towards thee wondrous high,
That would have need to be pitied by thee?
Kiss Him, and with Him into Egypt go,
With His kind mother, who partakes thy woe.

4
TEMPLE

With His kind mother who partakes thy woe,
Joseph turn back; see where your child doth sit,
Blowing, yea blowing out those sparks of wit,
Which Himself on the Doctors did bestow;
The Word but lately could not speak, and lo
It suddenly speaks wonders, whence comes it,
That all which was, and all which should be writ,
A shallow seeming child, should deeply know?
His Godhead was not soul to His manhood,
Nor had time mellowed Him to this ripeness,
But as for one which hath a long task, 'tis good,
With the Sun to begin his business,
He in His age's morning thus began
By miracles exceeding power of man.

5
CRUCIFYING

By miracles exceeding power of man,
He faith in some, envy in some begat,
For, what weak spirits admire, ambitious hate;
In both affections many to Him ran,
But Oh! the worst are most, they will and can,
Alas, and do, unto the immaculate,
Whose creature Fate is, now prescribe a Fate,
Measuring self-life's infinity to a span,

Nay to an inch. Lo, where comdemned He
Bears His own cross, with pain, yet by and by
When it bears Him, He must bear more and die.
Now Thou art lifted up, draw me to Thee,
And at Thy death giving such liberal dole,
Moist, with one drop of Thy blood, my dry soul.

6
RESURRECTION

Moist with one drop of Thy blood, my dry soul
Shall (though she now be in extreme degree
Too stony hard, and yet too fleshly), be
Freed by that drop, from being starv'd, hard, or foul,
And life, by this death abled, shall control
Death, whom Thy death slew; nor shall to me
Fear of first or last death, bring misery,
If in Thy little book my name Thou enrol,
Flesh in that long sleep is not putrefied,
But made that there, of which, and for which 'twas;
Nor can by other means be glorified.
May then sin's sleep, and death's soon from me pass,
That wak'd from both, I again risen may
Salute the last, and everlasting day.

7
ASCENSION

Salute the last and everlasting day,
Joy at the uprising of this Sun, and Son,
Ye whose just tears, or tribulation
Have purely washed, or burnt your drossy clay;
Behold the Highest, parting hence away,
Lightens the dark clouds, which He treads upon,
Nor doth He by ascending, show alone,
But first He, and He first enters the way.
O strong Ram, which hast batter'd heaven for me,
Mild Lamb, which with Thy blood, hast mark'd the path;
Bright Torch, which shin'st, that I the way may see,
Oh, with Thy own blood quench Thy own just wrath,
And if Thy holy Spirit, my Muse did raise,
Deign at my hands this crown of prayer and praise.

HOLY SONNETS

I

Thou hast made me, and shall Thy work decay?
Repair me now, for now mine end doth haste,
I run to death, and death meets me as fast,
And all my pleasures are like yesterday;
I dare not move my dim eyes any way,
Despair behind, and death before doth cast
Such terror, and my feeble flesh doth waste
By sin in it, which it towards hell doth weigh;
Only Thou art above, and when towards Thee
By Thy leave I can look, I rise again;
But our old subtle foe so tempteth me,
That not one hour myself I can sustain;
Thy Grace may wing me to prevent his art,
And thou like Adamant draw mine iron heart.

II

As due by many titles I resign
Myself to Thee, O God, first I was made
By Thee, and for Thee, and when I was decay'd
Thy blood bought that, the which before was Thine;
I am Thy son, made with Thyself to shine,
Thy servant, whose pains thou hast still repaid,
Thy sheep, Thine Image, and, till I betray'd
Myself, a temple of Thy Spirit divine;
Why doth the devil then usurp on me?
Why doth he steal, nay ravish that's Thy right?
Except Thou rise and for Thine own work fight,
Oh I shall soon despair, when I do see
That Thou lov'st mankind well, yet wilt not choose me,
And Satan hates me, yet is loth to lose me.

III

O might those sighs and tears return again
Into my breast and eyes, which I have spent,
That I might in this holy discontent

Mourn with some fruit, as I have mourn'd in vain;
In mine Idolatry what showers of rain
Mine eyes did waste? what griefs my heart did rent?
That sufferance was my sin; now I repent;
'Cause I did suffer I must suffer pain.
Th' hydroptic drunkard, and night-scouting thief,
The itchy Lecher, and self-tickling proud
Have the remembrance of past joys, for relief
Of coming ills.   To poor me is allow'd
No ease; for, long, yet vehement grief hath been
Th' effect and cause, the punishment and sin.

IV

OH my black Soul! now thou art summoned
By sickness, death's herald, and champion;
Thou art like a pilgrim, which abroad hath done
Treason, and durst not turn to whence he is fled,
Or like a thief, which till death's doom be read,
Wisheth himself delivered from prison;
But damn'd and hal'd to execution,
Wisheth that still he might be imprisoned.
Yet grace, if thou repent, thou canst not lack;
But who shall give thee that grace to begin?
Oh make thyself with holy mourning black,
And red with blushing, as thou art with sin;
Or wash thee in Christ's blood, which hath this might
That being red, it dyes red souls to white.

V

I AM a little world made cunningly
Of Elements, and an Angelic sprite,
But black sin hath betray'd to endless night
My world's both parts, and, oh, both parts must die.
You which beyond that heaven which was most high
Have found new spheres, and of new lands can write,
Pour new seas in mine eyes, that so I might
Drown my world with my weeping earnestly,
Or wash it if it must be drown'd no more:
But oh it must be burnt! alas the fire
Of lust and envy have burnt it heretofore,

And made it fouler; let their flames retire,
And burn me O Lord, with a fiery zeal
Of Thee and Thy house, which doth in eating heal.

VI

THIS is my play's last scene, here heavens appoint
My pilgrimage's last mile; and my race
Idly, yet quickly run, hath this last pace,
My span's last inch, my minute's latest point,
And gluttonous death, will instantly unjoint
My body, and soul, and I shall sleep a space,
But my ever-waking part shall see that face,
Whose fear already shakes my every joint:
Then, as my soul, to heaven her first seat, takes flight,
And earth-born body, in the earth shall dwell,
So, fall my sins, that all may have their right,
To where they 're bred, and would press me, to hell.
Impute me righteous, thus purg'd of evil,
For thus I leave the world, the flesh, the devil.

VII

AT the round earth's imagin'd corners, blow
Your trumpets, Angels, and arise, arise
From death, you numberless infinities
Of souls, and to your scatter'd bodies go,
All whom the flood did, and fire shall o'erthrow,
All whom war, dearth, age, agues, tyrannies,
Despair, law, chance, hath slain, and you whose eyes,
Shall behold God, and never taste death's woe.
But let them sleep, Lord, and me mourn a space,
For, if above all these, my sins abound,
'Tis late to ask abundance of Thy grace,
When we are there; here on this lowly ground,
Teach me how to repent; for that 's as good
As if Thou hadst seal'd my pardon, with Thy blood.

VIII

IF faithful souls be alike glorified
As Angels, then my father's soul doth see.

And adds this even to full felicity,
That valiantly I hell's wide mouth o'erstride:
But if our minds to these souls be descried
By circumstances, and by signs that be
Apparent in us, not immediately,
How shall my mind's white truth by them be try'd?
They see idolatrous lovers weep and mourn,
And vile blasphemous Conjurers to call
On Jesus' name, and Pharisaical
Dissemblers feign devotion.   Then turn
O pensive soul, to God, for He knows best
Thy true grief, for He put it in my breast.

IX

If poisonous minerals, and if that tree,
Whose fruit threw death on else immortal us,
If lecherous goats, if serpents envious
Cannot be damn'd; alas! why should I be?
Why should intent or reason, born in me,
Make sins, else equal, in me more heinous?
And mercy being easy, and glorious
To God; in His stern wrath, why threatens He?
But who am I, that dare dispute with Thee
O God? Oh! of thine only worthy blood,
And my tears, make a heavenly Lethean flood,
And drown in it my sin's black memory;
That Thou remember them, some claim as debt,
I think it mercy, if Thou wilt forget.

X

Death be not proud, though some have called thee
Mighty and dreadful, for, thou art not so,
For, those, whom thou think'st, thou dost overthrow,
Die not, poor death, nor yet canst thou kill me.
From rest and sleep, which but thy pictures be,
Much pleasure, then from thee, much more must flow,
And soonest our best men with thee do go,
Rest of their bones, and soul's delivery.
Thou art slave to Fate, Chance, kings, and desperate men,

And dost with poison, war, and sickness dwell,
And poppy, or charms can make us sleep as well,
And better than thy stroke; why swell'st thou then?
One short sleep past, we wake eternally,
And death shall be no more; death, thou shalt die.

XI

SPIT in my face you Jews, and pierce my side,
Buffet, and scoff, scourge, and crucify me,
For I have sinn'd, and sinn'd, and only He,
Who could do no iniquity, hath died:
But by my death can not be satisfied
My sins, which pass the Jews' impiety:
They kill'd once an inglorious man, but I
Crucify him daily, being now glorified.
Oh let me then, His strange love still admire:
Kings pardon, but He bore our punishment.
And Jacob came cloth'd in vile harsh attire
But to supplant, and with gainful intent:
God cloth'd himself in vile man's flesh, that so
He might be weak enough to suffer woe.

XII

WHY are we by all creatures waited on?
Why do the prodigal elements supply
Life and food to me, being more pure than I,
Simple, and further from corruption?
Why brook'st thou, ignorant horse, subjection?
Why dost thou bull, and boar so sillily
Dissemble weakness, and by one man's stroke die,
Whose whole kind, you might swallow and feed upon?
Weaker I am, woe is me, and worse than you,
You have not sinn'd, nor need be timorous.
But wonder at a greater wonder, for to us
Created nature doth these things subdue,
But their Creator, whom sin, nor nature tied,
For us, His Creatures, and His foes, hath died.

XIII

WHAT if this present were the world's last night?
Mark in my heart, O Soul, where thou dost dwell,

The picture of Christ crucified, and tell
Whether that countenance can thee affright,
Tears in His eyes quench the amazing light,
Blood fills His frowns, which from His pierc'd head fell.
And can that tongue adjudge thee unto hell,
Which pray'd forgiveness for His foes' fierce spite?
No, no; but as in my idolatry
I said to all my profane mistresses,
Beauty, of pity, foulness only is
A sign of rigour: so I say to thee,
To wicked spirits are horrid shapes assign'd,
This beauteous form assures a piteous mind.

XIV

BATTER my heart, three-person'd God; for, you
As yet but knock, breathe, shine, and seek to mend;
That I may rise, and stand, o'erthrow me, and bend
Your force, to break, blow, burn and make me new.
I, like an usurp'd town, to another due,
Labour to admit you, but Oh, to no end,
Reason your viceroy in me, me should defend,
But is captiv'd, and proves weak or untrue.
Yet dearly I love you, and would be loved fain,
But am betroth'd unto your enemy:
Divorce me, untie, or break that knot again,
Take me to you, imprison me, for I
Except you enthral me, never shall be free,
Nor ever chaste, except you ravish me.

XV

WILT thou love God, as He thee? then digest,
My Soul, this wholesome meditation,
How God the Spirit, by Angels waited on
In heaven, doth make His Temple in thy breast.
The Father having begot a Son most blest,
And still begetting, (for he ne'er begun)
Hath deign'd to choose thee by adoption,
Coheir to His glory, and Sabbath's endless rest;
And as a robb'd man, which by search doth find
His stol'n stuff sold, must lose or buy it again:

The Son of glory came down, and was slain,
Us whom He had made, and Satan stol'n, to unbind.
'Twas much, that man was made like God before,
But, that God should be made like man, much more.

XVI

FATHER, part of His double interest
Unto Thy kingdom, Thy Son gives to me,
His jointure in the knotty Trinity
He keeps, and gives to me His death's conquest.
This Lamb, whose death, with life the world hath blest,
Was from the world's beginning slain, and He
Hath made two Wills, which with the Legacy
Of His and Thy kingdom, do Thy Sons invest.
Yet such are Thy laws, that men argue yet
Whether a man those statutes can fulfil;
None doth; but all-healing grace and spirit
Revive again what law and letter kill.
Thy law's abridgement, and Thy last command
Is all but love; Oh let this last Will stand!

XVII

SINCE she whom I lov'd hath paid her last debt
To Nature, and to hers, and my good is dead,
And her Soul early into heaven ravished,
Wholly on heavenly things my mind is set.
Here the admiring her my mind did whet
To seek Thee God; so streams do show their head;
But though I have found Thee, and Thou my thirst hast fed,
A holy thirsty dropsy melts me yet.
But why should I beg more Love, when as Thou
Dost woo my soul for hers; off'ring all Thine:
And dost not only fear lest I allow
My Love to Saints and Angels, things divine,
But in Thy tender jealousy dost doubt
Lest the World, Flesh, yea Devil put Thee out.

XVIII

SHOW me, dear Christ, Thy Spouse, so bright and clear.
What! is it She, which on the other shore

Goes richly painted? or which rob'd and tore
Laments and mourns in Germany and here?
Sleeps she a thousand, then peeps up one year?
Is she self truth and errs? now new, now outwore?
Doth she, and did she, and shall she evermore
On one, on seven, or on no hill appear?
Dwells she with us, or like adventuring knights
First travail we to seek and then make Love?
Betray kind husband thy spouse to our sights,
And let mine amorous soul court thy mild Dove,
Who is most true, and pleasing to thee, then
When she is embrac'd and open to most men.

XIX

Oh, to vex me, contraries meet in one;
Inconstancy unnaturally hath begot
A constant habit; that when I would not
I change in vows, and in devotion.
As humorous is my contrition
As my profane Love, and as soon forgot:
As riddlingly distemper'd, cold and hot,
As praying, as mute; as infinite, as none.
I durst not view heaven yesterday; and to day
In prayers, and flattering speeches I court God:
To-morrow I quake with true fear of His rod.
So my devout fits come and go away
Like a fantastic Ague: save that here
Those are my best days, when I shake with fear.

THE CROSS

Since Christ embrac'd the Cross itself, dare I
His image, th' image of His Cross deny?
Would I have profit by the sacrifice,
And dare the chosen Altar to despise?
It bore all other sins, but is it fit
That it should bear the sin of scorning it?
Who from the picture would avert his eye,
How would he fly his pains, who there did die?

From me, no Pulpit, nor misgrounded law,
Nor scandal taken, shall this Cross withdraw,
It shall not, for it cannot; for, the loss
Of this Cross, were to me another Cross;
Better were worse, for, no affliction,
No Cross is so extreme, as to have none.
Who can blot out the Cross, which th' instrument
Of God, dew'd on me in the Sacrament?
Who can deny me power, and liberty
To stretch mine arms, and mine own Cross to be?
Swim, and at every stroke, thou art thy Cross;
The Mast and yard make one, where seas do toss;
Look down, thou spiest out Crosses in small things;
Look up, thou seest birds rais'd on crossed wings;
All the Globe's frame, and sphere's, is nothing else
But the Meridians crossing Parallels.
Material Crosses then, good physic be,
But yet spiritual have chief dignity.
These for extracted chemic medicine serve,
And cure much better, and as well preserve;
Then are you your own physic, or need none,
When still'd, or purg'd by tribulation.
For when that Cross ungrudg'd, unto you sticks,
Then are you to yourself, a Crucifix.
As perchance, Carvers do not faces make,
But that away, which hid them there, do take;
Let Crosses, so, take what hid Christ in thee,
And be His image, or not His, but He.
But, as oft Alchemists do coiners prove,
So may a self-despising, get self-love;
And then as worst surfeits, of best meats be,
So is pride, issued from humility,
For, 'tis no child, but monster; therefore Cross
Your joy in crosses, else, 'tis double loss,
And cross thy senses, else, both they, and thou
Must perish soon, and to destruction bow.
For if the eye seek good objects, and will take
No cross from bad, we cannot 'scape a snake.
So with harsh, hard, sour, stinking, cross the rest,
Make them indifferent all; call nothing best.

But most the eye needs crossing, that can roam,
And move; to th' other th' objects must come home.
And cross thy heart: for that in man alone
Points downwards, and hath palpitation.
Cross those dejections, when it downward tends,
And when it to forbidden heights pretends.
And as the brain through bony walls doth vent
By sutures, which a Cross's form present,
So when thy brain works, ere thou utter it,
Cross and correct concupiscence of wit.
Be covetous of Crosses, let none fall.
Cross no man else, but cross thyself in all.
Then doth the Cross of Christ work fruitfully
Within our hearts, when we love harmlessly
That Cross's pictures much, and with more care
That Cross's children, which our Crosses are.

RESURRECTION, IMPERFECT

Sleep sleep old Sun, thou canst not have repass'd
As yet, the wound thou took'st on Friday last;
Sleep then, and rest; Thy world may bear thy stay,
A better Sun rose before thee to-day,
Who, not content to enlighten all that dwell
On the earth's face, as thou, enlighten'd hell,
And made the dark fires languish in that vale,
As, at thy presence here, our fires grow pale.
Whose body having walk'd on earth, and now
Hasting to Heaven, would, that He might allow
Himself unto all stations, and fill all,
For these three days become a mineral;
He was all gold when He lay down, but rose
All tincture, and doth not alone dispose
Leaden and iron wills to good, but is
Of power to make even sinful flesh like His.
Had one of those, whose credulous piety
Thought, that a Soul one might discern and see

Go from a body, at this sepulchre been,
And, issuing from the sheet, this body seen,
He would have justly thought this body a soul,
If not of any man, yet of the whole.
Desunt cætera.

UPON THE ANNUNCIATION AND PASSION

FALLING UPON ONE DAY. 1608

TAMELY, frail body, abstain to-day; to-day
My soul eats twice, Christ hither and away.
She sees Him man, so like God made in this,
That of them both a circle emblem is,
Whose first and last concur; this doubtful day
Of feast or fast, Christ came, and went away.
She sees Him nothing twice at once, who 's all;
She sees a Cedar plant itself, and fall,
Her Maker put to making, and the head
Of life, at once, not yet alive, yet dead.
She sees at once the virgin mother stay
Reclus'd at home, public at Golgotha;
Sad and rejoiced she 's seen at once, and seen
At almost fifty, and at scarce fifteen.
At once a Son is promis'd her, and gone,
Gabriel gives Christ to her, He her to John;
Not fully a mother, She 's in orbity,
At once receiver and the legacy.
All this, and all between, this day hath shown,
Th' Abridgement of Christ's story, which makes one
(As in plain Maps, the furthest West is East)
Of the Angels' *Ave*, and *Consummatum est.*
How well the Church, God's Court of faculties
Deals, in some times, and seldom joining these!
As by the self-fix'd Pole we never do
Direct our course, but the next star thereto,
Which shows where the other is, and which we say
(Because it strays not far) doth never stray;
So God by His Church, nearest to Him, we know,
And stand firm, if we by her motion go;

His Spirit, as His fiery Pillar doth
Lead, and His Church, as cloud; to one end both.
This Church, by letting these days join, hath shown
Death and conception in mankind is one;
Or 'twas in Him the same humility,
That He would be a man, and leave to be:
Or as creation He hath made, as God,
With the last judgment, but one period,
His imitating Spouse would join in one
Manhood's extremes: He shall come, He is gone:
Or as though one blood drop, which thence did fall,
Accepted would have serv'd, He yet shed all;
So though the least of His pains, deeds, or words,
Would busy a life, she all this day affords;
This treasure then, in gross, my Soul uplay,
And in my life retail it every day.

GOOD FRIDAY, 1613.   RIDING WESTWARD

LET man's Soul be a Sphere, and then, in this,
The intelligence that moves, devotion is,
And as the other Spheres, by being grown
Subject to foreign motions, lose their own,
And being by others hurried every day,
Scarce in a year their natural form obey:
Pleasure or business, so, our Souls admit
For their first mover, and are whirl'd by it.
Hence is 't, that I am carried towards the West
This day, when my Soul's form bends toward the East.
There I should see a Sun, by rising set,
And by that setting endless day beget;
But that Christ on this Cross, did rise and fall,
Sin had eternally benighted all.
Yet dare I almost be glad, I do not see
That spectacle of too much weight for me.
Who sees God's face, that is self life, must die;
What a death were it then to see God die?
It made His own Lieutenant Nature shrink,

It made His footstool crack, and the Sun wink.
Could I behold those hands which span the Poles,
And turn all spheres at once, pierced with those holes?
Could I behold that endless height which is
Zenith to us, and our Antipodes,
Humbled below us? or that blood which is
The seat of all our Souls, if not of His,
Made dirt of dust, or that flesh which was worn,
By God, for His apparel, rag'd, and torn?
If on these things I durst not look, durst I
Upon his miserable mother cast mine eye,
Who was God's partner here, and furnish'd thus
Half of that Sacrifice, which ransom'd us?
Though these things, as I ride, be from mine eye,
They 're present yet unto my memory,
For that looks towards them; and Thou look'st towards me
O Saviour, as Thou hang'st upon the tree;
I turn my back to Thee, but to receive
Corrections, till Thy mercies bid Thee leave.
O think me worth Thine anger, punish me,
Burn off my rusts, and my deformity,
Restore Thine Image, so much, by Thy grace,
That Thou may'st know me, and I 'll turn my face.

THE LITANY

I

THE FATHER

FATHER of Heaven, and Him, by whom
It, and us for it, and all else, for us
  Thou madest, and govern'st ever, come
And re-create me, now grown ruinous:
    My heart is by dejection, clay,
    And by self-murder, red.
From this red earth, O Father, purge away
All vicious tinctures, that new fashioned
I may rise up from death, before I 'm dead.

II

THE SON

O Son of God, who seeing two things,
Sin, and death crept in, which were never made,
By bearing one, tried'st with what stings
The other could Thine heritage invade;
O be thou nail'd unto my heart,
And crucified again,
Part not from it, though it from Thee would part,
But let it be, by applying so Thy pain,
Drown'd in Thy blood, and in Thy passion slain.

III

THE HOLY GHOST

O Holy Ghost, whose temple I
Am, but of mud walls, and condensèd dust,
And being sacrilegiously
Half wasted with youth's fires, of pride and lust,
Must with new storms be weather-beat;
Double in my heart Thy flame,
Which let devout sad tears intend; and let
(Though this glass lanthorn, flesh, do suffer maim)
Fire, Sacrifice, Priest, Altar be the same.

IV

THE TRINITY

O Blessed glorious Trinity,
Bones to Philosophy, but milk to faith,
Which, as wise serpents, diversely
Most slipperiness, yet most entanglings hath,
As you distinguish'd undistinct
By power, love, knowledge be,
Give me a such self different instinct
Of these; let all me elemented be,
Of power, to love, to know, you unnumber'd three.

THE LITANY

V

THE VIRGIN MARY

For that fair blessed Mother-maid,
Whose flesh redeem'd us; that she-Cherubin,
  Which unlock'd Paradise, and made
One claim for innocence, and disseiz'd sin,
     Whose womb was a strange heav'n, for there
     God cloth'd Himself, and grew,
Our zealous thanks we pour. As her deeds were
Our helps, so are her prayers; nor can she sue
In vain, who hath such titles unto You.

VI

THE ANGELS

And since this life our nonage is,
And we in Wardship to Thine Angels be,
  Native in heaven's fair Palaces,
Where we shall be but denizen'd by Thee,
     As th' earth conceiving by the Sun,
     Yields fair diversity,
Yet never knows which course that light doth run,
So let me study, that mine actions be
Worthy their sight, though blind in how they see.

VII

THE PATRIARCHS

And let thy Patriarchs' Desire
(Those great Grandfathers of Thy Church, which saw
  More in the cloud, than we in fire,
Whom Nature clear'd more, than us Grace and Law,
     And now in Heaven still pray, that we
     May use our new helps right,)
Be satisfied, and fructify in me;
Let not my mind be blinder by more light
Nor Faith, by Reason added, lose her sight.

VIII

THE PROPHETS

Thy Eagle-sighted Prophets too,
Which were thy Church's Organs, and did sound

That harmony, which made of two
One law, and did unite, but not confound;
  Those heavenly Poets which did see
  Thy will, and it express
In rhythmic feet, in common pray for me,
That I by them excuse not my excess
In seeking secrets, or poeticness.

IX

THE APOSTLES

And Thy illustrious Zodiac
Of twelve Apostles, which engirt this All,
  (From whom whosoever do not take
Their light, to dark deep pits, throw down, and fall,)
  As through their prayers, Thou 'st let me know
  That their books are divine;
May they pray still, and be heard, that I go
Th' old broad way in applying; O decline
Me, when my comment would make Thy word mine.

X

THE MARTYRS

And since Thou so desirously
Did'st long to die, that long before Thou could'st,
  And long since Thou no more could'st die,
Thou in thy scatter'd mystic body wouldst
  In Abel die, and ever since
  In Thine; let their blood come
To beg for us, a discreet patience
Of death, or of worse life: for Oh, to some
Not to be Martyrs, is a martyrdom.

XI

THE CONFESSORS

Therefore with thee triumpheth there
A Virgin Squadron of white Confessors,
  Whose bloods betroth'd, not married were,
Tender'd, not taken by those Ravishers:

They know, and pray, that we may know,
   In every Christian
Hourly tempestuous persecutions grow;
Temptations martyr us alive; a man
Is to himself a Dioclesian.

XII

THE VIRGINS

The cold white snowy Nunnery,
Which, as Thy mother, their high Abbess, sent
   Their bodies back again to Thee,
As Thou hadst lent them, clean and innocent,
      Though they have not obtain'd of Thee,
      That or Thy Church, or I,
Should keep, as they, our first integrity;
Divorce thou sin in us, or bid it die,
And call chaste widowhead virginity.

XIII

THE DOCTORS

Thy sacred Academy above
Of Doctors, whose pains have unclasp'd, and taught
   Both books of life to us (for love
To know Thy Scriptures tells us, we are wrote
      In Thy other book) pray for us there
      That what they have misdone
Or mis-said, we to that may not adhere;
Their zeal may be our sin.   Lord let us run
Mean ways, and call them stars, but not the Sun.

XIV

And whilst this universal Quire,
That Church in triumph, this in warfare here,
   Warm'd with one all-partaking fire
Of love, that none be lost, which cost Thee dear,
      Prays ceaselessly, and Thou hearken too,
      (Since to be gracious

Our task is treble, to pray, bear, and do)
Hear this prayer Lord: O Lord deliver us
From trusting in those prayers, though poured out thus.

XV

From being anxious, or secure,
Dead clods of sadness, or light squibs of mirth,
From thinking, that great courts immure
All, or no happiness, or that this earth
Is only for our prison fram'd,
Or that Thou art covetous
To them Thou lovest, or that they are maim'd
From reaching this world's sweet, who seek Thee thus,
With all their might, Good Lord deliver us.

XVI

From needing danger, to be good,
From owing Thee yesterday's tears to day,
From trusting so much to Thy blood,
That in that hope, we wound our soul away,
From bribing Thee with Alms, to excuse
Some sin more burdenous,
From light affecting, in religion, news,
From thinking us all soul, neglecting thus
Our mutual duties, Lord deliver us.

XVII

From tempting Satan to tempt us,
By our connivance, or slack company,
From measuring ill by vicious,
Neglecting to choke sin's spawn, Vanity,
From indiscreet humility,
Which might be scandalous,
And cast reproach on Christianity,
From being spies, or to spies pervious,
From thirst, or scorn of fame, deliver us.

XVIII

Deliver us for Thy descent
Into the Virgin, whose womb was a place
 Of middle kind; and Thou being sent
To ungracious us, stayed'st at her full of grace;
    And through Thy poor birth, where first Thou
      Glorified'st Poverty,
And yet soon after riches didst allow,
By accepting Kings' gifts in the Epiphany,
Deliver, and make us, to both ways free.

XIX

And through that bitter agony,
Which is still the agony of pious wits,
 Disputing what distorted Thee,
And interrupted evenness, with fits;
    And through Thy free confession
    Though thereby they were then
Made blind, so that Thou might'st from them have gone,
Good Lord deliver us, and teach us when
We may not, and we may blind unjust men.

XX

Through Thy submitting all, to blows
Thy face, Thy clothes to spoil; Thy fame to scorn,
 All ways, which rage, or Justice knows,
And by which Thou could'st show, that Thou wast born;
    And through Thy gallant humbleness
    Which Thou in death did'st show,
Dying before Thy soul they could express,
Deliver us from death, by dying so,
To this world, ere this world do bid us go.

XXI

When senses, which Thy soldiers are,
We arm against Thee, and they fight for sin,
 When want, sent but to tame, doth war
And work despair a breach to enter in,

When plenty, God's image, and seal
    Makes us Idolatrous,
And love it, not Him, whom it should reveal,
When we are mov'd to seem religious
Only to vent wit, Lord deliver us.

XXII

In Churches, when the infirmity
Of him which speaks, diminishes the Word,
    When Magistrates do mis-apply
To us, as we judge, lay or ghostly sword,
        When plague, which is Thine Angel, reigns,
        Or wars, Thy Champions, sway,
When Heresy, Thy second deluge, gains;
In th' hour of death, th' Eve of last judgment day,
Deliver us from the sinister way.

XXIII

Hear us, O hear us Lord; to Thee
A sinner is more music, when he prays,
    Than spheres, or Angels' praises be,
In Panegyric Alleluias;
        Hear us, for till Thou hear us, Lord
        We know not what to say;
Thine ear to our sighs, tears, thoughts gives voice and word.
O Thou who Satan heard'st in Job's sick day,
Hear Thyself now, for Thou in us dost pray.

XXIV

That we may change to evenness
This intermitting aguish Piety;
    That snatching cramps of wickedness
And Apoplexies of fast sin, may die;
        That music of Thy promises,
        Not threats in Thunder may
Awaken us to our just offices;
What in Thy book, Thou dost, or creatures say,
That we may hear, Lord hear us, when we pray.

XXV

That our ears' sickness we may cure,
And rectify those Labyrinths aright,
   That we, by heark'ning, not procure
Our praise, nor others' dispraise so invite,
     That we get not a slipperiness,
     And senselessly decline,
From hearing bold wits jest at Kings' excess,
To admit the like of majesty divine,
That we may lock our ears, Lord open Thine.

XXVI

That living law, the Magistrate,
Which to give us, and make us physic, doth,
   Our vices often aggravate,
That Preachers taxing sin, before her growth,
     That Satan, and envenom'd men
     Which well, if we starve, dine,
When they do most accuse us, may see then
Us, to amendment, hear them; Thee decline:
That we may open our ears, Lord lock Thine.

XXVII

That learning, Thine Ambassador,
From Thine allegiance we never tempt,
   That beauty, paradise's flower
For physic made, from poison be exempt,
     That wit, born apt high good to do,
     By dwelling lazily
On Nature's nothing, be not nothing too,
That our affections kill us not, nor die,
Hear us, weak echoes, O thou ear, and cry.

XXVIII

Son of God hear us, and since Thou
By taking our blood, owest it us again,
   Gain to Thyself, or us allow;
And let not both us and Thyself be slain;

> O Lamb of God, which took'st our sin
> Which could not stick to Thee,
> O let it not return to us again,
> But Patient and Physician being free,
> As sin is nothing, let it nowhere be.

UPON THE TRANSLATION OF THE PSALMS

BY SIR PHILIP SIDNEY,

AND THE COUNTESS OF PEMBROKE HIS SISTER

ETERNAL God, (for whom who ever dare
Seek new expressions, do the Circle square,
And thrust into strait corners of poor wit
Thee, who art cornerless and infinite)
I would but bless Thy Name, not name Thee now;
(And Thy gifts are as infinite as Thou:)
Fix we our praises therefore on this one,
That, as Thy blessed Spirit fell upon
These Psalms' first Author in a cloven tongue;
(For 'twas a double power by which he sung
The highest matter in the noblest form;)
So Thou hast cleft that spirit, to perform
That work again, and shed it, here, upon
Two, by their bloods, and by thy Spirit one;
A Brother and a Sister, made by Thee
The Organ, where Thou art the Harmony.
Two that make one *John Baptist's* holy voice,
And who that Psalm, *Now let the Isles rejoice*,
Have both translated, and apply'd it too,
Both told us what, and taught us how to do.
They show us Islanders our joy, our King,
They tell us *why*, and teach us *how* to sing;
Make all this All, three Quires, heaven, earth, and spheres;
The first, Heaven, hath a song, but no man hears,
The Spheres have Music, but they have no tongue,
·Their harmony is rather danc'd than sung;

But our third Quire, to which the first gives ear,
(For, Angels learn by what the Church does here)
This Quire hath all.   The Organist is he
Who hath tun'd God and Man, the Organ we:
The songs are these, which heaven's high holy Muse
Whisper'd to *David*, *David* to the Jews:
And *David's* Successors, in holy zeal,
In forms of joy and art do re-reveal
To us so sweetly and sincerely too,
That I must not rejoice as I would do
When I behold that these Psalms are become
So well attired abroad, so ill at home,
So well in Chambers, in thy Church so ill,
As I can scarce call that reform'd until
This be reform'd; would a whole State present
A lesser gift than some one man hath sent?
And shall our Church, unto our Spouse and King
More hoarse, more harsh than any other, sing?.
For *that* we pray, we praise Thy name for *this*,
Which, by this *Moses* and this *Miriam*, is
Already done; and as those Psalms we call
(Though some have other Authors) *David's* all:
So though some have, some may some Psalms translate,
We thy Sidneian Psalms shall celebrate,
And, till we come th' Extemporal song to sing,
(Learn'd the first hour, that we see the King,
Who hath translated those translators) may
These their sweet learned labours, all the way
Be as our tuning, that, when hence we part,
We may fall in with them, and sing our part.

TO MR. TILMAN AFTER HE HAD TAKEN ORDERS

THOU, whose diviner soul hath caus'd thee now
To put thy hand unto the holy Plough,
Making Lay-scornings of the Ministry,
Not an impediment, but victory;
What bringst thou home with thee? how is thy mind
Affected since the vintage? Dost thou find
New thoughts and stirrings in thee? and as Steel
Touch'd with a Loadstone, dost new motions feel?
Or, as a Ship after much pain and care,
For Iron and Cloth brings home rich Indian ware,
Hast thou thus traffick'd, but with far more gain
Of noble goods, and with less time and pain?
Thou art the same materials, as before,
Only the stamp is changed; but no more.
And as new crowned Kings alter the face,
But not the money's substance; so hath grace
Chang'd only God's old Image by Creation,
To Christ's new stamp, at this thy Coronation;
Or, as we paint Angels with wings, because
They bear God's message, and proclaim His laws,
Since thou must do the like and so must move,
Art thou new feather'd with celestial love?
Dear, tell me where thy purchase lies, and show
What thy advantage is above, below.
But if thy gainings do surmount expression,
Why doth the foolish world scorn that profession,
Whose joys pass speech? Why do they think unfit
That Gentry should join families with it?
As if their day were only to be spent
In dressing, Mistressing and compliment;
Alas poor joys, but poorer men, whose trust
Seems richly placed in sublimed dust;
(For, such are clothes and beauty, which though gay,
Are, at the best, but of sublimed clay.)
Let then the world thy calling disrespect,
But go thou on, and pity their neglect.

What function is so noble, as to be
Ambassador to God and destiny?
To open life, to give kingdoms to more
Than Kings give dignities; to keep heaven's door?
Mary's prerogative was to bear Christ, so
'Tis preachers' to convey Him, for they do
As Angels out of clouds, from Pulpits speak;
And bless the poor beneath, the lame, the weak.
If then th' Astronomers, whereas they spy
A new-found Star, their Optics magnify,
How brave are those, who with their Engine, can
Bring man to heaven, and heaven again to man?
These are thy titles and pre-eminences,
In whom must meet God's graces, men's offences,
And so the heavens which beget all things here,
And the earth our mother, which these things doth bear,
Both these in thee, are in thy Calling knit,
And make thee now a blest Hermaphrodite.

A HYMN TO CHRIST

AT THE AUTHOR'S LAST GOING INTO GERMANY

In what torn ship soever I embark,
That ship shall be my emblem of Thy Ark;
What sea soever swallow me, that flood
Shall be to me an emblem of Thy blood;
Though Thou with clouds of anger do disguise
Thy face; yet through that mask I know those eyes,
  Which, though they turn away sometimes,
    They never will despise.

I sacrifice this Island unto Thee,
And all whom I lov'd there, and who lov'd me;
When I have put our seas 'twixt them and me,
Put thou Thy sea betwixt my sins and Thee.

As the tree's sap doth seek the root below
In winter, in my winter now I go,
    Where none but Thee, th' Eternal root
      Of true Love I may know.

Nor Thou nor Thy religion dost control,
The amorousness of an harmonious Soul,
But thou would'st have that love Thyself: as Thou
Art jealous, Lord, so I am jealous now,
Thou lov'st not, till from loving more, Thou free
My soul: who ever gives, takes liberty:
    O, if Thou car'st not whom I love
      Alas, Thou lov'st not me.

Seal then this bill of my Divorce to All,
On whom those fainter beams of love did fall;
Marry those loves, which in youth scattered be
On Fame, Wit, Hopes (false mistresses) to Thee.
Churches are best for Prayer, that have least light:
To see God only, I go out of sight:
    And to 'scape stormy days, I choose
      An Everlasting night.

THE LAMENTATIONS OF JEREMY

FOR THE MOST PART ACCORDING TO TREMELLIUS

Chap. I

1 How sits this city, late most populous,
    Thus solitary, and like a widow thus!
Amplest of Nations, Queen of Provinces
    She was, who now thus tributary is!

2 Still in the night she weeps, and her tears fall
    Down by her cheeks along, and none of all
Her lovers comfort her; perfidiously
    Her friends have dealt, and now are enemy.

3 Unto great bondage, and afflictions
  Judah is captive led; those nations
With whom she dwells, no place of rest afford,
  In straits she meets her Persecutor's sword.

4 Empty are the gates of Sion, and her ways
  Mourn, because none come to her solemn days.
Her Priests do groan, her maids are comfortless,
  And she's unto herself a bitterness.

5 Her foes are grown her head, and live at Peace,
  Because when her transgressions did increase,
The Lord struck her with sadness: the enemy
  Doth drive her children to captivity.

6 From Sion's daughter is all beauty gone,
  Like Harts, which seek for Pasture, and find none,
Her Princes are, and now before the foe
  Which still pursues them, without strength they go.

7 Now in her days of Tears, Jerusalem
  (Her men slain by the foe, none succouring them)
Remembers what of old, she esteemed most,
  Whilst her foes laugh at her, for what she hath lost.

8 Jerusalem hath sinn'd, therefore is she
  Remov'd, as women in uncleanness be;
Who honour'd, scorn her, for her foulness they
  Have seen; herself doth groan, and turn away.

9 Her foulness in her skirts was seen, yet she
  Remember'd not her end; miraculously
Therefore she fell, none comforting: behold
  O Lord my affliction, for the Foe grows bold.

10 Upon all things where her delight hath been,
  The foe hath stretch'd his hand, for she hath seen
Heathen, whom thou command'st, should not do so,
  Into her holy Sanctuary go.

11 And all her people groan, and seek for bread;
   And they have given, only to be fed,
All precious things, wherein their pleasure lay:
   How cheap I 'm grown, O Lord, bèhold, and weigh.

12 All this concerns not you, who pass by me,
   O see, and mark if any sorrow be
Like to my sorrow, which Jehovah hath
   Done to me in the day of His fierce wrath?

13 That fire, which by Himself is governed
   He hath cast from heaven on my bones, and spread
A net before my feet, and me o'erthrown,
   And made me languish all the day alone.

14 His hand hath of my sins framed a yoke
   Which wreath'd, and cast upon my neck, hath broke
My strength.   The Lord unto these enemies
   Hath given me, from whom I cannot rise.

15 He under foot hath trodden in my sight
   My strong men; He did company invite
To break my young men; He the vinepress hath
   Trod upon Judah's daughter in His wrath.

16 For these things do I weep, mine eye, mine eye
   Casts water out; for He which should be nigh
To comfort me, is now departed far;
   The foe prevails, forlorn my children are.

17 There 's none, though *Sion* do stretch out her hand,
   To comfort her, it is the Lord's command
That *Jacob's* foes girt him.   *Jerusalem*
   Is as an unclean woman amongst them.

18 But yet the Lord is just, and righteous still,
   I have rebell'd against His holy will;
O hear all people, and my sorrow see,
   My maids, my young men in captivity.

19 I called for my lovers then, but they
   Deceiv'd me, and my Priests, and Elders lay
Dead in the city; for they sought for meat
   Which should refresh their souls, they could not get.

20 Because I am in straits, *Jehovah* see
   My heart o'erturned, my bowels muddy be,
Because I have rebell'd so much, as fast
   The sword without, as death within, doth waste.

21 Of all which hear I mourn, none comforts me,
   My foes have heard my grief, and glad they be,
That Thou hast done it; but Thy promis'd day
   Will come, when, as I suffer, so shall they.

22 Let all their wickedness appear to Thee,
   Do unto them, as thou hast done to me,
For all my sins: the sighs which I have had
   Are very many, and my heart is sad.

CHAP. II

1 How over Sion's daughter hath God hung
   His wrath's thick cloud! and from heaven hath flung
To earth the beauty of *Israel*, and hath
   Forgot His foot-stool in the day of wrath!

2 The Lord unsparingly hath swallowed
   All Jacob's dwellings, and demolished
To ground the strengths of Judah, and profaned
   The Princes of the Kingdom, and the land.

3 In heat of wrath, the horn of *Israel* He
   Hath clean cut off, and lest the enemy
Be hindered, His right hand He doth retire,
   But is towards *Jacob*, All-devouring fire.

4 Like to an enemy He bent His bow,
   His right hand was in posture of a foe,
To kill what *Sion's* daughter did desire,
   'Gainst whom His wrath, He poured forth, like fire.

5 For like an enemy *Jehovah* is,
  Devouring *Israel*, and his Palaces,
Destroying holds, giving additions
  To *Judah's* daughters' lamentations.

6 Like to a garden hedge He hath cast down
  The place where was his congregation,
And *Sion's* feasts and sabbaths are forgot;
  Her King, her Priest, His wrath regardeth not.

7 The Lord forsakes His Altar, and detests
  His Sanctuary, and in the foes' hand rests
His Palace, and the walls, in which their cries
  Are heard, as in the true solemnities.

8 The Lord hath cast a line, so to confound
  And level *Sion's* walls unto the ground;
He draws not back His hand, which doth o'erturn
  The wall, and Rampart, which together mourn.

9 Their gates are sunk into the ground, and He
  Hath broke the bars; their King and Princes be
Amongst the heathen, without law, nor there
  Unto their Prophets doth the Lord appear.

10 There *Sion's Elders* on the ground are plac'd,
  And silence keep; dust on their heads they cast,
In sackcloth have they girt themselves, and low
  The Virgins towards ground, their heads do throw.

11 My bowels are grown muddy, and mine eyes
  Are faint with weeping: and my liver lies
Pour'd out upon the ground, for misery
  That sucking children in the streets do die.

12 When they had cried unto their Mothers, where
  Shall we have bread, and drink? they fainted there,
And in the streets like wounded persons lay
  Till 'twixt their mothers' breasts they went away.

13 *Daughter Jerusalem*, Oh what may be
    A witness, or comparison for thee?
Sion, to ease thee, what shall I name like thee?
    Thy breach is like the sea, what help can be?

14 For thee vain foolish things thy Prophets sought,
    Thee, thine iniquities they have not taught,
Which might disturb thy bondage: but for thee
    False burthens, and false causes they would see.

15 The passengers do clap their hands, and hiss,
    And wag their head at thee, and say, Is this
That city, which so many men did call
    Joy of the earth, and perfectest of all?

16 Thy foes do gape upon thee, and they hiss,
    And gnash their teeth, and say, Devour we this,
For this is certainly the day which we
    Expected, and which now we find, and see.

17 The Lord hath done that which He purposed,
    Fulfill'd His word of old determined;
He hath thrown down, and not spar'd, and thy foe
    Made glad above thee, and advanc'd him so.

18 But now, their hearts against the Lord do call,
    Therefore, O walls of *Sion*, let tears fall
Down like a river, day and night; take thee
    No rest, but let thine eye incessant be.

19 Arise, cry in the night, pour, for thy sins,
    Thy heart, like water, when the watch begins;
Lift up thy hands to God, lest children die,
    Which, faint for hunger, in the streets do lie.

20 Behold O Lord, consider unto whom
    Thou hast done this; what, shall the women come
To eat their children of a span? shall Thy
    Prophet and Priest be slain in Sanctuary?

21 On grounds in streets, the young and old do lie,
 My virgins and young men by sword do die;
Them in the day of Thy wrath Thou hast slain,
 Nothing did Thee from killing them contain.

22 As to a solemn feast, all whom I fear'd
 Thou call'st about me; when Thy wrath appear'd,
None did remain or 'scape, for those which I
 Brought up, did perish by mine enemy.

CHAP. III

1 I AM the man which have affliction seen,
 Under the rod of God's wrath having been,
2 He hath led me to darkness, not to light,
 3 And against me all day, His hand doth fight.

4 He hath broke my bones, worn out my flesh and skin,
 5 Built up against me; and hath girt me in
With hemlock, and with labour; 6 And set me
 In dark, as they who dead for ever be.

7 He hath hedg'd me lest I 'scape, and added more
 To my steel fetters, heavier than before.
8 When I cry out, He out shuts my prayer: 9 And hath
 Stopp'd with hewn stone my way, and turn'd my path.

10 And like a Lion hid in secrecy,
 Or Bear which lies in wait, He was to me.
11 He stops my way, tears me, made desolate,
 12 And He makes me the mark He shooteth at.

13 He made the children of His quiver pass
 Into my reins, 14 I with my people was
All the day long, a song and mockery.
 15 He hath fill'd me with bitterness, and He

Hath made me drunk with wormwood. 16 He hath burst
  My teeth with stones, and covered me with dust;
17 And thus my Soul far off from peace was set,
  And my prosperity I did forget.

18 My strength, my hope (unto myself I said)
  Which from the Lord should come, is perished.
19 But when my mournings I do think upon,
  My wormwood, hemlock, and affliction,

20 My Soul is humbled in rememb'ring this;
  21 My heart considers, therefore, hope there is.
22 'Tis God's great mercy we 're not utterly
  Consum'd, for His compassions do not die;

23 For every morning they renewed be,
  For great, O Lord, is Thy fidelity.
24 The Lord is, saith my Soul, my portion,
  And therefore in Him will I hope alone.

25 The Lord is good to them, who on Him rely,
  And to the Soul that seeks Him earnestly.
26 It is both good to trust, and to attend
  The Lord's salvation unto the end:

27 'Tis good for one His yoke in youth to bear;
  28 He sits alone, and doth all speech forbear,
Because he hath borne it. 29 And his mouth he lays
  Deep in the dust, yet then in hope he stays.

30 He gives his cheeks to whosoever will
  Strike him, and so he is reproached still.
31 For, not for ever doth the Lord forsake,
  32 But when He hath struck with sadness, He doth take

Compassion, as His mercy 's infinite;
  33 Nor is it with His heart, that He doth smite;
34 That underfoot the prisoners stamped be,
  35 That a man's right the Judge himself doth see

To be wrung from him, 36 That he subverted is
In his just cause; the Lord allows not this.
37 Who then will say, that aught doth come to pass,
But that which by the Lord commanded was?

38 Both good and evil from His mouth proceeds;
39 Why then grieves any man for his misdeeds?
40 Turn we to God, by trying out our ways;
41 To Him in heaven, our hands with hearts upraise.

42 We have rebell'd, and fall'n away from Thee,
Thou pardon'st not; 43 Usest no clemency;
Pursuest us, kill'st us, coverest us with wrath,
44 Cover'st Thyself with clouds, that our prayer hath

No power to pass. 45 And Thou hast made us fall
As refuse, and off-scouring to them all.
46 All our foes gape at us. 47 Fear and a snare
With ruin, and with waste, upon us are.

48 With watery rivers doth mine eye o'erflow
For ruin of my people's daughter so;
49 Mine eye doth drop down tears incessantly,
50 Until the Lord look down from heaven to see.

51 And for my city's daughters' sake, mine eye
Doth break mine heart. 52 Causeless mine enemy,
Like a bird chased me. 53 In a dungeon
They have shut my life, and cast on me a stone.

54 Waters flow'd o'er my head, then thought I, I am
Destroy'd; 55 I called Lord, upon Thy name
Out of the pit. 56 And Thou my voice didst hear;
Oh from my sigh, and cry, stop not Thine ear.

57 Then when I call'd upon Thee, Thou drew'st near
Unto me, and said'st unto me, Do not fear.
58 Thou Lord my Soul's cause handled hast, and Thou
Rescued'st my life. 59 O Lord do Thou judge now,

Thou heardst my wrong. 60 Their vengeance all they have
    wrought;
  61 How they reproach'd, Thou hast heard, and what they
    thought,
62 What their lips uttered, which against me rose,
  And what was ever whisper'd by my foes.

63 I am their song, whether they rise or sit,
  64 Give them rewards Lord, for their working fit,
65 Sorrow of heart, Thy curse. 66 And with Thy might
  Follow, and from under heaven destroy them quite.

Chap. IV

  1 How is the gold become so dim? How is
    Purest and finest gold thus chang'd to this?
The stones which were stones of the Sanctuary,
  Scatter'd in corners of each street do lie.

  2 The precious sons of Sion, which should be
    Valued at purest gold, how do we see
Low rated now, as earthen Pitchers, stand,
  Which are the work of a poor Potter's hand.

  3 Even the Sea-calfs draw their breasts, and give
    Suck to their young; my people's daughters live,
By reason of the foes' great cruelness,
  As do the Owls in the vast Wilderness.

  4 And when the sucking child doth strive to draw,
    His tongue for thirst cleaves to his upper jaw.
And when for bread the little children cry,
  There is no man that doth them satisfy.

  5 They which before were delicately fed,
    Now in the streets forlorn have perished,
And they which ever were in scarlet cloth'd,
  Sit and embrace the dunghills which they loath'd.

6 The daughters of my people have sinned more,
   Than did the town of *Sodom* sin before;
Which being at once destroy'd there did remain
   No hands amongst them, to vex them again.

7 But heretofore purer her Nazarite
   Was than the snow, and milk was not so white;
As carbuncles did their pure bodies shine,
   And all their polish'dness was sapphirine.

8 They are darker now than blackness, none can know
   Them by the face, as through the streets they go,
For now their skin doth cleave unto the bone,
   And withered, is like to dry wood grown.

9 Better by sword than famine 'tis to die;
   And better through-pierc'd, than through penury.
10 Women by nature pitiful have eat
   Their children dressed with their own hands for meat.

11 *Jehovah* here fully accomplish'd hath
   His indignation, and pour'd forth His wrath,
Kindled a fire in *Sion*, which hath power
   To eat, and her foundations to devour.

12 Nor would the Kings of the earth, nor all which live
   In the inhabitable world believe,
That any adversary, any foe
   Into *Jerusalem* should enter so.

13 For the Priests' sins, and Prophets', which have shed
   Blood in the streets, and the just murdered
14 Which when those men, whom they made blind, did stray
   Thorough the streets, defiled by the way

With blood, the which impossible it was
   Their garments should 'scape touching, as they pass,
15 Would cry aloud, Depart defiled men,
   Depart, depart, and touch us not: and then

They fled, and stray'd, and with the *Gentiles* were,
   Yet told their friends, they should not long dwell there;
16 For this they are scattered by Jehovah's face
   Who never will regard them more; no grace

Unto their old men shall the foe afford,
   Nor, that they are Priests, redeem them from the sword.
17 And we as yet, for all these miseries
   Desiring our vain help, consume our eyes:

And such a nation as cannot save,
   We in desire and speculation have.
18 They hunt our steps, that in the streets we fear
   To go: our end is now approached near,

Our days accomplish'd are, this the last day.
   19 Eagles of heaven are not so swift as they
Which fellow us, o'er mountain tops they fly
   At us, and for us in the desert lie.

20 The anointed Lord, breath of our nostrils, He
   Of whom we said, Under His shadow, we
Shall with more ease under the Heathen dwell,
   Into the pit which these men digged, fell.

21 Rejoice O *Edom's daughter*, joyful be
   Thou which inhabit'st *Huz*, for unto thee
This cup shall pass, and thou with drunkenness
   Shalt fill thyself, and show thy nakedness.

22 And then thy sins O *Sion*, shall be spent,
   The Lord will not leave thee in banishment.
Thy sins, O *Edom's daughter*, He will see,
   And for them, pay thee with captivity.

Chap. V

  1 Remember, O Lord, what is fallen on us;
    See, and mark how we are reproached thus,
  2 For unto strangers our possession
    Is turn'd, our houses unto Aliens gone,

3 Our mothers are become as widows, we
   As Orphans all, and without father be;
4 Waters which are our own, we drunk, and pay,
   And upon our own wood a price they lay.

5 Our persecutors on our necks do sit,
   They make us travail, and not intermit,
6 We stretch our hands unto th' *Egyptians*
   To get us bread; and to the *Assyrians*.

7 Our Fathers did these sins, and are no more,
   But we do bear the sins they did before.
8 They are but servants, which do rule us thus,
   Yet from their hands none would deliver us.

9 With danger of our life our bread we gat;
   For in the wilderness, the sword did wait.
10 The tempests of this famine we liv'd in,
   Black as an Oven colour'd had our skin:

11 In *Judah's* cities they the maids abus'd
   By force, and so women in *Sion* us'd.
12 The Princes with their hands they hung; no grace
   Nor honour gave they to the Elder's face.

13 Unto the mill our young men carried are,
   And children fell under the wood they bare.
14 Elders, the gates; youth did their songs forbear,
15 Gone was our joy; our dancings, mournings were.

16 Now is the crown fall'n from our head; and woe
   Be unto us, because we have sinned so.
17 For this our hearts do languish, and for this
   Over our eyes a cloudy dimness is.

18 Because mount *Sion* desolate doth lie,
   And foxes there do go at liberty:
19 But thou O Lord art ever, and Thy throne
   From generation, to generation.

20 Why should'st Thou forget us eternally?
   Or leave us thus long in this misery?
21 Restore us Lord to Thee, that so we may
   Return, and as of old, renew our day.

22 For oughtest thou, O Lord, despise us thus,
   And to be utterly enrag'd at us?

HYMN TO GOD MY GOD, IN MY SICKNESS

SINCE I am coming to that Holy room,
   Where, with thy Quire of Saints for evermore,
I shall be made thy Music; as I come
   I tune the Instrument here at the door,
   And what I must do then, think here before.

Whilst my Physicians by their love are grown
   Cosmographers, and I their Map, who lie
Flat on this bed, that by them may be shown
   That this is my South-west discovery
   Per fretum febris, by these straits to die,

I joy, that in these straits, I see my West;
   For, though their currents yield return to none,
What shall my West hurt me? As West and East
   In all flat Maps (and I am one) are one,
   So death doth touch the Resurrection.

Is the Pacific Sea my home? Or are
   The Eastern riches? Is *Jerusalem*?
Anyan, and *Magellan*, and *Gibraltar*,
   All straits, and none but straits, are ways to them,
   Whether where *Japhet* dwelt, or *Cham*, or *Shem*.

We think that *Paradise* and *Calvary*,
   Christ's Cross, and *Adam's* tree, stood in one place;
Look Lord, and find both *Adams* met in me;
   As the first *Adam's* sweat surrounds my face,
   May the last *Adam's* blood my soul embrace.

So, in His purple wrapp'd receive me Lord,
  By these His thorns give me His other Crown;
And as to others' souls I preach'd Thy word,
  Be this my Text, my Sermon to mine own,
    Therefore that He may raise the Lord throws down.

A HYMN TO GOD THE FATHER

I

Wilt Thou forgive that sin where I begun,
  Which is my sin, though it were done before?
Wilt Thou forgive that sin, through which I run,
  And do run still: though still I do deplore?
    When Thou hast done, Thou hast not done,
      For, I have more.

II

Wilt Thou forgive that sin by which I have won
  Others to sin? and, made my sin their door?
Wilt Thou forgive that sin which I did shun
  A year, or two: but wallowed in, a score?
    When Thou hast done, Thou hast not done,
      For I have more.

III

I have a sin of fear, that when I have spun
  My last thread, I shall perish on the shore;
Swear by Thyself, that at my death Thy son
  Shall shine as He shines now, and heretofore;
    And, having done that, Thou hast done,
      I fear no more.

LATIN POEMS AND TRANSLATIONS

TO MR. GEORGE HERBERT,

WITH ONE OF MY SEALS, OF THE ANCHOR AND CHRIST

QUI prius assuetus Serpentum fasce Tabellas
    Signare, (haec nostrae symbola parva Domus)
Adscitus domui Domini, patrioque relicto
    Stemmate, nanciscor stemmata jure nova.
Hinc mihi Crux primo quae fronti impressa lavacro,
    Finibus extensis, anchora facta patet.
Anchorae in effigiem Crux tandem desinit ipsam,
    Anchora fit tandem Crux tolerata diu.
Hoc tamen ut fiat, Christo vegetatur ab ipso
    Crux, et ab Affixo, est Anchora facta, Jesu.
Nec Natalitiis penitus serpentibus orbor,
    Non ita dat Deus, ut auferat ante data.
Quâ sapiens, Dos est; Quâ terram lambit et ambit,
    Pestis; At in nostra fit Medicina Cruce,
Serpens; fixa Cruci si sit Natura; Crucique
    A fixo, nobis, Gratia tota fluat.
Omnia cum Crux sint, Crux Anchora facta, sigillum
    Non tam dicendum hoc quam Catechismus erit.
Mitto nec exigua, exiguâ sub imagine, dona,
    Pignora amicitiae, et munera; Vota, preces.
Plura tibi accumulet, sanctus cognominis, Ille
    Regia qui flavo Dona sigillat Equo.

A SHEAF of Snakes used heretofore to be
My Seal, The Crest of our poor Family.
Adopted in God's Family, and so
Our old Coat lost, unto new arms I go.
The Cross (my seal at Baptism) spread below,
Does, by that form, into an Anchor grow.
Crosses grow Anchors; bear, as thou shouldst do

289

Thy Cross, and that Cross grows an Anchor too.
But He that makes our Crosses Anchors thus,
Is Christ, who there is crucified for us.
Yet may I, with this, my first Serpents hold,
God gives new blessings, and yet leaves the old;
The Serpent, may, as wise, my pattern be;
My poison, as he feeds on dust, that 's me.
And as he rounds the Earth to murder sure,
My death he is, but on the Cross, my cure.
Crucify nature then, and then implore
All Grace from Him, crucified there before;
When all is Cross, and that Cross Anchor grown,
This Seal 's a Catechism, not a Seal alone.
Under that little Seal great gifts I send,
Wishes, and prayers, pawns, and fruits of a friend.
And may that Saint which rides in our great Seal,
To you, who bear his name, great bounties deal.

TRANSLATED OUT OF GAZÆUS, *VOTA AMICO FACTA*. Fol. 160

God grant thee thine own wish, and grant thee mine,
Thou, who dost, best friend, in best things outshine;
May thy soul, ever cheerful, ne'er know cares,
Nor thy life, ever lively, know grey hairs.
Nor thy hand, ever open, know base holds,
Nor thy purse, ever plump, know plaits, or folds,
Nor thy tongue, ever true, know a false thing,
Nor thy word, ever mild, know quarrelling.
Nor thy works, ever equal, know disguise,
Nor thy fame, ever pure, know contumelies.
Nor thy prayers, know low objects, still Divine;
God grant thee thine own wish, and grant thee mine